First Baptist Church
1616 Pacific Ave.
Everett, Wa 98201

DATE DUE

AF
PET

#3

Peterson, Tracie
These Tangled Threads

Books by Tracie Peterson

www.traciepeterson.com

Controlling Interests
The Long-Awaited Child
Silent Star
A Slender Thread • *Tidings of Peace*

BELLS OF LOWELL*
Daughter of the Loom • *A Fragile Design*
These Tangled Threads

DESERT ROSES
Shadows of the Canyon • *Across the Years*
Beneath a Harvest Sky

WESTWARD CHRONICLES
A Shelter of Hope • *Hidden in a Whisper*
A Veiled Reflection

RIBBONS OF STEEL†
Distant Dreams • *A Hope Beyond*
A Promise for Tomorrow

RIBBONS WEST†
Westward the Dream • *Separate Roads*
Ties That Bind

SHANNON SAGA‡
City of Angels • *Angels Flight*
Angel of Mercy

YUKON QUEST
Treasures of the North • *Ashes and Ice*
Rivers of Gold

NONFICTION
The Eyes of the Heart

*with Judith Miller †with Judith Pella ‡with James Scott Bell

TRACIE PETERSON
AND
JUDITH MILLER

THESE TANGLED THREADS

BETHANYHOUSE
MINNEAPOLIS, MINNESOTA

These Tangled Threads
Copyright © 2003
Tracie Peterson and Judith Miller

Cover design by Dan Thornberg

Photo of house on cover is courtesy of Library of Congress, Prints and Photographs Division, Historic American Buildings Survey or Historic American Engineering Record, Reproduction Number HABS, CONN,8–CANBU,1–2.

Photo of girl standing by chair on cover is courtesy of Denver Public Library, Western History Collection, photo by Scott, X-21539.

Published by Bethany House Publishers
11400 Hampshire Avenue South
Bloomington, Minnesota 55438

Bethany House Publishers is a Division of
Baker Book House Company, Grand Rapids, Michigan.

Printed in the United States of America

Library of Congress Cataloging-in-Publication Data

Peterson, Tracie.
    These tangled threads / by Tracie Peterson and Judith Miller.
        p.   cm. — (Bells of Lowell ; 3)
    ISBN 0-7642-2690-8 (pbk.)
      1. Women—Massachusetts—Fiction. 2. Women textile workers—Fiction.
3. Textile industry—Fiction. 4. Fugitive slaves—Fiction. 5. Lowell (Mass.)—
Fiction. I. McCoy-Miller, Judith. II. Title.
    PS3566.E7717T48   2003
    813'.54—dc21
                                                2003013906

Dedicated to Beth Weishaar

With grateful thanks for your
enduring friendship throughout the years.
God's blessing on you, dear friend.

—Judy

First Baptist Church
1616 Pacific Ave.
Everett, Wa 98201

TRACIE PETERSON is a popular speaker and bestselling author who has written over fifty books, both historical and contemporary fiction. Tracie and her family make their home in Montana.

Visit Tracie's Web site at: *www.traciepeterson.com*.

JUDITH MILLER is an award-winning author of five novels and three novellas, two of which have placed in the CBA top-ten fiction lists. In addition to her writing, Judy is a certified legal assistant. Judy and her husband make their home in Topeka, Kansas.

Visit Judy's Web site at: *www.judithmccoymiller.com*.

CHAPTER *1*

Lowell, Massachusetts
Sunday, September 8, 1833

"I object to this marriage—the woman is not free to wed!" The indictment reverberated off the walls and then plummeted to the slate floor of St. Anne's Episcopal Church. The wedding guests craned their necks, a few murmuring and shifting in their pews before finally retreating into a cocoon of silence.

Arabella Newberry whirled toward the voice, her bridal satin rippling in waves behind her. "What are *you* doing here?" she cried out, her strained words slicing through the hushed quietude of the sanctuary.

Franklin Newberry edged out of a pew near the rear of the church, moved to the center of the aisle, and squared off with his daughter. Raising a paper into the air like a flag, he waved it above his head. "I hold proof of my words," he avowed, continuing to brandish the paper overhead while moving down the aisle toward Bella. "She is bound by contract to the United Society of Believers in

Christ's Second Appearing." His voice boomed through the church.

Bella reached out and clutched Daughtie's hand, pulling her friend close. "How did he know? You wrote to him, didn't you?" she accused, staring into Daughtie's doe-eyed gaze.

"N-n-n-no," Daughtie stammered. "How could you even think such a thing?"

There was no time to answer Bella's claim, for Franklin Newberry was now upon them, pushing Bella to one side as he thrust the document atop Reverend Edson's open Bible.

"See for yourself!" He stepped back a pace after issuing his command.

Theodore Edson stared at the document lying before him. Quickly scanning the contract, he glanced at Bella's ashen face and graced her with a look of compassion before turning his attention to Franklin Newberry. "I don't believe this document to be of legal consequence. It appears to have been signed by Miss Newberry when she was still a child of tender years—and she's female. I'm not a lawyer, but I don't believe a judge would find she had capacity to contract."

"She had capacity among the Shakers. She was old enough to understand the gravity of her decision, and the Shakers believe in equality between the sexes. She held the same ability to contract as any man and she is bound." Franklin reached out and grasped his daughter's wrist.

Bella tugged against his hold and winced as her father's fingers tightened. Her creamy white skin quickly turned red and was now beginning to resemble the bluish-purple shade of an overripe plum. She wiggled her fingers. Pin-pricks ebbed through her hand, and she pumped her fingers in and out, praying the action would permit a smidgen of blood to pass through her father's constricting grasp.

"You're hurting me. Turn loose my wrist." The words hissed from between her clenched teeth.

Disregarding the plea, he gave her an icy stare, one that would freeze the warmest of hearts. She willed herself to maintain a steady gaze. Should she look away, her father would believe he had the advantage. "You are coming with me." His voice was cold, void of emotion.

Bella ignored the ripple of fear flowing through her body and with an air of determination jutted her chin forward. "No! I intend to marry, and nothing you say or do will prevent this wedding from taking place. Create a scene if you must, but when I leave this church, my name will be Mrs. Taylor Manning."

"Indeed it will," Taylor agreed. His chest puffed out a bit. "I think you'd best leave," he said, raising his voice loud enough for the entire congregation to hear.

Bella shot him a look of gratitude. She was beginning to think he'd lost his ability to speak.

Franklin turned his frosty stare upon Taylor. "*You're* the one who invited me. Now that I've arranged to be present, you want me to leave? I'll depart right now, so long as my daughter accompanies me."

Bella leaned around her father's large frame in order to see Taylor. "*You?* You invited my father to attend our wedding? How could you do such a thing without asking me?"

"I was hoping the two of you could resolve your differences and mend your relationship. What better time to apologize and grant forgiveness than on this happy occasion?"

"Apology? You think I owe this disrespectful, vow-breaking girl an apology?" Franklin Newberry's voice once again boomed through the church.

"Forgiveness? I don't need *his* forgiveness." Bella's voice was no match for her father's, but she knew he heard her words, and that was all that mattered. She looked at Taylor.

"Did you truly invite him?" Her voice was now soft and filled with disbelief.

Taylor nodded and gave her a feeble smile. "My intentions were honorable."

"Indeed they were," Franklin agreed. "Who can say what it cost him to send a coach to Canterbury in order to have his man deliver an invitation. A noble gesture."

Reverend Edson cleared his throat. "If this discussion is going to continue, I would suggest we move to another place outside the hearing of the wedding guests. Perhaps we could request they excuse us for a short time," he suggested.

"I've nothing to say that can't be heard by these people. You asked openly if there was an objection to this marriage, and I've voiced my protest for all to hear. Why should we move elsewhere? If Bella truly believes she has a right to marry, let her defend herself in front of her invited guests," Franklin replied.

Taylor directed his gaze toward Bella. "Had your father sent a response agreeing to attend, I would have told you he was expected. But he sent no reply with the coach driver, nor did he respond later. Consequently, I assumed he would not attend." Taylor hesitated a moment and arched his eyebrows. "I expected him to follow proper etiquette."

Her father's hold loosened, and Bella shook off his hand. "You thought my father would adhere to the rules of etiquette? The only rules he follows are those that take him down a path of ease. That's why he joined the Shakers—to escape the responsibilities of a wife and daughter. Isn't that correct, *Brother* Franklin?" She spoke quietly, her words audible only to Reverend Edson and Taylor. "You were an adult who broke your marriage vows to my mother—vows you made before God. You have no right to speak to me of broken contracts. Your words are fouled by your own behavior. Please leave this place."

The minister turned his gaze from Bella to her father. "I don't want to have you forcibly removed, Mr. Newberry. Either take a seat or quietly leave this church. Please."

Bella watched as her father tugged at his indigo blue surtout and meticulously fitted each cloth-covered button through its buttonhole. Then, with head high and lips twisted in a tight line, he turned on his heel and walked down the aisle, the click of his shoes coldly tapping out his farewell. She squinted against the sunshine that streamed through the arched doors of the foyer, momentarily encircling Franklin Newberry with a dazzling light. Once again her father was turning his back on her.

Bella swallowed hard against the sudden urge to call him back. He hadn't wanted her years ago when he'd decided to join the Society of Believers, and he still didn't want her. Why couldn't he love her for who she was? Why couldn't her earthly father offer the same unconditional love she'd found in Jesus?

Reverend Edson lightly touched Bella's arm and brought her back to the present. "Bella? You look pale. Do you want to proceed or shall we wait?" The pastor's words were a hushed whisper.

Bella glanced at Taylor. He met her gaze, his eyes filled with concern. "We should proceed," she replied, turning toward the pastor. "But," she continued, turning her attention back to Taylor, "we need to discuss this entire matter after the ceremony."

"We don't want your marriage to begin on a sour note. Perhaps a short interlude *would* be best," Reverend Edson encouraged.

Bella gently adjusted the pleats along the waistline of her ivory satin gown. "No need to delay, Reverend Edson. Our marriage will survive the brief discussion of today's events," Bella replied with a sweet smile. "Nothing has changed my love for Taylor."

"Very well. We'll proceed from where I left off," he told the congregation.

"Let's begin *after* the part where you asked for objections," Taylor suggested.

Nervous laughter followed by warnings of *shh* drifted through the sanctuary, eliciting a faint smile from the minister. "Repeat after me," he instructed Taylor.

Bella listened as Taylor recited his vows and then slipped a gold band onto her trembling finger while he pledged his love. She followed with her own vows before looking up to receive his kiss. Her face tinged scarlet as they turned to face their smiling guests. Tugging at Taylor's arm, she propelled him forward, down the steps, and out of the church.

"I didn't realize you were so anxious to be alone with me. I believe we were at a full trot coming down the aisle," he teased while helping her into their awaiting carriage.

She turned to face him, ready to defend her actions, but burst into laughter when he began imitating their quick escape from the sanctuary. She patted the seat beside her. "Come along. If we hurry, we'll have a few minutes alone before the guests arrive."

"Yes, my dear," he said, giving her a mock salute. "I'll fortify myself for the tongue-lashing I'm about to receive for my boorish behavior." He slapped the reins, sending the horses into motion.

She giggled at his remark. "You do realize you almost ruined our wedding."

"*Almost.* That's the key word, my love. Even with my lack of common sense, we still managed to become husband and wife. And having you as my wife is all that matters."

She gave his arm a playful slap. "How can I remain

angry when you're so willing to be reprimanded?"

"Because I know I was wrong," he said, his voice suddenly becoming serious. "I realize my actions were foolhardy, and I apologize for taking such liberty without first consulting you, Bella. I give you my word: it won't happen again. With both of my parents deceased and the remainder of my family in England, and with your mother deceased, I thought it would be nice if your one remaining parent could be in attendance. My genuine wish was for you to experience reconciliation with your father. I foolishly thought our wedding might provide an opportunity for the two of you to make amends. Little did I realize your father would use such an important event to wreak havoc."

"The wedding gave him a perfect opportunity to return the embarrassment I caused him when I ran off from the Shaker village to work at the mill. I'm sure he viewed my departure from Canterbury as a personal affront rather than what it truly was—an unwillingness to embrace the Shaker beliefs and way of life he had chosen for our family. I only wish my mother could have lived to see me happily married."

Taylor's expression filled with concern. "Bella dear, I didn't mean to make you sad with all of this talk. I had simply hoped your father would come for the right reasons, such as wanting to resolve differences . . . and to see his lovely daughter in her wedding gown," Taylor added.

Bella looked heavenward. "If seeing me in my gown was his intent, he could have done so without causing a scene. Instead, he brought along my contract with the Shakers; he obviously desired a confrontation."

"You're right. I suppose I wanted to give him the benefit of the doubt," Taylor said while pulling back on the reins and drawing the horses to a stop. "I'll be pleased when we're able to move into our own house, and with a bit of luck, it should be finished by the time we return from our wedding trip to England," he said, helping her down from the carriage and escorting her up the steps of John and Addie Farnsworth's house.

"Perhaps if you hadn't insisted on all the intricate stonework, the house would already be completed," she said, gracing him with an engaging smile.

"Uncle John is the one who insisted upon having Liam Donohue design and build the fireplaces and decorative stonework. When I objected, he said I couldn't refuse him since he considered it our wedding present—over and above the gift of our journey to England."

"Yes, but had you not gone on and on about the new fireplaces and beautiful stonework Matthew Cheever had Liam complete in his house, I doubt whether your uncle John would have hired Mr. Donohue. However, I find his choice a unique and wonderful gesture, one we'll enjoy for years to come."

Taylor gave her a broad smile. "I certainly hope so. And here I thought we had hastened back to the house so you would have time to chastise me before our guests arrived."

Her face grew serious at his comment. "Chastising my husband in public is not something I plan to do. However, I *would* like you to promise you won't contact my father again without first discussing such an invitation with me."

"You have my word *and* my apology, Mrs. Manning," he replied, pulling her into his arms and kissing her soundly.

"That was a thoroughly delightful kiss," Bella whispered before disengaging herself from Taylor's hold around her waist. He attempted to once again pull her close. "Taylor, we have guests arriving," she said in her most prim and proper tone.

Taylor glanced toward the procession of horse-drawn carriages now moving down the road toward the house and emitted a loud guffaw. With a swoop of his arm, he pulled

Bella back into his arms. "You're my wife, Bella. It's perfectly acceptable for me to kiss you," he replied, holding her close.

Taylor released her from his embrace before the entourage pulled into the driveway, but Bella's cheeks remained flushed a deep ruby red long after he'd turned her loose. "It may be acceptable to kiss me, but it's hardly appropriate to do so in the middle of the street."

"We are nowhere near the middle of the street, my love."

Addie and John Farnsworth hurried up the steps to the house, their carriage the first to arrive. Addie looked at Bella with definite concern. "You're overheated. Look at your face—all red and flushed. Come along upstairs and I'll tend to you," she ordered, taking Bella by the hand. Addie had been mothering Bella since Bella came to work for the mills and resided at the boardinghouse she ran. Now, as a newly married woman herself, Mrs. Addie Farnsworth clearly didn't intend to neglect her duties.

"I'm not overheated," Bella protested while following Addie upstairs. "It's downright cool outdoors."

Addie touched Bella's cheek. "Your cheeks are warm—you're sick."

Bella giggled. "I'm not sick, Miss Addie. Taylor embarrassed me and I blushed," she explained.

Addie nodded, her eyebrows furrowed in concern. She went to a pitcher and poured water into a bowl. "You need to understand that Taylor was attempting to present you with a wonderful gift—the opportunity for a restored relationship with your father."

"Yes, we've . . ."

"Now don't interrupt, dear. I want to finish my explanation. Granted, Taylor should have given the matter thorough consideration before inviting your father. It would have been wise for him to seek out his uncle's advice or gain your permission, but his intentions were admirable. I pray you won't overly fault him," Addie rattled on. She wrung a cloth in the water and continued to fuss. "He truly is a good and thoughtful man. Don't let the sun go down on your anger." She dabbed the cool wet towel on Bella's face.

Bella reached up and pulled the cloth away. "I'm not sick, Miss Addie, and I've already forgiven Taylor."

Addie's eyebrows arched and her mouth dropped open. "You have? Well, why didn't you tell me? I've been going on and on when I should have been downstairs seeing to our guests."

"I tried, Miss Addie. You told me not to interrupt," Bella explained.

"You're right, I did." Addie chuckled and pulled Bella into a hug. "And you must remember I'm no longer a boardinghouse keeper that you refer to as Miss Addie nor the wife of John Farnsworth that you address as Mrs. Farnsworth; I'm now your aunt."

"Yes, *Aunt* Addie," Bella replied, the words sounding foreign though delightful to her ears. "I'll try to remember."

"Good. Now let's go downstairs and greet your guests."

CHAPTER 2

First Baptist Church
1616 Pacific Ave.
Everett, Wa 98201

Bella leaned close and whispered to Daughtie and Ruth, "Come upstairs and help me change into my traveling dress. I want to spend a little time alone with the two of you before we leave for England. We can sneak off and go up the back stairway without being detected."

The three girls wended their way through the crowd, coming to a halt several times to respond to a guest or answer a question before reaching the stairway. They giggled in delight when they finally entered the bedroom upstairs.

"Let me help you with the buttons," Daughtie offered. "I couldn't believe your father actually appeared at the wedding today," she confided while helping her friend out of her gown.

Bella nodded. "I could barely believe my eyes or ears. I knew it was my father's voice, but I couldn't believe he was actually in the church. The whole ordeal with my father is like a bad dream."

Ruth sat down on the edge of the bed and ran her hand

over the smooth satin fabric of Bella's wedding gown. "Didn't Taylor realize you and your father weren't on good terms?"

"That's exactly why he invited him. Taylor hoped the wedding might be a way to bring us together. Unfortunately, he didn't realize the depth of my father's anger. Even though my father willingly relinquished his claim to parenting me when he became a Shaker, he still believed he had the right to force his will upon me. Taylor didn't realize the only reason my father would attend the wedding was if he thought he could force me to return to Canterbury. Taylor was distressed by my father's behavior," Bella explained.

Ruth cast her gaze downward. "Perhaps I ought not complain about my family quite so much."

Daughtie held up the fitted jacket of Bella's carriage dress. "This emerald green print is perfect with your blond hair, Bella."

"Thank you," she replied, a faint blush rising in her cheeks. "I'm going to miss both of you so much, but I want you to know I've been praying an agreeable new roommate will arrive to take my place at the boardinghouse."

Ruth bounded off the bed. "Tell her our news, Daughtie."

Daughtie hesitated a moment and then gave Bella a faint smile. "We're going to move out of number 5. Mrs. Arnold next door has a bedroom open that Ruth and I are going to share. The room had been rented to two sisters, but they've returned home to Vermont. Isn't that the best of news?"

Before Bella could respond, a knock sounded at the bedroom door. "May I come in?" Lilly Cheever inquired while peeking into the room.

"Of course; please join us," Bella replied.

"I hope I'm not interrupting."

"No, not at all. Actually, you may be able to lend some insight to this conversation. We were just discussing the fact that Daughtie and Ruth have decided to move into Mrs. Arnold's house. Based upon Mr. Arnold's past behavior, I have some concerns about their decision. What do *you* think?" Bella asked, taking Lilly by the arm and drawing her toward a chair.

Lilly seated herself in the upholstered walnut rocker and seemed to briefly contemplate her reply before speaking. "Well, it's obvious Mr. Arnold isn't likely to change his ways. After all, he received ample warning from his supervisors to correct his behavior with both the mill girls and his wife. Although his conduct improved for a period of time, he ultimately returned to his unseemly actions. However, it isn't as though he's living here in Lowell any longer—nor does anyone expect him to ever return."

Bella's gaze remained fixed upon Ruth and Daughtie while Lilly spoke. She had hoped Lilly would caution her friends against such a move. Unfortunately, it appeared both Daughtie and Ruth had been comforted by Lilly's statements. Crossing her arms, Bella plopped down on the bed and faced Daughtie. "He's a despicable man. Once he discovers the two of you have moved in, I believe he'll enjoy coming to the house and nosing about. And with his terrible temper, I'm concerned for your safety. Besides, isn't there a rule that girls can't be assigned to Mrs. Arnold's house unless the other boardinghouses are full? After all, that house wasn't designed to be a boardinghouse, was it, Mrs. Cheever?"

"The other houses *are* full. A new girl has already moved in to take your place and there are two more girls arriving who will move into number 5 as soon as we move out," Daughtie interjected. "You do think it's safe, don't you, Mrs. Cheever?"

Lilly glanced back and forth between Daughtie and

Bella. "I don't know which question to answer first," Lilly replied, giving the girls a broad smile. "You're correct, Bella. The Arnold house wasn't designed as a boarding-house. The houses at the end of the rows were built specif-ically for the overseers and their families, with a common wall joining them to the boardinghouses. The Corporation gave Mrs. Arnold special permission to remain in the house and board two girls because of her difficult circumstances and because the new overseer wasn't married. It worked out well because he preferred to remain a boarder at Miss Mintie's boardinghouse." She leaned in as if to share a secret. "I think he's completely gone over Miss Mintie's cooking." The girls giggled.

Ruth picked up a tortoise-edged comb and began fash-ioning Bella's hair into long curls. "Why did they limit Mrs. Arnold to only two boarders? There's certainly space for additional girls in the house."

"The house would have required remodeling to become a true boardinghouse. While the Associates desired to help Mrs. Arnold, they didn't want to make structural changes to the dwelling, for they realize that another over-seer and his family will eventually occupy the house."

A lock of Bella's thick blond hair was tightly wrapped around Ruth's finger as she turned toward Lilly. "You mean Mrs. Arnold will eventually be forced from the house?"

"No, I don't think that's going to happen, Ruth. But when her child becomes older, Mrs. Arnold may decide to go to work in the mills herself or become a keeper, should a position become available at one of the regular boarding-houses," Lilly replied.

Bella tugged on Ruth's hand. "You're pulling my hair, Ruth." With an apologetic smile, Ruth released her hold and handed Bella the comb. "It's the reappearance of Mr. Arnold that most concerns me," Bella said. "Surely he returns to visit his daughter. What if he becomes abusive on one of those visits? Daughtie or Ruth could become the subject of his rage. Furthermore, I don't like the idea of my friends being anywhere near that unscrupulous man."

"Well, I think you're borrowing trouble," Daughtie replied. "Besides, I'm looking forward to being around little Theona. You know how much I enjoy children, Bella."

Bella nodded. "Daughtie was always requesting assignment to the children's dormitory at the Shaker village," she told Lilly and Ruth.

Ruth grimaced. "I spent enough years at home looking after younger brothers and sisters. What attracts me is having a bedroom we won't have to share with four or five other girls—and there will only be four of us around the table for meals. Won't that be delightful?"

Lilly nodded. "I understand completely, Ruth—about living with fewer people. Although I must admit I'm like Daughtie when it comes to children. Having a little girl in the same house *is* most agreeable. Our little Violet has truly brought joy into my daily routine," Lilly replied, a faint smile touching her lips at the mention of Violet's name. "I truly doubt there's any need to worry about Mr. Arnold. I think he would fear being placed in jail should he cause a ruckus. Now, why don't we turn to a more pleasant topic. I understand you and the Farnsworths are sailing for England in only a few days, Bella."

"Yes. Taylor and I are taking the *Governor Sullivan* to Horn's Pond, where we'll spend the night before going on to Boston tomorrow. Then John and Addie will join us in Boston later in the week. Can you imagine anything more exciting? I've never even been to a city the size of Boston, much less traveled to another country. Having the opportunity to meet Taylor's family makes the trip even more wonderful. He's quite anxious to see his grandfather Farnsworth and grandmother Manning. I'm certain his grandmother must be a wonderful lady. She graciously moved to

London in order to help care for Taylor's grandfather Farnsworth when his physical ailments worsened. Considering they're only related through the marriage of their children, I find her actions commendable. Taylor's younger sister, Elinor, is now nine years old, and she writes Taylor the most endearing letters. We'll be visiting her, of course. However, it's still uncertain whether there will be sufficient opportunity to meet his older brothers and sister," she explained.

"Bella! Here you are. Taylor was beginning to fear he'd lost his bride," Addie said while entering the bedroom. She gave the younger ladies a bright smile. "I dislike being the one to break up this little gathering. However, Bella, you really must come bid your guests good-bye. It's nearly time for you and Taylor to depart for Horn's Pond. You're due at the canal within the hour."

Bella stood and turned for Addie to inspect her outfit. "Do you think Taylor will like my dress?"

"Taylor Manning will be pleased with anything you choose to wear, whether it be coarsely loomed cotton or this beautiful printed challis." Addie quickly adjusted the neckline pleats and gave a nod of approval. "He is quite smitten with you; of that there is no doubt."

Taylor made his way through the garden and then surveyed both the parlor and dining room. Bella was nowhere to be seen. He glanced at his pocket watch. Perhaps Addie was correct—perhaps she'd gone upstairs to change into her traveling apparel. Though they'd been married only a few hours, Taylor wanted Bella close by his side. His misstep of inviting Mr. Newberry had given him a fleeting glimpse into a future without Bella. What foolishness! Why he had ever considered such a notion now astounded him. Certainly his plan had been well intentioned, but he should have realized there was a potential for failure, a calamity that could cause his bride embarrassment and pain. He didn't deserve the gentle forgiveness Bella had extended.

Taylor startled as Matthew Cheever slapped him on the back and observed, "It appears as if the womenfolk have deserted us. Best get used to these unexpected disappearances. Isn't that right, John?"

John Farnsworth gave Matthew a nod. "Indeed. I'm constantly looking about for Addie. She's generally fluttering about the kitchen rather than enjoying herself with our guests. But I suppose that's one of the things I love about her. She's more concerned about others being cared for than being cared for herself."

"We can only hope that Taylor has been as fortunate in his choice of a wife as we've been," Matthew replied. "Kirk and Anne asked me to extend their apologies. Anne wasn't feeling well, and they were forced to make an early departure."

John gave a hearty laugh. "I doubt it was Mrs. Boott's health that caused the early departure. When I last saw her, she appeared to be enjoying herself. I fear attending Taylor and Bella's wedding was a huge concession for our Mr. Boott. I don't think he'll soon forgive Bella for her public arguments in favor of the new school system. After all, a man willing to withdraw his membership from a church named after his wife is one who doesn't easily forgive those who take a stand against him."

Matthew's lips turned upward into a broad smile. "You're probably correct, John. I'm sure Anne nudged him into attending the wedding, but I doubt it took much effort. Let's not forget that he values both you and Taylor. He knows you've contributed immeasurably to the success of the mills. It was appropriate for him to be here even though Kirk is not overly comfortable in these social settings."

"Especially when he's unsure how some of the guests feel about *him*," Taylor replied with a grin.

"Well, you must admit you have quite a variety of social classes represented today," Matthew said.

John nodded. "Ah, Matthew, but that's the joy of a wedding. It's acceptable to force the socially elite to mingle among us commoners."

"You're no commoner, John. You hold a position of high esteem in this community. Look at this home the Corporation built for you. Why, I'd venture to say you live better than I do," Matthew replied with a grin. "I know you're paid better."

Patting Matthew on the shoulder, John said, "I'm a man of the working class, Matthew. My position in this town was elevated because I hold valuable knowledge and ability needed by the Corporation. That asset has proved beneficial to all of us, and I'm most grateful. But the fact remains that my social class remains with the laborer, and I'm delighted to have them in attendance. It pleased me immensely to see Hugh Cummiskey and Liam Donohue make an appearance here today. And if all these mill girls hadn't attended, why, Bella and Addie would have been devastated."

"Don't forget—I'm married to a young woman who once worked in the mills, also," Matthew replied. "I have no problem with anyone who's here today. However, I think some of those in attendance came as a surprise to Kirk."

"And hastened his departure," John promptly added.

"Perhaps," Matthew said, "but he did want me to advise you against taking any unnecessary actions while the four of you are in England. Kirk and I both fear there are still those in England who would like to see you brought to justice for what they consider treason."

"We plan to keep to ourselves," John said while waving

off the remark. "I seriously doubt anyone in England remembers I ever worked for the mills, much less cares if I ever return for a visit."

Matthew shook his head. "Don't discount what I'm saying, John. We both know danger could befall you. The English economy has suffered greatly because we've been able to duplicate their machinery."

Several girls moved closer, their laughter and animated chatter infiltrating the men's conversation. John nodded toward the library, and the three men moved into the unoccupied, inviting room before continuing their discussion.

John seated himself in front of an alcove lined with shelves of leather-bound books. "If memory serves me, it was your man, Francis Cabot Lowell, who stole the plans for the machinery. They hold *him* responsible for that particular act, not me. My part in the growth of the mills is minuscule. Had I not assisted with the improvement of your printworks, someone else would have soon done so. I doubt the English still bear a grudge."

Matthew took a seat opposite John. "I'll not argue with you, John, but you and I both realize you are in some danger. We can't be certain how much, but I would ask that you give your word you'll be careful."

"If it makes you feel better, you have my word. Weather permitting, we may journey to Portsmouth, but other than that, the majority of our time will be spent in London. I've no plans to visit Lancashire. With my family all relocated in London, there's no reason to venture anywhere near the mills."

"I understand, but I'm sure there are mill owners who visit London, just as members of the Associates travel between Boston and Lowell."

"Those men of importance didn't know who John Farnsworth was even when he worked for them. I doubt they'll remember me or bear a grievance after five years."

"Some wounds take a long time to heal, especially when they affect the financial investments of powerful people," Matthew warned. "Remember, I have a stake in your welfare, too. I'm the one who convinced the Associates we could do without you and Taylor for this extended period. If you'll not consider cautious behavior essential to your own well-being, then consider it a favor to me."

John leaned toward Matthew and rested his forearms on his thighs. "If it will cease your worrying, then you have my word I'll remain alert."

"Thank you, John. And on a more pleasant note," Matthew said, now turning his attention toward Taylor, "I wanted to let you know Kirk and I will be attending a meeting of the Associates next week in Boston. I plan to present your new designs, Taylor. I find them very exciting. I'm certain the owners will be impressed and eager to begin production of them once you've returned from England."

Taylor attempted to hide his pleasure, not wanting to appear portentous. He had spent a great deal of time on the drawings, discussing them with his uncle as he proceeded to ensure the machinery could be adjusted to accommodate the patterns. When both Addie and Bella had given their delighted approval to the designs, he had finally believed the plans were ready for production. He had anxiously awaited approval, but when none came, he believed they had been determined unacceptable.

"I'm pleased you like them. I only hope the Associates will share your opinion."

John smiled broadly and rose from his chair. "I told you there was nothing to worry over. Those new designs are wonderful, innovative. They can't help but like them—and if they express concern, Matthew, you need only call upon their wives to change their minds."

Matthew gave a hearty laugh. "I showed them to Lilly and she was enchanted, so I know you're correct on that account, John. If need be, Kirk and I will insist upon inter-rupting the women in their music room and asking for their opinion," he agreed.

"If you'll excuse me," Taylor said, rising from his chair, "I believe I'll see if I can locate my bride. We really need to make our departure or we'll miss our boat."

"Certainly, my boy. You don't want to do that or you'll be stuck here at home with us old folks."

Taylor gave his uncle a lopsided grin before leaving the men to continue their exchange. Stepping into the hallway, he glanced over his shoulder. The two men were once again deep in discussion, his uncle's brows furrowed and his lips set in a narrow, tight line. Perhaps his uncle John was more concerned about their journey than he'd indicated earlier.

Bella's voice pulled him away from his thoughts, and he glanced up the stairway. She was a beautiful vision with her creamy yellow hair tucked under a bonnet trimmed in the same emerald green that was woven into the fabric of her dress. Suddenly spotting Taylor, she graced him with a bright smile as their guests gathered around. Upon reaching the final step, Taylor leaned forward and placed a tender kiss on her cheek. She blushed uncontrollably, and Taylor knew he would love her forever. John and Matthew joined the crowd, and Taylor's glance momentarily rested upon his uncle's face. His thoughts returned to their earlier discus-sion, and a wave of concern overcame him. Surely this journey wouldn't put any of them in jeopardy. He attempted to push thoughts of danger from his mind, but Matthew's words of caution would not be silenced. Taylor looked back at his wife's smiling face. He fervently prayed this journey would not place Bella in any peril.

CHAPTER 3

Boston, Massachusetts

Tracy Jackson leveled a scowl directed at everyone in the room. Matthew Cheever shifted his gaze to Kirk Boott in an attempt to gauge Boott's reaction. Tracy was obviously intent on imposing his will upon the other Associates. Kirk's expression was indecipherable; however, Matthew was certain the stoic mask was a facade, for Kirk's passion regarding anything that affected Lowell and its paternalistic operation was legendary.

"Comments, gentlemen? Nathan? Josiah? Kirk—surely *you* have something to say," Jackson urged.

Swirling the small amount of port remaining in his glass, Kirk shook his head. "I'll defer." He tipped the glass to his lips and finished his drink.

Josiah Baines cleared his throat. "Well, I vote to remain practical and move slowly. You all know I believe in the railroad, but I certainly don't think we need to consider steam locomotion. We're talking about transporting goods between Boston and Lowell. We can use horse-drawn wagons pulled on rail just as effectively."

"Now, why would we even want to consider such a proposition, Josiah?" Tracy rose from his chair and gave Baines an icy stare before turning toward the other men. "Could we all consider being a little more forward thinking?"

"There's no need to become offensive, Tracy. You asked for our opinions, but it's obvious you really don't want them unless they concur with your own. Well, I for one, have always believed in carefully calculating my risks and not taking unnecessary chances investing money."

"I haven't noticed any unwillingness to share in the vast profits that have come from any of my previous suggestions or proposals, Josiah. You're always against me in the vote but first in line for your money."

"Now, now, gentlemen," Nathan Appleton interrupted, "let's remain civilized. We can discuss this without coming to odds among ourselves. I understand your excitement over the prospect of using steam locomotion, Tracy. However, some of us aren't as informed and enlightened. A calm examination of ideas will be much more helpful than exchanging barbs, don't you think?"

The cue was obvious to all in attendance, and Tracy nodded his agreement. "My apologies, Josiah. As you know, I tend to be overzealous when I'm trying to make a point."

"Apology accepted," Josiah replied. "Anyone else care to voice an opinion? Surely some other member of this group has a view he'd wish to share."

Nathan rubbed his jaw and nodded. "You say Robert Stephenson had good results with the steam engine on the Liverpool and Manchester Railroad, and I don't doubt your word, Tracy. But you must admit that making the huge financial investment required for steam locomotion is a bold stand, especially on an invention that hasn't proven the test of time. I'm having difficulty justifying the capital outlay based upon the population and commerce of Lowell. We can't compare the cities of Boston and Lowell to Manchester and Liverpool. Such a concept would be foolhardy, for our numbers are vastly dissimilar, both in trade and inhabitants."

"Our primary concern is to have reliable transportation during the winter months when the canals are frozen," Thomas Clayborn commented.

Tracy poured himself another glass of port before turning his attention to Clayborn. "We need to think beyond today's needs. If we don't make plans for the future before it arrives, we'll never be the forerunner, the one to set the standard. I, for one, prefer taking the lead rather than playing catch-up."

"Come now, my good man. We're hardly a bunch of backward bumpkins. Look at what we've accomplished over the past few years. I think you'll have to agree that all of us have willingly cooperated with most anything you've presented. You ought not take us to task the first time we question a major decision," Clayborn rebutted.

Matthew glanced out the tall, narrow window where a golden autumn sun now rested upon the distant horizon. He wondered if an amicable agreement could possibly be reached among the members, and although he had a definite stance, the only opinions that mattered here were those of the Associates. Matthew's stomach emitted a loud growl and he quickly pressed a hand to his midsection, hoping to silence the noise.

Kirk shifted in his seat. "I'm going to weigh in on Tracy's side this time. Personally, I believe his concept will transform Lowell from a mercantile community to an industrial powerhouse—and create extraordinary wealth in the process. This is no time for diffidence. If we move forward with the railroad, we'll no longer need to depend upon navigability of the canals. There's no doubt steam is the direction of the future. I don't see how we can decide against Tracy's proposal and continue to think of ourselves as capitalists."

Clayborn rubbed the back of his neck as though the massaging motion would clear his head. "You're probably correct, Kirk, but I think I'm going to need some additional time to decide. Tracy, if you could supply us with some definitive costs, it would be helpful."

"I think I can manage that within the next few weeks. Again, I apologize to those of you who think I've been overly aggressive with my proposal."

"Well, at least we haven't been subjected to William Thurston's legendary ranting about the Irish and their blight upon the town. I'd much rather listen to your fresh ideas than one of Thurston's tirades. That man's absence as a member of the Associates is refreshing as far as I'm concerned," Josiah replied. A murmuring of agreement and a few guffaws followed the remark.

"I concur with your assessment, but I would certainly like to see that man brought to justice," Nathan stated. "Who would have ever thought someone as inept as William Thurston could have eluded the police and kept them at bay for this long? Rather unfair, I think, that J. P. Green is in jail while Thurston is probably involved in some other illegal scheme."

Josiah nodded. "However, with Thurston's egotistical nature, there's no telling when he might reappear and attempt to do further harm to the Corporation. My poor wife still can't believe William was in the business of kidnapping and selling Yankee and Irish girls into the slave market. Of course, I didn't reveal all of the unpleasant details, nor did I tell her that he hadn't been captured. I fear she would have taken to her bed."

Henry Thorne scratched his head and grinned. "I think all this talk of William Thurston is nonsense. He associated with thugs and ruffians and has likely come to an early death. I'd guess he's probably rotting in a shallow grave somewhere. Besides, even if he has escaped harm, I doubt if he'd be foolish enough to show his face in Lowell again."

Kirk selected a cigar from the box that was being passed and carefully clipped the end. He inhaled deeply on the imported extravagance before expelling a large cloud of grayish-blue smoke. Lips pursed into a tight pucker, he watched in obvious satisfaction as the haze lifted toward the ceiling. "Let's don't forget the matter of the doctor," he reminded the others.

"Thank you, Kirk. The matter had slipped my mind," Nathan replied. "For those of you who may not know, Dr. Ivan Ketter has accepted our offer to set up his practice in Lowell the first of the year. With Dr. Fontaine's departure some months ago and now Dr. Barnard retiring at the end of the year, the town will be without a physician. Dr. Ketter seems a good choice, and Matthew has agreed to find suitable accommodations. We had hoped he could commence his duties immediately. Unfortunately, he's advised me he can't accept the position until January."

"I take it Dr. Ketter isn't interested in purchasing Dr. Barnard's house?" Josiah inquired.

Kirk flicked the ash from his cigar. "Dr. Barnard isn't interested in selling. He plans to remain in Lowell. There *are* those of us who prefer Lowell to Boston," he replied with an amused grin.

"My apologies. The question wasn't meant to be offensive," Josiah replied.

"No offense taken. Why don't we adjourn? I'm famished," Kirk said as he snuffed out his cigar.

CHAPTER 4

England
October 5, 1833

Bella quivered, unable to contain her excitement. After weeks at sea, the sails of the *Sea Sprite* were now finally furled and the passengers were jostling each other for a better view of England's sights. A sharp elbow in her ribs and a heavy foot coming down upon her stamped kid shoe caused Bella to grimace and then move closer to Taylor's side. He glanced down and gave her a broad smile.

As a cool ocean breeze swirled across the deck of the boat, Taylor encircled her waist with his arm, pulling her close. "I can't believe we've finally arrived. It seems an eternity since I left England and my family," he said. "Of course, with Rowland and Edward off at sea and Beatrice now married to a Scotsman and living in the north, it leaves only my grandfather Farnsworth, grandmother Manning, and Elinor for you to meet."

"If we're very fortunate, one of your brothers may be home between voyages, and perhaps your grandmother has written your sister Beatrice and she'll come for a short visit while we're here."

Taylor gave her a faint smile. "You are an optimistic young woman. I suppose anything is possible, but I'm not holding out much hope of seeing them. I fear Elinor will have to suffice."

A sigh of exasperation escaped Bella's lips, and she gave him a look of mock indignation. "You should be every bit as anxious to see your little sister as your other siblings," she lectured.

"Elinor can be a pesky child, constantly vying for attention. Unless she's changed—which I seriously doubt—I'm certain you'll soon come to share my opinion."

"Little girls are known to adore their older brothers. You should feel honored. And she *has* grown older. Her letters to you have been enchanting."

Taylor made a snorting sound and then pointed toward the shoreline as the small ship drew closer to town. "I can hardly wait to show you the sights in London. Some of my fondest memories are the yearly visits to London with Uncle John. The summer each of us turned ten and every year thereafter, he would treat my brothers and me to a few days in London. What fun we would have."

"And your sisters? Were they ever included?"

A chuckle escaped his lips. "You're going to give me your equality speech again, aren't you?"

"No, but just remember—when we have our daughters, I'll expect equal treatment for each of them."

"Each of them? I didn't realize you were planning such a large family. However, since you are, I'd like to put in my bid for *several* boys."

"What's this I hear, young man? You're already expecting to father several sons?" John asked while maneuvering Addie close to Bella on the deck.

"To be honest, it was more a discussion on equality that

somehow took a turn," Taylor admitted. "Thankfully we've finally arrived and can call a cessation to this conversation."

John laughed and slapped his nephew on the back. "I'd think that procreation is a topic you'd be happy to discuss with your wife."

"John! Such talk." Addie gave him a stern look of admonition.

Her husband smiled. "Well, we're all married, and there's . . ."

Addie's eyebrows arched and her lips formed a tight line. She moved her head back and forth in a quick, definitive movement. The conversation ceased.

———————

Bella stood beside Addie as they waited patiently while the men located their trunks. John motioned them forward, having wasted no time securing transportation to his father's residence. Once the trunks were loaded, John gave the driver the address and settled down beside Addie.

"I'm so excited I can hardly contain myself," Bella said, gazing out the window. "I keep thinking of all the places you've told me about."

Taylor nodded but couldn't get a word in edgewise as Addie took over the conversation. "John has shared so many descriptions of places. I just want to see them all."

The men chuckled as Bella adamantly agreed. "Yes. It hardly seems there will be time enough for everything."

"Then we'll simply have to come back at a later time," Taylor said, patting Bella's hand, "for a person can do only so much in a day."

The carriage driver maneuvered them through the busy traffic while Bella and Addie continued to chatter and look for anything that matched the descriptions their husbands had given during their storytelling. Addie leaned forward and peeked out of the carriage. "Oh, look! That's St. Paul's

Cathedral, isn't it?" She looked to John for confirmation. He followed her gaze and nodded.

Addie clapped her gloved hands together. "This is so exciting. I must pen a letter to Mintie and let her know we've arrived safely and that I've already had a view of this glorious cathedral."

John emitted a loud guffaw. "The poor woman will likely keep herself in a state of distress the entire time you're here in England."

"Now, John, it's not kind to laugh at her. After all, Mintie *is* my sister," Addie replied.

"I know, I know. But you'd think the woman would finally accept the fact that the United States and England are no longer at war. She continues to see spies and traitors at every turn. Such nonsense!"

"She's gotten better. After all, she attended *our* wedding even though she had been certain you were a spy back when you were living at her boardinghouse," Addie replied with a chuckle.

"You see? That's exactly what I mean. The minute Mintie realized I had recently arrived from England, she was certain I was in the country to spy on behalf of the English. Besides, we both know that if she could have talked you out of our marriage, she'd have done so. She conceded only after she realized you wouldn't change your mind," he reminded her.

"True, but at least Mintie accepted the defeat graciously," Addie said as the carriage came to a halt in front of a row of Georgian town houses. The white panel door, lined on either side by pillar-type facades, offered a cheery welcome behind the walkway's wrought iron gate. Addie was already on the edge of her seat.

"Oh, do hurry and help us down, John."

The men quickly complied, alighting the carriage in

short order. Taylor stepped aside to allow John to help Addie down.

"This is just lovely, John. I had no idea it would be such a pretty place," Addie noted. John reached up to help Bella down before Taylor could protest.

"It costs a pretty price, so it should be," John answered, smiling at Bella.

The front door opened and a dimple-cheeked girl bounded out, her nutmeg brown hair flying loose behind her. Taylor fell backward against the carriage as the girl enveloped him in a tackling embrace. "Elinor," he said while attempting to gain his footing, "you've grown considerably."

"Yes," she agreed. "I'm already taller than Grandmother. Do hurry up—she's quite anxious to see you."

"Though not quite so anxious as you," he said with a chuckle. "Elinor, this is my wife, Arabella—Bella. She's been eager to meet you."

Elinor gave a quick curtsy. "Pleased to meet you, Bella."

Bella graced Elinor with a charming smile. "The pleasure is mine," she said before turning toward Taylor. "You didn't tell me she was such a beautiful young lady."

Elinor beamed. "That's because he thinks I'm still a little girl."

John strode toward Elinor and pulled her close. "You *are* a little girl. Now come over here and you can meet *my* wife. Elinor, this is Adelaide Beecher Farnsworth, and I'm certain she's going to be delighted to have you address her as Aunt Addie."

"Pleased to meet you, Aunt Addie. Grandfather Farnsworth is *very* anxious to meet you," Elinor said while dropping into an exaggerated curtsy. "All these weddings," she mused. "I do wish I could have come to see them. I'm sure they were grand."

Addie's face had visibly paled at the child's remark, and

Bella went quickly to her side. "I'm sure John's father is anxious to meet you in the very best of ways," Bella whispered while squeezing the older woman's hand. "I, too, am feeling a bit nervous over meeting our new relatives."

"Are you attempting to frighten my wife into leaving before we've even gotten settled, Elinor?" John asked with a chuckle. "See if your brother would like some help."

Elinor hurried back to her brother, who was now wrestling a large humpbacked trunk. She eyed him momentarily and then grasped Bella's hand. "I'll show you inside," she offered.

Though her stomach lurched at the prospect of being scrutinized by Taylor's family, Bella nodded her agreement and took hold of Elinor's hand. What if Taylor's grandmother didn't like her? She followed the younger girl up the steps and into the house, with Elinor tugging upon her hand each time she attempted to lag behind. Stopping to admire a quaint hand-loomed rug inside the front door, Bella grinned at Elinor before finally surrendering to the child's insistent yank.

"Come on. Grandmother Cordelia is in the parlor," Elinor urged, pulling her forward. "Here she is, Taylor's wife," the girl announced with a beaming smile.

Bella felt as though she were a prize animal placed on display for approval and possible purchase. She glanced back and forth between the older woman and the gentleman who had now risen from his chair, his few wisps of white hair falling forward as he nodded his head into a bow.

"I'm Jarrow Farnsworth, Taylor's grandfather on his mother's side of the family, although I'm sure you've already come to that conclusion. And this is your husband's grandmother on his father's side, Cordelia Manning. Come have a seat," he said while directing her to the tapestry-covered settee. "Go on, sit down," he encouraged. "We'll not bite."

Bella forced herself to smile at the remark and seated herself across from Cordelia Manning. The older woman was obviously appraising her. "The others will be in shortly. Elinor insisted I come ahead," she stammered, looking to Grandfather Farnsworth as he took a seat once again.

"Elinor can be very insisting," Jarrow said with a hint of amusement in his tone.

"I hope you're a woman of high moral fiber. Taylor was always drawn to the wrong type of women when he lived in England. Ever since he sailed for the United States, I've prayed he'd find a good God-fearing woman who would steer him onto the straight and narrow," Cordelia said.

A loud thud, followed by the sound of footsteps, echoed from the hallway. "I wasn't sure where you wanted me to put the trunks," Taylor said as he strode into the parlor. Moving directly to his grandmother, he pulled her into a warm embrace and kissed her on the cheek. "You look beautiful, as always," he flattered.

The admiration brought a faint smile to Cordelia's lips. "You always did have a way with words," she remarked.

"At least with the women," his grandfather interjected.

"*You're* still quick with a rebuttal, Grandfather," Taylor replied as he grasped his grandfather's hand in a warm handshake.

Jarrow winked. "It's my body that's the problem, not my mind."

As if prompted by his words, Cordelia leaned to the right and tucked the lap robe more tightly around the old man's legs. "Now, then, tell us about your bride," she said.

Taylor smiled at Bella as he dropped down beside her. "Your prayers have been answered, Grandmother. I know Bella will meet your every expectation."

Cordelia folded her hands and then rested them in her lap. "We shall see," she murmured.

Bella gazed at Cordelia, uncertain what was meant by

the older woman's response. Perhaps Taylor's grandmother had some personal test in store for her. However, John and Addie's appearance in the parlor forestalled any immediate discussion of the matter.

Jarrow's lips turned upward into a broad smile, and his blue eyes twinkled. "John! It is so good to see you. And this must be Adelaide," he said. "Very pleased to meet you. I suppose you realize you've snagged yourself a fine husband," he continued with an exaggerated wink.

"Indeed I do," Addie replied, returning his smile.

"I'm the fortunate one in this marriage. Addie has the patience of Job and the kindness of an angel."

Jarrow gave a hearty laugh. "I'm certain you're right on that account, John," he replied.

Bella smiled, enjoying the verbal exchange between the Farnsworths. It appeared the elder Mr. Farnsworth was pleased with John's choice for a wife. She wasn't, however, so certain about Cordelia Manning's feelings toward her. Perhaps Mrs. Manning thought her grandson deserved someone prettier or perhaps a woman of higher social standing. Elinor sidled closer and then carefully wedged herself between Bella and the arm of the settee.

"We're anxious to hear about life in Massachusetts, but I would guess the ladies would like to freshen up while I make some tea," Cordelia said. "Jarrow insisted on making arrangements for dinner at the Bloomsbury."

"It appears as if we're going to be treated like royalty our first night home. The restaurant is located in a hotel by the same name. Quite nice—and good food, too," Taylor explained to Bella and Addie.

"Hurrumph," Cordelia snorted. "I told Jarrow you'd probably prefer to relax here at home and have a nice mutton stew. Besides, he ought not be out and about in the cool night air. But, of course, he wouldn't listen."

Jarrow narrowed his eyes and shook his head. "I wanted

to celebrate the arrival of our family. They can eat mutton stew tomorrow night, and I'll feel no worse outdoors than I do sitting inside this house."

"Waste of good money, and say what you will, your health will suffer," Cordelia muttered before turning her attention to her granddaughter. "Elinor, you can show the ladies to their rooms and then promptly return and help me in the kitchen."

Elinor wrinkled her nose at the request, her behavior drawing an immediate reprimand from Mrs. Manning.

"Sorry, Grandmother," the girl meekly apologized. "Follow me, ladies," she said, motioning Addie and Bella up the wooden staircase.

Once Addie had been directed into her room, Elinor led Bella to another bedroom at the end of the hallway. "Don't permit Grandmother to frighten you. She's really quite nice, and I think she likes you. She'll question you severely once she gets you alone, so you'd best be prepared," Elinor confided.

"I'm not nearly as convinced she's fond of me—and why would she want to question me privately?" Bella inquired.

Elinor wiggled onto the bed. The child waited until Bella finished pouring water from the china pitcher into the matching bowl before replying. "I'm not supposed to tell. It's a secret."

"Then you ought not tell me," Bella replied. "I wouldn't want to be the cause of your breaking a confidence."

"It's not really a confidence because I didn't give my word not to tell," she retorted. "I overheard Grandmother say she's going to see if you and Taylor will take me back to Massachusetts when you leave."

The comment rendered Bella momentarily speechless.

She stared at the girl, who was now peering back at her in wide-eyed anticipation.

"You mustn't tell anyone—not even Taylor. And when Grandmother brings up the topic, you'll appear surprised, won't you? She doesn't think I know a thing about her plan, and she'll think I was eavesdropping on her conversation."

"Weren't you?"

"Not really. I happened home early and she was talking to Grandfather. They didn't hear me come in the house."

Bella arched her eyebrows. "Once you realized they were discussing a matter that wasn't meant for your ears, did you announce your presence?"

Elinor wagged her head back and forth.

"Then you *were* eavesdropping."

"Well, I suppose just a little. But *please* act surprised. And I do hope you'll agree to her request. I truly want to go to America, and even though Taylor would probably consider me a nuisance, I'm hopeful you'd find my presence to your liking."

Elinor's words had rushed out like a torrent of rain, and Bella couldn't help but smile. "All of this is quite a surprise. Right now I think you'd best hurry down and help your grandmother with tea. Otherwise, she may be required to come looking for you."

Elinor jumped down from the bed. "You won't tell, will you?"

"I won't volunteer any information, but I won't lie, either. If I'm asked a direct question, I must tell the truth. That's the very most I can promise."

"That will do just fine. Thank you," Elinor said, flashing Bella a bright smile before scurrying off.

Bella stared at her reflection in the oval mirror above the walnut commode. The thought of a nine-year-old girl returning home with them was daunting. Yet how could she possibly deny the request? She considered the consequences of Elinor making her home with them until her head ached. *I'm borrowing trouble. No need to worry until I actually know there's a problem,* she decided, rubbing away the furrows that now creased her brow.

Barlow Kent turned and watched as the Farnsworths and Mannings were escorted to an oval table in the main section of the restaurant. Surely his eyes deceived him. He stood just outside the doorway and waited.

"A moment, sir," he said as the waiter returned. "Those people you seated—did they have a reservation?"

The man pursed his lips and sniffed. "Yes, of course," the man replied.

Barlow leaned in close to the waiter. "I believe I recognized one of the men, an old friend named John Farnsworth."

"Yes, Farnsworth," he agreed. Seeing that the man clearly knew the party in question, he became rather talkative. "Mr. Jarrow Farnsworth made the reservation. He said he wanted to have a surprise dinner reunion when his relatives arrived from America with their new wives. Perhaps you'd care to join them for a glass of wine?" he suggested.

Barlow grasped the waiter's arm. "No, absolutely not. I wouldn't want to disrupt their reunion. If I could beg your indulgence, I'd prefer you not tell John I inquired. I'd like to surprise him at a later date."

"Yes, of course. I enjoy a good surprise myself. Your secret is safe with me."

CHAPTER 6

Litchfield, New Hampshire
Late October

Thaddeus Arnold reached inside the breast pocket of his greatcoat and retrieved the missive he'd placed there earlier in the day. He wanted an opportunity to relax and read the letter without interruption. Downing a mug of ale, he waited while the alcohol spread its warmth through his chilled body and then pulled the flickering candle closer. Although the tavern was noisy, Thaddeus had strategically chosen a table in a rear corner where he could ignore the din.

He scanned the letter for any urgent message it might contain and then began to read it more carefully. It appeared William Thurston was enjoying himself in England, living on all the money he'd managed to accumulate while selling girls into the slave market and appropriating goods manufactured in the mills for sale to other unscrupulous marketers. Thaddeus imagined Thurston dining in a stylish English hotel, mingling among socially noteworthy people, and imbibing in the finest epicurean delights while Thaddeus remained in New England drinking ale in a seedy tavern. After all, William had committed crimes that far exceeded his own, yet William was enjoying life to its fullest. Thaddeus slumped down in his chair. Nothing had changed—life always treated him unfairly.

"Another mug?" the barkeep inquired.

Thaddeus nodded.

"The men at the table across the room wondered if you might want to join them for a few hands of poker."

Thaddeus leaned to one side in order to gain a better view. "You know any of them?"

"Two of them are locals. Don't know the other one."

"Are they any good at cards?"

"Average—never known 'em to cheat. You want your ale delivered here or over there?" he asked with obvious impatience to move on.

"May as well join them. Perhaps my luck will change," Thaddeus replied, pushing back from the table.

Wending his way through the tavern, Thaddeus moved toward the far table, assessing the men as he approached. He'd never seen any of them before and wondered what could have precipitated their invitation. He nodded before extending his hand. "I don't believe we've been properly introduced. I'm Thaddeus Arnold."

"Right. I'm James Wooner. This here's my brother, Sam, and that's Michael Sidley," James replied while nodding at the men surrounding the table.

"Pleased to make your acquaintance. Any particular reason you asked *me* to join you?"

James glanced at the others before looking back at Thaddeus. "You were the only person alone in the place," he stated simply.

Thaddeus relaxed and seated himself in the empty chair. He hoped the cards would fall in his favor; he could use a few extra coins to tide him over. Unfortunately, William

Thurston's letter hadn't mentioned any money coming his way in the near future. He picked up his cards and absently fanned them apart while his thoughts returned to the last time he'd met William Thurston. It had been in this very pub. The only piece of good fortune to have come his way in years, Thaddeus decided.

"You in?" the man named Michael asked.

Thaddeus looked at the hand one final time before snapping the cards together and placing them face down on the table. "Not with this hand." Like it or not, he'd have to play cautiously. He couldn't afford to lose any money.

The men continued their game, but Thaddeus quickly lost interest. What was it William had said when they'd met in the tavern? *"The gods must be smiling on both of us."* Yes, that was it, and the statement had held some truth. Had it not been for that meeting, Thaddeus would have been forced into some sort of manual labor. He loathed the very idea. Working as the supervisor of all those lovely young girls in the spinning room had been idyllic. Had it not been for Lilly Cheever and a few other girls who couldn't keep their mouths shut, he'd still be enjoying his position. There were days when he'd been required to help with machine repairs, but overall, he had enjoyed his time watching the girls as they moved about the room. And they had proved to be such easy prey, most of them afraid to say a word when he'd make advances. In fact, some of them had been more than willing to cooperate when given special privileges. Instinctively, he wet his lips.

Sam slapped his hand on the table. "You don't act like a man wanting to play cards."

Thaddeus startled at the interruption. "I apologize. My thoughts were elsewhere."

"That was mighty obvious," James replied. "Where you hail from, Mr. Arnold? Don't think I've seen you afore."

"I was in Lowell before coming here."

Michael shuffled the deck of cards and began to deal. "Lowell? I hear there's some high-paying wages for women-folk in that town. I gave a few minutes thought to going down there myself. I figure if they're paying them girls such good wages, I might find *me* a high-paying job. What you think, Mr. Arnold? S'pose there's work for the likes of me in Lowell? What kind of work was you doing?"

Thaddeus couldn't restrain his pride. "I was the supervisor of the spinning room in the Appleton Mill."

"Spinnin' room, huh? That don't sound too hard. Bet I could do that. What'd they pay you?"

Thaddeus took a drink of ale and wiped the back of his hand across his upper lip. "I doubt you would qualify, Mr. Sidley. A thorough knowledge of the machinery is required, not to mention the ability to supervise forty or fifty girls."

Michael emitted a boisterous laugh. "I might not be able to handle the machinery, but I sure could handle the women. How 'bout it, James? You think you could *supervise* a roomful of women?"

"What're you talking about, Michael? You can't even handle your own wife," James replied before turning toward Thaddeus. "How come you left such a good position, Mr. Arnold? I wouldn't think a man would soon give up a job like that."

Thaddeus pretended to be concentrating on his cards while he silently chastised himself. He should have kept his mouth shut. "I had other opportunities," he replied. "Your bid, Sam."

"What opportunity could possibly be better here in Litchfield?"

Obviously, Michael wasn't going to be deterred. "A confidential business venture. Until we're operational, I can't discuss it," Thaddeus replied while pulling out his pocket watch. "I didn't realize it was so late. I'm sorry to pull out of the game so early on, gentlemen, but I really must be on my way."

He didn't wait for a response. Shoving back from the table, he bid the men farewell and exited the tavern. He'd not soon become mired in another situation in which strangers could question him. The evening had proven a failure. Not only had he managed to raise suspicion about himself, but he had come away from the gaming table without so much as a few extra coins. He would pen a letter to Thurston this evening telling him John Farnsworth's nephew had been recently wed. Thaddeus doubted whether he would find the information of great interest, but William *had* promised to pay for any details relating to the mills, its employees, or those highfalutin' Boston Associates. Of course, he couldn't expect much remuneration for such an insignificant morsel. Another journey to Lowell would be necessary to ferret out the latest happenings, he decided.

Mrs. Hobson was peeking from behind the dust-filled draperies that hung like red-clad sentries protecting the front window of her boardinghouse. Thaddeus gave a quick wave of his hand, for he wanted the snooping woman to know he had seen her. Mrs. Hobson was everything he detested in a woman: she was meddlesome, devious, and gossiping. But as far as Thaddeus was concerned, most women filled that description. Her boardinghouse, however, was inexpensive and, as much as he hated to admit it, she did serve a decent meal. He entered the foyer and immediately walked into the parlor, where Mrs. Hobson sat demurely stitching a piece of embroidery.

He leveled a beady-eyed glare in the woman's direction. "Is there some particular reason you were peeking through the draperies, Mrs. Hobson?"

"I heard a rapping noise outside the house and was checking to see if an animal was on the porch."

"I didn't know animals were endowed with the ability to rap," he replied with a sneer.

Mrs. Hobson's cheeks flushed bright pink. Pleased with himself, Thaddeus turned on his heel and marched up the stairs and then down the narrow hallway to his room. After loosening his collar, he seated himself at the small table, took up his pen, and began composing a letter to William Thurston. After embellishing the report as much as he dared, Thaddeus folded the missive and placed it on the chest. He'd post it first thing tomorrow, he decided while disrobing for bed.

A short time later he settled his wiry body beneath the bedcovers, but sleep eluded him. His mind was filled with thoughts of his former wife. Even though he loathed the prospect of once again returning to their former home in Lowell, he relished the discomfort his visits to Lowell caused Naomi. His jaw tightened at the thought of her. He knew when he married her she would require a heavy hand if she were to become a suitable wife. He had attempted to make Naomi into a decent, respectable woman. Unfortunately, he hadn't succeeded in changing her. Their marriage had been a disaster—all because of Naomi's behavior, of course. And yet everyone had taken her side, accusing *him* of mistreatment. Even the management at the mills had aligned themselves with Naomi. Why, Matthew Cheever had even gained corporate consent for Naomi and his daughter to remain in the house their family had occupied while he was supervisor of the spinning floor. Such an occurrence was previously unheard of—and yet Naomi and their daughter, Theona, still remained in the house, an ever-present thorn in his side.

Calling at the house on the pretense of visiting their daughter did, however, give him a valid excuse for his return trips to Lowell. Unfortunately, his former wife hadn't proved the font of information he had hoped for. In fact, she preferred to remain silent while he was in the house. However, one of her boarders would occasionally pass along some interesting scrap—that's how he had discovered Taylor Manning was to be married. In order to garner any information of value on his next visit to Lowell, he would most likely be forced to visit the Acre or at least a local pub. He didn't relish the thought, for too many of the locals remembered the reason he'd been dismissed from the mills. They enjoyed the opportunity to look down their self-righteous noses at him. But one day that would all change.

Taking pleasure in the satisfying thought, Thaddeus pulled the scratchy wool blanket under his chin. Yes, one day those supercilious Associates and the haughty townspeople of Lowell would pay for what they'd done to him.

CHAPTER 6

Lowell
November

Daughtie rushed down the stairs carrying a stack of fabric, her navy blue cottage bonnet swinging back and forth from one finger as she made her descent. "I hope everyone is ready, because we're going to be late if we don't hurry," she called out toward the kitchen.

"I'm helping Theona with her cape and then we'll be with you," Mrs. Arnold replied, her voice drifting into the hallway from the rear of the house.

Ruth came through the parlor. "I'm ready," she said while tying the wide green ribbons of her bonnet into a fashionable bow beneath her chin. She nodded toward the fabric in Daughtie's arms. "Do you want me to carry some of that?"

Daughtie loosened her grip, and Ruth gathered half of the cloth into her own arms. "I didn't realize you had accumulated so much fabric since our last meeting," Ruth remarked.

"It's wonderful, isn't it?" Mrs. Arnold said as she led

Theona by the hand. "I think we're ready. Do you need some additional help with the cloth?"

Daughtie shook her head. "No, we can manage. You look after Theona. Are you excited to be visiting the Cheevers, Theona?"

The little girl bobbed her head up and down, her dark curls springing about with each nod. "I wike Viowet," she said in her lisping toddler voice.

"I'm certain you do. She's a sweet little girl—just like you," Daughtie said, using her free hand to tug the hood of Theona's cape up over the child's head. "There. It's chilly outside. You'll want to keep your ears warm."

They walked more slowly than usual since Theona's short legs were unable to accommodate the stride of her elders. Finally the child's mother swooped her up. "I think I can carry her the remaining distance," Mrs. Arnold told them.

"We're right on time," Daughtie reassured Mrs. Arnold as they walked up the steps of the Cheevers' front porch and lifted the brass door knocker.

The front door opened and Theona squealed in delight. "Viowet!" The child squirmed for release from her mother's arms.

The women smiled as they watched the two girls nearly fall atop each other while attempting to embrace. "Rowena is going to care for the girls upstairs in Violet's nursery," Lilly told Mrs. Arnold.

"Oh, but that seems unfair. I'm sure she'd rather be downstairs with the other women. I can go up with the girls."

Rowena came out of the parlor in a flurry. "Oh no. *I* get to watch after the girls. My stitching is atrocious, and I utterly detest any type of sewing. My mother considers herself a failure because I can't stitch a straight hem," Rowena confided with a giggle.

Naomi gave Rowena a sweet smile. "If you insist. But if Theona becomes a burden or if she fails to mind properly, please come and get me," she said before turning to Theona and removing the child's cape. "You be a good girl and mind Miss Rowena."

"I will," the child promised, giving her mother a dimple-cheeked smile.

"She's a beautiful little girl," Lilly remarked as the women walked into the parlor.

Naomi nodded. "Yes, sometimes I can't believe she's actually mine. I mean, when you consider the appearance of Thaddeus and me, it's rather difficult to believe we could produce such a beautiful child."

Lilly grasped Naomi's hand in her own. "Nonsense! You're a lovely woman, Naomi, and God's very own creation."

Naomi grinned. "One of His lesser accomplishments, I fear. Now, let's get started with our sewing or we'll not have sufficient time to complete our final quilt this evening."

The women had been working consistently throughout the year at their weekly gatherings and, as time permitted, at home. Lilly Cheever, along with Addie and Mintie Beecher, Bella, Daughtie, and Ruth, had formed a Ladies Aid group that had grown over the past two years. Originally they had organized to stitch a few blankets and garments for the needy residents of Lowell. The number of participants in their group that first year had been limited and production had been meager. But thanks to Lilly Cheever's influence, they had, since the beginning of the year, been able to secure the end pieces of cloth made in the mills. That fact alone had caused the members to enlist the help of additional women. The variety of fabrics now made it possible to create an array of goods rather than the few quilts they'd managed to produce during those first years.

The founders of the group, however, continued to maintain secrecy concerning a portion of the goods that they distributed to the Irish community. "No need to borrow trouble," the women had decided before expanding their membership. It was difficult to determine in advance who might be offended by the prospect of assisting the disadvantaged Irish folks living in the Acre. While the larger group met weekly at the Episcopal church, the original members plus one or two trusted newcomers, such as Mrs. Arnold, had remained intact and continued to meet at the Cheever residence on Thursday evenings.

"I've been wondering about our distribution this year, ladies," Lilly started. "Miss Beecher, Naomi, and I have been attending the weekly gatherings at the Episcopal church during the daytime as well as our Thursday evening group. I think they will agree that production this year far exceeds our expectations. We've even had a number of ladies bringing older clothing to donate. With the exception of those goods going to the Acre, I wonder if we should rely upon the churches to distribute the goods. What do you think?"

"We'd certainly have to determine how much would go to each church. There may be a larger membership at St. Anne's, but the needs of the parishioners aren't as great there, either. I would guess that some of the Baptists and Methodists could use more help," Mintie replied.

"We certainly don't want to offend or humiliate anyone," Daughtie quietly offered. "Could the preachers make an announcement during church services? The preachers could prepare a list of needs for us to fill and then distribute the items. That way the names of the recipients could be kept private—only their pastor would know."

Lilly gave Daughtie's hand a reassuring pat. "That's a

wonderful idea, Daughtie. I think folks would appreciate maintaining their privacy."

Mintie's forehead creased in deep lines before she jabbed her needle into the quilt. "Pride! When folks are set on keeping their need private, it's nothing but pride."

"Well, I for one, don't think it's any of our business who receives these items," Mrs. Arnold replied. "It's difficult enough admitting to yourself when you need help. Even if other folks realize you're in dire straits, a person needs to be able to hold her head up in public."

"As I said—pride," Mintie repeated, her pinched features revealing the lines of her age.

"And what foible is it that requires one to know who is the recipient of one's charity? Wouldn't that, too, be a form of pride, Miss Beecher?" Daughtie's voice was barely audible, yet the attention of every woman in the room focused upon her before slowly shifting back to Mintie Beecher.

Mintie's eyes flashed with anger. "Well, I never," she sputtered.

Daughtie gave the older woman a retiring smile and prayed God would provide the perfect words to resolve this situation. "I'm sure you never considered the concept prideful. I am certain a woman of your stature and Christian compassion would never intentionally promote an attitude of pride," she said in a gentle tone. She held her breath, awaiting Mintie's reply.

Mintie twisted her neck, shifting her head upward as though she were attempting to keep her nose above water. "You're absolutely correct, Daughtie. I wouldn't want to act in a prideful manner. Thank you for that kind revelation. I think we should follow Daughtie's suggestion."

Daughtie softly exhaled and returned Mintie's smile. "Thank *you,* Miss Beecher."

"Tut, tut, right is right. Let's finish this quilt or we'll still be stitching come Christmas. I hear tell there's to be an antislavery meeting at the Pawtucket church in December," the older woman noted, skillfully changing the topic of discussion.

Lilly cut a piece of thread and deftly drew it through the eye of her needle. "I'm hoping Matthew will agree to attend, although I'm not certain he'll find it wise."

"Why would your husband find it imprudent?" Naomi inquired.

"Matthew is reliant upon the Corporation for his employment. The Corporation is reliant upon plantation owners for cotton. The plantation owners are reliant upon slaves to cultivate the cotton. It's a vicious circle. However, Matthew doesn't believe in slavery," she added.

"That's what the Associates say when they're in Boston and the other big northern cities, but they tell a different story when they are in the South," Daughtie said. She glanced up from her stitching. The other women were once again staring at her. "At least that's what I'm told," she added.

"And who told you this?" Mintie inquired as she outlined a yellow flower with tiny, evenly spaced stitches.

"It's on the handbills advertising the meeting."

"I read the broadsides and saw no such thing," Mintie countered.

Daughtie shook her head. "That information isn't on the broadsides posted about town, but there are printed circulars being handed out. They give additional information concerning the antislavery movement that's beginning to take root. The paper lists groups that have taken a stand and those that seem to be straddling the fence. That's what they say about the Boston Associates—that they're straddling the fence."

"I wonder if Matthew has seen those circulars," Lilly murmured.

Ruth picked up a pair of scissors and clipped her thread.

"I doubt it. The circulars are reserved for those people truly aligned with the antislavery cause. That wouldn't include the mill management."

"What else does this circular say?" Lilly asked.

"Mostly it lists those people who are pro slavery and others, like the Associates, who speak from both sides of their mouths. The handbill contains a little more information about Prudence Crandall, the woman who will be speaking at the meeting. Other than that, the particulars are very similar."

"Oh, and you'll never guess the interesting similarities between Daughtie and Prudence Crandall," Ruth exclaimed.

"They're both antislavery," Lilly replied with a grin.

"Well, yes, but in addition to that," Ruth said with a giggle.

Mintie tapped her forehead for a moment. "Is Prudence Crandall one of those Shakers, too?"

"No, but she's a Quaker."

"Practically the same thing," Mintie said.

"It isn't," Daughtie protested.

"No, but they're both from Canterbury," Ruth interjected delightedly.

Mintie pursed her lips. "You see, I'm right. They're both Shakers."

"No, Miss Mintie. Prudence Crandall is a Quaker, and she lives in Canterbury, Connecticut, whereas Daughtie was a Shaker and lived in Canterbury, New Hampshire. Isn't that astonishing?" Ruth asked.

"Well, it's interesting," Mintie agreed. "It would be more astonishing if they were both *Shakers,*" she insisted. "What does this Prudence Crandall have to say that's so important to the Negroes and the antislavery movement?"

"She is the headmistress at a girls' boarding school," Daughtie replied.

"Well, I would certainly think they could find someone

other than the headmistress of a boarding school to speak about the slavery issue."

Daughtie smiled. "It's a boarding school for Negro girls."

"*What?* I've never heard of such a thing," Lilly replied. "And this school is in Connecticut? What do the towns-people say about this?"

"That's what she'll be talking about at the meeting," Daughtie replied. "I can hardly wait to hear what she has to say."

"It does sound interesting. Perhaps Matthew will agree to attend once he hears this information," Lilly replied.

"Did I hear my name mentioned?" Matthew Cheever inquired as he entered the hallway.

"Only briefly, dear. I'll tell you about it later," she replied. "Oh, good evening, Liam," Lilly greeted.

"Evening," Liam replied pleasantly.

"Nice to see all of you ladies," Matthew said to the group of women and then turned back toward his wife. "We'll be in my office should you need me, Lilly."

"Isn't that an Irishman with Matthew?" Mintie inquired.

"Why, yes, Liam Donohue. He's the stonemason who is doing all this marvelous handiwork about town. Liam did our fireplaces," Lilly replied.

"He's obviously talented, I'll give him that," Mintie replied. "But it seems odd Matthew would bring him here—to your home."

Daughtie leaned forward and looked directly at Miss Mintie. "Why is that, Miss Beecher? Because Mr. Donohue is Irish?"

Mintie leaned forward. "Well, they are given to the—" she raised her hand up and down to her mouth for a moment before adding—"drink."

"Surely you don't believe that just because some Irish

are given to imbibing that all Irish behave the same way."

Mintie arched her eyebrows and leveled a look of irritation in Daughtie's direction, but before she could speak, Lilly put down her needle and stood. "Would you help me prepare tea, Daughtie?" she asked.

"Of course," Daughtie replied. Lilly had never requested assistance at any of their previous gatherings, and Daughtie silently chastised herself for prodding Mintie. Obviously Lilly was requesting her assistance in the kitchen in order to prevent any further unpleasant conversation among the ladies.

They had barely entered the kitchen when Daughtie spoke. "I apologize for my unpleasant behavior this evening. I've spoken out of turn twice, and I now fear Miss Beecher won't return to our meetings."

Lilly laughed aloud while donning an apron of blue-striped cotton. "It would take more than a few disagreeable comments to keep Mintie away. You think that's why I've asked you to help in the kitchen, isn't it? To reprimand you for your behavior?"

"Isn't it?" Daughtie asked.

"No, of course not. Mintie Beecher is quite capable of defending herself in any circumstance—especially when she has a parasol in her hand. Why don't you arrange these biscuits on the tray while I prepare our tea." Lilly pointed toward a hand-painted china serving platter, and Daughtie immediately set to work. "I did have another reason for requesting you join me, however," Lilly admitted.

Daughtie glanced up from the tray, her interest aroused. "What is it?"

"Would you consider coordinating our gifts for the people in the Acre?"

"But *you've* taken charge of distribution in the Acre ever since we began this project, and it has worked well. Why change now?"

Lilly gave her a tentative smile. "It's clear you have a heart for others, Daughtie. You're a good choice. Matthew asked me to minimize my activities for a while. I haven't been feeling well of late."

"You're ill?" Daughtie's heart began to pulse in quick, heavy thumps against her chest. Her mother had talked the same way when she became ill. Two months later she had died.

"I'm not yet certain, but we may have another child next year. Matthew insists I take care of myself."

Daughtie breathed a sigh of relief. "How very wonderful for all of you. Well, in that event, I'll do my best. But I'll need your guidance. I don't even know anybody in the Acre."

"There's not much involved. You won't actually be required to go into the Acre. In fact, Liam Donohue, the Irishman who came in with Matthew, will be your Irish liaison. Would you like to meet him?"

Daughtie brushed a strand of hair behind one ear. "If you'd like. We won't be interfering with their business, will we?"

"Of course not. Matthew never discourages my interruptions when he's working at home. However, I'm sure he'd be even more welcoming if we took a few of these pastries for them. I've discovered that men are always hungry."

Lilly led the way while Daughtie followed close behind with a plate of biscuits, scones, and marmalade. "Look what we've brought you," Lilly announced as they entered Matthew's library. "You can put their refreshments on the desk," she instructed Daughtie.

"Not the desk," Matthew said, jumping up and taking the plate from Daughtie's hands. "This table will be fine. We have drawings on the desk. I wouldn't want to get food on my paper work," he explained.

Daughtie nodded and glanced toward the desk where Liam Donohue stood hunched over a sheaf of papers, his dark curly hair falling across his forehead. Daughtie watched his arms bulge in muscled strength as he pushed himself into an upright position and nodded in greeting.

"I wanted to introduce Liam and Daughtie since they will be handling the charitable goods for the Acre this year," Lilly said. "Daughtie, this is Liam Donohue, Lowell's illustrious stonemason. And Liam, this is Daughtie Winfield, a fine young lady who works at the Appleton."

Liam smiled and his entire face appeared to soften, his dark eyes sparkling. "Pleased to make yar acquaintance, Miss Winfield," Liam said, reaching for the cup of tea she offered.

His hand encircled hers warmly. She met his gaze and quickly looked away, breathless and unable to speak. He continued to hold her hand, finally giving a tiny squeeze that brought her to her senses. "A pleasure, Mr. Donohue," she croaked, pulling back on her hand.

"I look forward to assistin' you with the distribution," he said.

"What? Oh yes, the distribution. I'm sure it will be an enjoyable experience," she replied. An enjoyable experience? What was she saying? She felt the hot sting of blood rushing to her cheeks.

"I'm certain it will," Liam stoically replied. "I've already begun coordinatin' a list with the priest at St. Patrick's. Ya can send word when the items are ready for delivery."

If he thought she had just made a total fool of herself, he didn't let on, and for that, Daughtie was thankful. She didn't know how she was to send word—she had no idea where he lived—but this wasn't the time or place to inquire. She'd get the necessary information from Lilly Cheever.

Lilly brushed Matthew's cheek with a kiss. "We'd best get back to our sewing."

Daughtie glanced toward Liam. He was staring at her, not a gawking, uncomfortable stare, but one of gentle kindness—as though he'd known her for years. His eyes were filled with a tenderness that somehow made her long to be loved. She looked away, confused by the feelings this man had stirred within her.

"We'd best serve tea to the ladies or they'll think we've deserted them," Lilly said as they left the room.

Daughtie clenched her fists into tight knots and willed them to cease their shaking as she followed Lilly back into the kitchen. Her fingers trembled while she finished arranging the tray of pastries. What was wrong with her? She was acting like a silly schoolgirl who had never before met a man.

"Liam is a very nice man; quite talented, also. Did you like him?" Lilly inquired while preparing the pot of tea.

"I think we will be able to work together quite nicely," Daughtie pleasantly responded.

"Yes, I believe you will," Lilly replied, the hint of a smile tugging at her lips.

Mrs. Arnold looked up from her stitching when they entered the room. "There you are, Lilly. We were just talking about the new doctor who will soon be moving to Lowell. Have you heard any word on exactly when he'll be coming?"

"Matthew did mention the fact that Dr. Ketter's arrival was discussed at the last meeting of the Associates. Although they had hoped he could begin his medical practice the end of the month, he's been detained until the end of the year. Did you tell the others he'll be setting up his office in your house, Naomi?"

Naomi nodded. "Yes, and of course, Ruth and Daughtie knew. The carpenters have already begun making the minimal changes necessary to the downstairs rooms."

"So old Dr. Barnard is finally going to quit practicing. It's about time," Mintie declared. "He can't hear at all, and his eyesight failed him long ago. He should have quit doctoring ten years ago."

Lilly giggled. "We can always depend upon you to speak your mind, can't we, Miss Beecher?"

Mintie gave an affirmative nod of her head. "Absolutely. If there's one thing I've always had, it's an opinion— and a willingness to share it with others. If my sister, Adelaide, were here, she'd give a hearty amen to that admission."

Lilly offered the plate of pastries to Mintie. "Speaking of your sister, I do hope they all have a wonderful time in England. What fun it will be for Addie to meet all of her new relatives and visit the places Mr. Farnsworth speaks of so fondly."

Mintie jabbed her needle in and out of the fabric. "Pshaw! I think all this traveling to England is nonsense. I can't imagine why anyone would want to associate with anyone living in that treacherous country. Believe me, I told Adelaide she'd do better to stay here in Massachusetts than traipse across the ocean. But did she listen? No! Off she went, pretty as you please, without a thought to what I said."

"I doubt there's any reason to fear for her safety. England and the United States are no longer at war, Miss Beecher."

"So they say," Mintie replied, giving her needle a resolute stab. "Tell me more about this new doctor. Where does he hail from? Not England, I hope. I could never utilize his skills if he were trained in England."

Mrs. Arnold took a sip of her tea. "No, I understand he completed his medical training a few years ago and has been doctoring in Vermont the past two years."

"Nothing but a young whippersnapper. I'd guess he prescribed the wrong tonic to one of those Vermont farmers, and now they've run him out of town on a rail," Mintie declared quite seriously. "He'll set up his practice here in Lowell and likely kill us all."

The room fell silent, the women obviously unsure how to react to Mintie's comment, until Lilly laughed aloud. Soon they all joined in, with Mintie appearing to delight in the revelry as much as the rest of them. "Let's at least give him a chance before declaring him incompetent," Lilly said between gasps of laughter.

"If you insist," Mintie replied, trying hard not to appear amused. The group once again burst into laughter.

"You ladies seem to be enjoying yourselves," Matthew genially remarked. He stood in the parlor doorway with Liam at his side.

"To tell you the truth, Mr. Cheever, I don't know *when* I've had such fun," Mintie replied. Matthew shared a surprised glance with Lilly and Daughtie.

"I'm delighted to hear it," he responded with a smile.

Daughtie looked past Matthew and watched Liam shrug his broad shoulders into a dark woolen coat. He suddenly glanced up and met her gaze while tugging his cap tightly onto his head. Before she could turn away, he gave her a broad smile and it appeared as if he winked at her. *Did* he wink? Surely he hadn't been so bold, although she felt a strange tingling sensation at the prospect. Likely he had something in his eye. After all, she shouldn't be hoping a man had winked at her—especially not an Irishman. Yet she couldn't turn her gaze away from him.

CHAPTER 7

London

Once he bid the doctor good-night, John Farnsworth stood at the front entryway and momentarily pressed his forehead against the door in a futile attempt to draw strength from the firm, cool wood. He had hoped for better news and now needed time to digest the doctor's prognosis before returning to his father's bedside. Methodically he turned the brass key, locked the door, and entered the parlor. Edging down into an overstuffed chair, he leaned back and rested his head on the cushion before silently reviewing the doctor's words.

"Ah, there you are," his wife said.

Addie stood in the hallway looking in upon him. He straightened in the chair and gave her a cheerless smile. "Come sit down. The doctor left only minutes ago."

"I do hope he gave you a good report on your father."

John shook his head. "I'm afraid not, my dear. In fact, I fear Father is much worse than any of us anticipated. Although the doctor is unable to explain this flare-up, he strongly recommended I cancel my return voyage until . . ."

John attempted to hold himself in check. It would serve no purpose to give in to his feelings of despair. He needed to remain positive for his father's sake.

Addie sat down in the chair next to John and clasped his hand. "Of course, my dear. We'll stay as long as necessary."

John leaned over and kissed her cheek. "Thank you, Addie. I know you wanted to be home before Christmas, and I'm certain remaining here is going to cause Mintie no end of worry on your behalf." He forced a smile. "She'll no doubt believe you to have been kidnapped by English spies."

Addie offered him a tender smile. "I'll write her a letter. Once she knows your father has taken a turn for the worse, she'll understand. Mintie has her faults, but she believes family should be together in their time of need."

"I'll need to pen a missive to Kirk and Matthew, also. I'm certain they'll be less than pleased with this turn of events."

Patting his hand, Addie encouraged, "They'll have no choice but to understand. In any case, these circumstances aren't of your own making. What exactly did the doctor say?"

"That's part of my dilemma. Dr. Adams says he doesn't understand what has occurred. Father was making excellent progress until this sudden turn for the worse, and the doctor can find no reason for the change. Therefore, he hesitates to change the medical regimen. He'll return tomorrow, but if Father doesn't begin a turnaround within a few days, he fears the worst. Of course, he was quick to add that he has no way of being certain when any change may actually occur. That's why he suggested we postpone our voyage."

Addie nodded. "We'll abandon our plans and leave our return date open, John. I'll have the opportunity to experience an English Christmas," she cheerily replied.

He smiled and rose from the chair with a little of his old sparkle returning. "And somehow we'll make it a very merry Christmas. In fact, we'll go out and do some Christmas shopping tomorrow. Our gifts may arrive in Lowell on time if we can get them on a ship very soon. What do you say? We ought to find at least a gift or two for Mintie and perhaps something for Matthew and Lilly. We'll take Bella and Taylor along and make a nice day of it. Cordelia will be here to look after Father. And, of course, we'll invite Elinor to join us."

Addie frowned, her brow furrowing into deep wrinkles. "Do you think we dare spend the day out in public? Up until this point, you've wanted to remain somewhat reclusive. After all, you know there are those in England who still consider you a traitor."

"I don't know that for a fact, my dear. I promised the Associates I would be cautious more because of their fears than my own. I truly doubt there's anyone who cares whether I've returned. Besides, London is a large city, and it's not my home. I imagine anyone possibly holding a grudge against me would be in Lancashire, not London," he explained. "It will be good for us to get out. Taylor and Bella are the only ones who have had much fun since our arrival."

"Well, it *is* their honeymoon. They should be going to see the sights and having fun," Addie replied. "I do know Bella has been completely agog over the places they've visited thus far. She told me all about seeing St. Paul's Cathedral. Oh, and she had a marvelous time strolling past a place called Buckingham House. They're in the process of converting it into a palace for the king."

"This excursion hasn't been fair to you, what with all this worry about keeping myself secluded. Well, from this point forward, we're going to find a spark of enjoyment amidst this gloom."

"I've not been unhappy, John. We've been able to share time with your father and each other. And I know you've finished several books you've been eager to read."

"That's true enough. But who knows if we'll ever be back in England again. You need to see London before we sail. We can plan a list of places you'd like to see, but first I'll go and visit with Father. I know he's anxious to hear the doctor's report. Thank you, Addie. I now feel as though I can keep focused while talking to Father," John replied. He leaned down and gave her a kiss before leaving the room. He turned to face her once he'd reached the bottom of the stairway. "You warm my soul, Addie Farnsworth."

"Thank you, John."

He nodded, continued up the stairs, and inhaled a deep breath before opening his father's bedroom door. "Father? Are you awake?" he whispered.

"Come in, son," his father replied in a weakened voice. He lifted a hand to wave John forward. The veins in his father's hand were a cloudy bluish-green against his aged, fragile skin. "What did Dr. Adams have to say?" He paused, looking intently at John. "I'm dying, aren't I? How much longer do I have?"

John pulled a straight-backed chair close to his father's bedside and sat down. "The doctor can't tell us much as he's not sure what has happened. However, he doesn't want to change his treatment—at least until he has a better idea of what's occurring. He'll be back tomorrow. In the meantime, he thinks you should continue to rest and take your medicine."

His father gave him a feeble smile. "I don't have much choice about that, now, do I? And what of your departure?"

"I talked with Addie before coming upstairs to visit

with you. We've decided we'll stay until you're stronger. Besides, Addie assures me she would like to observe Christmas in England. This will be the perfect opportunity," John replied, hoping the note of cheerfulness in his voice would forestall any questions his father might raise.

"Having you home for Christmas will be very special." He paused for a moment and then said, "I think I'd like to rest awhile, and I'm sure you're hungry. Why don't you go downstairs and partake of the noonday meal with your wife while I take a nap?"

John gently patted his father's hand. "You rest, then, and I'll be back later this afternoon."

"Oh, I've simply had the most marvelous day," Addie said as their carriage came to a stop.

"I'm glad to hear it," John replied as he stepped from the carriage and turned to assist his wife. "I fear we've traveled enough ground to have ridden all the way back to America."

Addie pulled her wool cape close. "You didn't mind too much, did you, dear?"

John smiled. "Not at all. Just seeing how happy it made you is enough to cause me to do it all again tomorrow if that would be your wish."

Addie laughed. "I never could have imagined the grandeur of it all." She looked up at the building in front of them. "Oh, a teahouse. How lovely. Could we stop in?"

John took hold of her arm. "It was exactly what I had in mind. It's time for proper genteel folk to have their high tea. This teahouse has been highly recommended to me— by one Mrs. Arabella Manning."

"Well, if it passed Bella's scrutiny, it must be wonderful."

John opened the door and escorted his wife into the

small shop. Without delay they were shown to a lovely linen-covered table.

"Oh, it's so charming. Warm and cozy and not at all pretentious," Addie exclaimed. John helped her out of her wrap, taking care to seat her before tending to his own coat and hat.

It wasn't long before they were presented with a steaming pot of tea and a platter of tiny sandwiches and cakes, fruit tarts, and scones. A bowl of jam and clotted cream rounded out the offering.

Addie sampled a bit of each thing, feeling contented and not at all embarrassed by her enthusiasm. "I suppose you must think me quite out of step with propriety," she told John, watching him for any sign that he did indeed feel that way.

John merely laughed. "Addie, you can be out of step with propriety any time you like, but I see nothing wrong with a woman enjoying herself at the table."

"Mintie would be aghast. She has always chided me about my plump waist. If she saw me with clotted cream, she would never let me hear the end of it."

John reached over to gently touch Addie's arm. "You must never concern yourself with such things. I find you perfectly sized and delightful company." He touched his hand to her cheek, causing Addie to feel flushed at the public display.

"John, you shouldn't. People will think we're lovers instead of husband and wife."

At this John laughed with an abandonment Addie hadn't seen since their arrival in London. Several of the other patrons looked their way and Addie felt her cheeks burn.

"John!"

He glanced over his shoulder and smiled at those who watched him. Then he quickly turned his attention back to

Addie. "You are such a delight."

Addie calmed and returned her focus to the pastries on her plate. "I want to do some more Christmas shopping if there is time. I'd like to find something special for your father, as well as Daughtie and Bella and Lilly."

"Sounds as though we'll have to buy another trunk, as well," John teased. "For how else will we be able to transport all of the things you purchased for Mintie, as well as these new gifts?"

Addie frowned. She hadn't thought of the cost. She'd been guilty of spending John's money quite freely, in fact. "Oh, I am sorry, John. I hadn't considered the extravagance of it all."

"I'm not chiding you for your choices, my dear. I'm teasing you. We will purchase whatever your heart desires. Even if we need to buy ten trunks to haul it all back. I have made my fortune and am quite capable of providing for you."

"But your generosity is beyond anything I've ever known." Addie gave her husband a smile. "Even the Judge didn't spoil Mintie and me as much as this." The thought of her departed father reminded her again of Jarrow Farnsworth's own impending death. "What do you suppose your father would enjoy as a gift?"

"I do believe there are some wonderful new books available in the shop just around the corner from the house. I was down there the . . ." John fell silent. Addie watched as he slowly turned.

"What is it?" she asked.

"I don't know." He turned back around, shaking his head. "I just felt a chill run up my spine—as if someone were watching me."

"Oh, John, you don't suppose . . ."

He smiled and lifted his cup. "It's nothing. Someone

probably opened the door, then changed their mind about coming in. That's all."

"Still, perhaps we should return home. We've been gone a long time."

John looked as though he might refuse but then nodded. "Perhaps you're right." He quickly paid the bill and collected their coats.

They said nothing as they exited the teahouse, but John continued to look over his shoulder. "Do you mind if we just walk?" he asked.

Addie couldn't help but notice the edge to his voice, but she made no comment. Nodding, she looped her arm through John's. His body was unyielding, almost rigid. Something wasn't right, but she could see he didn't want to discuss it. Forcing a smile, she pulled him along. "Look, it's starting to snow."

John glanced to the lead gray skies overhead and back to Addie. "Yes. It's grown colder—we'd best hurry."

CHAPTER 8

Lowell

Irresistible excitement captured Daughtie's imagination as she thought of the note she'd received earlier that day. She quickly gathered the goods to be distributed in the Acre, anxious to be on her way. Over these past weeks, her routine had not varied. Each Tuesday evening she would take the items completed by the Ladies Aid to the storage room in the circulating library. But tonight was different. Tonight Liam Donohue was to meet her and load the boxes into his wagon for delivery to the Catholic priest, who would distribute the items to the Acre's Irish residents. Weeks had passed since she'd last seen Liam. She thought of the wink he'd leveled in her direction at the Cheevers' house. Once again, she pulled the scrap of paper from her skirt pocket and read it.

I look forward to seeing you this evening. Liam Donohue

Daughtie's lips curved into a faint smile while considering these words. He could have simply written *I'll arrive at eight o'clock*. Instead, his message revealed he was looking forward to seeing her. Her heart quickened at the thought.

Then Daughtie chastised herself. She was likely reading more into his message than he'd intended. Liam was simply being polite, she decided. Yet there had been no need for him to send her a note at all. He knew Lilly Cheever was going to advise her of his arrival. Perhaps he *was* looking forward to seeing her. She packed the last hand-stitched quilt into the box and bounded down the stairs, a bright smile on her face.

Ruth was seated in the parlor and glanced up from the book she was reading. "You appear cheerful this evening," she remarked.

Daughtie pulled her cloak from one of the wooden pegs that lined the wall beside the front door. "I always enjoy working at the library. I'll talk to you when I get home if you're still awake."

"If you happen to see a book I might enjoy, would you sign it out for me? I've only a few pages to read before I'll be finished with this one."

"I'll inspect the shelves for any new offerings," Daughtie promised before hurrying out the door. She didn't want Ruth to draw her into a lengthy conversation. Even though it was early, Daughtie didn't want to run the risk of missing Liam.

The weight of the box had caused her steps to slow, but the library clock revealed she was still a half hour early. "Good evening, Mrs. Potter," she called out while placing the heavy box on the floor just inside the front door.

"Good evening, Daughtie," the older woman greeted, rounding one of the bookshelves and walking toward the front of the store. She glanced toward the clock above the checkout desk. "You're early this evening."

Daughtie nodded. "If you'd like to get home a few minutes early, I don't mind if you leave now."

"Only if you're certain it wouldn't be an inconvenience. I haven't been overly busy today. In fact, I was dusting shelves to keep myself occupied."

"The new books we ordered haven't arrived, have they?"

Mrs. Potter shuffled through the papers on top of the desk. "We received a partial shipment the day before yesterday, but I've already cataloged and shelved them, and I've posted the past due notices."

"No wonder you're dusting shelves," Daughtie replied with a grin. "I'll have to hope there are a lot of people anxious to borrow books this evening if I'm to keep myself busy."

Mrs. Potter fastened her cape and then removed a small reticule from the bottom drawer of the desk. "Well, I'll be off. You're on the schedule for next week," she reminded Daughtie while pointing toward the list atop the desk.

Once Mrs. Potter had exited the building, Daughtie picked up the list of recently purchased books. Making her way up and down the aisles, she pulled a number of volumes from the shelves and carried them to the front desk. Surely among all these selections she could find something intriguing for Ruth.

The clock above the desk slowly ticked off the minutes. Several girls came in looking for specific titles, a few girls returned books they had borrowed, and one or two sheepishly returned overdue books and quickly paid their fines. Mrs. Potter would be pleased. Daughtie carefully drew a line through the names posted on the past due notice and once again returned to the volumes she'd pulled from the shelf. The bell over the front door jingled, and Daughtie glanced up from her reading. Liam Donohue was pulling off his cap as he approached the desk.

"Good evenin', Miss Winfield."

"Good evening, Mr. Donohue. I was beginning to wonder if you had forgotten," she said, giving him a sweet smile.

He stood directly in front of her, looking down into her eyes. "I'd never be forgettin' something so important as comin' here tonight."

The odd sensation she'd experienced when she last saw Liam returned in full force, once again taking her by surprise. However, she wasn't certain if Liam meant he wouldn't forget something as important as picking up the items for the Acre or if he meant he wouldn't forget coming to see her. She hoped it was the latter yet felt embarrassed to admit such a thing—even if only to herself.

"Is it this box here?" he asked while pointing toward the items she'd carried into the library earlier in the evening.

"No. Well, yes—but that's not everything."

He gave her a hearty laugh. "I was wonderin' why I'd be needin' my wagon if there was only this one box to be hauled off. Have you been keepin' yarself busy this evenin'?"

"Not too busy. I've been glancing through a few of these books to pass the time."

"Perhaps I should be seein' if you 'ave a book on how to fancy up a house. Do you have a book such as that?" His Irish lilt delighted her senses.

"A home decorating book? You want something that explains how to enhance the beauty of your home?"

Liam grinned and nodded. "Aye. The construction of me house has finally been completed. I'm generally pleased with the outer appearance, but the inside lacks a woman's touch."

"Oh—that's the most exciting part—decorating the interior. Of course, flower gardens can also provide a challenge," she quickly added. "The Shakers believed in stark simplicity, which I found boring. I believe God wants us to create and enjoy beauty. Lilly Cheever has decorated her home with simple elegance, don't you think? She must have found such pleasure in beautifying their home."

"I'm thinkin' my house could best be described as Spartan tawdriness," he said with a chuckle. "If ya'd like to be tryin' your hand at some decorating, I'd be happy to employ you to give mine a bit o' that simple elegance."

"Truly?" Daughtie could barely contain her excitement. "When can I begin?"

"Whenever you like. You pick out the items ya'll be needin'. Just go to the shops, have them record the purchases against me name for payment, and let me know when ya're ready to begin."

Daughtie hesitated for a moment. "I'd best see the house first, don't you think? I'd hardly know how to decorate it until I've seen the rooms."

Liam laughed. "And for sure ya're right. A tour of the house would likely be helpful. How about Saturday evenin'? You get off work early on Saturdays, don't ya?"

"Yes, I can come immediately after work if you'll give me directions."

He paused for a moment, a frown crossing his expression. "Ya don't think people would be condemnin' ya if ya were to be alone with me?" His Irish intonations were more prominent as he voiced this new concern.

"I truly don't care what other people think, Mr. Donohue. Besides, this isn't Boston. Lowell is much more open to women moving about and doing things on their own. After all, if they allow us to sweat and toil at the mills, they must give us time to move about and tend to business. They call us progressive here, but I simply believe it's just as the good Lord intended."

Liam studied her a moment and smiled. "Well, then, let us not hinder progress."

Liam took the paper she offered, penned his address, and drew a simple map. "If I'm not there by the time you arrive, just be lettin' yarself in. The key is under the flagstone to the right of the front door. Now that I've resolved my decoratin' problems, I suppose I should get busy loadin' the boxes," he said.

"The other items are in the storage room. I carried them with me each week when I came to work. There's more room for storage here at the library than at Mrs. Arnold's house," she explained. "Back here," she said, stepping from behind the desk and directing him to the rear of the library.

"*All* of these?" he asked, glancing into the room and then back at Daughtie.

"Yes," Daughtie replied. "And those along the wall, also."

"*Now* I understand the need for a wagon," he said, folding his cap in half and tucking it into the back pocket of his work trousers. He stacked several boxes on top of one another and hoisted them into his arms. Daughtie followed his lead and began to lift one of the parcels. "You needn't be liftin' these heavy boxes," he quickly said. "If you'll just take care of openin' and closin' the door, I'd be most appreciative. I don't want to be lettin' all that cold air blow in here."

Daughtie hurried ahead of him to open the front door. She watched him in fascination as he made trip after trip. When the last boxes had been loaded, Liam returned inside. "I'm guessin' that's everythin'?"

Daughtie bobbed her head up and down. However, she didn't want him to leave so soon. "Will you be delivering the parcels this week?" she asked.

He moved away from the door and drew closer. "That's up to Father Rooney to decide. I told him I'd be bringing the boxes by later tonight. I'll leave them with him for distribution. I'm thinkin' he's goin' to be mighty pleased. I doubt he was expectin' so much."

"I'm glad we can help. There are so many people who

need help and so few willing to lend a hand. Don't you think?"

Liam raked his fingers through the mass of dark curls, pushing them back off his forehead. "That's a fact. And I know for certain there's plenty o' needy folks down in the Acre that appreciate *any* help they can get."

"I grew up among the Shakers, where everyone was cared for and none of us lived any better than the other. We shared in the work as well as the fruits of our labor. Living in the world is much different. I hadn't realized there was such an immense division between classes of people. Bella tried to explain to me before we left—she'd lived in the world before her family joined the Shakers. But, of course, I couldn't completely understand the concept. Are you planning to attend the antislavery meeting?"

Liam had a puzzled expression on his face. "My, but you do go jumpin' from one topic to another very quickly, don't you? I'm not certain what a Shaker is, and now you're askin' about the antislavery meetin'," he said with a broad smile.

She cocked her head to one side. "No, I don't suppose you would know about the Shakers. It's a religious sect. The United Society of Believers in Christ's Second Appearing organized in England, and the group has now become commonly known as Shakers. I don't know if any of them made their way into Ireland, but they were run out of England," she added.

"I see. Well, there appear to be any number of those in this country. It's difficult for a person to decide what to believe."

Daughtie snapped to attention. "You don't know what you believe?"

"Oh, I believe in God," he replied. His tone was non-committal. "But I think it's a wee bit late in the evenin' to be gettin' into a religious discussion. We'll save that for another time when I don't have to make a delivery. But in answer to your earlier question, I *am* plannin' on attendin' the antislavery meeting."

"Would you like to go with me? I mean, since you're going and I'm going, we could attend together," she stammered.

He twisted his cap with both hands and looked her straight in the eyes. "Do ya not realize that a lass such as yarself ought not be seen in public with the likes o' me? Ya'll be shunned by yar own kind for such behavior. It would not be good for either of us." Again, his Irish brogue thickened with every word.

"I don't understand. Obviously you didn't see a problem with my helping decorate your home. Why is attending a meeting with me any different?"

"Ah, but it is. I'm employin' ya to work in my home. Now, I realize most Irish can't even afford to own a home, much less hire someone to adorn it. I am very fortunate. But all of that doesn't change the fact that I'm Irish. People will likely be understandin' if ya're workin' for me, but anything beyond work would be considered unacceptable behavior."

"As I mentioned earlier, what others think has never been of great importance to me. I've always been more concerned about God's opinion regarding my conduct. We're both His creatures, and I doubt He'd frown upon the two of us attending an antislavery meeting together."

Liam shook his head. "Ya've led a sheltered life, Miss Daughtie Winfield, of that there's little doubt. I'll not come calling at yar door, but I'd be pleased to sit beside ya should there be a vacant seat when I arrive," he replied with a grin. Tugging his cap down on his forehead, he went to the door, turned back toward her . . . and winked.

The bell over the front door jingled, and Liam jumped aside, barely avoiding the heavy door as Ruth thrust it

open. Daughtie watched Ruth edge past him while drawing her cloak close about her, as though touching Liam
might somehow contaminate her.

Liam tipped his cap. "Good night to you, Miss Winfield," he said and then was gone.

Ruth stared at the door momentarily and then turned
her attention back to Daughtie. "What is an Irishman
doing in the library? I'd think if he wanted to borrow a
book, he'd go to the Mechanics Association library before
he'd come here and bother you. I doubt he can even read."
Her words were filled with utter disdain.

"That was Liam Donohue. Didn't you recognize him?
He came to collect the items going to the Acre, Ruth. And
what's wrong with the Irish using this library? They have a
right to improve their minds the same as anyone else, don't
they?"

Ruth shuddered, a look of dismay etched upon her
face. "You know I'm willing to help with making goods
and donating old clothing to the downtrodden, and I'm in
favor of lending our assistance to the Irish. But the Irish
belong in their part of town, and we belong in ours. I don't
go into the Acre, and it's probably best if they don't come
into our part of town."

Daughtie wagged her head back and forth, as though
the movement might somehow clear the invisible cobwebs
gathering in her mind. "I thought you were *against* slavery
and segregation."

"Of course I'm against slavery. What has slavery to do
with the Irish? They're free men and women, paid for their
work, and able to come and go at will."

"Are they? If we don't want them anywhere but the
Acre, are they truly free? Isn't the blood that runs through
the veins of an Irishman the same as ours?"

"Oh, Daughtie, let's do not get into one of your phil-
osophical discussions. Sometimes I think those Shakers

filled your head with extremely odd ideas."

"I don't see anything odd about believing in the equality of *all* people—men and women, black and white . . ."

"Irish and Chinese," Ruth said with a giggle.

Daughtie nodded enthusiastically. "Absolutely!"

Ruth eyed her with obvious curiosity. "You've developed an interest in this Liam Donohue, haven't you? I can see it in your eyes when you talk about him."

"Don't be foolish. I've seen him on only two occasions. That's hardly enough time to develop an interest in someone. Although I shall be seeing more of him since he has employed me."

Ruth's eyebrows arched high on her forehead. "*What?* Employed you? To do what? And exactly how is it an Irishman has money to employ anyone?"

"He's an extremely talented man, Ruth, specifically chosen and brought to Lowell in order to design and lay the stonework at St. Patrick's. His talent has taken him into the finest homes in Boston and Lowell—and other cities in Ireland, I suspect. He's built a home and has asked for assistance with the interior decorations. He offered to employ me and I agreed, although I don't intend to take pay for the service. The opportunity to be creative will be payment enough."

"I can't believe my ears. I think you've lost your senses, Daughtie Winfield."

"And your attitude is small-minded and downright annoying," Daughtie replied, unable to keep her mouth closed. "I've invited Liam to attend the antislavery meeting with me," she added with a note of defiance.

Ruth was stunned into momentary silence. When she opened her mouth to speak, her lips quivered as though she would cry. "I don't believe you. Do you realize that if you're seen in public with an Irishman, no respectable man will ever call on you? Your reputation will be completely ruined. You absolutely must reconsider. Don't do it, Daughtie!"

"If it helps to assuage your fears, Liam refused to call for me at the boardinghouse. He seems to share your concern about my reputation."

"Well, at least he has a modicum of common sense, even if you don't," Ruth rebutted.

Daughtie chose to ignore the remark, returning to the desk with her paper work in hand. "I found you a book. I've already signed it out in your name," she said, handing Ruth the volume. "It will be a while before I finish my work. You needn't wait for me."

"Remember what I've said, Daughtie. That Irishman will be your ruination—stay away from him." Faint red stains accentuated Ruth's pronounced cheekbones. Other than her blushing cheeks, there was no indication she considered her words ignoble in the least. With her head tilted upward in a haughty position, she tucked the book beneath her arm and walked out.

The reverberating jingle of the bell above the door permeated the stillness of the room long after Ruth's departure. The echoing sound seemed to quietly repeat Ruth's admonition: *Don't do it. Don't do it.* Defiantly, Daughtie slapped the book she was holding upon the thick wooden desktop and murmured, "I *will* do it. He's a good man who happens to be Irish. I don't care what anyone thinks—especially Ruth Wilson!"

———

Liam washed his hands and glanced for the fifth time at the clock. It wouldn't be long before Miss Winfield would be coming. He could still see her dark eyes staring up at him in wonder, her dark curls dancing soft on her shoulders. She was a fine figure of a woman—delicate in appearance, yet sturdy in design. And it was clear she wasn't afraid of hard work.

With Daughtie on his mind, Liam put water on for tea and forced himself to think of something other than the petite woman. He thought of his homeland and all that he'd left behind. His family . . . his mother. He missed Ireland sometimes; missed the rich green hills and stone fences, missed the thatched cottages and the lively music that spilled out from the pubs.

He'd lived differently than most Irishmen. He'd trained early as a stoneworker, learning the skills and designs of setting stone and creating a masterpiece. His skills were famous in his homeland. Why, he'd even been approached by a traveling English architect to come work in London— something he'd not even considered for a moment. He'd never do anything to aid the English. They were harsh masters—landowners who came where they weren't invited and stole what was never theirs to own.

It was this rage toward the injustices heaped upon his people that had caused Liam to come to America in the first place. He knew he could never make the kind of money in Ireland that was possible in America. Here, stonemasons were fewer and whether Irish, English, or something else, they were afforded a bit of respect.

Daughtie had told him she'd been taught to respect all mankind, regardless of race or gender. How could it be that a handful of . . . what did she call them? Ah, yes, Shakers. How could it be that a handful of Shakers could understand the need to give respect and value to each human life, but it somehow eluded the rest of the English-speaking race?

The kettle whistled, steam pouring from its spout. Liam glanced at the clock again and smiled. She'd be here soon and she would share his company—share his tea. The thought brought a liveliness to his step and a hope to his heart.

The tower bell dutifully tolled the dismissive clangs releasing the mill workers for another day. Daughtie pushed her straight-backed wooden chair away from the drawing-in frame and stood up. Setting aside the long metal hook used to draw warp threads through the harness and reed, she donned her indigo blue Shaker cape and tied her bonnet strings in place before scurrying down the circular stairwell taking her out of the mill.

She'd barely made it to the edge of the mill yard when Ruth's words sliced through the crisp air. "Daughtie! Wait for me."

Daughtie hesitated. Much as she desired to hurry on and ignore Ruth's request, she came to a halt. Half of the girls in the mill yard had turned in Ruth's direction. Daughtie could scarcely claim that she alone had been unable to hear Ruth calling out her name.

"Where are you hurrying off to? Why didn't you wait for me?" Ruth panted, the words spurting out in short, explosive puffs.

The wind whipped at Daughtie's cloak and swept across her body, chilling her to the bone. "I have an errand and won't be going directly to the boardinghouse," she said, pulling her woolen cape more tightly around her body and beginning to walk away.

"I'm in no hurry to get home," Ruth said, quickening her pace to match Daughtie's stride. "I'll walk along with you."

"I'd rather you didn't." Daughtie's words were simple and to the point.

Ruth stopped midstride. "Why!" It was more accusation than question.

"Because I prefer to be alone." Daughtie continued walking.

"Oh, *now* I remember," Ruth called after her. "You're going to meet *him*, aren't you?" she quizzed, hastening her steps until she came alongside Daughtie. "Aren't you?" She seized Daughtie's arm and pulled her to a stop. "Answer me!" she demanded.

Daughtie yanked free of Ruth's grasp. "Quit acting like an overly protective parent, Ruth. What I do is not your concern. Go home," she exclaimed with a note of finality in her voice.

"Don't go there. You're making a mistake," Ruth cautioned. "It's not proper that you should be alone with any man, much less someone like him!"

Daughtie turned and walked away, though Ruth's disdainful attitude served to dampen her spirits. She glanced toward the sky. The air had now turned cold and appeared to be threatening snow showers. Likely a dismal forecast of things to come, she decided. Trudging onward through the shopping district and then toward the outskirts of town, Daughtie turned at the fork in the road but then stopped short, her gaze suddenly focused upon the house that surely must belong to Liam Donohue. Surrounded by trees and perched alone on a small rise, the house was centered by a gabled flagstone entry with an extension on each side. The structure appeared to rise up and lengthen itself in a welcoming gesture, much like an open-armed lover awaiting the return of his sweetheart. There was an inviting warmth about the dwelling that seemed to beckon her forward.

Hurrying up the steps leading to the front door, Daughtie lifted the iron knocker and waited, a smile now on her face. The door opened, and the hallway lamp cast a dim light behind Liam, haloing his raven hair with an auburn hue. Daughtie's breath caught at the sight of him. "Good evening," she croaked, her voice sounding foreign to her ears.

"Good evening," he greeted, stepping aside to permit

her entry. "Please come in." He pushed the door closed behind her and then gave it an extra thump with his broad hand. "It sometimes doesn't latch well. I'll be needin' to plane it just a trace," he explained. "May I take your cape?"

"Yes, thank you," Daughtie replied, thankful her voice had returned to its normal pitch. A crackling fire burned in the Rumford fireplace. She moved into the parlor, her gaze locked on the granite mantelpiece.

"Your fireplace—it's, it's . . ." she stammered, unable to think of words to express herself.

"Granite."

"No. Beautiful," she contradicted in a soft, contemplative tone. "Honestly. It's more than beautiful, but just now I can't think of a word to adequately describe the workmanship."

His head tilted at an angle, and he gave a hearty laugh. "Thank you. I'm quite fond of it myself. However, it *is* granite."

She moved closer and, drawing near, ran her hand across the smooth, charcoal-black facade. Tracing one finger around the outline of the etched eagle in flight that embellished the center of the arch, she whispered, "It's lovely. Your carving shows such strength, yet the delicate wings make the bird appear almost vulnerable. Why did you choose an eagle?" she inquired, looking up into his dark eyes.

"The eagle is a part of the Donohue family coat of arms. I didn't want to carve the entire coat of arms, so I decided to extract one portion for the fireplace."

"You have a family coat of arms? How impressive."

"My people were once powerful and influential. At least in Ireland."

"What happened?"

Liam gave her a sad smile. "The British happened."

She hated having led him into sad memories. "So you

carved only part of the coat of arms. Still, it seems quite perfect."

"I doubt my mother would approve of the idea. She'd be tellin' me I've disgraced our heritage."

"You might be surprised. I don't see how she could find this carving anything other than compelling artistry."

Liam pushed the dark curls off his forehead and grinned. "You *do* have a way with words, Miss Winfield. Still, I believe my mother would take one look at this fireplace and ask when I was going to carve the greyhounds."

"Greyhounds? Dogs?"

Liam nodded his head. "Aye. There are two of them that make up a portion of the Donohue coat of arms. Now, if the beasts were lying there peaceful and cozy, I might 'ave considered adding them. But the greyhounds that are pictured in the Donohue coat of arms are standin' on their hind legs and appear to be dancin' with each other more than anythin' else."

Daughtie giggled. "Well, I think you've made a wonderful choice," she replied, finally looking away from the fireplace and permitting herself to observe more of the house.

"I told the truth—I've done little to fix up the inside. Would you like to see the rest of the house?"

"Yes, of course. But you must tell me which rooms you want adorned."

He glanced over his shoulder and gave her a grin. "All of them."

"All?"

He nodded his head. "As my mother used to say, 'No need in doin' anything halfway.'"

"I see. Well, that may take a little more time than I anticipated—and money," she added.

"Money's not an issue. As I said, just tell the merchants to keep a tally. And if it's yar own wage that's causing concern, I'll be glad to pay ya whenever ya say—right now, if that's what ya prefer."

Daughtie could feel the heat rising in her cheeks. "No, I'm not worried about myself. I consider it a privilege to have this opportunity. I expect no payment, but we'll need to discuss how much you're willing to spend."

"Right you are. But for now, ya needn't worry about the money issue. Just go ahead and buy what ya need to make the inside of this place look as respectable as the outside," he instructed while walking her through the dining room, kitchen, and the room he referred to as his office. "I'll not need ya fixing up my office, I don't suppose," he added. "So there's at least one room you can take off the list. Oh, and not too many lacy frills—except in the guest bedroom. Ya can use ruffles and the like in that one, I suppose."

The mention of the bedrooms caused her to swallow hard. She knew she was risking her reputation simply by being alone with a man—much less an Irishman. And now he was talking about bedrooms and showing her around his house . . . all alone. Daughtie quickly covered her nervousness with a chuckle. "I'll attempt to keep the lacy frills to a minimum, but I hope you won't object to some color—not overly bright," she quickly added.

They made their way downstairs, returning to the parlor. Liam stood before her, his feet planted a short distance apart and arms folded across his chest. "As ya can see, I've not purchased any furniture, except the wood pieces I had specially made. You can choose any colors ya like for the overstuffed furniture. Except for bright pink. I'm thinkin' that would be a little too womanly for a single man. 'Course, I don't plan on stayin' single all my life, but until then, I think it might be best to use another color."

Daughtie gave him a solemn nod of agreement. "I agree. Pink won't even be considered. Unless I should find something absolutely irresistible, that is."

Liam turned back in her direction, nearly snapping his neck. He stood before her in stunned silence, gazing down into her eyes.

Daughtie giggled at him. "I was teasing, Mr. Donohue."

"Please don't address me as Mr. Donohue. Liam. My name is Liam," he cordially replied. "And I certainly *hope* you were teasing."

A clock chimed in the hallway, signaling nine o'clock. "I really must be going. It's getting late, and your house is quite a distance from where I live."

"Oh, I'll be takin' ya in the wagon. I wouldn't consider letting you walk home alone after dark. Besides, I'm sure it's gotten a mite colder since you arrived. I'll deliver you close to the boardinghouse and then watch until you get to your doorway. Probably best we're not seen together, especially after dark."

"I believe you worry overmuch, Mr. Dono—Liam."

"Trust me. Living in the Shaker village has left you inexperienced in the ways people think," he said while fetching her cloak. He slipped the woolen wrap over her shoulders. "I'll only be a moment. I'll bring the wagon around front. The horses are still hitched."

As soon as Daughtie heard the rear door close, she moved to the front porch and waited until the team of horses came clopping and snorting around the side of the house. Once the wagon came to a halt, she hurried down the steps. "No need to get down, Liam. I can make it up by myself."

"Not likely I'd permit such a thing," he said, jumping down from the wagon and hurrying to the other side.

"Thank you," she said as he handed her up. "I see you've already delivered all of the goods to the Acre."

Liam flicked the reins and the horses moved off toward

the lane. "Indeed. And Father Rooney was more than a little happy to receive every last article. He was still busy sifting through the lot of it when I finally left 'im the other night."

"I'm glad he was pleased."

"Not nearly as pleased as the folks that'll be keeping warm under those quilts this winter," he said with a smile. "It's a fine thing you ladies have done."

"Not nearly enough, I'm sure," she whispered. "There's always someone needing help. The children, those are the ones we need to be helping the most."

"True enough, but remember you're only one person; you can't lend a hand to everyone."

"I suppose, but I believe the Bible commands us to do our utmost to help those in need, to share our bounty, so to speak."

"You've a good heart, Miss Daughtie Winfield. So do ya think I should be givin' away my money to the poor instead of livin' in a big house and fixin' it up with nice furniture and the like?"

Daughtie gave him a pensive look. "I think you should do whatever your heart tells you to do."

Liam leaned back against the wooden seat of the wagon and gave a hearty laugh. The moon reflected down upon them while his gaze moved from her eyes and then settled upon her lips. "If I did what my heart's telling me to do at this very moment, I'm afraid I'd find myself in more trouble than an Irishman could handle."

CHAPTER 9

Thaddeus Arnold looked down into the Merrimack Valley as the rickety old wagon in which he was riding rumbled down the dirt road nearing the outskirts of Lowell. "Stop here, if you don't mind," he requested pensively.

The wagon driver complied and Thaddeus thanked him before donning his black beaver hat. He patiently waited until the wagon was out of sight, a malicious grin playing upon his lips. He'd had no difficulty convincing the old man to give him a ride. A simple lie about a dying child was all that had been necessary. The gullible old fool had even refused the paltry few coins Thaddeus had offered. *His stupidity is my gain,* he thought while walking briskly down the road toward the house occupied by Naomi Arnold.

Digging deep into his pocket, Thaddeus slid his fingers around the old pocket watch his father had given him on his sixteenth birthday. He glanced down and noted the time before snapping the lid closed and shoving the timepiece back into place. Nearly five o'clock. A disgusted grunt escaped his lips. He had hoped to arrive earlier, but the old man wouldn't lay a whip to his horse. Naomi would be busy preparing dinner for those girls she boarded in the house that *he* had acquired through his overseer position. No matter that the house belonged to the Corporation. Naomi's possession of the dwelling had come through *his* effort, not hers. But the Corporation had elected to grant Naomi the privilege of remaining in the house. The thought still rankled him, yet he needed an excuse to return to Lowell. His wife and daughter provided justification for those visits.

Tugging at his jacket, he brushed out the wrinkles while approaching the front door of what had once been his home. It chafed him to knock, but he yielded and did so. Three loud raps. The front door opened as he began to once again lower his fist against the door.

Naomi stood before him, wiping her hands on a checkered towel, a flour-covered apron tied about her waist. "I wasn't expecting you." Her expression made it obvious she was neither anticipating nor pleased by his visit.

He gave her an insolent grin. "No need to look so dour. You should be pleased to see your husband. Isn't that what they teach you in that church you've been wagging off to every Sunday?"

Her jaw went slack at the question. "I'm no longer your wife, Thaddeus. And who told you I've been attending church?"

Pushing his way past her into the entryway, he removed his hat and wool coat, then meticulously hung them on the same pegs he'd used while living in the house. He turned and faced her. "I'm aware of *everything* you do, Naomi. The fact that I live in New Hampshire doesn't preclude me from knowing your every move." She shuddered visibly at the remark. He rubbed his hands together, enjoying her discomfort. "You know I don't want Theona's mind glutted with nonsensical religious babble."

Naomi straightened her shoulders and met his stare with what appeared to be a modicum of defiance. "Theona *needs* God in her life. Besides, attending church gives her the opportunity not only to learn she has a heavenly Father who loves her but also to observe men modeling that same type of love for their families. I want her to know there are such men so that one day when she's considering marriage, she'll seek a man who loves and serves the Lord. I don't want Theona marrying a man she can't love and respect."

Thaddeus felt his anger rise. "A man like me—is that what you're saying?" he growled, clasping her face, his thumbs pushing hard into her hollow cheeks.

She pulled back from him, pushing his arms away. "Why are you here? You knew Theona would be napping and I'd be busy preparing supper."

He bit the inside of his cheek, forcing himself to remain calm. He wanted to slap her until she said aloud that he was a wonderful man, worthy of her love, but he knew he dared not. Naomi turned away and took a step toward the kitchen before he caught her by the arm. "Don't you ever walk away from me when I'm talking," he said, jerking her forward until her body was against his. Grasping her chin in a rough hold, he lowered his face to hers. Too soon she realized his intent and pulled away. "I'm entitled to my rights as a husband," he snarled.

"You're entitled to nothing in this house, Thaddeus. You're no longer my husband. If your abusive behavior continues, I'll be forced to report you to the Corporation and the judge. You're only permitted to visit Theona in this house based upon the judge's order and the Corporation's agreement. And, if you'll recall, the judge was concerned about your temper in Theona's presence. I doubt he would look favorably upon your behavior today."

Thaddeus backed away, his anger seething inside him.

He knew, however, he had to make her believe he was contrite.

"I apologize. It's just that I miss you and Theona so much, and when I come back here, I become angry realizing all that I lost with my foolhardy behavior," he lied.

Naomi gave him a sidelong glance. "You have a strange way of showing your remorse. Now if you'll excuse me, you may wait for Theona in the parlor. I must finish preparing supper."

He silently chastised himself for his boorish behavior. If he was going to succeed in extracting information from Naomi, he needed to hold his temper in check. His very existence depended upon discovering some morsel of gossip to pass along to William Thurston. "Is there anything I can do to help?"

Naomi stopped midstep. "You? Help in the kitchen?"

He stifled the urge to spew what he was truly thinking and instead said, "Certainly there must be something I could manage to do without ruining the meal."

"You could set the table," she curtly replied before walking off toward the kitchen. "The dishes and utensils are out here," she called over her shoulder.

There was a hint of mistrust in her tone, but he forced himself to appear unperturbed. Following along behind, he grimaced and replied, "I'll do my best."

Naomi pointed toward the dishes and picked up a wooden spoon. She gave the ham and bean soup a quick stir, then scooped a measure of cornmeal into a large bowl. Thaddeus grabbed the dishes, quickly placed them on the table, and returned to the kitchen. "It appears the mills are continuing to operate in fine fashion," he ventured.

"Did you assume your departure would shut down the Corporation?"

He gritted his teeth. "I was merely attempting to make polite conversation. I thought the mills would be a neutral topic we could discuss." It took all the determination he could muster to maintain a note of civility in his tone.

"I hear little of what goes on in the mills, and what I do hear, I soon forget. Most of it has little effect upon my life or Theona's."

He stood staring at her back while she poured the corn bread mixture into an iron skillet. "Since your home and livelihood are dependent upon the Corporation, I'd say what goes on there does affect you."

"Umm, perhaps," she murmured, obviously more intent on her baking than carrying on a conversation.

The sound of Theona's voice drifted into the kitchen, and Naomi quickly rushed off to fetch her. The child came hurrying into the room but stopped short at the sight of her father.

"Aren't you going to give me a hug?" Thaddeus held his arms open in a welcoming gesture and waited until the child hesitantly moved toward him. He pulled her into an embrace but quickly released his hold when she began squirming. "She seems to grow taller every time I see her."

Naomi nodded. "That tends to happen with children."

A short time later the front door slammed, followed by the sound of female voices. "Good evening, Mrs. Arnold," someone called out.

"Good evening, Daughtie; good evening, Ruth. Supper will be on the table by the time you wash up."

"Thank you," the girls replied in unison.

Thaddeus pushed his pride aside and said, "Am I invited to supper?"

"I suppose, but please don't make a habit of arriving at mealtime. I can't afford to feed you."

Digging into his pocket, Thaddeus pulled out a coin and slapped it on the table. "I wouldn't want it bantered about that I'm begging food from your table."

He watched as Naomi took the coin and slipped it into

her apron pocket. After managing to save coach fare for his journey, he now found himself paying to eat in his own home. The gall of the woman! He silently followed her into the dining room, where the two girls were already seated at the table entertaining Theona.

"Mr. Arnold will be joining us for supper, girls."

They looked at him with the same suspicion and wariness he'd observed only moments earlier in his own daughter's eyes. It was obvious Naomi had kept the gossip about him uppermost in their minds. "Good evening, ladies. Ruth and Daughtie, if memory serves me correctly," he said in his most gentlemanly fashion. "How are you this fine evening?"

"I'm doing very well, Mr. Arnold," Daughtie responded. "Are you visiting Lowell for long?"

Brazen girl, he thought, but he gave her a pleasant smile. "I'm hoping to depart this evening if all goes well."

"Did you injure yourself, Mrs. Arnold? There are red marks on your face. In fact, there's one along the left side of your face that appears to be turning blue. I hope you didn't meet with an accident this afternoon," Daughtie said, pointing toward Naomi's jaw.

Thaddeus came to attention at the comment. "You always were a bit clumsy, weren't you, my dear?" Thaddeus dismissively questioned before quickly shifting his attention back to Daughtie. "Tell me, Miss Winfield, have there been any changes occurring at the Appleton? Even though I no longer work for the Corporation, I still maintain an avid interest in the mills."

"I'm unaware of anything that would interest you, Mr. Arnold. I merely go to work, perform my labor, and return home. If there were plans for change, I'm guessing that the mill girls would be the last to know. Did I mention I received my first letter from Bella, Mrs. Arnold?"

"No. How exciting. Did she say if they encountered

any problems on their voyage?" Naomi asked.

Thaddeus perked to attention, his gaze fastened upon Daughtie as he anxiously awaited any details she might reveal.

"She said the ship was quite beautiful, and they met with rough waters on only one occasion. Her missive detailed that the captain was extremely capable and maneuvered their ship through the storm with relative ease. I know Bella must have been relieved. Before they sailed, she expressed grave concern over becoming seasick. I told her I would be praying for smooth waters."

"I'm certain that must be what calmed the seas," Thaddeus replied, unable to keep the sarcasm from his tone. "Where did your friend's voyage take her?"

"England," Daughtie curtly answered. She shifted in her chair, turning her back toward Thaddeus. "She said that she and Taylor had attended a concert, but the letter was written only a few days after their arrival. The missive was certainly filled with joy and excitement. I can hardly wait to hear all the details of the journey upon her return."

"And Mr. Farnsworth's father—how is he faring?" Naomi questioned.

"Apparently his move to London was a wise decision. Bella says that the day they arrived, he was in fine spirits and appeared much improved. The family believes his regular visits to the doctor have been helpful."

"So the Mannings and Farnsworths are in England? I'm surprised John Farnsworth would return to his motherland," Thaddeus commented offhandedly.

"Why is that?" Ruth asked as she helped herself to another piece of corn bread.

Thaddeus peered down his long, thin nose. "Men skilled in the art of fabric printing were valued in England. In addition, the English certainly didn't want their secrets shared with the mill owners in this country."

Ruth's dead-eyed stare affirmed what Thaddeus had always known: women had no comprehension of the business world. It was obvious the silly girl hadn't begun to grasp the seriousness of his words and so he continued in his attempt to explain. "If English printers came here and worked for the mills in this country, the English mill owners knew it wouldn't be long until we'd no longer need to import their cloth. Their profits would be drastically reduced. And that's exactly what has occurred. Consequently, men like John Farnsworth are considered traitorous in some circles." He enunciated each word, his voice taking on a singsong tone as though he were talking to Theona rather than a grown woman.

Ruth's head began bobbing up and down. "Oh, I see. Well, I don't think Mr. Farnsworth would ever place his wife or Taylor and Bella in jeopardy. Besides, their visit was a surprise so I doubt any of those English mill owners will know they've visited until long after they've returned home."

"You're probably correct," Thaddeus agreed with a glint in his eyes. "And when *will* your friends be returning to the fair city of Lowell?"

"I'm not certain. I think their return depends upon the health of Mr. Farnsworth's father. However, since he's making good progress, they may return soon. I certainly hope that's the case," Daughtie replied. "I'm hoping for another letter from Bella. Perhaps they've already boarded a ship for their return."

Thaddeus cringed at the thought. He was certain this news would interest William Thurston, but only if he could get word to him before John Farnsworth departed from England. Snatching up his napkin, he quickly swiped it across his mouth and shoved his chair away from the table. "I hate to rush off and leave such excellent company, but I've just remembered a matter that needs my immediate attention. Thank you for dinner, Naomi, and do be careful. I'd hate to see you suffer any other bruises. No need to see me to the door. I know my way out."

He shrugged his wiry frame into the wool coat and grabbed his hat from the peg before rushing out the front door. He would hurry to the stationer's shop for supplies and pen a letter to Thurston this very night.

CHAPTER *10*

London

William Thurston stared into the mirror while fastening his collar. He took a moment to brood over his reflection, rather disturbed he now bore the receding hairline and long protruding brow that were both lineaments of his heritage. He had always hoped to avoid the strong familial resemblance to his father.

His dull gray eyes stared back from the mirror and reminded him of his dreary wife and the marriage they had shared for nearly twenty years—utterly lifeless. Shortly after his departure from the United States, William had realized certain advantages flowed in his direction solely because he was a fugitive. The greatest of these benefits was being inaccessible to his wife, who continued to live in Massachusetts, ignorant of his whereabouts. Another was the opportunity to mingle with true bluebloods, a feat he would accomplish within the hour.

It mattered little that his presence wasn't truly desired at tonight's gathering; he had managed to wangle an invitation from Chauncy Fuller, and he *would* attend, tipping his nose up in the air along with the rest of the gentry. He'd make them believe he was one of them. No one would be the wiser. This little get-together could provide access to some of the greatest fortunes in England. These men were the backbone of England's industrial wealth. He smiled into the mirror. The Boston Associates paled in comparison to the men with whom he would dine this evening.

Thurston walked down the stairs, a shiver of delight coursing through his body. Nathan Appleton, Kirk Boott, and the other Associates who so freely despised him would be amazed to find him mingling among the elite of English industry. He stepped out the front door of the small boardinghouse where he'd rented a room when he had first arrived in England. A coach and driver awaited him. William considered the cost of hiring the carriage and driver to be an investment in his future and willingly paid the fee. To be seen arriving afoot could cause questions regarding his suitability to attend tonight's gathering.

The ride was bumpy and the driver was careless in handling the horses, but William remained silent. He kept his mind focused upon the evening that lay ahead. "You can park and wait with the other drivers," he instructed while clambering down from the carriage. The driver tipped his hat and flicked the reins, urging the horses forward, moving off toward the end of the circular driveway.

William squared his shoulders and walked up the steps of the Fuller mansion. A butler, with silver tray in hand, stood guard at the front door, artfully extending the scallop-edged plate as each guest entered the front door. Placing his card in the center of the tray, William patiently waited until the butler returned and beckoned him forward. At the door of the main drawing room, the butler stepped aside and nodded. William walked into the room with its gilded walls and flickering candles, the shimmering light dancing down upon the Fullers' jewel-bedecked female guests.

His gaze flitted about the room, finally resting on Chauncy Fuller, who was standing alongside two women greeting the guests. William made his way toward the group and anxiously awaited his host's acknowledgment. Chauncy nodded and welcomed William rather off-handedly with a slight bow.

"Good evening," he said, introducing him neither to the women nor to any of the gentlemen who stood nearby.

Knowing he had never achieved anything in life by adhering to strict social mores, William realized he could ill afford to begin now. Edging his way into the circle of men, he stood listening attentively until the topic of American industry began seeping into the otherwise lackluster dialogue.

William took a deep breath, infusing himself with courage. "I'd not talk too harshly against the textile industry in America. If their progress continues, they'll soon be selling their cloth here in England."

A hush fell over the group as the men turned to face him. A tall, elegantly dressed gentleman stroked his mustache and narrowed his eyes. "You speak with an American accent." The blistering words jabbed through the silence like a thrusting rapier.

William nodded. "I was born in Massachusetts, although I come from a long line of fine Englishmen. My heart and loyalty are to the motherland, not America."

"Your words sound as though you have more belief in the ability of the Americans than the English. We've had years of industrialization in this country. The United States will not easily usurp our power," the gentleman argued.

William held out his hand to the man. "I'm William Thurston. I don't believe we've met."

"Reginald Archer. I own a controlling interest in

several cotton mills in Lancashire."

"I don't mean to offend any of you fine men, but the fact remains the Americans are moving forward by leaps and bounds in the textile industry. Surely you've already experienced a decline in sales. I know they now import very little from England."

Archer nodded his head. "Of course. But they'll never achieve the quality of our cloth. There are Americans who will still demand cloth woven in England."

"I'm not as certain as you, Mr. Archer. The mills in Lowell are now weaving every imaginable type of cloth, even carpets for American and foreign markets."

Archer glanced about the circle of men and then eyed William suspiciously. "How is it that you are privy to information that permits you to speak with such authority on the topic of the American textile industry?"

Chauncy Fuller had drawn closer and now placed his hand on Archer's shoulder. "Mr. Thurston is personally acquainted with some of the *industrial giants* of America."

Several of the men sniggered while casting glances at one another. "*Industrial giants,*" one of them guffawed.

"The Americans have never had an original idea. Everything they've accomplished has been developed by the English. The only achievement those American capitalists can claim is thievery," Reginald asserted.

William nodded in agreement. "That's a fact, Mr. Archer. Oh, they may have refined a thing or two, but Francis Cabot Lowell relished telling how he had visited the homeland and managed to finagle an invitation to tour the mills. Of course, I must give the man credit. He possessed an exceptional memory, and it served him well. He died a wealthy man while causing a dip in profits for the rightful owners of the design living here in England."

A lanky bespectacled man moved closer, his eyebrows knit into a tight line above his wire-rimmed eyeglasses.

"Just how did you come by this information that you're so willing to share with us, Mr. Thurston?"

"I was a member of the Boston Associates."

A gasp could be heard from somewhere among the group. Thurston peered around the circle, wishing the uncomfortable silence would soon end.

"Well, that's quite a revelation," Chauncy finally remarked.

The lanky gentleman removed his spectacles and leveled a beady-eyed stare in William's direction. "Indeed! And you left the financial security of your membership in the Boston Associates because you suddenly have an abiding love for the motherland. Is that what you expect us to believe, Mr. Thurston?"

The man's accusatory tone sent a ripple of irritation flowing through William. "It would appear you find difficulty accepting my explanation, sir."

The man nodded, a smirk etched upon his lips. "Any sane man in this room would find it difficult to believe a man would leave a thriving investment merely because he's suddenly decided he loves the motherland—especially when he's never even lived here before."

William rested his chin in one hand and gave the man a look of contemplation. "You're right. Were the circumstances reversed, I'd probably harbor at least an iota of disbelief. I can't force you to accept the truth of what I've said. However, I think that you'll find all of my information verifiable. In fact, the Associates were busy spreading ugly rumors about me before I ever sailed for England. Feel free to contact any of them. I'm sure they'll tell you all manner of lies about me. They consider my departure nothing short of a crime—in fact, sources tell me they've accused me of any number of criminal deeds since my departure. They're fearful I'll somehow undermine their plan to overtake England as the leading industrial nation." He leaned forward and lowered his voice to a hoarse whisper. "And, in fact, gentlemen, that is exactly what they're planning—to send England into a spiraling business slump—a depression, so to speak."

"Depression?" The word spread among the men like a flame licking its way through dry kindling.

William gestured for quiet. "Gentlemen, gentlemen. There's no need for concern—at least not yet. Armed with information and a few good men, we'll be able to outsmart the Americans at their own game. I have sources in America who are willing to, shall we say, *share* information for a small price. There's no reason we can't *borrow* information and use it here in England."

"I'm not certain we want to stoop to their level. After all, we can't prove what they've done is illegal—at least not all of it," Fuller stated.

Thurston plucked a glass of port from the tray of a passing servant. "If you don't stoop to their level, you'll soon find yourselves swept aside by the industrial tidal wave in America. I don't think any of you want to suffer the kind of financial disaster such inaction will reap, but of course, I wouldn't consider forcing your decision."

William peered over the rim of his glass, taking great satisfaction in the manifestation of fear that had already etched itself upon all the faces now staring back in his direction. "To your health and good fortune, gentlemen," he said while lifting his glass into the air.

"How reliable is your information?" one of the men called out.

"Reliable enough to know that all of your printing designs have been copied and are presently being sold in the United States. In fact, they've expanded upon your printing technology through several Englishmen who sold out to the Americans. When I left Massachusetts, the Associates were developing new print designs that surpassed anything

I've seen in England. Any of you familiar with John Farnsworth?"

Reginald Archer hoisted his cigar into the air. "I am. He was my employee in Lancashire. Good man, talented. I hated to lose him, but he said he had an opportunity that would provide him a more substantial lifestyle than he could make in the mills."

"Perhaps Mr. Farnsworth meant to say he had an opportunity that would provide him more money than he could make in the *Lancashire* mills. He left England and is working in Massachusetts for the Boston Associates. He spoke the truth about a substantial lifestyle. He's managed to make himself invaluable and is handsomely paid," William divulged.

"Treason!" Archer shouted. "Employees of the mills are forbidden to divulge trade information to foreign powers. It's difficult to believe John Farnsworth would behave in such a self-seeking manner. I thought his allegiance to the crown was above reproach."

A surge of delight swept over William. His plan was working. "Money is a treacherous master, Mr. Archer. John Farnsworth has obviously bowed to its power. Not only that, but he later sent for his young nephew, Taylor Manning. Granted, the young man had no previous experience, but Farnsworth has taught him everything he knows, and his nephew appears to have a natural talent for design. I understand that between Farnsworth's mechanical prowess and the nephew's artistic design, they're developing what will be undeniably beautiful fabric."

Discordant murmurs sifted throughout the room. "Gentlemen, gentlemen. We'll not resolve any of this tonight; in fact, I've already received several disapproving looks from my wife. Perhaps we should agree to meet in another setting. I believe we'll soon be going in for dinner," Chauncy advised.

"We can meet in my London office if you like," Reginald Archer offered. "When are you available, Mr. Thurston? Your attendance is imperative."

William attempted to hide his feeling of smug satisfaction. "My priority is to assist you gentlemen in any way possible. You decide what time and date will work for all of you, and I'll be present."

———

Chauncy Fuller escorted William to the door, confirmed their meeting for the following Wednesday, and returned to the drawing room, where Barlow Kent, his wife's pitiable cousin, was obviously attempting to gain his attention. Chauncy's wife had recently begun inviting Barlow to their social functions, obviously hoping to somehow cheer her distant relative. Since his wife's untimely death several years ago, Barlow had been wallowing in self-pity. But although Chauncy dearly loved his wife, her relatives were another matter altogether. They were a beggarly lot, not one of them ever amounting to much, and Barlow was a prime example.

The half-crazed man continued to wave a lit cigar overhead until Chauncy finally reached his side. "Put that thing down before you set someone's hair afire," he warned.

"Let's step outside for a few minutes. We need to talk," Barlow said.

"Outside? It's freezing outdoors. If it's privacy you want, we can go to my library," Chauncy replied, leading the way down the hallway and into the room. Firmly closing the door, he turned to face Barlow. "What's so important?"

"I heard what that Thurston man had to say, but John Farnsworth is in London at this very moment. I've seen him."

"What are you talking about, Barlow? You don't even

know John Farnsworth. It was Reginald he worked for down in Lancashire." Chauncy gave the man a sympathetic look, fearing Barlow's grief had finally caused him to become delusional.

"I'm not crazy, Chauncy. John Farnsworth and I worked together for a number of years—before Reginald hired him. I know it was Farnsworth whom I saw going in and out of several shops and the museum last week. I followed him. He was with four or five people—relatives, I surmise. Then a few days ago, I happened upon him at a teahouse. I kept out of sight and followed him back to his father's house. Look, I know John left England to help the Americans. He told me as much when he quit his position with Reginald. There's no doubt in my mind he's returned to gather more information and seek out our latest innovations to take back to the Americans."

"You're certain about this?"

"Absolutely."

Chauncy hesitated, wondering if he should trust Barlow's rationality, yet a sense of urgency gripped him. He knew they must act. "Then we must put together a plan to stop Farnsworth. I'll contact the authorities first thing in the morning."

"No! I don't think that's wise. The police will want to investigate, and they'll scare him off. Worse yet, he may complete his espionage and leave the country before they arrest him. We can take care of this ourselves. Once we've formulated and carried out our plan, we can turn him over to the Crown and he can be tried for treason, but we don't want to let him get out of the country. You know how the authorities tend to mishandle the simplest of matters."

"Perhaps you're right," Chauncy conceded. "I'm to meet with William Thurston next Wednesday. Would you feel comfortable confiding in him? Possibly we could join forces with him to bring Farnsworth down."

Barlow nodded. "I would rather talk to Thurston than the authorities, and with his knowledge of the United States and his obvious disdain for the Boston Associates, he may prove useful."

"Well, then, let's set this matter aside until Wednesday. I really must return to my guests," Chauncy said. "Perhaps you should get some rest, Barlow. You look exhausted."

"I think I will excuse myself if you won't think me an ungrateful guest."

"Not at all," Chauncy replied. "I'll send the butler for your coach."

Barlow raised his hand in protest. "No. I'll see to it. You attend to your guests. I've already taken too much of your time."

Chauncy flinched as Barlow Kent grasped his hand in a death grip and pumped his arm up and down. Barlow would bear close scrutiny.

CHAPTER 11

Lowell

Daughtie tied her bonnet and impatiently waited at the bottom of the steps. "Come on, Ruth, or we'll be late," she called out while intently watching the stairway.

Daughtie didn't want to be delayed this evening. Over the past several weeks, she had been growing increasingly annoyed at Ruth's persistent tardiness. Thus far, Daughtie had been able to hold her tongue, but it was becoming increasingly difficult. She waited, tapping the toe of her shoe on the shining hardwood floor and watching the hands of the mantel clock march onward.

"Ruth! I'm leaving right now."

Ruth appeared at the top of the steps and cast a look of disdain in Daughtie's direction. "I'm doing my best. We have plenty of time."

"I want a good seat where I can see and hear everything. I specifically told you I wanted to leave early."

Ruth raced down the steps at breakneck speed and came to a skidding halt directly in front of Daughtie. "Well, here I am. *Let's go,*" she said, holding the door open.

Daughtie frowned at the remark. Ruth's tone made it sound as though she'd been ready and waiting for hours instead of the other way around. "We're leaving, Mrs. Arnold," Daughtie called out. "Are you certain you don't want to attend the meeting?"

Naomi Arnold came from the kitchen, wiping her damp hands on a frayed white dishcloth. "I'd love to hear Miss Crandall speak, but I don't want to keep Theona out after bedtime, and I fear the meeting will run late. You girls go along. I'll look forward to hearing everything when you return—if it's not too late. I may be in bed," she added with a smile.

"If you're not up when we return, I'll be sure and set aside some time before I go to the library tomorrow evening," Daughtie promised.

The girls walked in silence for several minutes, the cold December wind whipping at their cloaks. "It's cold. Let's walk a little faster," Ruth said, picking up the pace. "I wish they were having the meeting at one of the churches here in town."

"You know that would have caused trouble for certain. There are too many folks who would object to Miss Crandall being permitted to use one of the bigger churches. It's better this way—maybe the folks who disagree with her views will just stay away."

A coach and several wagons rumbled down the street past them. "As cold as it is, maybe *everyone* will stay away," Ruth retorted.

"I doubt that. After all, *we'll* be in attendance, and I know there are a lot of others planning to be present."

"You lasses care for a ride?"

Both girls looked up toward the driver as he pulled back on the reins, bringing the team of bays to a halt alongside them.

"Yes," Daughtie delightedly replied.

"No!" Ruth responded while tugging at Daughtie's arm. She leaned in close to Daughtie's side. "We can't ride with *him*."

"You can walk if you want, but I'm going to ride. As you pointed out only a few minutes ago, it's cold." Daughtie accepted Liam's outstretched hand and allowed him to assist her up. "Are you walking or riding, Ruth?"

"Riding," Ruth grumbled while reluctantly accepting Liam's assistance. She settled beside Daughtie and whispered, "This is a mistake and you know it."

Daughtie chose to ignore the comment. Liam gave a slap of the reins, the horses moved out, and the wagon lurched forward, jostling her closer to Liam. Ruth jabbed Daughtie in the ribs, motioning her to scoot away from him. Instead, she held fast and made no effort to move. In fact, Ruth would be appalled if she knew just how much she was enjoying Liam's nearness, Daughtie decided.

"From the look of all those wagons, it appears there'll be a good crowd this evenin'," Liam said as the churchyard came into view. Wagons, coaches, and saddled horses filled the area that surrounded the small country church. He pulled into a spot between two coaches and helped the girls down from their perch before moving to the front of the wagon to secure the horses.

"Come on, Daughtie," Ruth urged, grasping Daughtie's hand.

Daughtie tugged back, freeing herself from Ruth's hold, squared her shoulders, and stood firm. "I'm waiting for Liam," she replied.

"Liam? You call him by his first name? I'm worried about you, Daughtie. What's going on up there?" Ruth asked while pointing a finger toward her head.

"I'm just fine, and nothing's gone awry with my thinking. I'm going to sit beside Liam at the meeting, and if you don't want to be seen with us, then you go ahead in and take a seat. I'll be careful not to sit beside you. I wouldn't want to cause you any embarrassment."

"Fine!" Ruth retorted, and Daughtie watched her roommate march off toward the front door of the church.

"I'm guessin' yar friend is a wee bit worried about being seen in public with an Irishman," Liam said as he approached Daughtie. "And ya should be, too. Why don't ya go on and join her?"

"Because I don't want to. I've given this a great deal of thought over the weeks, and I feel like a hypocrite every time I avoid you. I'm not embarrassed, and if folks don't like it, that's their problem. I'm not going to permit narrow-minded people to interfere in my life."

"I don't know that ya'll be gettin' a choice in the matter," he said, walking alongside her into the church.

Daughtie took the lead and found a pew near the front with only a few occupants. She edged her way into the row, seated herself, and patted the space beside her. Liam lowered his gaze and seated himself as far from her as space permitted, hugging the end of the pew.

"Liam! Good to see you." Matthew and Lilly Cheever were standing at the end of the pew. "May we join you?"

"Certainly," Liam replied while standing to permit the Cheevers entrance into the row.

Matthew seated himself and then leaned forward to meet Liam's gaze. "Did we interrupt something?"

"No, 'course not. Miss Winfield and Miss Wilson were afoot, and I offered them a ride in me wagon. There were only a few seats remaining when we arrived," he hurried to explain.

"Well, I'm pleased there's a good crowd. I had to twist Matthew's arm to get him here," Lilly replied before turning her attention to Daughtie. "Have you received any correspondence from Bella or Addie since their arrival in England? I'm anxious to hear how they're doing."

"Yes. I had a letter from Bella, and they had a safe voyage," Daughtie replied. She glanced toward Matthew and then lowered her voice to a whisper. "Did you discover Mr. Cheever is pro slavery after all? Is that why you had difficulty getting him to attend the meeting tonight?"

"Pro slavery? No—but as I explained at our Ladies Aid meeting, he must be very careful where he places his allegiance, what with the mills and all. I'm sure you understand."

"No, I'm not certain I do understand. Why would he let his position in the mills affect his stand on slavery?"

Lilly leaned closer. "As I explained at the meeting, the mills are dependent upon cotton, and cotton is raised in the South. Without slaves, the Southern plantation owners say they are doomed for failure."

Daughtie nodded her head. "I see. So it's not a matter of what's right or wrong but what's economically in the best interest of the Southerners?"

"Not exactly. You may have twisted my words just a bit. However, it's the economic future not only of the Southern plantation owners but all of us that would be affected if slavery were abolished. However, I don't know how much serious thought has been given to the total impact abolition would have upon the country. Don't misunderstand—I'm an abolitionist through and through."

"Well, I think we'll all be called to make sacrifices if slavery is ever to be abolished. It will require a commitment to place others ahead of our personal economic security. I'm extremely eager to hear Miss Crandall speak this evening. From what I've been told, she's a very brave woman, and she's been forced to make difficult decisions. One can't help but applaud her willingness to model a lifestyle that exemplifies the cause she so capably champions."

Reverend Walters moved to the lectern and rapped with a wooden gavel several times before the assembled crowd turned their attention to the front of the church.

"If I could have your attention," Reverend Walters said. "Miss Crandall has arrived, and we'll begin as soon as the room quiets."

The sound of murmurs and shuffling feet subsided, and Reverend Walters cleared his throat. "Because Miss Crandall must leave for Connecticut early in the morning, I'll reluctantly forego the urge to spend at least an hour telling you of her bravery and fine accomplishments. Instead, I'm hoping she'll include the many details of her struggle over the past year, and I believe what she says tonight will heighten your awareness of the bigotry and hatred that sometimes occurs when a person takes a stand for egalitarianism."

Reverend Walters turned to his right and motioned Miss Crandall forward. The speaker's long fawn-colored hair was swept into a decorative coil that framed her face and added fullness to her long, narrow features. Her piercing blue eyes and the white bodice of her russet dress accentuated the porcelain fairness of her skin. She gazed into the audience as though taking account of each person in attendance before uttering a word.

"Thank you for braving the cold in order to attend this meeting. I come to speak to you about a matter of grave concern, and I pray you will give consideration to what I say this evening. I believe each of us will one day be required to take a personal stand on the issue of slavery. Now, I'm not talking about whether we're from the North or the South and what the general opinion of that locale may be; I'm talking about deep down inside our beings, what you as an individual believe. I tell you this because you may be required to put your convictions to the test. Unfortunately, I have already been forced to take a stand. Little did I realize I would be met with such hostility and anger—and this type of behavior was from people who profess to be abolitionists. I find there are many who say they oppose slavery, yet few of them believe in equality for the Negro. I say that the Negro must be given his freedom *and* treated as an equal to the white man. There is a mighty chasm between freedom and equality. What I am about to tell you is proof of that statement."

Daughtie gave Miss Crandall her rapt attention, anxious to hear the unfolding story.

"This whole affair began through no instigation on my part. In 1831 I was approached by a number of families residing in Canterbury who valued my Quaker upbringing. They'd heard I was an experienced teacher and encouraged me to open a school for their daughters, who had already completed their primary education requirements. I made arrangements with the bank to purchase a home on the Canterbury Green, a house large enough to accommodate the girls who would be boarding with me. Everything progressed nicely. The residents of Canterbury were pleased, enrollment soon reached capacity, and from all appearances, opening the school was a sound decision that worked to the benefit of all concerned.

"However, in 1833 Miss Sarah Harris, a young lady of color who was living with her parents in Canterbury, approached me. Miss Harris had attended the district schools in Norwich, Connecticut, and dreamed of becoming a teacher herself. This fine young lady believed that once she received additional education at my academy, she would be equipped to teach people of her own race. Naturally, I applauded her desire and agreed that she could attend classes. She remained at home with her parents and merely came to the school each day for classes. Nonetheless, once word spread about town that I had admitted Miss Harris, the residents of Canterbury were outraged."

A smattering of murmurs could be heard throughout the church. Daughtie wasn't certain if folks were whispering their approval or displeasure over Miss Crandall's actions. Daughtie, however, was in awe of Miss Crandall's moral fiber and was anxious to hear every word the woman uttered.

"Needless to say," Miss Crandall continued, "I was surprised and saddened by the attitudes and behaviors with which I was confronted. All of my white students withdrew from the school, for their parents were unwilling to accept a Negro girl being educated beyond the boundaries of the district schools. Realizing that I would soon be destitute, yet unwilling to bow to the demand of ejecting Miss Harris, I consulted with several abolitionists. After much thought-provoking discussion and prayer, I made the decision to reopen my school. However, this time I organized it as a school for the education of young ladies of color. I began recruiting pupils throughout the Northeast for the first boarding and teacher training school for young women of color."

Miss Crandall hesitated for a moment and gazed about the church. "I was astounded when the people of Canterbury immediately retaliated by sending representatives to the Connecticut General Assembly. The Assembly quickly passed a law prohibiting the education of out-of-state Negroes in private schools. Although there was no doubt the law was specifically aimed at closing my school, I have defied that ill-conceived law and continue to operate. I have been arrested, spent the night in jail, endured one trial, and will soon suffer the disruption of another, yet I plan to fight on for the equality of educating these fine young ladies. Many of those who oppose my school also say they oppose slavery. Perhaps they do; I am not their judge. However, I believe *all* people must be treated with the same equality and opportunity. So on this cold winter's night, I come to tell you that if you stand for abolition, you may be forced to bear some discomfort. But if you believe in equality, be prepared—for you will surely suffer.

"My students and I continue to be bullied and harassed, but we will withstand as long as humanly possible. Should the safety of the girls become a factor, and I fear one day it shall, I may be forced to reevaluate my position. But for now, I stand resolute in my determination to educate any young woman desiring an education, regardless of color."

Applause filled the church, though not as boisterously as when Miss Crandall had taken the podium earlier in the evening. Several people left the building before the question-and-answer session began, while others, obviously pro slavery, stayed and queried her unmercifully. Daughtie watched with admiration as Miss Crandall patiently responded to the inquiries without evidence of anger.

A tall, well-dressed man stood near the back of the church. "In case you people of Lowell don't remember what's needed to keep this town operating, let me remind you that it's cotton," he called out. "It takes slaves to raise that cotton. If we're to survive, these mills need to operate. Without cotton, the mills will fail and you'll be without jobs. Before you adopt Miss Crandall's ideology, you'd best decide if you can survive with the ramifications of such a decision."

"Thank you, sir. I concur with your last remark," Miss Crandall stated. "I'm not encouraging anyone to blindly follow along with my beliefs. Each person in this room needs to prayerfully evaluate the truth that God speaks to his or her heart and be prepared for the consequences of the decision, whether for or against slavery. I'm well aware this town is dependent upon the cotton raised in the South. I disagree, however, that the only way to raise cotton is through the use of slaves. Granted, those wealthy plantation owners may suffer some losses if they're required to pay wages, but cotton *can* be raised without slavery."

The man wagged his head in obvious disagreement. "Just remember, folks, if the plantation owners are required to pay wages, the price of cotton will increase, which means the cost of production increases, so the cost of cloth will increase. If folks can buy imported cloth cheaper, production will dwindle and your wages will decrease—if you're able to maintain a job at all."

"That makes sense," another man agreed. "And I can't afford to lose my job."

"Yeah, and what if those Negroes move up here and are willing to take lower wages for our jobs? We'd have them *and* the Irish to deal with!"

A sense of anger rose within Daughtie, and she stood to her feet. "People need to have a willingness in their hearts to do what's right no matter what the personal cost. Wouldn't you want the Negroes to sacrifice for you if the situation were reversed and *you* were held in bondage?" With legs trembling, she plopped down on the pew, her meek nature having returned full force.

"They could all go back to Africa and be free. They wouldn't be competing for our jobs thaddaway," another man remarked.

"You gonna pay their passage, Emil?" someone called out. A few chuckles followed, and an embarrassed-looking Emil Kramer sat down.

There was more Daughtie wanted to say, but the few words she had spoken earlier left her feeling drained and inadequate. She listened as members of the audience continued to speak and, on several occasions, clenched her fists in anger at the comments being made. Yet she knew little would be accomplished through hostility and brash words and was relieved when Reverend Walters finally called the meeting to a close.

The moment the crowd was dismissed, Daughtie rushed forward, determined to speak with Miss Crandall. For a short time she was forced to move against the crowd, much like a fish swimming upstream, but finally she freed herself from the other attendees and waved her handkerchief in the air. "Miss Crandall! May I have a moment?" she called out, hoping her voice could be heard over the din.

Miss Crandall turned in her direction and then motioned Daughtie forward.

Breathless, Daughtie rushed up the two steps to the stage and came to a halt in front of the speaker. "Thank you for waiting. I'm Daughtie Winfield," she said, almost feeling as though she should curtsy.

Miss Crandall's face warmed in a bright smile. "Prudence Crandall. I'm pleased to meet you, Miss Winfield. What may I do for you?"

"I wanted to personally express my admiration for you and the work you're doing. I was hoping we could discuss in more detail what might be done to overcome the attitudes opposing equality for all races. I agree with everything you've said this evening, especially your words that we must not only free the slaves but also have a willingness to embrace them as equals. I find some of the people in this community unwilling to treat the Irish as equals, and that attitude causes me to question the sincerity of their stand for abolition. Do you believe they can treat the Negroes as equals when they won't do that much for the Irish immigrants?"

Miss Crandall patted Daughtie's hand. "Or women, for that matter," Miss Crandall said. "Based upon my own experience, I seriously doubt the black man will be considered an equal when he is finally freed, but that doesn't mean we should blindly accept such an attitude. Change will not occur if we silently agree to whatever the majority imposes upon us."

"I apologize for interrupting, but we really must leave, Miss Crandall," Reverend Walters said.

"Of course," she replied and then turned back to Daughtie. "Above all, pray for guidance, my dear. I'm sorry we don't have more time to visit, but should you feel so inclined, you may write to me."

"Oh, thank you. Corresponding with you would give me immeasurable satisfaction."

"Then by all means, please do so. I promise to answer each and every letter," Miss Crandall said while pulling on her doeskin gloves. She fastened her gray woolen cape, then bid Daughtie good-bye before following Reverend Walters out the back of the church.

Ruth was waiting outside the door and quickly latched on to Daughtie's arm. "Where have you been? We'd best hurry if we're going to make it back to the house before curfew."

"Matthew and I will take you home, won't we?" Lilly offered as she glanced up at her husband, who was conversing with Liam Donohue. "It's too cold to walk all that distance."

Daughtie glanced toward Liam, but he said nothing. Why didn't *he* offer to take her home? Instead, he pulled up his collar against the cold, bid the Cheevers good-night, and after nodding in her direction, hurried off toward his wagon.

"What did you think of Miss Crandall?" Lilly inquired after they were seated in the carriage with warm woolen blankets tucked around their legs.

Ruth squirmed forward. "I was very impressed with what she said. Her courage is remarkable, and I completely agree with what she said regarding equality. It truly does little good if the slaves are freed and then prevented access to the same opportunities as their white brothers."

"Which white brothers?" Daughtie asked, meeting Ruth's surprised gaze.

Ruth's mouth gaped open in an exaggerated oval. "Why, whatever do you mean, Daughtie?"

"Equality doesn't exist between the 'white brothers.' So

I'm wondering if the fairness you speak of would provide Negroes the same equality we give the mill workers and farmers, or would it be the same access we give the Irishmen? The Irish are permitted to dig canals and haul stone, but they're relegated off to the Acre to live in shanties, their children are required to attend separate schools, and they are treated with disdain," Daughtie passionately replied.

"You just want to argue," Ruth responded. "Just because I don't think you should be keeping company with Liam Donohue, you attack everything I say regarding fair and equal treatment of differing people."

"Daughtie has a valid point, Miss Wilson. The Irish are mistreated and underappreciated. They don't receive the same advantages as other white people in this community—or any other, for that matter," Matthew replied. "However, Daughtie, you might want to talk to my wife regarding the sensibility of a courtship with Mr. Donohue. Don't misunderstand; Liam's a fine man and we value his friendship. But I doubt whether the community will harbor the same attitude."

Daughtie gave momentary thought to pinching Ruth's arm. How dare she make such unsolicited remarks about Liam? Even if they were keeping company, it was improper of Ruth to speak of the matter.

Lilly gave Daughtie an enchanting smile. "I think Daughtie has a very sound mind, and I doubt she needs my assistance sorting out the details of her personal life. In fact, I believe she's quite mature and certainly capable of deciding what's best for her future." Lilly reached across the carriage and patted Daughtie's arm. "That isn't to say I wouldn't be happy to discuss the matter, if you desire. However, it's not a topic I would broach should you come for tea."

Daughtie returned Lilly's smile. "Nor is it one I would expect you to solve. Quite honestly, I fear Mr. Donohue is even more concerned than Ruth about the ramifications of such a social relationship—if it's possible to be any more alarmed than Ruth," she added.

Ruth stiffened beside her, and Daughtie felt a modicum of satisfaction. Perhaps Ruth would think twice before attempting to embarrass her again.

"As I said, Liam's a fine man, but right or wrong, there are undeniable prejudices against the Irish. You should be careful," Mr. Cheever warned.

"Daughtie tells me she's had word from Bella, and they're enjoying their time in England," Lilly said, obviously intent on changing the topic of conversation.

"That reminds me, I failed to tell you we received a missive at the mill office just the other day. It was from John—seems his father's health took a downward turn, and with winter setting in, he doubts they'll return until early spring."

Lilly turned to face her husband. "Oh, my. That means they'll be gone over the holidays. I was so hoping they'd be returning any day—before the weather turned any colder. How disheartening . . . yet I'm being selfish. I *am* pleased John and Addie can be with John's father and lend their assistance."

"I know, my dear. I miss them, too."

Thoughts of defending Liam quickly slipped from Daughtie's mind. Bella would be gone until next year. An undeniable pang of despair clutched her heart as the carriage pulled up in front of Mrs. Arnold's house.

"Here we are," Matthew said. He opened the carriage door and assisted both girls down. "We've gotten you home with at least fifteen minutes to spare."

"Thank you for the ride," Daughtie said.

"Do let me know if you hear further from Bella or Miss Addie," Lilly called out before the carriage began to pull away.

"I will," Daughtie called after them.

The house was dark save a burning candle Mrs. Arnold had left for them on the candlestand beside the stairway. While Daughtie removed her cloak and hung it on a peg by the doorway, Ruth grasped the candle and silently led the way to their room.

Once inside, Daughtie closed the bedroom door and began preparing for bed.

"You're angry with me, but I'm only looking out for what's best for you," Ruth said, breaking the heavy silence that permeated the room.

Daughtie seated herself on the bed. "I don't need you to mother me, Ruth. If I want your opinion regarding the choices I make, I shall ask. Your intent to embarrass me in front of Mr. and Mrs. Cheever was obvious. But I'm more angered by your statements regarding equality than by what you said to the Cheevers. I can't imagine how you can say you believe in equality for the Negroes and then, in the next breath, defame me for seeking to befriend an Irishman. Your words and deeds are in opposition."

"I *do* believe in abolition. I don't think people should *own* each other. However, permitting Liam Donohue to court you is a totally different issue. You listen to me, Daughtie Winfield. You stand to lose more than you think if you continue down this path of defiance. It may be a step up the social ladder for Liam Donohue to be seen with you on his arm, but it is certain death to any future marriage plans of yours. Do you think any respectable man is going to escort you, much less marry you, after you've been associated with an Irishman? If you have any sense at all, you'll cease this imprudent behavior immediately."

Daughtie sat momentarily silent, mystified and quite unable to comprehend Ruth's behavior. "I was taught from the time I was a little girl that we all have equal value in the eyes of God. Two Negro women joined the Shakers and lived with us at Canterbury. They were our sisters, treated no differently than anyone else. Nothing more and nothing less was expected of them; the same rules applied to everyone; the same benefits were enjoyed by all. Why must it be so different out here among the world's people?"

"Greed and selfishness, I suppose," Ruth replied simply.

Daughtie nodded. "Life isn't so simple away from the structured existence of the Shakers, where personal belongings are nonexistent. However, I believe change can occur—if we're willing to pay the price."

Liam prepared for bed, thinking all the while of Daughtie Winfield and her passion for equality in mankind.

"For sure she's like no lass I've ever met," he murmured to himself.

And indeed she was unique. Her upbringing seemed to envision a world that Liam was sure could never exist—a world where no one would think twice if Liam were to show up on her doorstep to escort her to a dance or a lecture.

"That world will never exist!" he declared, crawling into bed. "The world would never be seein' the likes of me on the arm of a Yankee girl like her."

It was best to put thoughts of such a nature completely from his mind. Better to concentrate on his work. He was scheduled to begin the creation of a stone staircase for a Mr. and Mrs. Price. Mrs. Price had recently been to England, where she was entertained in the home of some grand lord and lady. Their staircase was of palatial proportions; however, Mrs. Price was confident Liam could recreate the entire thing, on a smaller scale, for her new home. Being an artist, she had made multiple sketches of the stairs, banisters, and newels. They would be paying him a nice tidy sum for the grand stonework they'd described, and he would have a good amount of cash to send home to his mother and family.

Taking a deep breath, Liam blew out the candle on his bed table and closed his eyes. He thought of his boyhood home—of racing across the stone bridge with his playmates, of learning to jump his mare over rock walls and streams. Those were the moments he'd been most happy as a child. Life had seemed quite simple then. He had enough food to fill his belly and a warm bed in which to sleep. Every night his mother would come to tuck him in, bending over to gently kiss his forehead and bid him pleasant dreams.

But memories of his mother soon faded, replaced by Daughtie Winfield's dark-eyed gaze. He could see her clearly enough in his mind that if he'd wanted to, he could have etched her in stone. Her face was almost heart-shaped, with huge brown eyes that seemed to take in every detail of life. Her nose was pert, turned up just a bit at the end, and her lips . . . He pushed the images aside and rolled over on his stomach.

"My mother would say I'm bewitched," he muttered. "She'd say the fairies had taken my mind, and no doubt she'd have a charm or potion to rid me of such misery and thoughts."

But in truth, he didn't want to stop such thoughts. In fact, he'd just as soon lose himself in dreams of what could never be.

CHAPTER *12*

London

Bella's lips formed a contented smile. She stared into the blazing fire, the warmth coloring her cheeks a rosy pink. "This was a lovely Christmas," she whispered, her fingers reaching to touch the cameo pin at her neckline while snuggling against Taylor's chest. With Grandfather Farnsworth asleep in his bed and the others out enjoying a short visit with their friends, Bella and Taylor were alone for the first time in days.

Taylor pulled her closer, then leaned down to place a kiss atop her head. "I know you would have preferred celebrating Christmas in Massachusetts, but you've been a good sport about all of this. Even though I haven't said so before, I hope you realize I'm very thankful for your sweet attitude. Had you been in a dour mood about remaining in England, I don't know what I would have done," he confessed.

"You need to be here with your family, especially now that your grandfather's health is no longer improving. I fear

I've done little other than lend moral support. I wish there were more I could do."

Taylor placed a finger beneath her chin and, tilting her head upward, gazed into her eyes. "You have been an immense help, especially with Elinor. I don't know what we would have done without you. Somehow you've miraculously managed to keep her entertained and out from underfoot. Believe me, that is quite an accomplishment. Grandmother has been ailing herself, and keeping up with Elinor takes more energy than she can muster."

"Elinor is a sweet girl. I find she uses her misbehavior to gain attention. Whenever I lend an ear to her woes or provide a bit of entertainment, she immediately settles. She's even begun reading with me each day," Bella replied.

Taylor nodded. "When I saw her sitting and stitching while you read to her the other day, I could hardly believe my eyes. Quite frankly, I didn't think Elinor had any idea how to use a needle."

Bella giggled. "She didn't. There were quite a few pricked fingers and several screams of pain before she mastered the technique. However, she's taken quite a liking to needlepoint. I'm going to see if I can interest her in tatting over the next few weeks."

"From what I saw of Grandmother's Christmas gift, you're quite the teacher. I'm not sure who was more excited over the gift, Elinor or Gran."

"We used to make sewing kits in the Shaker Village and sell them to the townsfolk or give them as gifts to visitors. They were one of our bestselling items. Elinor is quite interested in the Shakers—she's been quizzing me incessantly."

Taylor's laughter filled the room. "I can't imagine our Elinor interested in the strict communal life of a Shaker. She can't even discipline herself to come to the dinner table on time. How would she ever survive?"

Bella joined his laughter. "You'd be surprised how quickly Eldress Phoebe could change bad habits. A hickory switch to the legs and extra laundry duties usually made an impression upon us. Of course, I'd never want to see Elinor forced into such a situation. A child needs the freedom to enjoy her early years without fear of constant reprimand. I'm ever so thankful I have memories of life with my parents before going to live in Canterbury. Poor Daughtie spent her entire life among the Shakers until we ran off."

"And I'm still surprised she agreed to leave with you," Taylor remarked.

Bella smiled and nodded. "I don't think she regrets her decision. Ever since she secured the drawing-in position at the Appleton, she's been content."

"Did she say anything in her last letter about finding a beau?" Taylor inquired.

"No. I am a bit concerned, however. She mentioned Liam Donohue several times in her letter. I'm beginning to fear that her interest in him goes beyond friendship."

"Liam's a fine man. Not many Englishmen could match his work ethic, and his talent is without challenge."

"A fine man, yes. But he's Irish. We both know such a relationship is unacceptable. Daughtie would be shunned by the entire town."

"You're worrying unnecessarily, my dear. I doubt either one of them would enter into such a thorny situation."

Bella gave him a sidelong glance. "Once love begins to bloom, people tend to forget the difficulties of 'thorny situations.' I do hope Daughtie will guard herself against heartache."

"Pen her a letter and speak of your concerns. After all, you're the closest to family she's ever known, and I'm certain she values your opinion."

"Perhaps I'll write her tomorrow while Elinor works on her stitching."

Taylor turned to face Bella and then clasped her hands in his own. "I'm truly pleased you and Elinor have been getting on so well, because Gran has approached both Uncle John and me about Elinor's future. She's asked that we consider taking Elinor back to Massachusetts with us. I told them I didn't feel we could undertake such a responsibility. After all, we're newlyweds not yet adjusted to marriage, and a nine-year-old is quite a handful, but Gran said to pray about it and talk to you."

Bella swallowed hard before speaking. "What did your uncle John say? Perhaps he and Aunt Addie would be the better choice to raise Elinor."

"Exactly what I thought. But Uncle John pointed out that we would be much better suited than he and Aunt Addie since we're young and would be more capable of keeping pace with a girl Elinor's age."

"Oh, pshaw! Aunt Addie was managing a boarding-house filled with young women not long ago, and her health hasn't deteriorated one iota since marrying your uncle. Don't misunderstand—I think your grandmother has a valid concern, but what about your older sister, Beatrice, and her husband? They're in Scotland, and that would be in closer proximity if Elinor wanted to return and visit your grandmother from time to time. Surely Elinor would be happier with her own sister."

Taylor's laughter was tinged with disdain. "Don't expect Beatrice to step forward and offer assistance. She's always been one to shirk any responsibility that happened her way, and I don't expect she's changed a jot. Besides, if Beatrice and that Scot she calls a husband *did* agree to rear Elinor, they'd expect the child to arrive with a pocketful of coins to pay for her keep and then require Gran to send money at every turn. They'd bleed Gran for every farthing she's managed to save. In addition, Elinor would likely run off before she'd ever agree to live with Beatrice. They can't seem to abide each other for more than a few minutes at a time."

Bella refused to panic. They would be in London until early spring. By winter's end, they would surely arrive at an agreeable solution. "Well, then, we'll do as your grandmother has requested. We'll pray that the Lord will provide a solution."

Taylor silently stared into the fire, his hands, fingertip to fingertip, forming a small pyramid. Finally, he turned toward her. "Yes, surely by spring we shall have an answer."

Just then a ruckus sounded at the front door. Taylor got up to see what was the cause and Bella followed him into the vestibule just as Elinor burst into the house.

"Oh, Bella, you missed the best fun. There was dancing and storytelling, and Uncle John even sang for us."

John assisted Addie and Cordelia through the door as Elinor made this announcement. He laughed and released the women. "A mistake I won't be repeating."

Bella smiled. "I'm sure your offering was as fine as could be had."

"If you heard me and still thought so," John said, helping Cordelia from her coat, "I would have to assume you to be tone deaf."

Taylor laughed and pulled his wife close. "Uncle John doesn't lie. He sounds rather like a hound to the fox."

Bella elbowed Taylor and moved to Uncle John's side. "Don't listen to him. He's just jealous because he can't carry a tune."

John winked. "It's a family curse."

"Not so," Addie threw in, "for Elinor sang like a bird. She has a sweet voice."

The girl beamed under the praise. "I love to sing."

"See there," John replied, pointing to the girl, "she's inherited all of the family talent."

"Come now," Cordelia stated stiffly, "let us go into the

parlor and warm up. I'm certain in spite of the hour we can still have a cup of tea and some refreshments."

Bella remembered her arrangements with the cook. "Indeed we can, for I had such thoughts earlier in the evening. I've already arranged for tea and some other goodies. Just come in by the fire and I'll see to it."

Cordelia eyed Bella for a moment, and then with a look of approval she nodded and motioned the family to the parlor.

Taylor followed Bella to the kitchen. "You've made points with her for sure. My grandmother is not easily won over, but I believe you have her in the palm of your hand."

"I hope she doesn't think me simply trying to impress."

"I'm sure she recognizes your good nature and ability to think ahead. She values sensible people," Taylor replied, halting Bella before she entered the kitchen. He pulled her into his arms. "And I value the warmth of your lips and the sweetness of your kiss." He lowered his mouth to hers.

"I see some of us are getting our refreshment sooner than others," John Farnsworth said, surprising them both.

Bella jumped back, feeling her face grow hot, while Taylor only laughed. "I couldn't help myself, sir." He threw Bella a look of pure mischief. "She insisted."

Bella gasped. "Taylor Manning! How dare you tell such falsehoods—and on Christmas!"

The men roared with laughter while Bella turned back for the kitchen. She couldn't help the smile that spread across her lips.

CHAPTER *13*

Lowell
January 1834

Church was over and the noonday meal completed. Ruth, Daughtie, Naomi, and little Theona sat in the parlor, the four of them primly lined up on the settee and chairs with their hands folded, poised, as if waiting to be cued into action. However, when a knock on the front door finally sounded, they all startled.

"I'll go," Mrs. Arnold announced, standing and pressing the wrinkles from her skirt with the palm of her hand while moving toward the front door.

Daughtie and Ruth leaned forward as the door hinges squeaked, straining to hear the exchange of voices or perhaps catch a glimpse of the doctor who would be depriving Mrs. Arnold of a portion of the house. Being hired as a physician for employees of the mills granted Dr. Ketter the right to occupy the greater portion of the first floor. Mrs. Arnold's voice sounded more animated than usual as she offered welcoming words. Moments later, the older woman returned to the parlor with the new doctor in tow.

Daughtie noted he was a slim, smallish sort of man with a narrow face and aquiline nose. His dark brown hair and eyes were his better attributes, she decided, for while he was not an ugly man by any account, neither was he truly handsome.

"Dr. Ivan Ketter, I'd like to introduce Miss Daughtie Winfield and Miss Ruth Wilson. And this," she said, taking Theona's tiny hand in her own, "is my daughter, Theona."

Dr. Ketter gave a slight bow. "It's a pleasure to meet you. When I was told of the disruption my arrival would cause, I became concerned that perhaps I should find another place to set up my practice. However, Mrs. Arnold's letter set me at ease. I want to thank all of you for your willingness to accept these changes."

They'd really had no choice in the matter, but Daughtie wouldn't embarrass him with that tidbit of information. The Corporation had declared Dr. Ketter would board with Mrs. Arnold, using the downstairs rooms for his living quarters and medical practice, with the exception of the kitchen and the dining area. Those two rooms would remain under Mrs. Arnold's authority. The parlor would be rearranged as a waiting room for his patients; the bedroom Mrs. Arnold and Theona had shared would become an examination room. Daughtie lamented the fact that there would be no parlor for entertaining guests or reading by the fireplace on a cold winter's evening, but Mrs. Arnold was at the mercy of the Corporation. Of course, the Associates *had* been generous in granting their permission for her to remain in the house after her husband's discharge from the Appleton. She could ill afford to be less than receptive to their recent announcement, but moving to an upstairs bedroom with little Theona would certainly make her life more difficult.

Obviously the changes would be most difficult for Mrs. Arnold and Theona, so Daughtie attempted to hide her irritation over the newest boarder. After all, she shouldn't make this any more difficult for Mrs. Arnold. *Besides,* she reasoned, *bearing a grudge against the doctor would be unfair: it isn't his fault the Corporation foisted him upon Mrs. Arnold.*

And so she smiled and gave a small curtsy in response to his welcoming gesture before glancing upward. As she met his eyes, he stared deep into hers. The boldness of his gaze caused her to quickly look away.

"I'm sorry," he murmured, appearing surprised by her discomfiture. "Daughtie. Is that a nickname for Dorothy?" he inquired, obviously hoping a bit of cordial conversation would set matters aright.

"No. I was told that my parents were certain they would have a son. Because of their confidence, they had not chosen a girl's name. My father called me Daughter, and my mother decided to shorten Daughter to Daughtie—at least that's what Sister Mercy told me." The doctor's face appeared to cloud with confusion, but Daughtie ignored the questioning gaze and directed him to Ruth. "Ruth, step forward and meet Dr. Ketter."

The doctor briefly greeted Ruth but immediately turned his attention back toward Daughtie. "I'm going to want to hear more about you, Miss Winfield."

"Perhaps you should get settled, Dr. Ketter. I'm certain your journey was tiring, and Mrs. Arnold has your rooms prepared—don't you, Mrs. Arnold?"

"Indeed. And I hope you're going to be comfortable with the way I've arranged the rooms. I thought you could use the parlor as your waiting room, and I've made very few changes. You may want to purchase some additional seating, for when word spreads that you've arrived, I'm certain there will be many townsfolk who wish to avail themselves of your services."

"Well, of course those employed by the Corporation will receive priority, but I do hope my practice will expand to include other residents of the community. I enjoy keeping busy," he replied as Mrs. Arnold led him toward his new office.

"He appears quite taken with you," Ruth whispered, envy etched upon her face as she glanced first at Daughtie and then over her shoulder toward the doctor.

Daughtie grasped Ruth's arm and pulled her toward the stairway. "If you'd quit acting so shy and talk to him, he'd likely be much more interested in you."

"I'll see you at supper, Miss Winfield?" Dr. Ketter inquired.

Ruth's eyebrows arched. She gave Daughtie a smug grin before racing up the stairs.

Daughtie turned toward Dr. Ketter. "I'm present for three meals a day, just like Ruth, Theona, and Mrs. Arnold," she advised before making a hasty retreat.

She ran up the stairs and into the bedroom. Ruth was already sitting on the bed, her gaze fixed upon a book she obviously wasn't reading. "That book is *much* easier to read when it's turned right side up," Daughtie remarked with a smile.

Ruth snapped the book closed and whacked it down on the bed.

Daughtie plopped down beside Ruth. "Please don't be angry with me, Ruth. I did nothing to encourage Dr. Ketter's attention. You know I'm not interested in him. Besides, he was only being cordial. He's probably got a fiancée back home."

"Strange that *you* were chosen as the sole recipient of his conviviality," Ruth retaliated.

Daughtie sighed and leaned back against the wooden headboard. "I promise to direct all the conversation to you at supper tonight. *Now* will you forgive me?"

"I never said I was angry with you."

"There's more frost inside this room than out on the front steps."

Ruth giggled. "I'm sorry for my unseemly behavior. I suppose I did feel jealous when Dr. Ketter appeared interested in you. Instead, I should be encouraging you to befriend him. After all, if you direct your attention toward Dr. Ketter, perhaps you'll stop making a fool of yourself with that Irishman."

Daughtie attempted to hold back the anger that suddenly rose in her chest. "When I want your opinion, I'll ask for it."

Ruth crossed her arms over her chest and gave a smug grin. "Now who's caused the chill in this room?"

"Arguably, I could say it's *you*. You're the one determined to make disparaging remarks about Mr. Donohue," Daughtie replied before stomping out of the room, down the steps, and directly into the arms of a surprised-looking Dr. Ketter. Instinctively, she flailed about to steady herself before finally gaining her balance.

She looked up and was greeted by Dr. Ketter's chocolate brown eyes, which were now sparkling with amusement. His head was tilted at a slight angle, and his full lips were turned up in a broad smile that caused his cheeks to plump.

"Excuse me! I lost my balance. I guess you realize that," Daughtie stammered, pulling out of the doctor's grasp.

"Well, I've heard tell of girls throwing themselves at eligible men, but having never been the recipient of such activity, I wasn't quite certain if this was to be my first encounter. Now you've gone and dashed my hopes," he said while maintaining his wide grin.

Daughtie felt the heat rise in her cheeks. "I had no intention of throwing myself at you. I tripped on the stairs."

Dr. Ketter laughed. "I realize you stumbled, Miss Winfield. I was merely teasing you and certainly didn't intend to cause you further embarrassment. Mrs. Arnold tells me you lived in the Shaker community in Canterbury, New Hampshire," he said, leaning back against the wall and crossing his arms. "Moving to Lowell must have posed innumerable difficulties for you."

"I doubt if I've had more difficulties to overcome than any of the other girls. After all, most of the mill girls left families behind. At least I didn't have to leave my parents and siblings, wondering if and when I might see them again," she replied while attempting to inch off toward the kitchen.

He reached out and gently grasped Daughtie's elbow, directing her into the parlor. "Why don't we sit down? I'd appreciate the opportunity to visit with you."

Daughtie stiffened. She didn't want to spend the remainder of the afternoon being questioned by Dr. Ketter. "I have some mending to complete" came her feeble excuse.

"That's quite all right. Why don't you fetch it, and we can talk while you stitch? I'll feel as though I've returned home. My mother used to sit by the fire and stitch while I worked on my school lessons years ago."

Daughtie knew she was trapped. Dr. Ketter was one of those people who would have a remedy for any excuse she might toss in his direction. "I'll get my sewing," she mumbled before retracing her steps to the bedroom.

"Back so soon?" Ruth inquired, looking up from her book.

"Yes. Dr. Ketter has requested company in the parlor. I came to fetch my sewing *and* you. I didn't want to fritter away the afternoon and not have my mending completed come morning," she replied. "Come along."

"How kind of Dr. Ketter to include me," Ruth said while they were descending the staircase. "Perhaps he *is* interested in me."

Daughtie cringed. She hoped that nothing would be said to lay blame on her for stretching the truth. After all, she hadn't told a blatant lie. That thought helped salve her nagging conscience for only a brief moment, for the instant they entered the room, Ruth flashed a smile in the doctor's direction.

"Thank you so much for inviting me to join your conversation," she said, fluttering her eyelashes with a wild abandon that caused her to appear absurd.

Dr. Ketter leveled a questioning glance at Daughtie before replying. "You are most welcome, Miss Wilson. I'm sure you will lend tremendous insight to our discussion."

Daughtie breathed a sigh of relief and aimed a grateful, albeit fleeting, smile in Dr. Ketter's direction before taking out her mending.

"Tell me, Miss Winfield, how did you happen to leave the Shaker community? I didn't think anyone ever left their communes."

Daughtie could feel Ruth's cold stare. "Oh, people leave from time to time for various reasons. I left with a friend in order to see what life was like among the world's people. Ruth grew up in New England and knows all about the farming communities in the area, don't you, Ruth?"

Ruth bobbed her head up and down. "Indeed. But I'm sure Dr. Ketter finds life among the Shakers much more intriguing, don't you?"

"Since I know little about the Shakers, I do find the topic of genuine interest."

Ruth leaned back in her chair and stared at Daughtie with a look of irritated satisfaction crossing her face.

"Well, that proves my point exactly. I've always been interested in hearing about Ruth's life—and I'm interested in hearing about yours," Daughtie hastened to add. "We're always interested in the unknown, aren't we?"

"Exactly!" Dr. Ketter replied, slapping a hand to his knee.

"Perhaps the solution would be for each of us to tell a little about our background," Ruth ventured.

"That's a marvelous idea, isn't it, Dr. Ketter?"

"Yes, I suppose it is. But I'm going to insist that you ladies call me Ivan. If we're going to be living in the same house, we should be less formal, wouldn't you agree?"

"By all means," Ruth agreed. "You may call me Ruth."

"And *you,* Miss Winfield? May I address you as Daughtie?" Dr. Ketter inquired.

Daughtie didn't immediately reply. She preferred to keep things as they were—more formal and distant. Yet a refusal would make her appear haughty, so she nodded her reluctant agreement. "I suppose that would be acceptable, although highly unusual. After all, we are hardly peers."

"But of course we are," Ivan replied. He allowed his gaze to linger on Daughtie, causing her to grow very uncomfortable.

"Why don't you begin by telling us about yourself?" Ruth requested, leaning forward and giving the doctor her undivided attention.

"I fear you'll find my life to date rather boring. However, I'm hoping that will change now that I've completed my studies. I wanted to excel in school and consequently didn't enjoy much social life, I fear."

"Where did you grow up?" Ruth inquired, her enthusiasm almost contagious.

"My family owns a fishing business in Maine. I grew up along the coast, enjoying the ocean and the seafaring life. My father determined early on that I'd best receive an education if I was going to support myself. My mother worried about the dangers at sea. In fact, I had to sneak aboard my father's boat in order to fish with him, and then when we'd return home, Mother would give me a tongue-lashing and sulk about for at least a week," he said with a grimace.

Ruth chuckled at his antics. "And who decided you should go to medical school?" she inquired.

"Medicine was my choice. My mother and father briefly mentioned studying law, but I thought I was more suited to medicine. I've not regretted my choice. I found medical school much to my liking, although there were times I longed to put away the books and get on with healing patients."

"I think medicine is an admirable calling," Ruth agreed.

"*Was* your decision to enter the medical profession a calling?" Daughtie inquired.

"I don't know that I'd say it was a calling, but I do want to help people. Does that count?"

"The question wasn't meant as a test. I merely asked because I believe the finest doctors are called to the profession."

"And upon what theory or study do you base your conclusion?" Dr. Ketter inquired.

"None—other than personal observation, that is. Throughout my life at the Shaker village, I worked alongside two different doctors and numerous Sisters who acted as nurses. It was a simple matter to identify those who were truly called to the medical field and those who were merely performing a task."

"And which were *you,* Daughtie?"

"My calling was in the children's dormitory. I found great pleasure working with children, and I'm told I was very good with them. Children enjoyed being around me."

"I can understand why," he replied.

Daughtie blushed and tried to ignore his remark. Ruth glared in her direction, but Dr. Ketter met Daughtie's gaze with an adoring smile.

"Supper is ready," Mrs. Arnold announced from the doorway.

"Prayer answered," Daughtie murmured. She jumped up from her chair and hastened into the dining room, strategically placing herself beside Theona. "Sit here beside me," Daughtie said while beckoning Ruth toward the chair to her left.

Ruth ignored her request and seated herself at the far end of the table, which permitted Dr. Ketter access to the seat beside Daughtie. He walked to the chair and sat down next to Daughtie. Ruth's annoyance was obvious, yet she'd done nothing to prevent the situation. Her actions were akin to those of a spoiled child, Daughtie decided.

Mrs. Arnold fluttered into the room with a bowl of fried potatoes in one hand and a platter of boiled chicken in the other. "Would you give thanks, Dr. Ketter?" she inquired after setting the bowls atop the table and sitting down.

"I'd be honored," he replied, reaching out to grasp hands with Mrs. Arnold and Daughtie. The rest of them followed his lead and joined hands. "This was a custom in my family at meal times. I hope you don't mind."

"Of course not," Mrs. Arnold replied. "It's a very nice custom."

Daughtie wondered if Dr. Ketter had intentionally squeezed her hand upon completion of his prayer but then decided she was likely overreacting. Reaching for the buttered turnips, she scooped a serving onto her plate and passed the bowl to Dr. Ketter.

"Has Daughtie told you of her excellent medical background?" Mrs. Arnold asked while placing a piece of chicken on Theona's plate. "Why, if it hadn't been for Daughtie's nursing skills, Theona would probably still be fighting a fever."

"Not at all," Daughtie explained. "I merely sat with her

so you could get some rest, Mrs. Arnold. And Ruth certainly took her turn at Theona's sickbed, also."

Mrs. Arnold nodded in agreement. "Yes, although I don't believe Ruth is quite so comfortable tending to illness, are you, Ruth?"

"No, I'm certainly no match for Daughtie. Now, if you'll excuse me, I'm not very hungry. I think I'll go upstairs and read my book. I feel certain I won't be missed," Ruth replied. The wooden chair legs scraped across the floor, their protest seeming to mirror Ruth's angry emotions.

"I have apple pie, Ruth. I'll call you when we're ready for dessert," Mrs. Arnold offered.

"Thank you, Mrs. Arnold, but please don't bother. Once I've finished reading, I plan to retire for the evening."

"In that case, I'll bid you good-night," she said. "Theona, tell Ruth good-night."

Ruth rushed from the room while Theona and Dr. Ketter were still in the midst of bidding her good-night. They don't realize she doesn't want to go up those stairs at all, Daughtie thought. What Ruth *really* wants is to hear them beg her to remain and tell her the gathering will be of no consequence without her. Instead, each of them wished her an amiable good-night and quickly returned to their food and conversation. Daughtie wondered if she should follow Ruth—if it would make her feel better knowing that only Mrs. Arnold and Theona would be garnering Dr. Ketter's attention. But what plausible reason could she give in order to excuse herself? She could think of none, so she remained, listening to Dr. Ketter's compliments and answering his onslaught of questions with as much brevity as she could manage.

"I would certainly enjoy seeing a bit more of the town. Is there any possibility you would agree to accompany me for a stroll, Daughtie?"

"Oh, absolutely not. I have my mending to complete and several other tasks that need my immediate attention. But thank you for the kind invitation," she added, feeling she must at least exercise proper etiquette.

"Tomorrow night?"

"I work at the library, but I'm certain Ruth would be pleased to accept your invitation. Shall I ask her when I go upstairs?"

"No, thank you. I'll wait until one evening when you're free," he replied, a trace of a smile on his lips.

Dr. Ketter was absent when the girls hurried home from the mill for breakfast the next morning.

"Apparently Dr. Ketter isn't an early riser," Ruth observed, heaping an empty bowl with oatmeal.

"He's already left the house. He's going to be busy throughout the day completing arrangements for the delivery of his office supplies. Some of the items should be arriving today," Mrs. Arnold explained.

The reply brought an obvious look of disappointment to Ruth's face; however, Daughtie was relieved. In fact, she hoped to avoid Dr. Ketter as much as possible since his attention was obviously going to cause difficulties in her friendship with Ruth. In truth, she hoped he would be delayed until after her departure for the library this evening.

When Dr. Ketter failed to arrive at the table for supper that evening, a sense of relief washed over Daughtie. She ate her supper more quickly than was necessary for the last meal of the day, jumped up from the table, and announced she was leaving for the library.

"Surely you have time for dessert," Mrs. Arnold said, attempting to coax her back to the table.

"No, I must be on my way. I'll be home by nine forty-five," she replied, grabbing her indigo blue wool cloak from a peg in the hallway and scurrying out the door.

Mrs. Potter gave a cheery greeting the moment Daughtie opened the front door of the library. "I'm glad you've arrived, my dear. We received a large box of books late this afternoon. They need to be evaluated and shelved. Most of them appear to be in good condition."

"How wonderful! Were they donated?"

"Yes. The wife of one of the Boston Associates heard the mill girls had begun a library, and she boxed up all these books and shipped them from Boston, along with this lovely note," Mrs. Potter said, waving a piece of engraved stationery in the air. "I've been giddy with excitement all day. They're all such treasures. Near the bottom of one box, I found *The Lady of the Lake* as well as *The Fair Maid of Perth,* both Sir Walter Scott offerings that I'm certain girls will enjoy."

"How wonderful!" Daughtie exclaimed, quickly shrugging out of her cape and hastening to reach deep into the box. "I can see I'm going to have a delightful evening," she said, pulling out a leather-bound volume of *Waverley.*

"Indeed. I selfishly wished they had arrived earlier in the day, but alas, I must go home and complete my chores. Please be certain you catalog the books before you place them on the shelves. I don't want to lose any of them."

Daughtie nodded her agreement and began leafing through another book. The hours ticked by, and for once, Daughtie was pleased there had been few patrons throughout the evening. She'd unpacked most of the books and had cataloged and shelved them according to Mrs. Potter's exacting instructions. After assuring herself the whale oil lamps were extinguished, Daughtie doused the embers in the fireplace and then donned her wraps. Exiting the library, she carefully turned the key and then jiggled the handle, assuring herself the library was securely locked.

"I thought you should be closing soon."

Daughtie whirled around and found herself face-to-face with Dr. Ketter. "What are you doing here?" she snapped.

"I frightened you—I apologize. I asked Mrs. Arnold for directions, hoping you might enjoy some company on your way home," he replied.

A wagon lumbered up the street and came to a halt in front of the library. "Good evenin', Miss Winfield. I was comin' by to see if ya had any additional boxes that needed to be delivered to the church and thought you might need a ride home on this cold night. But I see ya've already closed up the library, and it appears you have an escort to see you home, so I'll bid ya good-night," Liam Donohue said. Without waiting for a reply, he flicked the reins and was gone.

Daughtie turned and glared at Dr. Ketter. The one night when Liam Donohue materialized, asking to escort her home, Ivan Ketter had to emerge on the scene. She wanted to thrash the good doctor. Instead, she hiked off toward home without so much as a word, Ivan Ketter following close on her heels.

CHAPTER *14*

Boston

Tracy Jackson moved behind the large desk and bellowed into the conversation-filled room, "Gentlemen! If I could have your attention, we really must begin. Otherwise, I fear we'll still be discussing matters at midnight."

Josiah Baines emitted a sigh. "The sky was threatening snow when I arrived. I certainly want to get home before we have a major storm."

"I don't think there's any need to worry, Josiah. It's looked like snow for the past two weeks, and we haven't seen so much as a flurry," Henry Thorne replied. "You'd best get comfortable. I'm certain there's going to be a great deal of discussion once I've completed my report."

"Then why don't we begin with Henry's report?" Josiah questioned.

Matthew Cheever observed Tracy as he closed his eyes momentarily and shook his head in obvious frustration. "If everyone will take a seat, we'll begin the meeting. We'll get to Henry's report in due time, Josiah. I believe Nathan would prefer to conduct the meeting in the same orderly fashion he's utilized in the past. Nathan, would you like to begin?"

Boott leaned toward Matthew. "I'm thankful Nathan agreed to take charge this evening. I'm guessing tonight's agenda will make for heated discussion," he said in a hushed voice.

Matthew nodded his agreement but remained silent. He wasn't quite so convinced the meeting would be lengthy. He doubted the agents were going to argue at length for the mill girls, but he kept his opinion to himself, anxious to observe the unfolding drama.

Nathan Appleton moved to Tracy's side and picked up a sheaf of papers. "Gentlemen, as we discussed at our last meeting, the profits have dropped considerably, and urgent steps are needed if we're to protect our investment. With all of the directors in attendance earlier this month, we voted to decrease the mill girls' wages by twenty-five percent. This proposal was discussed with the supervisors at the mills. They asked to meet with us in order to expound upon their ideas and concerns."

"Excuse me, Nathan, but wouldn't it expedite matters if Kirk spoke on behalf of the supervisors? After all, he attended their meeting as well as our previous meeting. *And* he's here tonight," Josiah said with a flourish while giving Kirk a broad smile.

Nathan turned toward Kirk Boott. "Would you like to respond to Josiah's question?"

"You're in charge of the meeting, Nathan," Kirk replied. He settled into his chair and glanced around the room from under hooded eyelids. Either he was attempting to avoid the smoke from his cigar or he didn't want any supposition regarding his thoughts. Matthew surmised it was the latter.

Turning his attention back toward Josiah, Nathan said, "As I believe you all know, Kirk is a director of the Boston

Associates and owns an interest in the Corporation. While he has his finger on the pulse of Lowell, the supervisors and agents are in an entirely different position. Although they have a vested interest in our success due to their employment, they don't own any shares in the Corporation. If Kirk were to speak for them, it could be said his suggestions and ideas were tainted by his monetary investment. You see—"

"Oh, all right, Nathan. I'm not a complete dolt. You don't need to go into further detail. I understand," Josiah interrupted. "Let's just get on with the meeting, shall we?"

"I would be delighted," Nathan replied with sarcasm dripping from each word. "Mr. Meanor, I believe the agents and supervisors have delegated you as spokesman for their group. Please step up here so that we may all hear what you have to say."

Matthew glanced toward Robert Meanor. He knew the man well. He was a good agent who capably managed the Tremont Mill and was respected by both workers and the other supervisors and agents. Both groups generally accepted his opinions with favor, and Matthew suspected that was why he had been chosen. The other agents hoped Robert could influence the Associates.

Robert took his place at the desk, the sheet of paper he held visibly shaking as he began to speak. "Thank you for giving us this opportunity to present our views," he began. "You asked that the agents meet and discuss your proposal for a twenty-five percent reduction in wages and respond to you. All agents are in agreement that a twenty-five percent reduction would be disastrous. We believe you would suffer irreparable damage by such a large reduction. If you move forward with this idea, the climate will be unfavorable for the procurement of good help in the future, and we believe there will be a mass migration homeward of many employees. Such an exodus will only lead to a further downward spiral. We need dependable, hardworking, trained employees if we are to keep production at the present output and maintain the current marginal profit."

"What do you suggest, Mr. Meanor?" Tracy Jackson inquired.

"The agents have proposed you consider nothing greater than ten percent."

"Oh, but that is preposterous. At that rate, we'll continue our losses without any hope of recovery. We need a change that will make a difference," James Babcock replied.

"What we need is for John Farnsworth to return home with additional new and exciting patterns for the print shop. Something that will send the women scurrying to buy our cloth and make it desired in every country around the world. And we need Taylor to return so he can begin production on the new prints we've already approved," Josiah replied. "We haven't been able to gain a large enough foothold in the foreign market."

"Those statements may be true, but we need relief right now. The only way I see that happening is a reduction in wages," Tracy replied.

"A wage reduction is an easy answer as we sit here tonight, gentlemen, but I do believe there will be repercussions if you continue down this road. I doubt whether the operatives will remain silent," Robert countered.

Nathan adjusted his collar and looked about the room. "There may be a few that quit and go home, but the majority have grown accustomed to earning a wage. Given time and thought, they'll adjust to the idea. After all, if we don't turn a profit, the mills will close and they'll have no jobs at all."

"The entire country is in total disruption with that scoundrel Andrew Jackson at the helm. As president he is surely causing more damage than good," Tracy began. "His ideas regarding the Bank of America and its dissolution are enough to create mass panic in the streets. Surely other businesses across the nation will find it necessary to cut expenses."

"Yes, but their cuts might well have less of a national effect than those of the textile industry," Babcock threw out. "It's just a collection of women, after all. They have no head for business or knowledge of the way our banking system is teetering on the edge of disaster."

Mr. Meanor cupped his chin in one hand and cast his gaze downward. "Forgive me for being so bold, sir, but most of you men have distanced yourselves from Lowell. I believe you may get more of a fight than you've bargained for. That collection of women you refer to has gone out of their way to educate themselves. Just last week a banking expert from Philadelphia came to lecture them. You might be surprised at what they have a head for. But either way, I'll follow your instructions."

"Perhaps we should test the waters. Why don't we have broadsides posted that explain there will be a decrease in wages beginning the first day of March? We can suggest that the amount may be as high as twenty-five percent. If we see the need, we can always rescind the proposal," Kirk suggested.

"Excellent idea, Kirk. It's no wonder we hired you to manage the city," Nathan replied. "What do you think, gentlemen?"

Agreement came quickly, and Mr. Meanor and the other agents who had accompanied him were soon dismissed with orders to post broadsides at each of the mills as soon as they could be printed. Any reactions were to be reported to Matthew, who was charged with investigating the seriousness of any agitation.

"Kirk, you can decide if we need to reconvene. If a meeting is necessary, send word to me," Nathan instructed. "Let's move on to Henry's report, and after that, I think we can adjourn. I'm certain Josiah will want to hurry home, but for any of you who care to remain, there's a fine bottle of port awaiting us in the drawing room."

London

William Thurston walked up the stairs to his small room and removed his woolen greatcoat before seating himself at the small desk. He had decided on his way home he would pen a letter to Thaddeus Arnold. He longed to feel the surge of delight caused by sharing his schemes with another. Writing a letter to Thaddeus would not give him the same heightened pleasure, but it would have to suffice. He dared not trust anyone else in England.

The last letter he'd received from Thaddeus was tucked into a small drawer. William withdrew the missive and reread the letter before carefully folding and returning it to the drawer. Thaddeus would be pleased to know the information he had supplied regarding John Farnsworth had proved correct.

Picking up his pen, William dipped the nib into a small bottle of ink and began to write. Thaddeus would be delighted to hear of his success this evening. The meeting with Barlow Kent and Chauncy Fuller, although brief, had exceeded William's expectations. Chauncy had completed some investigating on his own and was quick to tell William he and Barlow agreed that Farnsworth was likely in England to pilfer additional information for the Americans. Much to Thurston's pleasure, they had agreed the authorities should not be involved. Little did they realize that their announcement had eliminated William's greatest fear. Surprisingly, Barlow Kent had made the statement and Chauncy had quickly voiced his agreement that they should be able to handle the Farnsworth matter on their own. In fact, the two men said they'd nearly completed a plan to ensure John Farnsworth would never return to America, and once the arrangements were in place, they would contact Thurston. Although he preferred the role of leader to that of follower, he knew his power was limited. If these men wanted to take charge, he'd adhere to their pronouncements—as long as their decisions concurred with his own.

With his lips curved in a self-satisfied smile, William continued with his letter.

CHAPTER *15*

February
Lowell

Daughtie slumped into the thick-cushioned chair and folded her arms. "I wish you hadn't invited a whole group of girls," she complained. "Did you ask Dr. Ketter's permission to use his waiting room?"

"*Yes,*" Ruth replied, her irritation obvious. "And even though I specially requested his permission, you may recall that Dr. Ketter told us we could use this room as a parlor on Sundays."

"Strange you can remember what Dr. Ketter said about the parlor, yet you can't seem to recall I wanted to have a private discussion about the turnout."

"Why does everything have to be on *your* terms, Daughtie? I'd rather have the opinions and ideas of several people. That way we'll have a well-balanced viewpoint. Besides, nobody's forcing you to sit in that chair. You can go upstairs if you don't want to be involved."

"I'll stay and listen, but I doubt whether I'll add much to the conversation. I barely know these girls, and they could be some of the very ones who have been reporting information back to the supervisors."

Ruth gave her a look of disdain. "You're overreacting. There is nothing preventing you from merely sitting there like a bump on a log and listening to what the others have to say. You can weigh the information and still have plenty of time to decide if you want to support a strike before the first of March arrives," Ruth replied before hurrying off to answer a knock at the door.

With Dr. Ketter having granted permission to use the parlor and Mrs. Arnold and Theona gone visiting for the afternoon, there was little doubt Ruth was planning on several hours of lively discussion. When Ruth returned with ten girls in tow, Daughtie knew there would be no shortage of opinions.

The introductions were brief. Two of the girls were employed at the Appleton; the remainder worked at the Lawrence, Tremont, and Suffolk mills. Daughtie recognized the girls from the Appleton, for they both worked on the spinning floor. However, she had never seen the others and carefully scrutinized each one as introductions were made. "I'm Daughtie Winfield. I work at the Appleton. I recognize you girls from the Appleton, but I don't believe I've seen any of you other girls before, *even at the library,*" she remarked. There was an edge to her voice.

"I don't have time for reading," one of the girls replied. "And I've never seen you, either," another remarked, returning Daughtie's condescending gaze.

"You should *make* time to expand your mind," Daughtie rebutted.

Ruth sighed. "We're not here to discuss library usage and mind expansion. We're here to discuss the merits of a turnout the first of March. If you want to discuss these other matters, I suggest we schedule another get-together for that purpose. Now, why don't we begin? Who would like to make a statement against turning out?"

One of the girls from the Suffolk raised her hand. "I'm afraid to go on strike. I need my job, and what if they find replacements to take our place? They could blackball us and never let us return to work at any of the mills. They do things like that, you know!"

"If we sit back and let them decrease our wages, they'll take it as our approval to do the same thing the next time they claim that their profits are going down. We can't idly sit by and let them get away with this," Marjorie, a girl from the Lawrence mill, replied.

Several girls nodded in agreement.

Jane Rinemore from the Suffolk shifted in her chair. "Perhaps we could circulate a petition setting forth our opposition to the lowering of wages. If we gathered enough signatures, the owners would see that we disapprove of their actions, yet we could continue working."

"A page full of signatures won't stop them from lowering the wages. Are you willing to do nothing but sign a protest and then smile and accept your wages being decreased?" Marjorie inquired.

Jane shrugged her shoulders. "I don't believe I have a choice. My family depends upon the money I send them."

"Well, your family will have less to count on come the first of March unless we do something," Marjorie countered.

"The Bible tells us that we honor Christ by submitting to each other. Wouldn't it then be a mark of faith if we acted in love and obedience to Christ's teachings and merely accepted the Corporation's offer?" Jane asked while surveying the room.

Marjorie's lips tightened into a knot. "Well, if you're referring to Ephesians 5:21, you've completely misinterpreted the passage. *That* passage means Christians shouldn't create disturbances within the church with their stubborn behavior."

"But what *is* the church if it's not the believers? The mills are owned by Christian men, aren't they? I certainly don't think that verse is speaking of a church building," Jane replied with authority. "And if you disagree with that Scripture, Ephesians also says that Christians should submit to their employers."

Ruth patted Marjorie's arm. "I don't think we need to discuss this matter based upon biblical truths, Jane. Our decision is purely related to right and wrong within our workplace. Don't the rest of you agree?"

There were nods of agreement around the room, except for Jane and Daughtie.

"Your remark makes absolutely no sense, Ruth. We may disagree over interpretation of the Scripture, but the Bible is *exactly* where we should look for our answers. If you're saying our behavior at work shouldn't reflect Biblical principles, I heartily disagree. I concur with Jane; I think a turnout is improper behavior," Daughtie said, having regained her composure.

"I should have known," Ruth murmured before squaring her shoulders and leveling a look of disdain at her roommate. "Your Shaker upbringing is surfacing."

Several of the girls giggled.

Daughtie observed the group for a moment and then stood. "I thought this was to be an exchange of thoughts and beliefs—an open discussion. However, it appears I misunderstood the intent of the meeting. Please excuse me. I'm going upstairs, since it appears those opposing the majority opinion will gain only hurt feelings."

———————

"Daughtie! Wait for me," Ruth called.

Daughtie hesitated and then stopped. She wanted to

continue on her way without a confrontation with Ruth. They hadn't spoken since the meeting yesterday, but there wasn't time to resolve their differences now.

Ruth hastened toward her. "Could we clear the air? I don't want us to quarrel."

"We can talk later if you like. I'm not going back to the boardinghouse right now. I've already told Mrs. Arnold not to expect me for supper."

"Would you like some company? I'd be happy to accompany you—or help with whatever is needing your attention."

"No, thank you. I don't need any help, and I prefer to be alone."

"How long are you going to continue pouting? I'm trying to apologize, but you're determined to make me suffer even longer, aren't you?"

"Don't be silly. I'm not pouting, and my prior arrangements have nothing to do with you or yesterday's meeting. I'm sorry if you're offended, but I really must be on my way," Daughtie replied before turning and hurrying out the mill yard gate. She could feel Ruth staring after her, but she continued onward without glancing back until she reached Whidden's Mercantile on Gorham Street.

The bell over the door jingled, announcing her presence as she walked into the store. "Good evening, Mrs. Whidden," she greeted. "I came back to pick up the fabric swatches."

The older woman smiled and motioned her back toward the rear of the store. "I have them all ready for you," she said while reaching beneath the counter and pulling out a bundle wrapped in brown paper and tied with cord. "Here you are. Be certain your measurements are exact. We wouldn't want to order incorrectly," she cautioned.

Daughtie nodded. "I'll make sure the dimensions are correct. Thank you for your assistance, Mrs. Whidden."

"You're welcome. I hope your customer is pleased with the choices."

Daughtie scurried from the store with the package tucked under her arm. She'd been awaiting the arrival of the fabrics and was anxious to see Liam's reaction to the prints. She hadn't had an opportunity to visit with him since he'd seen her with Dr. Ketter outside the library. By the time she reached Liam's house, her fingers were cold and stiff inside her knitted mittens. She knocked, her knuckles aching as they struck the hard wood of the front door. A pair of the Shakers' coonskin mittens would be a welcome delight, she decided when a rush of cold air swept across the front porch.

Liam pulled open the door, and a gentle draft of heat rose up to warm her face. She opened her mouth to greet him, but instead her teeth chattered incessantly. Try as she would, even with her mouth clamped tightly shut, the clicking sound continued. Her jaw was jiggling like a freshly opened jar of grape jelly.

Liam smiled and quickly moved aside. "Come in before ya freeze to death."

"Th-th-th-thank you," Daughtie finally chattered.

"Let me take yar cloak," he said, assisting her with the garment. "Go in by the fire and warm yarself."

Daughtie didn't offer to wait for him. She scurried into the parlor and yanked a wooden chair in front of the fireplace. Plopping down, she leaned forward, stretching toward the pleasant warmth of the fire.

"This is yar package?" Liam inquired, carrying the paper-wrapped parcel in his large callused hands.

Daughtie remained in her extended position while nodding her head. "Yes. Open it."

Liam sat in a nearby chair, carefully untied the cord, and pulled back the paper. "Are ya goin' to make a bedcover from all these pieces of cloth?" he inquired.

Daughtie giggled. "No. These are pieces of different fabrics we can choose from." It was obvious he was confused by her remark. "For your draperies and furniture," she explained.

He smiled and nodded. "Oh, I see! From the mills. Ya've brought me samples o' cloth from the mills."

"No—I ordered these from a book at Whidden's Mercantile. Most of them are from England. Once we make our decision, I'll order the fabric."

Liam appeared dumbstruck.

"I know it's going to be difficult to choose. There's such a lovely variety, and then attempting to envision the fabric on the furniture or hanging at the windows is an overwhelming task. I'd be happy to share my first choices if you like," she offered, a winsome smile turning up the corners of her pink lips.

"No." Liam placed the pile of fabric on the settee.

" 'No' you don't want my opinion, or 'no' you can't come to a decision right now?" Daughtie questioned.

"No, I'll not be wantin' any of these fabrics."

"What? Why not? Just look at this claret damask. It would be beautiful for your bedroom windows. And please notice that I didn't bring you any pink." She graced him with a bright smile while holding the piece of plum-colored fabric in her outstretched hand.

Liam shook his head. "I'm thinkin' it best to use fabric produced at the mills here in Lowell. Buyin' cloth made in this city is the proper thing to do. Besides, I'm not for spendin' any money in England; goes against my beliefs."

Daughtie leaned back in her chair. "Well, I wish you would have mentioned that fact before I put Mrs. Whidden to all the trouble of ordering these samples. I don't know how I'll ever explain."

Liam rested his ankle across his opposing knee and produced a hearty chuckle. "Just tell her the truth. Ya're workin' for a hardheaded Irishman who won't give in to buyin' from the English."

Daughtie was silent for a moment, contemplating Liam's edict. "You're absolutely right," she finally agreed. "Residents of the community *should* support the industrial efforts right here in Lowell. I don't know why I didn't think of that."

"Ya were merely attemptin' to give me more choices. Don't be hard on yarself."

"Instead of rushing off to Whidden's to select fabric, I should have prayed about my new assignment. Perhaps then I would have had a similar thought about the fabric."

Liam grinned at her, his eyes sparkling in the firelight. "And do you go prayin' about *everythin'*, Miss Daughtie Winfield?"

"Are you laughing at my beliefs?"

Liam held up his hand as though to ward off an attack. "I would never be laughin' at your beliefs. I think prayin' is laudable. Much good has been wrought through prayer."

"Do you speak from personal experience?"

"I'm afraid not. 'Tis one of my mother's famous quotes. Though I'm not opposed to prayer," he hastened to add.

"I can't explain very well, but my life goes more smoothly when I pray about things."

He scooted down into his chair in a relaxed manner and gave her his full attention. "And since you weren't prayin' about the decoratin' of me house, what have you been prayin' about lately?"

She felt comfortable with his easy manner and returned his smile. "My position at the mill. The Corporation has posted broadsides informing us that our wages are going to be cut. They're proposing a twenty-five percent decrease in our wages. The very day the announcement was made, the girls began talk of a turnout. Girls from all of the mills are urging a strike."

"And you, Daughtie? What do *you* believe is best?" Liam asked, his gaze unwavering.

"I believe we should continue working. I know a loss of wages is difficult to accept, especially for the girls who are helping support their families, but I fear that if we go against the Corporation, the Associates may vote to close the mills entirely. In my opinion, closing the mills would cause irreparable harm to the whole community. Besides, I don't believe a turnout is the Christian thing to do."

"And what do the girls who favor the strike argue?"

"They say that if we agree to a pay cut, there's nothing to stop the owners from continuing down this path of decreasing our income. Ruth called a meeting last night, and most of the girls favor the turnout for that particular reason. Of course, they believe the Corporation is acting in an unchristian manner and therefore they feel no responsibility to respond in a fair and prudent manner."

Liam nodded his head but said nothing.

"You disagree with me?"

"I didn't say that. I don't believe I have enough information to agree or disagree about a strike, but I do admire yar willingness to base yar decisions on what the Bible has to say. 'Course, people tend to argue about what the Bible says, too. My mother was always at loggerheads about the Scriptures."

"Your parents are still in Ireland?"

"Aye. They promised to come to America once I had a steady job; then my mother postponed, sayin' I should be buildin' a house first. Now she says it needs to be properly furnished. Once it's furnished, she'll be findin' another excuse to remain at home. Yet she'll be pleased because she can be tellin' all the women in the village that her Liam has a good job, a large house, and fine furniture," he said with a laugh.

"And are your parents Christians?"

With his eyebrows arched, Liam gazed heavenward for a moment. "I'm not certain that's a word I'd use to describe them. My father doesn't speak of his beliefs or faith. He goes to church with my mother from time to time, mostly to stop her incessant nagging, I think. My mother's beliefs are a puzzlement to me. As far as I can tell, she goes shiftin' back and forth between the church and witchcraft . . . or maybe it's idolatry. I quit tryin' to figure her out."

Daughtie smiled in understanding. "And you, Liam? What do you believe?"

"To be honest, I'm not certain. O' course I went to catechism and attended church every week when I was growin' up. My mother wouldn't have had it any other way, but like me da, I quit going. Seems as though people in this country have some different ideas about religion and God—not the Irish over here in the Acre, but the rest of ya."

"Maybe you never noticed the differences in Ireland because people in your village didn't talk about their faith," Daughtie suggested. "Who have you been talking to since you arrived in Lowell?"

"About what? My belief in God?"

She cupped her chin in one hand with an elbow perched upon her knee. "Yes."

"Mostly just to Matthew Cheever, although John Farnsworth and I have had a conversation or two. I first talked to Matthew back when I was working on the masonry at St. Patrick's Church. That was shortly after I'd come to Lowell. We talked a little about the stonework I was doin' in the church, and then Matthew said he'd be likin' to get together again and continue our discussion. I laughed at the thought of it—Matthew Cheever associatin' with a lowly Irishman. I'm tellin' ya, I was surprised when he did just that. We've spent some fine times talkin' about God. I'm not sayin' he's convinced me just yet, but I'd say

I'm a lot closer to believin' than I was when I stepped foot in this country. Matthew's a good man and he has strong beliefs—like you and your friends."

"Not all of my friends share my beliefs. In fact, one of the reasons there are so many churches is because people disagree about interpretation of the Scriptures and then rush off to start a church of their own. I disagreed with some of the Shaker beliefs, and that's one of the reasons I left the community," she explained.

His eyes grew wide at her reply. " 'Course, ya didn't go startin' your own church . . . or did ya?" he asked with a grin.

"No. But I suppose I get as opinionated as the next person. Sometimes I wonder just what God thinks of all of us running around down here on earth acting the fool over petty matters."

"Thing is, it's a petty matter only if it doesn't go against what ya believe, right?"

"I suppose you have a valid point, and I do believe some things are blatantly unscriptural. In that event, and if you know the beliefs are not going to change, I think it's better to leave than cause problems within the group. The Bible says we're not to cause disruption within the body of believers. I knew the Shakers would not change, and that is part of the reason I left the Society. I truly prayed for guidance. Once I felt my prayers were answered, I didn't have time to look back," she said, giving him a wistful smile. "Clearly, my decision was for a mixture of reasons. My friend Bella was determined to leave, and from the time she came to the Shaker village in Canterbury, we were the best of friends. I didn't think I could bear the pain of losing her friendship. I had grown to love many of the Sisters; I still miss some of them. On the other hand, there were two or three Sisters I could barely abide. I spent much time in prayer about how to love those particular Sisters. I'm somewhat ashamed to make that admission," she said, giving him a sheepish grin.

He laughed at her remark. "And now ya have no regrets, even though yar friend has married and left you alone?"

"Bella will be back from England soon. Besides, I'm not alone. I have other friends," she defended.

"And I hope ya'll be countin' me as one of them."

There was an intensity in Liam's words that caused her face to warm at his remark. "Yes, that would be nice." Suddenly the fact that they were alone seemed very noticeable. Daughtie cleared her throat. "Now, about the fabrics? I suppose I'd best go back and have a talk with Mrs. Whidden."

"My talk of friendship has embarrassed ya. I apologize. I'd never overstep me bounds. You know that, don't ya?"

Impulsively, Daughtie reached across the chasm between them and touched Liam's hand. "I'm honored that you consider me a friend, and you need not worry about overstepping boundaries. Surely you know I don't choose friends based upon where they were born or the color of their skin. *That* is one principle of the Shakers to which I gladly conform," she said, finally gaining the courage to look into his eyes. Liam's gaze, however, was fixed upon her hand resting atop his own. Daughtie's eyes followed his gaze, and she immediately found herself overwhelmed with the impropriety of her own behavior. She snatched her hand away quickly, as if she'd been jabbed with a hot poker. Scooting back in her chair, she primly wove her fingers into a prayerful pose.

Liam laughed aloud. "Ya jumped like ya were being attacked by a band of leprechauns. There's no need to go concernin' yarself—I didn't mistake your warmth for anything more than the kindness of a friend. And since I do count ya as a friend, and because I know how ya feel about the slavery issue, there's a matter of confidence I was hoping we could be discussin'."

Daughtie nodded in agreement, pleased to discuss anything other than her recent conduct.

"I've given me name as a contact for runaway slaves," he said.

Daughtie stared at him in stunned silence.

"Did ya hear me? I said—"

"I heard you. I'm just, just—amazed. Of all the things you could have possibly said, I never expected to hear those words."

"Why? Do ya think I have no sympathy for a people torn from their homeland and forced into slavery?"

"No, that's not what I think, not at all," Daughtie immediately replied. "You're a compassionate man. It's just that we've talked little of the slavery issue since Prudence Crandall's visit. Your announcement came as a total surprise. When did you arrive at this decision?"

"I went back and talked with several of the men who accompanied Miss Crandall to the meeting. They told me there's a need for safe houses for runaways trying to get to Canada and assured me that once the slaves 'ave made their way this far north, the owners have generally given up on tryin' to get them back. I don't think there's much danger. Besides, I have this big house and the barn out back. Not many folks have as much space to offer, and it's only me I'd be puttin' in any danger."

Daughtie began wringing her hands, a habit for which she'd been soundly rebuked as a child in the Shaker village. "I admire your willingness to help, but I fear the assurances you've been given may be overstated. We had a Sister join the Society. She was a runaway who had escaped from a cruel owner, and by the time she reached Canterbury, the Elders doubted whether anyone would continue searching for her."

"What happened?"

Daughtie's eyes glazed. The long-forgotten memory returned anew. "It was a few weeks after Sister Bessie arrived. We were in Sunday meeting. As usual, a group of spectators had entered the church to observe our worship. Everything progressed normally—we had begun to dance—when a man pointed toward Sister Bessie and began yelling out he'd found his runaway slave. He had two other men with him—big burly men. With total disregard, all three of them bullied their way through the sanctuary and dragged poor Sister Bessie out of the room. I can still hear her screaming for help."

"And no one tried to stop the men?"

"The Brothers and the other spectators tried. But two of the men pointed their weapons and threatened to shoot the first person who made any further move toward them. They said if anyone followed them, they'd return and burn down our buildings. I suppose it does sound quite cowardly that we all stood staring after her, doing nothing. I thought so at the time. I wept and told Sister Mercy there wasn't one soul among us that deserved a heavenly reward. She hugged me close until I quit crying and then explained that either Sister Bessie or someone else in the church would have been killed had the Shaker men continued their pursuit. I suppose she was correct, but I lay awake many a night thinking about Sister Bessie, wondering if she'd been beaten and what had become of her." Daughtie raised her head and met his concerned gaze. "So you see, there are slave owners who will pursue their runaways even farther north than Lowell. I doubt what I've told you will change your decision, but you should have accurate information. You could be placing yourself in serious danger."

"So ya think I've made a bad choice?"

"No, I think you've made a courageous decision. I applaud your willingness to help, but I want you to understand that there could be danger involved. I'm honored you would take me into your confidence."

Liam gave her a broad smile. "I don't know if anythin' might ever arise so that I'd need help, but if I did . . ."

"Just send word, and I'll do anything I can," she said. "Anything."

"I knew I could be countin' on you," he said, slapping an open palm on his knee. "But from the way the men talked, I'm not expectin' I'll ever be needed. Seems as though they try to find people willin' to help in every town they visit."

"That makes sense. It's wise to have a solution before a problem settles on your doorstep. Perhaps you should do the same."

His forehead creased in concern. "What do ya think I should do?"

"If runaways arrived tonight, would you be prepared to care for them and help them move on? Think about what items are necessary to feed and clothe them. You may need to offer some medical care. Where would you hide them? Is the area safe for men, women, children, and babies? You never know who may arrive or how many. Would you use the house for some and the barn for others? If so, you'll need provisions in both places and good hiding places in the event unexpected visitors arrive."

Liam scratched his head and laughed aloud. "Appears I'll be needin' your help with more than just decoratin' this house."

CHAPTER *16*

Dr. Ketter stood poised in the doorway to his office as Daughtie and Ruth returned home from work late Saturday afternoon. Daughtie cast a sidelong glance in Ruth's direction. Her friend appeared pleased to see the doctor, but there was something more—a look that passed between them—almost as if Ruth expected Dr. Ketter to be awaiting their arrival.

"Good afternoon, ladies," he greeted. A gust of cold air whisked across the threshold. The doctor rubbed his hands together and shivered. "Seems as though it hasn't warmed up outside."

Daughtie pushed the door closed before removing her cape and gloves. "If you're chilled, perhaps you should move back into your office. That way you'll be out of the draft."

"If you'll join me, I'll do exactly that. It's at least an hour before supper."

Not even taking time to contemplate the request, Daughtie moved toward the stairway. "I'm sorry, but I have several matters I wish to accomplish before supper. If you'll excuse me—we can talk during the evening meal."

She had taken two steps up the staircase when Dr. Ketter's words stopped her. "I have a patient I wish to discuss, and I don't think the conversation would lend itself to mealtime, especially with a child present. I'm hoping your knowledge of herbs may be helpful."

Turning, she retraced her steps and he led the way to his office. "What is it you wish to talk about?" Daughtie inquired from just inside the doorway.

"Do sit down," he encouraged, gesturing toward a chair.

"No, thank you. How may I help?"

Dr. Ketter gave her an embarrassed smile. "I hope you'll forgive me, but I've actually gotten you into my office under false pretenses."

"Truly? So you don't need my assistance?"

"Not with a patient, but I did want the opportunity to speak with you privately."

"What is it you want to discuss, Dr. Ketter?"

"I've been told that there is a ball March 21, the Blowing Out Ball. I was hoping you would attend with me."

With her eyes wide, Daughtie stared at him. "You wanted to invite me to a dance? Is *that* your important question?"

"Yes," he replied, his face suddenly taking on a red tinge.

"I think the Blowing Out Ball may be an uncertainty this year given the fact that the girls are threatening a turn-out. Who knows? The mills could be closed down five or six weeks from now," she replied tersely.

Dr. Ketter's crimson complexion paled. "Do you truly believe a strike is possible? I set up practice in Lowell because the Corporation said there was security and that I

wouldn't have to rely upon farmers paying me with produce or animals. If the mills close—even one or two of
them—it could adversely affect the whole community.
Surely the girls will consider the impact their actions could
have upon the rest of us. Such behavior would be completely irrational."

Dr. Ketter's outburst annoyed Daughtie. He seemed not
concerned about the workers or the city of Lowell; instead,
his fretfulness was for himself and the inconvenience a
strike might cause in the plans he'd made for a flourishing
medical practice. For the first time since she'd heard talk of
a turnout, Daughtie considered siding with the girls who
favored the strike.

"I believe a turnout is highly possible, though it will
depend upon the supporters rallying enough workers to
their cause," she replied.

"A bright girl like yourself doesn't favor the plan, do
you?"

"I haven't given it my support, as yet. I believe much
depends upon how the Corporation presents its final offer
regarding the cutback of wages. If they remain determined
to lower wages by the full twenty-five percent, there's no
doubt many of the girls will strike in opposition."

"But a level-headed woman like yourself could be the
voice of restraint. You're educated and articulate. You could
sway many of the undecided."

Daughtie gave him a faint smile. "It's up to each girl to
determine the merits and vote her own conscience.
They've all listened to the positive and negative aspects of a
walkout. There have been many meetings over the past two
weeks. I'm surprised you aren't more aware of the goings-
on in the town, especially since you express a strong desire
to remain in Lowell."

"I've been so busy—I haven't had an opportunity to
talk with many of the businessmen in town or become

involved in community activities."

His tone was defensive, and Daughtie knew her words had hit the mark. "Priorities, Doctor," she said, turning to leave the room. "It would appear that becoming involved in the community could yield some of those benefits you seem to value and currently enjoy. Now if you'll excuse me, I really must go upstairs."

"Wait," he said, grasping her arm. "If there is a ball, will you do me the honor of attending with me?"

"I don't—"

He held up a hand to stave off her answer. "Perhaps I should do as you suggested earlier. I'll wait to see if the Associates will be hosting the celebration."

Daughtie gave a nod of her head and ran up the stairs. Just as she reached the bedroom, she heard a knock at the front door—likely an ailing patient needing the doctor's assistance. She'd let him answer.

Ruth perked to attention when Daughtie entered the room. "Did you and Dr. Ketter have a nice visit?"

"You knew he was going to ask me, didn't you?"

"Ask you what?"

"To accompany him to the Blowing Out Ball. Don't try to act innocent. The two of you arranged that entire encounter, didn't you?"

"You two are perfect for each other. With all you have in common, you're an ideal match. He's a doctor, and you know so much about medicine. I know I was a bit jealous at first, but honestly, you should consider him a fine match. Together, you could do so much good—and be so happy. My mother says that a husband and wife need to have common goals."

"Husband and wife? If you think Dr. Ketter would be a perfect husband, why don't *you* attend the ball with him?"

"Because it's you he's interested in," Ruth snapped.

"Besides, you need to focus your attention on a *decent* man."

"Does that mean you think I'm paying attention to an indecent man?"

"Liam Donohue is certainly an inappropriate suitor for anyone except, perhaps, one of his own kind," Ruth replied.

A fount of righteous indignation rose up within Daughtie and then spilled over. "How *dare* you speak ill of Liam Donohue! He's a fine man with outstanding principles. Dr. Ketter would be hard-pressed to exhibit the kind of moral fiber I've seen in Liam Donohue."

"Truly? And exactly what display have you seen from Mr. Donohue?"

After realizing she'd spoken out of turn, Daughtie hesitated, attempting to regroup her thoughts. "He attended the antislavery meeting, and he's done a good deal to help the struggling Irish in the Acre. He cares deeply for the less fortunate."

"And you think Dr. Ketter doesn't? I haven't heard you say anything about Mr. Donohue that couldn't apply equally to Dr. Ketter. Certainly you should be considering the fact that Dr. Ketter has chosen a profession in which he is constantly helping others."

"So long as they pay for the service," Daughtie countered. "His biggest concern right now is whether the mills will strike. And do you know why that concerns him? Not because he fears the workers are being ill treated, not because he fears others will suffer if there's a strike, not even because he's concerned for the investment of the Associates. Oh no! Your fine Dr. Ketter is worried because he was promised a flourishing medical practice, and should the workers strike and a mill or two close down, the number of patients would decrease and his income would suffer. His concern is his own livelihood. I don't think Dr. Ketter is the humanitarian you make him out to be."

"You can't fault a man for being concerned over his own welfare. He has expenses to pay like any of us." She lowered her voice momentarily. "He might even have debts. I'd think less of him if he *weren't* concerned about making a living. The way you continually defend Liam Donohue makes me wonder if there isn't more going on between you two than meets the eye. If it's nothing more than friendship, why would you turn down Dr. Ketter's invitation to the ball? I'm beginning to think you're less than forthright about Mr. Donohue."

The smug look on Ruth's face was more than Daughtie could bear. There was little doubt that Ruth would soon be spreading false rumors. "If going to the ball with Dr. Ketter will serve to convince you I'm telling the truth, then so be it. In reality it proves nothing except that I've tired of this debate."

Ruth jumped up and clapped her hands together. "So you *will* go with him?"

"If there's a ball, I'll go with him—but not because I've any romantic interest in the good doctor. My agreement is given solely to silence your nagging."

"And you'll tell him you accept his invitation?"

Obviously the reasoning behind Daughtie's agreement mattered little to Ruth. "Yes, I'll tell him. But not this evening."

"Well, when?" Ruth whined.

"Once there's an actual announcement by the Corporation that the ball is going to be held. And don't you say a word to him, either. If you do, I'll take it all back and stay at home."

"Oh, all right, but I do wish you'd reconsider. I know it would make him ever so happy to have your acceptance this evening."

"Ruth! Not another word about this subject. I'm going

to need headache powders if you don't cease this bother-
some behavior."

———————

A short time later, Daughtie rounded the doorway and
skidded to a halt. "Mr. Arnold! I didn't realize you were
here," she said, backing away. His beady-eyed stare caused
her to give an involuntary shiver.

A wicked smirk tugged at his lips. "No harm done. In
fact, it's a shame you stopped short of reaching my arms. I
rather like the thought of holding you in a warm embrace."

"What did you say, Thaddeus?" Mrs. Arnold inquired
while carrying a heaping platter of roasted pork into the
dining room. "I wasn't able to hear you out in the kitchen."

"Nothing. I was merely admiring Miss Winfield's
charm and grace. She is a lovely young lady, isn't she?"

Mrs. Arnold's gaze shifted between her former husband
and Daughtie. "Yes, she's quite lovely," she replied before
retreating to the kitchen.

"Why did you say such a thing?" Daughtie hissed.

"You *are* lovely, my dear," he said, drawing nearer and
stroking her arm.

Instinctively, Daughtie pulled away and hurried across
the hallway. "Aren't you coming to supper, Dr. Ketter?"

Ivan looked up from his papers and gave her a broad
smile. "Yes, of course. How kind of you to remind me of
the time."

Daughtie slipped her hand through the crook of his arm
and permitted him to escort her back across the hall to the
dining room. Thaddeus Arnold appeared amused by the
sight, Mrs. Arnold surprised, and Ruth—Ruth's face was
etched in delight.

Thaddeus speared a slice of roast pork and looked
toward Dr. Ketter. "Are you enjoying the hospitality of my
house, Dr. Ketter?"

Ivan appeared taken aback by the question. "It's my understanding this house belongs to the Corporation, Mr. Arnold. However, I do find the accommodations to my liking."

"I'm certain you find more than the accommodations to your liking," Thaddeus retorted as he eyed the three women. "Having the pleasure of dining with these lovely women each night is certainly enough to make me envious." He leisurely wet his lips with the enjoyment of a cat licking the last droplet of cream from its whiskers, leaned back in his chair, and awaited Ivan's reply.

"I find the company as pleasurable as the accommodations," Ivan simply stated.

Thaddeus gave a wicked laugh. "Don't become too comfortable in your new surroundings, Dr. Ketter. Women can be a fickle lot—telling lies and causing all manner of problems."

Daughtie ceased eating, carefully watching the exchange. It was obvious Thaddeus was toying with Ivan, enjoying the doctor's obvious discomfort, while Mrs. Arnold fidgeted with Theona in an understandable attempt to draw her husband's attention away from Dr. Ketter.

Uncertain whether it was sympathy for Mrs. Arnold and Dr. Ketter or a distinct dislike for Thaddeus Arnold that caused her boldness, Daughtie said, "I was taught at an early age that good digestion is dependent upon pleasant table conversation. I'm certain we can find something more enjoyable to discuss."

Thaddeus squeezed his face into a condescending mask of tolerance and pointed his fork in Daughtie's direction. "If you'd rather change topics, why don't you tell me about work at the Appleton? I continue to miss the pleasure my duties at the mill afforded me."

Neither Mr. Arnold's smirk nor the evil glint in his eye was lost on Daughtie. How a kind woman such as Naomi

Arnold could have ever chosen to marry him was beyond Daughtie's comprehension. "Work at the mills continues as usual," Daughtie replied.

Ruth twisted in her chair and leveled a look of amazement in Daughtie's direction. "Daughtie! How can you make such a remark? The Corporation is threatening to lower wages by twenty-five percent, the operatives are organizing for a turnout, and you say everything is normal?"

Thaddeus arched his neck in Ruth's direction. "A decrease in wages, you say? Profits must be down, which means sales have decreased and production, of course, has increased. I know someone who projected this is exactly what would happen. They've expanded too rapidly for their own good. And you say the operatives are going to strike?"

Ruth came to attention. "Yes, they—"

"Merely talk, nothing more," Daughtie interrupted. "I doubt whether this topic is any better for the digestion than your earlier discussion of women's foibles, Mr. Arnold."

"Quite the contrary, Miss Winfield. I find the discussion excellent for my digestion. Tell me, Miss Wilson, have the girls organized? I find that organization is the key to efficiency in all things."

"I absolutely agree. We began organizing the day the broadsides were posted. Since then, we've been holding meetings in an attempt to persuade all of the operatives to join those of us who have already committed to the cause."

"Good, good," Thaddeus encouraged, nodding in agreement, "and when will you strike?"

"We're awaiting a final decision on the amount of the wage decrease. The Associates want twenty-five percent. However, we've been told Mr. Boott and Mr. Cheever, along with other members of management here in Lowell, have requested the amount be reassessed."

"No matter the amount, the wages should not be lowered. You must rally the operatives and explain they must stand their ground," he replied with a thump of his fist on the table.

"For a man who no longer works at the mills, you appear to be keenly interested in this difficulty," Dr. Ketter suggested.

Thaddeus ignored the remark and remained focused upon Ruth. Her eyes had widened at Mr. Arnold's impassioned declaration, and she glanced toward Daughtie.

"Don't look to Miss Winfield for advice. You're obviously a young woman of vision and leadership. I have no doubt you can convince the other workers they should strike. And the sooner, the better. You must send a clear and concise message to the Associates that the workers will not tolerate their greedy actions. Those men in their fancy mansions will continue to live in the lap of luxury, no matter the consequence to the lowly mill workers. They care little whether there's a crust of bread in your mouth."

"I think your statement is somewhat melodramatic, Mr. Arnold," Daughtie said in a lighthearted tone, hoping to ease the tension permeating the room. "Our discussion is not going to resolve the problems in the mill, and I'm certain your former wife and daughter would find another topic much more edifying."

"Don't attempt to tell me what will or will not interest Naomi or Theona, Miss Winfield. They'll listen to whatever I care to present."

Daughtie wanted to continue the argument, but one look at Mr. Arnold's ashen complexion convinced her to reevaluate her position. He might hold his temper in check during dinner, yet Daughtie knew afterward it would be Mrs. Arnold and Theona who would suffer the brunt of his anger. She should have known better than to provoke him, but in a momentary lapse of memory, she'd forgotten his detestable behavior. Well, she'd not leave Mrs. Arnold and Theona alone with Thaddeus this evening, of that she was certain.

"Please accept my apology, Mr. Arnold. I didn't mean any offense," she replied in a conciliatory tone.

His chest swelled slightly, obviously pleased by her act of contrition. "As I was saying, Miss Wilson, you should make due haste in gaining support. Is there no word from management as to when you can expect a decision?"

Ruth cast a sidelong glance at Daughtie before replying. "We're told the first of March, but some say it may be later."

"Have the supervisors met with you and set forth exact reasons for this callous behavior?"

"It's as you stated earlier. Profits have diminished."

"And you poor girls are going to be the Corporation's scapegoats, suffering the disastrous effects of their inept ability to manage their assets. Disgraceful!"

Daughtie stared in disbelief. When had Thaddeus ever cared about the girls in the mills? For that matter, when had he ever cared about anyone other than himself? And why was he still so interested in the mills? He quizzed them every time he came to visit, obviously anxious for any morsel he might acquire. His behavior made no sense. The moment Ruth began to spoon-feed him the information he so desperately desired, his wrath subsided. Still, she wouldn't leave Mrs. Arnold alone in his presence. The man was a chameleon, altering his behavior at every twist and turn.

Pushing away from the table, Thaddeus crooked his finger and beckoned Ruth. "Let's finish our discussion in the parlor—or, should I say, Dr. Ketter's waiting room? You don't mind if we use your waiting room, do you, Doctor? Come, come, my dear," he urged. "We have important matters to discuss."

CHAPTER *17*

London

William Thurston threaded his way through the shoppers and sightseers lining the streets, careful to keep John Farnsworth and his group within sight. If he grew too close, he feared one of them might see his reflection in a store window. He attempted to edge past a group of elderly women moving at a snail's pace, obviously more intent upon their own conversation than the fact that they were blocking the path of others.

He inadvertently brushed the shoulder of one woman as he passed by. "Well, I *never!* You might excuse yourself," she scolded. When William didn't respond, she thumped him soundly with her cane. "I *said* you need to excuse yourself!"

William turned and tipped his beaver top hat. "My apologies. I'm in a hurry."

"That much is obvious," the old woman called after him.

William ignored the remark and rushed onward, now concerned John Farnsworth might disappear from sight.

"Foolish old woman," he muttered, scanning the crowd. Spotting Farnsworth, he breathed a sigh of relief.

He waited outside each time they entered a shop until his gloved fingers grew numb from the cold. When they entered a large establishment, he pulled up his collar and followed them inside. The freezing temperatures had forced him to discontinue his observations outdoors.

Moving down an adjacent aisle, he wended his way through the shelves and counters until he found a spot within listening distance of the group, where he heard John mention their dinner reservations were for seven o'clock at the Blue Boar.

Relieved when the group finally completed its shopping expedition, William retraced his steps back toward his boardinghouse. If luck was on his side, he'd be seated somewhere near the Farnsworth dinner party this evening.

William's lips turned upward in a smile of satisfaction. Citing his dislike of large groups, he had convinced the waiter to place a small table in a secluded area behind an ornate marble column near the Farnsworth table—close enough to overhear their conversation, yet concealed enough to remain undetected.

He sipped a glass of deep red port and watched as the Farnsworth party was seated, enjoying the surreptitious infringement his location would afford him throughout the evening. "It's almost as though they've invited me to their little party," he muttered in self-satisfaction.

"I do believe we're privileged to have the most beautiful women in the room seated at our table," John commented to Taylor.

Taylor nodded in agreement. "I believe Bella spent more time fashioning Elinor's hair than her own."

"And well worth the effort, I might add. You look

beautiful, Elinor," John said. "And you, my dear, are too lovely for words."

"Enough of this drivel," William mumbled.

"Excuse me? Did you want something, sir?"

William glanced up to see a waiter standing in attendance at his table. "No, just thinking aloud. I'll wait until later to place my order," he replied, turning his attention back to the conversation that was taking place on the other side of the stone pillar.

"I'm not sure that's wise, John. I think we should wait until the first of the month before making a final decision. After all, Taylor has been able to locate those new print ideas to take back to Mr. Boott, and he seems to have reconnected with some of his old acquaintances. Haven't you, Taylor?" Addie inquired.

"Absolutely. Believe me, we know that what we're doing here in England is necessary. Bella and I are committed to staying until Uncle John is certain there is enough information to return home with confidence."

William's eyes widened, and he strained closer to listen.

"I appreciate your willingness to remain in England. The fact that you both realize the importance of this visit means a great deal to me. I know you've put your future on hold, but I promise you'll be rewarded for your efforts."

"No need for that, Uncle John. You're family—we do whatever we can for family. Right, Bella?"

Bella smiled and nodded. "Yes, for your family, we're pleased to help wherever and however needed."

"I still think it wise to check on passages home. If things go as we're hoping, we still may be able to sail by early March," John replied.

"As you wish, my dear. Whatever will make you most contented," Addie replied.

William startled at the remark, nearly toppling over his glass of port. The conversation at the other table swirled through his mind. Manning had said he wanted Farnsworth to return home with enough information to feel confident. *No doubt he's made promises to the Associates that he'll produce valuable information. If Farnsworth returns to Massachusetts without anything of real value, he'll appear the fool and, more importantly, lose stature with the Corporation,* William decided. And the fact that Farnsworth had the total agreement of his entire family to assist him in this sabotage was even more baffling.

Certainly *he* would never have confided any business information to his wife, yet both of the women appeared fully informed, entering into the conversation as though they were equals in the decision making. William's wife would never have agreed to help him, much less keep her mouth shut. The idiocy of these men astounded him! But, he reasoned, both of the women had worked for the Corporation. Perhaps they felt some overwhelming loyalty to the mills—or perhaps it was merely an allegiance to their husbands.

The fact that Farnsworth and his family might soon be returning to America was most disconcerting. Having all but promised to deliver Farnsworth and proof of his espionage activities, there was now a strong possibility Thurston might lose his foothold with the British aristocracy. Tomorrow he would follow Farnsworth to the ticket offices at the wharf; perhaps the ticket agent would be forthcoming. If not, a few coins would likely loosen his tongue. On Wednesday he would follow Taylor Manning to find out how he was stealing fabric patterns.

William stroked his chin in absolute delight. What more could he have asked for? A recent letter from Thaddeus telling him of a possible strike in the Lowell mills, coupled with the information he'd assembled about John

Farnsworth and his family over the past week, should raise his stature a notch or two with Chauncy Fuller and his pompous English associates. He ordered ale and watched the front door of the pub.

Barlow Kent and Chauncy Fuller entered the Ale House. William waved the men toward his table and then rose to greet them. "Exactly on time," he said.

"I personally abhor tardiness," Barlow replied while signaling to the barkeep.

Chauncy pulled a gold watch from his pocket and checked the time. "Since the topic of time seems to be of the utmost importance to both of you, I'd best mention that I have only an hour to spare before my next meeting."

Thurston clenched his jaw. However, he didn't want Chauncy to discern his irritation. "Then we'd best move along swiftly, as I have much to report." He hesitated for a moment, assuring himself he had their full attention—he *deserved* their full attention. "Since our last meeting, I have been engaged in numerous activities, all of them garnering valuable information. I began my quest for additional facts by following John Farnsworth on numerous occasions. My first piece of significant information was gained through secreting myself at dinner—"

"I'm sorry to interrupt, my good man, but if we're to accomplish anything today, you'd best cut to the chase. As I said, I've only an hour," Chauncy cautioned impatiently.

Unable to hide his irritation, William leaned across the table and met Chauncy's gaze. "I spent innumerable hours in the freezing cold gathering this information, and now you want me to hurry along so that you may attend to other business? I think not! Perhaps you need to reevaluate your priorities."

Chauncy didn't appear offended, yet he didn't waver from his proclamation. "Tell the information at your own pace, but the fact remains that I must leave in an hour.

Unlike you, I have more than one matter that beckons my attention."

William inwardly flinched at the remark but gave no visible sign he was offended. Instead, he offered a perfunctory nod. "In that case, I assume you're even more grateful for my assistance. As I was saying, I followed the Farnsworth family to numerous locations and, through my observations, became privy to information that Taylor Manning, Farnsworth's nephew, may have discovered a way to steal print designs, and the group may be departing England in the very near future."

Chauncy's eyebrows arched. "If they're leaving and none of the mills has reported espionage problems, what makes you certain designs have been stolen or anything has gone amiss? Perhaps they were here for the obvious reasons—to visit family and spend the holidays in England."

William wagged his head back and forth, clearly enjoying the moment. "I assume you're playing devil's advocate since I know you're already convinced Farnsworth is up to no good. The information I've uncovered will prove exactly that—Farnsworth is a traitor. And please remember that the earlier espionage committed by the Americans was not detected until their mills were already operating in Massachusetts."

"That's true. He has a valid point," Barlow agreed.

William flashed a glance at Barlow Kent. At least he'd succeeded in convincing Kent there was reason for concern. Twisting in his chair, William focused his attention upon his enthusiastic supporter. "As it turns out, Farnsworth didn't book passage; instead, he merely inquired when ships were scheduled to depart in the months of March, April, and May. The ticket agent has agreed to send word to me when Farnsworth actually books passage. As I expected, it took a few coins to persuade him to cooperate.

However, by the time I left his office, I had secured his complete cooperation."

Barlow Kent rubbed his hands together, obviously enjoying the revelation. Leaning forward, he gave William his full attention. "Go on," he encouraged.

William offered an appreciative smile. "The next day, I followed young Taylor Manning. He's the one who has been helping with design work back in Massachusetts. I don't suppose either of you would like to venture a guess where he might have gone, would you?"

"I don't think we have time for guessing games," Chauncy curtly replied.

"He waited outside Armstrong and Talley—the company that designs for the print work mills in Lancashire. He met one of their employees and the two of them walked off together. I followed but could never get close enough to hear their conversation. However, I'm certain the man handed him some papers."

Barlow Kent straightened in his chair. The information had obviously captured his interest. William momentarily basked in the attention before continuing. "You realize, of course, the possibility exists for him to steal any new ideas they may be formulating."

Chauncy still didn't appear convinced. "They may be old friends enjoying a brief opportunity to become reacquainted."

"You've obviously had little experience in the area of industrial espionage, my good man. All these men need is a foot in the door, so to speak. He could be doing something as unassuming as meeting an acquaintance, but mark my words, he'll find a way to secure any scrap of information that will assist the Americans."

"I think you may be overreacting."

"I concur with Thurston, Chauncy. I think William is correct in his assumptions. These men have already hoodwinked us once. Are we going to permit them to do it again?" Barlow Kent asked.

Chauncy rubbed his forehead and glanced across the table. "I agree they must be stopped. I've already conceded that point, but I think we need to be absolutely certain of their plans. We don't want to make fools of ourselves."

"Nor do we want to miss the opportunity to thwart this espionage. It appears their return will depend upon Manning's ability to steal the design plans. Why else would Farnsworth be checking on so many alternate dates for their return?"

"Didn't you say Jarrow Farnsworth is ill? They may be awaiting medical advice," Chauncy suggested.

William took a drink from his tankard and settled back in his chair. "That's all a ploy. I'm beginning to doubt whether the old man is even sick. Likely his illness is a ruse to keep us at bay."

"You may be right," Chauncy replied. "I suppose those who would willingly turn traitor against the motherland would also manipulate and exploit their own families. Perhaps I should have a visit with Wilbur Talley. He's a business acquaintance and family friend. Once we tell him of our suspicions, I'm certain he'll be pleased to assist with investigating young Mr. Manning."

"Excellent! I was hoping you might have a contact at Armstrong and Talley. If you'd be willing to write a letter of introduction, I'd be pleased to meet with Mr. Talley— since you're so busy with other matters," William added. "If he's willing to cooperate, we could plot out a plan of action. I certainly wouldn't want to disrupt his business or upset his valued employees."

Chauncy hesitated for only a moment. "Since I can't possibly meet with him for at least a week, I believe I'll take you up on your offer. I'll write a letter for you later today. You can stop by my office at your convenience."

"Any word from your contacts in Massachusetts?" Fuller inquired.

"As a matter of fact, I have," William replied, pulling Thaddeus Arnold's missive from his breast pocket. "You'll be pleased to hear there is talk of a turnout among the working class."

A glint of pleasure shone in Barlow's eyes. "Do tell! That *is* pleasurable news. Apparently all this talk of their happy employees working in a utopian existence is little more than propaganda."

Chauncy drew closer. "If the employees are striking, it's because their wages are being lowered or their workload is being increased without an offer of additional wages. Lower wages could mean production has dropped off and their profits are down, which would be excellent news for us. However, if the Corporation is wanting to increase the workload without an increase in wages, it could mean they're receiving more orders than they can fill and they see this as an opportunity to recoup their investment in rapid fashion."

William nodded. "My informant states that orders have remained steady; however, with the increased number of mills in operation, they need to see an increasing market if they're to operate with a profit. The easiest way to increase their profit margin is to lower wages."

"What have they proposed to their employees?" Barlow inquired.

"Twenty-five percent."

Chauncy exhaled a deep breath between his teeth that culminated in a long, low whistle. "I can see why they may be faced with a strike."

"Apparently a final decision hasn't been made—at least it hadn't at the time this letter was written. By now the workers may already be on strike."

"And wouldn't that be grand news for us? If they

remain on strike for any length of time, our orders could double by spring," Chauncy rejoiced. "Barkeep! Another round," he called out. Suddenly his two o'clock appointment seemed not quite so important.

CHAPTER *18*

Lowell

"Escaping to the library again this evening?" Ruth inquired, her voice distant and cold.

Daughtie tightened her jaw. She wasn't going to engage in another verbal contest over the turnout. "Not escaping—merely helping shelve books," she replied.

"You can run out of the house, but tomorrow morning you'll be forced to make your final decision for all to see, Daughtie. You'd do better to sit here and discuss the merits of both sides and make a choice tonight. Or have you already decided and you're merely afraid to tell me?"

"Why would I fear *you,* Ruth? *I'm* the one who must live with my choice. I'm seeking what God would have me do in this matter. My decision doesn't reflect upon what you or anyone else is supposed to do, only what I believe *I* am supposed to do. So, you see, further discussion with you will be of little assistance. Now, if you'll excuse me, I really must be going."

Daughtie pulled on her cloak and hurried out the door without looking back. She could feel the cold stares of

Ruth and the other girls, and she knew they thought her cowardly. Well, perhaps Mrs. Arnold didn't harbor such views, but certainly Ruth and the others who had gathered at the house shortly after supper believed she was weak and indecisive. She pulled her cape tight against the cold, damp wind until she reached the welcoming warmth of the circulating library.

"Daughtie! Dear me! Where is my mind? I should have sent word to you. I completed shelving all the books earlier today and have two other girls scheduled to work. I'm afraid there will be little to keep you busy. Of course, there are books to read," Mrs. Potter said with a bright smile. "I hope you'll forgive me. I doubt you wanted to be out on this cold night."

Rubbing her hands together near the fire, Daughtie gave Mrs. Potter an easy smile. "No need to concern yourself. There are some new fabrics being produced at the Tremont. I understand they've been stocked at Whidden's Mercantile. I'll go and take a look at those."

"If you'll wait just a minute, I'll accompany you as far as Gorham Street."

Daughtie nodded. "Certainly. I'd enjoy your companionship."

Several minutes passed while Mrs. Potter issued instructions and donned her coat and muff. When they were finally on their way, the older woman looped her arm through Daughtie's. "I've overheard talk of a strike. But I'm hoping it's merely idle gossip," she said with a note of expectancy in her voice.

"It appears as if there are many girls who support a turnout. However, it's impossible to know what will actually occur until the time arrives for them to make their choice. A part of me wonders if those who are speaking so favorably about a strike will, at the last moment, change their minds. Most of them realize that there's no guarantee they can return to their jobs if they participate in the walk-out."

Mrs. Potter nodded. "I hope they'll weigh their decisions carefully. I know many of the girls help support their families, and this situation could prove devastating for them. Now, tell me about these fabrics you're going to inspect at the mercantile. Are you making yourself a new dress?"

"No. I've been hired to assist with choosing some fabrics and furnishings for a new home."

"Really? How exciting. And do you get to make all the choices?" Mrs. Potter asked with a smile.

"No. Mr. Donohue makes the final decisions. In fact, I had chosen fabrics made in England, but he wants to use only textiles produced here in Lowell."

"Mr. Donohue? The stonemason?"

"Yes. Do you know him?" Daughtie inquired.

"He's Irish."

"Yes, I know."

Mrs. Potter stopped midstep. "Is it *his* house you're decorating?"

Daughtie continued walking. "Yes. It's a beautiful home," she replied.

Mrs. Potter hastened to keep in stride, tugging at Daughtie's elbow. "Associating with an Irishman will jeopardize your future. You know that, don't you?"

"My future with whom? I've been told by various well-meaning people that I'll never find a *decent* husband if I'm seen with Liam Donohue. However, I would have no desire to marry a man who didn't consider Liam Donohue his equal. You see, I believe we're all alike in the eyes of God. After all, He created all of us, didn't He? I would find it impossible to respect a man who thought himself better than another merely because his skin color or birthplace differed. Consequently, I'm unwilling to concern myself with what others think of my association with Liam Donohue."

"That's a noble thought for a girl of tender years, but I'm older than you, and I hope you'll give serious consideration to my words. Virtuous deeds won't warm you on a cold winter night, furnish food for your table, or care for you in your old age. We've all made improper decisions in our youth. Most of those choices are forgotten. But socializing with an Irishman is a millstone about your neck that you'll not escape."

Daughtie patted Mrs. Potter's hand. "I do value your opinion and thank you for your concern, but this is merely a task I've been employed to complete."

Mrs. Potter smiled weakly. "You intend to continue down this path of destruction, don't you?"

"I intend to finish what I've already begun. I believe this is where you turn, isn't it?" Daughtie inquired as they reached Gorham Street.

"Yes. You have a pleasant evening, my dear."

"Thank you, and you do the same."

Daughtie stood and watched until Mrs. Potter reached the corner before walking off toward Whidden's Mercantile. She shivered, uncertain whether the involuntary gesture was caused by the freezing temperature or by Mrs. Potter's reproving words. Why were people continually judged by external appearance? Was it not a person's heart that truly mattered?

Pushing open the front door of the store, the warmth beckoned her in like a mother's welcoming smile. "Good evening, Mrs. Whidden."

"Good evening to you, Miss Winfield. Have you come to view more fabric?"

Daughtie nodded. "Yes, but as I told you when I returned the English textiles, only fabrics manufactured here in Lowell. I'm told there are some new offerings from the Tremont Mill."

"Indeed. And they are quite lovely. I'm certain you'll find something to your liking," the older woman replied as she led Daughtie toward the middle of the store. "All of these," she said, pointing toward a long wooden table piled high with folded cloth.

Daughtie approached the table and giggled in delight. "It's hard to believe I have so many choices. These are beautiful." The sight of the gorgeous fabrics was almost enough to erase the painful headache she had suffered throughout the day.

"I thought you might be pleased," Mrs. Whidden remarked while pulling out an especially colorful piece of damask fabric from the bottom of the pile.

Daughtie carefully evaluated the choices, finally limiting her selection to six before glancing at the clock. Eight o'clock. There would be sufficient time to take the samples to Liam for his inspection. Grasping the package of cloth under her arm, she waved good-bye and hurried out the door.

She was nearing Liam's house when the thought of actually seeing him and delivering the fabrics caused an unfamiliar stirring. Was it seeing Liam's reaction to the textiles or purely seeing Liam that was creating her excitement? The thought startled her. She regarded Liam with the same respect and attention she had always afforded others. Why, then, did she feel this strange exhilaration? Her mind raced back to conversations she'd had with Bella when her friend had first fallen in love with Taylor Manning. Daughtie's eyes widened. Bella had mentioned her heart occasionally fluttering with excitement when she first began to fall in love with Taylor. Was *she* falling in love with Liam Donohue? Yet he was a friend—nothing more, nothing less, she cautioned herself while walking up the steps to his porch.

She reached out and knocked on the door, realizing her hand was trembling! "It's the cold," she said aloud, hoping to convince herself. *It's anticipation over seeing Liam,* a small voice inside her head whispered. A bewildering uncertainty plagued her. Instinctively, she rubbed her throbbing temples, hoping the pressure would ease her distress.

A smile captured Liam's lips the moment he opened the door. "Would you look who's here! Come in, come in."

He stepped aside and waved Daughtie forward. "Let me take yar cape. Ya've chosen a frigid night to be out and about, lassie." He hung her cloak and turned back to his guest. "Don't misunderstand—I'm always delighted to have a lovely lady appear on me doorstep."

Daughtie felt the heat rise in her cheeks. She doubted Liam would notice. Surely the freezing temperature had already colored her complexion to a bright pink. "I stopped by Whidden's," she explained, holding out the package to justify her visit.

"Ah, I see. I'm guessin' this is the fabric," he replied, untying the cord and pulling back the brown paper. "Let's take them in the parlor and see what ya've brought me." He hesitated a moment. "But first, let me show you something else," he said, beckoning her down the hallway.

Daughtie followed behind him, stopping when they arrived in the kitchen. Her eyes widened at the sight. There were barrels and wooden boxes stacked all about the room. "What is all of this?" she quizzed.

"Provisions!" His voice was filled with a joyful pride. "I've been doin' as ya told me, gathering as many provisions as I dared. Mrs. Whidden did question the number of blankets I'd been buyin'," he said with a chuckle. "I told her my family might be coming to visit and they were a cold-blooded lot. She appeared to accept my explanation."

Daughtie stood on tiptoe, peered into several of the boxes, and nodded her approval. "This is wonderful," she said while still lifting lids and eyeing the contents. "However, you must get it put away—hidden from sight. What if someone came in here and saw all of this?"

"Besides myself, ya're the only person that's been in this kitchen since the day I moved in. I'm not expectin' visitors."

"But, Liam, if you're suspected of harboring slaves, they'll go through your entire home. If the authorities should find all of this out in plain sight, there's little doubt of what they would think. They'd never even give you a chance to answer questions before hauling you away."

"I s'pose ya're right about that. Guess I'll be needin' to make me some good hidin' places. I think the men and boys will be safe enough out in the barn, and there's ample space to store some blankets and a few clothes. For sure we can't be storin' any food out there, though—the coons and possums would have it eaten before any runaways arrived. I've made a couple of good places upstairs for any women and their youngsters. I built a false wall in two of the bedrooms. Long as they're quiet, there's no one could detect what I've done," he proudly announced.

"I'm amazed at all you've accomplished. It doesn't appear you need any help with your preparations."

"I sent word me house was ready. Now I just have to wait and see if anyone comes," he said, leading her back down the hallway.

Daughtie patted the folds along the side of her dress. "I have something here to share with you, too," she said, reaching deep inside her pocket and retrieving a letter. "From Prudence Crandall."

"Really? She wrote you a letter?"

"She encouraged me to correspond with her. This is her second letter."

"You never mentioned you intended to write her."

"I know. I feared she wouldn't reply," Daughtie stated simply. "But she seems quite pleased to answer my missives. Listen to this," she said, lowering her voice as though she planned to include Liam in some dark conspiracy.

Seating himself, Liam folded his brawny arms and gave her his full attention. "All right, I'm listenin'."

"I want you to hear this one paragraph," she said before looking back down at the letter. " 'The girls and I continue to persevere, although many of the townspeople are steadfast in their determination to see me and all of my girls removed from their community. Their anger grew deeper this week when I enrolled two more girls. The house was pelted with rotten eggs and rocks. Two windows were broken, but I give thanks that none of us were injured. Continue to pray that we'll be protected and that God will soften the hearts of those who persecute us. I will not give in to these tormentors unless I fear for the lives of my charges. They are such capable young ladies, eager to be educated. Each one will make fine contributions to our country, if only given the opportunity.' " Daughtie refolded the letter and tucked it back inside her pocket. "I'm deeply saddened Miss Crandall and the girls must endure such treatment."

"I agree, but 'tis good to know she hasn't given in to the ruffians. She's determined to educate her students, and I believe it will be takin' more than rotten eggs and a few rocks to frighten her off."

"You're right. The best thing we can do is what she's asked: pray."

Instead of responding, Liam jumped up from his chair like he'd been hit by a bolt of lightning and began spreading the pieces of cloth across the cherry dining room table. "These are quite lovely. All from the Lowell textile mills?"

"All from the Lowell textile mills," she affirmed, loving

the sound of his lyrical Irish lilt. "You can choose the drapery fabric from among this group, and we'll use your choice of two other favorites for the overstuffed furniture in this room."

"Only two? That may prove difficult."

"We can use some of the others in the bedrooms, dining room, and library," she suggested while seating herself in one of the chairs that would soon be upholstered with fabric. While Liam directed his attention to the cloth, Daughtie began to once again massage her temples.

"Headache?" Liam inquired, turning toward her.

"Yes. I can't seem to rid myself of the pain. It's been a nuisance most of the day."

"Here, let me," he said. Without awaiting her consent, he moved behind the chair and began to gently massage her temples with his broad fingers while gently moving his thumbs in a circular motion at the nape of her neck. The chokehold of pain banding her head began to ease as he continued to massage her head. Her eyes closed in relaxation. She knew she should stop him—but she didn't. His ministrations were much too soothing.

When the throbbing finally began to subside, she raised her hand. "Thank you. I'm feeling much better," she said. "It appears you're a man of many talents."

"My mother suffered with headaches. From the time I was a wee lad, I would massage her head until the pain would leave. It's good to know I haven't lost my touch. Now tell me, what's causin' your muscles to knot up in pain? Is it Miss Crandall's letter?"

"No," she murmured.

"When the muscles get knotted up like this, it's usually caused by worry. You know, keepin' yarself tense, not lettin' the body relax itself. If it's not Miss Crandall's situation that's causin' ya to fret, what is it that's been weighin' so heavy on yar mind?"

Daughtie gave him a forlorn look as he pulled a chair directly in front of her. "It's all the discord at the mills. The turnout's been scheduled for the first of March, and that's only a few days away. Unless the Associates change their minds about the decrease in wages, I fear many of the girls are determined to strike."

Liam nodded. "I thought you'd made up your mind about that issue back when the idea of a turnout was first proposed by Ruth and the others."

"You're right, and I was vocal in my disagreement. Then a few days later, when I refused to sign the petition they were circulating, Ruth wouldn't even speak to me. She gave me the silent treatment for two full days."

"That was probably a blessin' in disguise," Liam said with a chuckle.

"True, for she hasn't stopped nagging me ever since. She presents the petition to me on a daily basis, telling me she knows I'll soon come to my senses."

"And does this petition say ya agree to walk out with them?" Liam inquired.

"It says we've been wronged by the Corporation and cheerfully agree not to enter and work in the mills on the first of March or any time thereafter unless our wages are restored to what we received prior to the date of the turn-out."

"And so it's not just an agreement but a *cheerful* agreement they're wantin'?" he asked, his full lips turning up into a wide grin.

"I think the girls want to emphasize to the Corporation that they're happy to go without their wages. I thought Ruth might come to her senses when they dismissed a girl over at the Suffolk Mill, but even that didn't faze Ruth."

Liam's eyebrows arched high on his forehead. "So they've actually fired someone?"

"Yes—Mary Wickert is her name. They said she was

holding meetings within the mill during dinner breaks and stirring the operatives into such a state of agitation that by the time they returned to work, the girls couldn't concentrate and production suffered. Of course, Ruth said the charges were totally unfounded. However, Lucinda Seawart works at the Suffolk. She was in the library last night and told me that the accusations were true. She said the supervisor told Mary to cease the meetings at the mill or she'd be terminated. So when Mary met with a group of girls the next day during the dinner hour in the mill yard, they sent the agent to escort her into the office and fired her—they even escorted her to the boardinghouse and waited while she packed her belongings. She was told to never set foot on Corporation property again. Wouldn't you think terminating Mary's employment would give the girls pause to wonder about their own futures?"

Liam nodded. "Aye. But just as we believe helpin' slaves escape is vital, these girls obviously believe their cause is justified. Perhaps it is; I don't be pretendin' to know."

"I don't think you can compare the two, Liam. The slaves didn't choose to leave their homes and become the chattel of white plantation owners. However, these girls made a decision to come here and work in the mills. I realize they thought their income would continue to increase rather than decrease, but the contracts don't even address the issue of a wage reduction."

"I understand, but there are times when people get swept up in the tide of a movement such as this and feel obligated to go along with the crowd. They fear bein' singled out as unsympathetic to the cause. 'Course, I'm not one for signin' things like petitions, so whether I agreed or not, I'd refuse to sign their paper. I believe a man's *word* should be his bond."

"Even if I did agree with the strike, I don't concur with the remainder of what they've tacked on to the petition."

"And what is that?"

"If you sign the agreement and then don't turn out with the others, you're then required to pay five dollars to be used for some benevolent action in the town. Even with that added language, the girls are signing; their anger over Mary's dismissal has caused many more to sign up."

"And has all of this now caused you to change your mind?"

"No, I don't think we should strike. It's just that the actions of Ruth and her supporters leave me feeling alone."

"Surely there are others who stand in opposition, aren't there?"

"Yes, but they don't have to sleep in the same room with Ruth. Besides, with Ruth acting as an organizer at the Appleton, all of those who come to our house favor the walkout."

"Isolation is a difficult thing. You find yourself in a position of bein' so much the same as those around you and yet very different," he said in a soft voice.

She glanced up into his eyes. "You know exactly how it feels, don't you?"

"Yes. I know about loneliness and separation. I've lived with them ever since comin' to this country."

"How have you managed?" she questioned, her voice no more than a whisper.

"I keep busy with me work and me dreams." His voice was low and husky.

Daughtie trembled at his nearness. She held her gaze on his face, unwilling to lose the feeling that was growing within her. The wonder of the moment filled her with awe.

"I'd be thinkin' that prayin' and such might come as a comfort to you," he added.

Daughtie forced her thoughts to reform. "Yes, it does. I rely heavily on God for comfort—especially when I'm . . . particularly . . . discouraged."

He leaned forward and surprised her by taking hold of her hands. "Like now?"

She nodded, almost afraid to speak. "Yes. Like now." She bit at her lower lip to keep Liam from seeing how it quivered. Her stomach did flip-flops, leaving her wavering between wanting to run away from Liam and longing to run to him.

"I know it's hard for you to endure, but I admire your strength. I admire most everything about you."

For a moment Daughtie thought he might kiss her, but the clock chimed the hour and Liam quickly released his hold and sat up straight. "We should be gettin' ya back to the boardinghouse. It's bad enough ya go keepin' company with me like this—with no other womenfolk around to keep things good and proper. But to be comin' home late . . . well, now, there'd be no end of grief for ya." His brogue thickened with the emotion of the moment.

Daughtie took up her things while Liam went quickly to hitch the horses. She floated to the door as if in a dream. There was something about this man . . . something that touched her deep inside.

They rode in silence, the cold pressing them close together in spite of propriety. Daughtie was actually glad to see that Liam was willing to drive her directly to the boardinghouse rather than drop her off at the end of the street.

Liam reined back the horses and fixed the brake before jumping down to help Daughtie. She was in no hurry to leave his company, but a pelting sleet began to blow down from the skies. Liam reached up and took hold of Daughtie's waist as if she were a small child. Setting her down gently, he continued to hold her for just a moment. Then, without warning, he kissed her lightly on the cheek.

Daughtie gave a gasp of surprise and touched her gloved hand to her cheek in wonder. Liam hurried back to the wagon and was gone before Daughtie could even speak. She watched him disappear into the night—suddenly not feeling nearly as alone as she had earlier in the evening.

Daughtie shoved her fist into the pillow, attempting to create the perfect cradle for her throbbing head. But the cruel pounding wore on, mimicking the thumping looms in the weaving room. She rolled to her side and tugged at the covers, longing for the deep, restful slumber of her childhood, when thoughts of a turnout hadn't invaded her sleep. She pulled the covers over her head and attempted to blot out all thoughts of the mill. She tried to focus on Liam and how he had kissed her cheek, but the worry and concern of what events might yet come to pass pushed the memory aside.

It seemed as though she had barely crawled into bed when the pealing of the tower bell startled Daughtie from her restless slumber. Her eyelids drooped heavy with sleep, but she forced herself to remain awake. Edging into a sitting position, she swung her legs over the side of the bed and attempted to stand. Her legs wobbled, protesting the weight she now forced upon them.

"I'm going downstairs," Ruth announced curtly.

Daughtie glanced over her shoulder. Ruth was perched upon the bed, dressed for the day with her hair properly braided and fashioned into a knot atop her head. "How long have you been awake?"

"Probably an hour or so. I woke up and couldn't go back to sleep. I'm meeting with some girls before final bell," she said as she moved toward the door.

"You're meeting here at the house?"

"No, we're going to meet on the weaving floor before Mr. Kingman arrives."

"Oh, Ruth, I don't think that's wise. Mr. Kingman is

likely at the mill at least a half hour before any of us. With Mary's dismissal, I think you're taking a foolish risk."

Ruth shrugged her shoulders. "I imagine you do, but if you're not willing to join our ranks, you need not force your opinions upon me."

"I'm not forcing my opinion upon you, Ruth. I'm expressing my concern."

"Well, you don't need to do that, either. I'll be fine."

The anger in Ruth's voice caused a lump to form in Daughtie's throat. "I'll be praying for you," she said while holding back her tears.

There was no reply. Tears flowed down Daughtie's cheeks as she listened to Ruth's footsteps clattering down the stairs.

———

Daughtie hastened off toward the mill, feeling strangely unsettled. Only on those rare occasions when Ruth was ill did Daughtie walk alone. Her discomfort abated when she peeked in the weaving room and saw Ruth standing by her looms. Ruth glanced in Daughtie's direction but didn't return her wave. No matter—at least there had been no repercussions to the early morning meeting Ruth had attended.

She sat down at her drawing-in frame and permitted herself a mental review of the fabrics she'd taken for Liam's assessment. He hadn't made his final choices by the time they had parted, and now she was hoping he would pick the deep rose damask fabric for the parlor. It would be lovely with the carpet of dark blue, beige, and rose he had chosen. Yet he had said he didn't want pink. Would he consider the rose hue to be a shade of pink? If he decided upon the lighter blue, she would focus his attention upon the shades of rose in the carpeting.

She couldn't help but think of Liam and how kind he

had been—gently massaging her head until the pain ebbed, tenderly holding her hands as he spoke to her about loneliness. Along with these thoughts, however, came reminders of Mrs. Potter's negative comments and Ruth's persistence that Daughtie would ruin her life by associating with the Irishman. Daughtie knew that most people would take the same stand as her dear friend. The Irish were despised; they were associated with brawling and papist views. *But Liam's not like that. He's neither a brawler nor a papist. The poor man isn't even sure about God, much less the complications of religious views,* she thought to herself.

Then her musings traveled to those silent moments outside the boardinghouse. *He kissed me.* Her hand went to her cheek again. What did it mean? Was it just the sweet gesture of a friend?

Drawing the threads through the harness, Daughtie worked with expert speed until her thoughts were interrupted by the sounds of Mr. Kingman's shouts, which could now be heard over the rumbling sound of the looms. Daughtie glanced over her shoulder. Mr. Kingman was moving toward her with Delia Masters following close by his side. Daughtie gazed toward Delia, and a hard knot formed in her stomach. Fear burned bright in Delia's pale gray eyes as she passed by Daughtie's frame.

The sounds from the weaving room began to subside as the looms groaned into a halting silence. Daughtie stared in disbelief as operatives began filing down the hallway and out of the building. "What's happening?" she shouted as Ruth neared.

"Those of us who signed up for the turnout are leaving now. They're discharging Delia, and we're leaving in protest."

"But the turnout isn't scheduled until the first of March," Daughtie argued.

Ruth nodded. "Yes, but when they terminated Mary,

we all agreed that if it happened again, we would immediately begin the turnout. I've got to go. I'm supposed to notify the girls at the Tremont that the turnout's begun. Are you going to join us?"

Daughtie bit her bottom lip. "No. I'm not going to participate."

Ruth appeared startled. "But Delia's our friend and she's losing her job. I can understand those girls who have families to support remaining at their machines. But surely *you're* going to support Delia's bravery."

"No, Ruth. You know my position. We've discussed this over and over. I wouldn't expect Delia to compromise her beliefs for me, and I won't change my own on her account," Daughtie replied unwaveringly.

Ruth's searing glare went through her like a sharp knife, and profound sorrow seeped into Daughtie's heart as she picked up her steel hook and once again began pulling threads through the harness. Two hours later, the dinner bell pealed from the tower, and the machinery droned into quietude as the remaining operatives rushed toward the stairway. Daughtie joined them and hurried down the stairs.

As the throng of workers bustled through the mill yard, a procession of girls marched past the entrance, heading off toward the center of town. Daughtie stood watching until the last few demonstrators disappeared around the corner. She should go and eat dinner, but her curiosity nagged like a puppy nipping at her heels. Glancing over her shoulder, she gazed at the girls who were already making their way toward the boardinghouses and their noonday meals. Her stomach growled, and she gave momentary consideration to following them. "I'd rather know what's going on in town than eat," she muttered, lifting her skirts and running down the street.

The sight of Delia standing atop a stack of boxes, her

hair blowing free as she waved her calash high into the air, brought Daughtie to an immediate halt. Ruth was standing near her side.

"We must take heed of our rights and prove to the moneyed aristocracy that they cannot trample on the rights of their female employees. I beseech you to sign our resolution vowing to discontinue your labors until terms of reconciliation are made. There are petitions circulating among you as I speak. Sign now and support your sisters in their crusade," Delia shouted to the cheering women.

A young operative tugged at Daughtie's cape and pointed toward Delia. "Isn't she wonderful? I'm going up to sign the petition right now."

The girl didn't wait for an answer. Instead, she rushed off toward one of the petitions Ruth was now waving heavenward like a flag of glory. Sorrow etched Daughtie's face as she bowed her head against the wind and turned toward home.

CHAPTER *19*

Boston
March

Josiah Baines scuttled across the room and threw himself into a chair like an ill-mannered child. "This turnout at the mills has completely interrupted my schedule. I thought the agents and supervisors had this matter under control. If they can't handle their employees, why are we paying them?"

Nathan inhaled and then removed an intricately carved pipe from between his clenched teeth. "If you find the meetings an undue burden, please don't feel obligated to attend, Josiah. I'd be happy to act as your proxy," Nathan said, his exhaled smoke mingling with the words and floating off toward the ceiling.

"Which would also ensure an earlier conclusion to the meetings," Tracy mumbled.

"I take that statement to mean you gentlemen believe I'm the sole cause of these infernal meetings that last well into the early morning hours. And where is Kirk?"

"Take it however you choose, Josiah. I'm weary of your petulant attitude. We all have busy schedules and other business interests that require our attention. Either give me your proxy and take your leave, or permit me to begin the meeting," Nathan replied. "As to Kirk's whereabouts, he is suffering with a bout of illness and has sent Matthew to represent him at this meeting."

Nathan turned away from Josiah and focused his gaze upon Matthew. "Although we wish Kirk could be in attendance, we all realize that the information you relate to us will be directly from his perspective. I know we will profit much from what you have to tell us, Matthew. Why don't you begin?"

"Thank you, Nathan, for your kind words. Gentlemen, I appreciate your understanding. Kirk's profound desire was to be here tonight. In fact, he gave serious consideration to overriding the doctor's warning against travel—until his wife got wind of his plans."

The room resonated with telltale laughter.

"As you are aware, the turnout is over, most of the operatives are back to work, and wages have been reduced by ten percent. I wish I could report that the workers are satisfied with what has occurred. Unfortunately, that is impossible. There are still rumblings of anger from time to time, although to our knowledge, there are no plans for future strikes."

"It's beyond me how Kirk ever permitted such an occurrence," Josiah growled.

Matthew leveled a thoughtful look in Josiah's direction. "Tell me, good sir, without the ability to leave wages intact, how did you expect Mr. Boott to prevent such an incident? We can hardly lock the employees in the building. And even if we could, how would you propose we force them to operate their machines?"

"Perhaps he should develop a better relationship with the workers so that they value his opinion and accept the decisions of the Corporation as being in their best interests," Josiah retaliated.

"The workers at the Lowell mills are endowed with the same reasoning powers and intelligence God gave you, Mr. Baines. They are not animals we can herd about and prod into submission. We had hoped the workers would not turn out when management agreed to a ten percent reduction rather than the original twenty-five percent. I might add that the agents, supervisors, and Mr. Boott believe that the number of strikers was dramatically decreased due to that very action on your part."

Josiah rose from his chair and began pacing in front of the fireplace. "Well, of course you're going to report there was a decrease in strikers due to our change in percentages because, truth is, there's no way of knowing how many would have walked out if we'd just left it at twenty-five percent."

Matthew nodded. "That's true. But we had reports that there were as many as fifteen hundred threatening to strike when the wage reduction was set at the higher figure. Our final count showed that there were only eight hundred who actually left the mills. I think we should give credit to the supervisors that we lost little in production time through the turnout. They managed to have us at full production within a week while maintaining a continuum of dignity and calm inside the mills."

"Hear! Hear!" Tracy said, raising his glass of port.

"Except for a few of the organizers who were discharged and a handful of others who decided to return to their farms, the employees returned to work and now are adhering to all rules of the Corporation. Quite frankly, it's as though the incident never took place."

"Hah! Do you read newspapers, Mr. Cheever? We're either notorious bandits taking food from the mouths of babes or shrewd businessmen who have perfected the art of coercing these young women to do our bidding."

"You exaggerate, Josiah. I've seen only one report that spoke ill of our tactics," Nathan argued. "Most reports state the girls are highly paid unskilled workers who are unable to comprehend the economics of business, and were their minds able to digest such information, they would be on their knees thanking God above for the kindness of the Corporation."

"He's right, Josiah. You always tend to overstate the negative," Tracy concluded. "Granted, this was an unfortunate event, and we can hope it never recurs. However, should we face these same problems in the future, I hope we will be blessed with the same fine results we've seen this time."

"Well, what else is there to say, then? You gentlemen are all pleased, and I don't see that we have any recourse against the employees. After all, we need them," Josiah replied, once again taking his seat. "So is that it? Are we through for the night?"

Nathan pulled a linen handkerchief from his pocket and mopped his brow. "As I said earlier, you're free to leave at any time. As for the rest of us, I'm planning to discuss plans for the railroad and possibly make some final decisions."

Josiah wriggled back in his chair. "The railroad is going to cost us money that we can ill afford to spend. Since I believe we need to reevaluate this whole railroad idea, I suppose I'll be remaining for the balance of the meeting."

Tracy leaned forward, resting his forearms across his thighs, and met Josiah's gaze. "There's that negative approach rearing its ugly head again, Josiah."

Matthew remained standing near Nathan's desk. "If I could have time for one more issue before you begin your discussion of the railroad?"

"Of course, my boy. I thought you had completed Kirk's report."

"Mr. Boott asked that I make you aware of the fact that farmers who live in proximity to Pawtucket Falls have become increasingly distressed due to the ongoing problems caused by the dam."

"Balderdash! That dam was erected years ago," Josiah responded. "Why is this even being brought up for discussion?"

"If you'll let me finish, Mr. Baines, I'll try to explain," Matthew replied patiently. "During the past couple of years, we've had more rain than usual. To a certain extent, the farms have flooded ever since the dam was erected. However, with the increased rains the past few years, the flooding has caused crop failures that are sending the farmers into ruination. And then there's the problem with the fish. The consistently high waters make it impossible for them to spawn, and we're receiving complaints from not only the farmers and citizens who depend upon the fish in those waters for their own dinner tables or to supplement their income but also the citizens living in Lowell. Kirk is concerned that this problem could escalate if we don't address it and at least attempt to look toward a solution— something we can report to the farmers that will hold them in abeyance or ease their minds."

Josiah grunted. "Hold them in abeyance? What are they planning to do? *They* can't strike. Personally, I don't see the need to appease them. Besides, we need the dam."

Henry Thorne had remained quiet throughout the evening but now raised his hand to be recognized. Nathan nodded. "Yes, Henry?"

"We don't want to be perceived as the villain in all of our dealings. The good people that farmed the Chelmsford soil already believe that they were wronged when the Corporation purchased land for the mills. Now the few farmers who've been able to remain believe their livelihood is being jeopardized. Perhaps we won't suffer financial losses due to this issue, but we do stand to lose the working relationship that's been cultivated with the farmers over the past years."

Nathan nodded. "That's true, Henry, but I don't know what we're to do. We can't release additional water without jeopardizing the operation of the mills."

"I know we can't do that. Has Kirk offered any solution? What about the possibility of increasing the size of the millpond? Is that feasible?" Henry asked.

"Mr. Boott gave me no possible solution to offer you," Matthew said. "I have no idea if it's possible to enlarge the millpond."

"What about having the engineers at the Locks and Canals Division study that prospect and report to Kirk?" Tracy inquired.

"Sounds reasonable," Nathan replied.

"The cost of labor alone to perform such a feat would be prohibitive," Josiah countered. "Let them present their argument to the courts if they think they have legal standing. Are we going to cave in at every whim?"

"Could we agree merely to investigate the possibility?" Tracy inquired. "At least it will give Kirk something he can tell the farmers. Before we begin worrying about the cost, Josiah, let's find out if it's even a possibility to expand."

"I think that's an excellent idea," Henry replied.

"Of course you do," Josiah muttered.

The measure passed, with Josiah casting the only dissenting vote.

"I'll write out instructions to Kirk," Nathan told Matthew. "Was there anything else you wanted to bring before us?"

"We are assuming the Corporation will sponsor the Blowing Out Ball as scheduled?"

"Yes, of course. It's business—and pleasure—as usual," Nathan replied.

Matthew gave a quick nod and took his seat. "Then that's all I have."

"We appreciate your reports, Matthew. Now let's get on with discussing the railroad. Spring is already upon us, and if the railroad is to progress as scheduled, we need to be prepared."

"Good idea, Nathan. I'd like all of you to consider the possibility of opening a machine shop to build locomotives. I believe we have the caliber of men in the Locks and Canals Division who can see this to fruition. We would save money as well as bolster the economy of Lowell and the Corporation," Tracy Jackson said.

Josiah sighed and slumped deeper into his chair. "Is there nothing you men won't think of to bring us into total decline? The *last* thing we should be doing right now is thinking of expansion. We need to rein ourselves in and pay heed to the financial condition of the company and the country. The banks may well all close their doors after Andrew Jackson's through with them. On top of that, there's the fact that steam locomotives are quite untested and unproven as far as I'm concerned. Just because the British are having success with them doesn't mean the same will be true for us. We need to practice caution, but you all seem to want to rush in on a whim."

"It's hardly a whim, Josiah. We are men of vision," Tracy replied frankly. "Men of vision are willing to risk the future on untried creations because, like it or not, it is the new inventions and industries that will take us forward in progress. Even if there are problems and failures, the situation will eventually be mastered and life will be better because of it. Mark my words, the railroad will transform this country. Within the next twenty years we'll see railroads crisscrossing this country as the major form of long-distance transportation."

"Don't be ridiculous," Josiah protested. "Such machinery

and the tracks necessary to move them about will be too costly. And, I might ask, who do you suppose is going to be willing to pay the thousands—no, the millions of dollars that it will cost to finance such inventions?"

Tracy smiled rather smugly. "Men of vision, Josiah. Men of vision will finance such inventions."

"Perhaps, but now is hardly the time for foolish investments." Josiah's face reddened as if the strain of the conversation were too much for him. "The mills can ill afford to add this expense. Think of it, gentlemen. We just reduced wages—how can we justify building a locomotive machine shop?"

Matthew listened intently as the discussion wore on. Kirk would expect extensive details of the meeting—especially Tracy's viewpoint—since Boott also favored the locomotive project. In fact, he'd heard discussion between the two men several weeks ago when Tracy had visited Lowell immediately after the turnout, so the topic came as no surprise. By the time Josiah finally convinced the men to reconvene at a later date before making a final decision on the machine shop, it was nearing midnight.

"You planning to remain in Boston for a few days?" Nathan asked as he escorted Matthew to the front door.

"No. I'll be leaving in the morning. I must be back in Lowell to make final arrangements for the Blowing Out Ball. I doubt my wife would forgive me if I were the cause of an improperly planned ball," he replied with a grin.

Nathan gave him a broad smile. "I understand. Please advise Kirk that most of us plan to be in attendance. I'm holding out hope that Josiah will remain at home."

"I heard that remark, Nathan, and I'm sorry to disappoint you, but I plan to attend. I want to have a few words with Kirk. Perhaps he'll listen to a voice of reason and see that this machine shop idea is pure folly. Besides, I might be able to give him a few pointers for handling those irate farmers."

Nathan arched his eyebrows, his lips turning up in a patronizing smile. "You do that, Josiah. I'm sure Kirk will be pleased to have your counsel."

CHAPTER *20*

Lowell

"I wish I hadn't agreed to attend the ball with Dr. Ketter," Daughtie lamented while stitching a row of lace along the neckline of her dress.

Ruth stretched out on the bed and wound a loose thread around her finger. "I was hoping the girls who participated in the turnout wouldn't attend the ball. Instead, they're fluttering around as though dancing with members of the Corporation is the greatest honor they could ever hope for."

"I don't know about dancing with the Boston Associates, but attending the ball is a treat for most folks—at least for those who work in the mills. You ought not fault the girls for wanting to have an evening of enjoyment."

Ruth snorted. "I'll fault them if I want to. When I told Mrs. Arnold I was thinking of staying home, she said it would be unwise, especially for anyone who participated in the strike. She thinks the supervisors may monitor our behavior for a while."

"Mrs. Arnold's probably correct. If anyone knows how

these supervisors think, surely she does. After all, she was married to one," Daughtie replied. "Besides, I told Dr. Ketter you would be attending with us."

"*What?* I'm not going with the two of you."

"Oh, yes, you are. After all, it was you that encouraged him to invite me, and don't bother denying it. I know you've been busy playing the matchmaker almost from the day he arrived. If you won't attend with us, then I'm going to tell him I must cancel on my commitment because I won't attend without my dearest friend."

Ruth flipped over on the bed like a salmon floundering on the banks of the Pawtucket. "Well, I'll not dance with those pompous men, I can tell you that much for certain. And should one of them ask, he'd get a firm refusal."

"So long as you're courteous, I doubt whether anyone could fault you for refusing. However, Sarah told me the girls actually line up in order to dance with the men, so I think you need not worry."

"Oh, what does Sarah know? She's never attended a ball," Ruth argued. "You'd best watch what you're doing. You're sewing that lace on crooked." Her brows furrowed into wavy lines of disapproval.

Daughtie poked her needle into the fabric and took another stitch. "My sewing is fine, but you're certainly in foul humor. What are you going to wear to the ball?"

Ruth scooted upward and leaned against the wooden headboard. "If I must go, I'll wear the same dress I wear to church on Sundays. If that's not fancy enough for those self-important men, they can tell me so and I'll give them an earful. I'll be quick to tell them that I can't afford to buy a new dress now that wages have been reduced."

"I believe you'd actually *enjoy* being confronted by one of them."

"Indeed I would!"

"There. I think I'm done," Daughtie said while inspecting her dress. "What do you think?"

"I still think the lace is crooked."

Daughtie giggled. "The lace is not crooked. I'm going out for a while, but I'll be back by nine-thirty. Why don't you go downstairs and visit with Mrs. Arnold and Theona?"

Ruth swung around on the bed, her shoes thumping as they hit the floor. "Where are you going? You're not scheduled to work at the library, and you don't quilt at Mrs. Cheever's home until next week. Are you going to buy something special for the ball? A new comb or reticule, perhaps? I'll go with you."

"No," Daughtie replied a tad too quickly.

Ruth's eyes darkened a shade as she leveled an accusatory look in Daughtie's direction. "You're going to see Liam Donohue! Don't even try to deny it."

Daughtie remained silent as she tucked away the sewing box and carefully returned her dress to a peg on the wall. Retrieving her cape, she walked toward the bedroom door.

"You *are* going to see him!" Ruth's voice was filled with surprise. "Otherwise, you would have denied my accusation."

Daughtie hastened out the door and down the stairway, with Ruth following close on her heels.

"What are you thinking?" Ruth hissed. "You can't keep running off to that Irishman's house."

Peeking into the dining room, Daughtie waved at Theona and Mrs. Arnold. "I'm going out for a while. I'll see you in the morning."

"Have a pleasant evening, dear," Mrs. Arnold said before turning her attention toward Ruth. "Are you going, too?" she asked Ruth, who had nearly appended herself to Daughtie's side.

"I believe I will," she said. "What do you think of

that?" she asked, giving Daughtie a smug grin.

Daughtie continued fastening her cloak. "If you'd like to join me, I'd be pleased to have your company. Shall I wait while you get your cape?"

Ruth furrowed her brows in obvious confusion. "So you're not going to Liam Donohue's house?" she whispered.

"I don't see what difference it makes. Are you coming or not? I really need to be on my way," Daughtie replied.

"I suppose I'll stay home since you won't divulge where you're going."

Daughtie nodded and walked out the door. A sigh of relief escaped her lips. Taking Ruth along would have ended in catastrophe. Not that Liam would have been inhospitable, but Ruth—well, no doubt she would have acted boorish and aloof.

Daughtie dabbed her nose with an embroidered linen handkerchief. "I believe I'm coming down with something. My throat feels scratchy, and I've had the sniffles for two days."

"It's nothing but the fibers in the air at work. You're not fooling me, Daughtie. You'd best get dressed. Dr. Ketter said we would leave for the ball in less than an hour. I'm still disappointed you didn't accept his invitation to have supper at the Merrimack House."

"If you had your way, I'd spend every free moment with Dr. Ketter. Why would I want to go to supper with him? After all, we dine together twice a day, occasionally three times if he manages to get out of bed early enough for breakfast. Going out to supper with him would be a wasteful expense."

Ruth wagged her head back and forth. "Well, it is his money, and if he wants to take you to a nice restaurant for supper, you should accept. He asked you to accompany him to see *The Heir at Law* when the professional players appeared in Lowell, but I understand you refused that invitation, also."

"And how would you know? Are you and Dr. Ketter conspiring? Have you been acting as his advisor and confidante?" Daughtie asked while fashioning her hair into a pile of cascading curls.

Ruth plopped down on the bed and gave a quick nod. "How do you manage to fix your hair without a mirror?"

"The Shakers believe that staring into a looking glass fosters vanity. There was only one small mirror for use by all of the Sisters, and if you were caught staring into it, you were reprimanded. Accordingly, I grew up styling my hair without a mirror. Of course, we didn't wear our hair in fashionable styles. I've discovered it takes more time to create curls, but I don't find it requires a mirror," she said. "You didn't answer my question. Have you been urging Dr. Ketter to pursue me?"

"I wouldn't say I've *urged* him."

"Just what would you say?"

Ruth tapped her index finger on the bedpost as though the matter took deep contemplation. "Encouraged! I've encouraged him."

Daughtie gave her a sidelong glance. "Well, I'd appreciate it if you'd cease your encouragement. I'm not interested in Dr. Ketter, and he should spend his energy wooing another."

"After tonight, you may change your mind. He has quite an evening planned," Ruth replied with a secretive grin.

———

Dr. Ketter stood waiting at the foot of the stairs. "You ladies look absolutely lovely," he said, his gaze fixed upon

Daughtie. He took her hand in his own and placed a fleeting kiss upon her extended fingers.

Daughtie flinched at his familiarity, but his grip tightened as she attempted to pull away.

"Shall we?" he inquired, pulling open the front door with his free hand while still holding on to Daughtie. Ruth giggled, obviously amused by Daughtie's noticeable discomfort. Dr. Ketter carefully looped Daughtie's arm through his own as though she were his prized possession. "I attempted to hire a carriage, but there were none available when I checked at the livery. However, Ruth tells me you enjoy walking, so I hope you won't mind since it's such a lovely starlit evening."

"Walking is fine," Daughtie replied. "I'm unaccustomed to riding in a carriage."

"Ruth tells me you have quite a talent for sewing and decorating," he said. "Perhaps you could assist me with my living quarters."

"I'm rather busy right now. I've committed to the library and several other matters, and I doubt I'd have adequate time. But Ruth has quite an eye for design herself. Since you two have become such close friends, perhaps she could help you."

"You would be a *much* better choice," Ruth insisted, leveling a glare in Daughtie's direction.

"Daughtie! Ruth!" Amanda Corbett called out. "Wait for us!" A group of six girls, with Amanda in the lead, came scurrying down the street in their best attire, with hair coifed to perfection and cheeks blushing with anticipation. "Isn't this exciting? I can hardly wait to begin dancing," she said, her blond tresses bouncing up and down as she expressed her delight. "And aren't you the most fortunate one of all, Daughtie. You'll be able to dance all of the dances with Dr. Ketter."

"I'm not fond of dancing, so I'm certain Dr. Ketter will

be happy to sign all of your dance cards," Daughtie offered as they reached Phineas Whiting's establishment.

"Oh, would you, Dr. Ketter? That would be *so* kind. I understand the girls always outnumber the gentlemen by at least six or seven to one." Amanda thrust her card into Dr. Ketter's hand.

Before Dr. Ketter could assist Daughtie with her cape, he was surrounded by a group of chattering girls, each one vying for his signature. "Could we each have two dances with you?" one of the girls pleaded.

Dr. Ketter handed the cards back and reached around Daughtie's shoulders to assist with her cloak. "I've promised each of you a dance and two dances to Ruth. Surely you wouldn't want me to ignore Daughtie. She'll never agree to accompany me again if I don't designate most of my time to her."

"Oh, I don't want to be selfish. I'm more than willing to share your time and attention," Daughtie replied.

"Dr. Ketter's correct. We're already taking advantage of his time. Let's don't be greedy," Ruth admonished.

Daughtie met Ruth's steely glare with a smug grin. "I see a table that will accommodate all of us," she said, pointing to the left side of the room and leading the way. The others fell in step behind her, and as they settled themselves at the table, Amanda strategically placed herself at Dr. Ketter's left while Daughtie sat to his right.

The musicians were seated along the north wall, and the sound of their stringed instruments filled the room with soft music. Daughtie kept her gaze focused upon the feet of the dancers as they waltzed to the melody. "This is nothing like Shaker dancing. I'm not certain I could dance like that," she whispered to Ruth.

"It's really quite simple. I'm certain you'd be willing to try if *Liam Donohue* was asking to be your partner," Ruth snidely replied.

Daughtie stared at Ruth momentarily and then turned away. The remark didn't deserve a reply, she decided.

"Oh, look! Mr. and Mrs. Cheever have arrived," Amanda said while pointing toward the door. "Doesn't she look exquisite?"

Matthew Cheever led Lilly onto the dance floor as Daughtie turned in their direction. "Indeed!" she replied, unable to think of adequate words to describe Mrs. Cheever's stunning appearance. Lilly Cheever's pale yellow gown was lined with satin the shade of summer daffodils and embellished with sheer ivory lace. Tiny yellow flowers that perfectly matched the dress surrounded her intricately arranged curls. There was little doubt anyone would out-shine Mrs. Cheever this evening; she was the epitome of loveliness.

"Did you know they're to have a baby?" Amanda questioned. "I heard it talked about just the other day."

Daughtie nodded, having known for some time that Lilly would give birth to another Cheever heir in July. She noted the woman's beautiful attire and slim figure that was only now starting to thicken at the waist. It was hard to believe Lilly was even expecting.

"I love babies," another of the girls added. "I would love to be a nanny instead of a mill girl."

"Oh, they look so wonderful together," Amanda said with a sigh.

Dr. Ketter leaned toward Daughtie. "I would enjoy the pleasure of this dance," he whispered into her ear. "I think we might look wonderful together, as well."

Daughtie stiffened. "As I explained when you invited me, I'm not accustomed to this type of dancing. Why don't you dance with one of the other girls, and I'll watch until I'm more familiar with the steps."

His lips tightened into a thin line, but he finally nodded in agreement. He moved to the other side of the table and held out his hand to Ruth with a smile on his face. She rose and he escorted her onto the dance floor. As promised, Daughtie watched the couples and attempted to memorize their movements as they twirled around the room. Each time Dr. Ketter returned and gazed in her direction, she signaled to wait just a little longer. After fulfilling his dance card obligations to most of the doting girls who had accompanied them into the hall, Daughtie finally succumbed to his request.

Ivan pulled her into his arms, his lips curved into a broad smile as he began to lead her to the steps of a waltz.

"Let's stay close to the outer perimeter. I don't want my clumsiness to interfere with the other dancers," Daughtie requested, pushing against the pressure of his hand on the small of her back as he attempted to lead her into the crowd.

He acquiesced, and they moved somewhat clumsily, with Daughtie making a valiant attempt to follow Ivan's lead.

She grimaced when her foot came down hard atop his boot. "I'm sorry," she apologized with a weak smile.

"No need to apologize. Practice makes perfect. We'll just keep trying," he replied in a cheery tone.

When the musicians announced the need for a few minutes to refresh themselves, Daughtie sighed with relief. Taking Ivan's arm, she joined the throng of dancers moving back toward their tables. However, Ivan pulled her to a stop when shouting voices and the sound of pounding feet drifted into the room. He drew her close to his side as several men burst through the front door of the Old Stone House.

"Where's Mr. Boott and Mr. Cheever?" one of the men shouted. His eyes glistened in the flickering light cast by the sperm-oil lamps. He gazed about the room, his panic obvious for all to see.

Kirk and Matthew approached the men and began talking in hushed whispers while the partygoers milled about, obviously hoping to overhear some snippet of their conversation. Several minutes passed before Kirk finally requested that the partygoers take their seats. The guests strained forward, watching as he mounted the small platform being used by the musicians.

"I've just received word that there are vandals attempting to destroy the Pawtucket Dam at this very moment. I need able-bodied men to accompany us, men prepared to block these evildoers by any means necessary. If you have easily accessible weapons, bring them with you. I don't want any bloodshed, but we don't know if these men are armed."

"Who are these miscreants? Do you have any idea, Mr. Boott?" someone called out from across the room.

"We've been told they are farmers from the surrounding area. However, there may be those among them who merely enjoy a fracas. We can't be certain. One thing is clear: this matter requires our immediate attention. Ladies, I apologize for leaving you without dance partners, but perhaps you can remain and enjoy the company of one another as well as the food that's been prepared. I'm hoping we'll soon return and the evening will not be totally spoiled. Gentlemen, please join me," he encouraged, obviously hopeful the men would rally to the cause.

The scraping of chairs echoed throughout the hall, and men scurried toward the door. Daughtie turned toward Ivan, who remained seated beside her. "You'd best get your medical bag and accompany them," she urged. "If the men resort to fisticuffs, they'll need medical aid."

"I suppose you're right," he acknowledged, though still not moving. "But my preference is to remain here with you."

"I imagine the other men would prefer to remain here,

too. However, they're already on their way."

He placed an arm across the back of Daughtie's chair and drew near. "But they didn't have the pleasure of escorting *you*. If they had, they'd still be here, too," he whispered.

Daughtie leaned back and met his gaze. Both his words and the look in his eyes caused her discomfort.

Matthew pulled back on the reins and brought the carriage to a halt in front of the Old Stone House. As the men began scurrying out of the building, Matthew directed them to the livery. "Kirk, Nathan, Josiah, and I will meet you at Kittredge's. Mr. Kittredge has two wagons we can use. He's hitching up the teams. It's best we travel as a group," Matthew called after them. He waited until the three men were settled into the carriage and then flicked the reins.

"Seems it's just one problem after another here in Lowell," Josiah complained, grasping Kirk's arm as the carriage wheeled around at breakneck speed. "Could you slow the horses down before this carriage turns over?" he shouted while tapping Matthew on the back with his silver-tipped walking stick. "Is there some sort of management problem, Kirk?"

Nathan turned in his seat and glared at Josiah. "As I recall, you're the one who said we should ignore the farmers' complaints and grumbled because we held a discussion of the issue. And let me see, weren't you the one who voted *against* exploring the possibility of expanding the millpond?"

"No need for sarcasm, Nathan," Josiah replied. "Did you tell the farmers we're attempting to renovate the millpond, Kirk?"

Matthew slowed the carriage as they neared the livery and motioned the men to follow. Both wagons were filled with men, a number of them bearing weapons—either their own or those loaned to them by Mr. Kittredge, Matthew surmised.

Once they were on the road to the dam, Josiah turned his attention back to Kirk. "You didn't answer my question. Did you talk to the farmers?"

"Yes, they've been advised. However, they expressed their dissatisfaction with the idea, saying they weren't going to wait until engineers did a survey and report. Instead, they said they'd handle it in their own way. I suppose this is what they meant. Let's hope they don't have a keg of gunpowder waiting to greet us."

"You actually think they might destroy the dam?"

"That's what I explained at our Boston meeting, Mr. Baines. They want the dam out of there," Matthew called over his shoulder.

The horses raced on, their hooves drumming out a warning of the approaching wagons. "Up there, Kirk!" Nathan shouted, pointing toward the dam. "It looks as though there may be thirty or forty men. Let's pray they don't have weapons leveled in our direction."

The instant Nathan's words had been uttered, Kirk leaned forward and shouted in Matthew's direction, "Stop the carriage. Now!"

Matthew pulled hard on the reins, hoping the wagons behind him would stop in time. "What's wrong?" he shouted to Kirk.

"Nathan's words made me wonder if they might have those men out in the open to entice us onward. There may be an ambush up ahead. I don't want to ride directly into harm's way. Have one or two of the men make their way closer. They can see if there's a trap and discover what's actually happening closer to the dam. Surely the farmers have men watching the road. They've likely heard us coming."

"I'll go," Matthew volunteered.

"No! I forbid it. I'll not have you risking your life. Ask one of the men in the other wagons to go."

Matthew swung about, startled at Kirk's request. "My life is no more valuable than any of those men!"

In the dim moonlight, Kirk's features appeared carved in granite. "Don't question my decisions. Do as you're told." His voice had taken on the harshness of a father reprimanding his errant son.

Matthew stalked off toward the wagons without a word. Anything he wanted to say would be disrespectful. He neared the first wagon. "Any volunteers to see if there's an ambush lying in wait up the road? We need two or three men."

"You afeared to go?" Thomas Getty hollered with a loud guffaw before jumping down from the wagon. Two other men joined Thomas, both of them obviously amused by his remark.

"I volunteered, but Mr. Boott refused my offer."

"Of course he did," Thomas replied, his retort followed by another round of laughter. "Let's get going before Matthew insists upon replacing one of us."

Matthew gazed heavenward. Attempting to defend himself had only made matters worse. "Get your instructions from Mr. Boott before you rush off. And each of you needs to take a weapon," he called after them. One of the men came racing back to the wagon and retrieved a rifle from one of his friends. He nodded at Matthew, his grin still intact as he scurried after the other two men, who were already making their way down the dark roadway.

"That was most embarrassing," Matthew mumbled while climbing back into the carriage.

A volley of gunfire cracked through the dark silence shrouding their carriage. "Better embarrassed than dead. I hope none of them is injured," Kirk matter-of-factly replied. "We need at least one of them to get back here with a report."

Matthew stared in disbelief. As far as he was concerned, Kirk's remarks went beyond callous. They were both self-serving and cruel. "These men volunteered to assist us. I can't believe you feel no distress over their welfare."

Kirk shook his head in disgust. "Distress? What good does it do if I sit here wringing my hands like a frightened child? I spent my early adulthood in England training for the military. Battle requires intelligent tactical decisions and people who carry out orders without question. I'll not apologize for exemplary battlefield behavior."

"But those men are not *soldiers* under your command; they're ordinary citizens," Matthew argued.

"Technically, you're correct, but they are also employees who are dependent upon their positions in the mills. If the dam is destroyed, they'll find themselves without wages until it's reconstructed. They may not be soldiers, but they *are* men fighting for their livelihood."

A rumbling explosion sounded in the distance, and the ground shuddered underfoot. The two men silenced their arguing while all eyes focused upon Kirk and awaited his direction.

"Hold fast!" he called out as Thomas Getty came racing toward them.

Chest heaving and gasping for breath, Thomas clung to the side of the buggy. "We need to advance around the woods to the left. They set off an explosion to block our path, and they're readying to blow up the dam."

Kirk shouted for the wagons to follow, and Matthew grasped Thomas by the arm. "Get in the carriage!" he hollered, assisting Thomas up before cracking the whip and sending the horses into a gallop. "Direct the way!" he shouted to Thomas.

Thomas pointed toward a growth of trees. "You'll need

to slow down. We've got to navigate through those tall pines. Horace and Zedediah are waiting for us."

"No injuries, then?" Matthew asked.

"No, we're all fine, but that explosion scared the stuffin' out of Zed," he said with a chuckle. "Lodged a particle of fear in me, but I didn't tell Horace or Zed. They don't think nothing bothers me." As their progress slowed, he stated, "Think we'll do better on foot from here on out. Too hard to get the wagons through the rocks and trees, and some of their men may be scattered about out here. Besides, the wagons make too much noise." Thomas then emitted an eerie hooting sound that brought Zed and Horace running toward them.

"There's more of us than them," Horace reported. "I made it over to the dam. They're getting powder kegs ready to set off, so we need to get moving. Best be careful where you shoot. If we hit one of them kegs, we'll all be blown to kingdom come."

Kirk gathered the men close. "Stay together until I signal. Then separate into four groups," he said, quickly pushing the men into four clusters. "When you hear a single gunshot, I want those of you with weapons to fire them into the air. When they hear gunfire coming from four different directions, I'm hoping they'll believe they're mightily outnumbered and surrounded. If we can frighten them off without bloodshed, I'll be satisfied."

Thomas aligned with one group of the men. "I don't aim to kill no one, but if they start shooting at us, we'll have to return fire. This could turn into a massacre. I don't think none of us want to see that happen, Mr. Boott."

Kirk nodded his agreement. "I don't, either, so let's be cautious and pray for the best," he said, signaling the men to move out.

"Apparently the suggestion of prayer was only a figure of speech," Matthew murmured before silently making his own plea for safety among them and taking his assigned position near the rear.

"Mr. Boott appears confident. If I didn't know better, I'd almost believe he was enjoying himself," one of the men beside Matthew remarked.

"I wouldn't go so far as to say he's enjoying himself. He's likely remembering all those years of military instruction years ago. I'd guess he's surprised to be putting the training into use at a small dam in Lowell," Matthew replied. "There's the signal to break off into our section and head south."

Kirk's lone shot resonated in the distance. The men followed instructions, answering his single blast with a volley of gunfire. The countryside was filled with the sound of gunfire, shouting men, and pounding feet trampling through the woods.

"Hold your fire!" The order echoed down through the ranks in a ripple effect.

When the shadowy wooded area had once again grown silent, Kirk summoned Matthew forward. "They want to talk," he told Matthew. "I want you to go with me. Some of them will recognize you. If we're lucky, they'll still consider you one of their own and be more responsive to us."

"I doubt my presence will aid you, but I'm happy to lend my assistance," Matthew replied.

It took but a few minutes to walk the short distance to a clearing near the dam. No less than twenty angry-looking men, all of them armed, stood waiting as they made their appearance. "We have no weapons," Kirk said. He moved slowly, careful to show the men he truly was unarmed. Matthew, following Kirk's example, moved forward and stood beside him.

Matthew squinted into the darkness. "Simon? Is that you?"

Simon Fenske edged his way forward between two men. "Yep—sure is."

"I'm surprised to see you among these men. I've always known you to be a man of reason, not one who would join forces with a group intent on taking the law into their own hands," Matthew said, moving closer.

"Don't try to influence me with your flattering words, Matthew. I'm here because I support this cause. Not all of us sold out to the Corporation. *We* still earn our living from the land," Simon replied harshly.

"If we're to continue fishing and farming this land, we need this water running free like God intended. Either tear down this dam or we will!" another man shouted.

A chorus of support rang out from the surrounding throng, and soon the men were shouting in cadence: "Tear down the dam! Tear down the dam! Tear down the dam!"

Kirk waited patiently and then slowly waved his arm in the air. "If you'll permit me to speak," he shouted, obviously hoping that his voice would be heard above the chanting men. "Gentlemen! Gentlemen!"

With the metal of his weapon gleaming in the moonlight, Simon Fenske gestured to the crowd. The pulsing mantra ebbed into a deafening silence before he finally spoke. "Let's see what Mr. Boott has to say. We don't have to agree, but we've got nothing to lose by hearing him out."

Reluctant nods and murmurs of uncertain compliance hung in the air like gloomy shrouds begging for elimination.

Kirk cleared his throat, tugged at his waistcoat, and gave Matthew a pat on the back. "This young man is one of your own. He's tilled the soil and loves this land like all of you. We've talked at length about the concerns you've expressed over the dam and how it impacts your land and livelihood. We are deeply grieved that while the dam has created industrialization and progress for many of us, it has caused grief and hardship for others. Our goal is to find a reasonable solution, but we can't accomplish anything in haste."

"We can completely destroy the dam in less than an hour," someone shouted from the rear of the group.

"Demolition of property is not the answer," Kirk replied firmly. "We're reasonable men who can solve this problem without harm to one another or the dam. Would you be willing to appoint one among you to act as a representative to meet with us? Someone you trust to speak and make agreements on your behalf?"

"What do you say, men? Do you want to talk or fight?" Simon bellowed.

"You talk to 'em, Simon," John Wells called out, "but we ain't willing to wait until they have all them fancy-pants fellers come from the city to do a report. There's enough men at the Locks and Canals that can figure out what needs to be done to free up this water."

"You willing to talk with 'em, Simon?" another man shouted.

Simon reached up under his cap and scratched his head. "If that's what you want, I'll meet with them. However, I'll not enter into any agreement without the consent of the group. I'm not looking to lose any friends over this."

"Why don't we meet tomorrow morning? Matthew and I can come out to your farm. And any of you other men who want to be present—please feel free to attend," Kirk said, raising his voice so the entire assemblage could hear the offer.

"Tomorrow's fine," Simon replied.

"Do I have your agreement that nothing further will happen here at the dam until we've talked?" Kirk inquired, extending his hand.

"You have our word," Simon said, shaking hands and sealing the agreement.

Daughtie hurried out of the mill, anxious to eat supper and be on her way to Liam's. "Hurry up, Ruth. You're plodding along like a lazy mule."

"I'm tired. Some of us were up very late last night."

"Don't whine. You chose to remain at the ball and lose sleep. I didn't."

"Oh, don't act so self-righteous, Daughtie. The only reason you left the ball was because you thought Dr. Ketter might return. You didn't fool me one jot with your story of a headache and being tired. Running off was an easy way to escape your obligation."

"Escape my obligation? I fulfilled my duty. I attended the ball. *He's* the one who departed the dance."

"At *your* urging. I heard you tell him there might be injuries and he should go along with the men," Ruth rebutted.

"I was thinking of the men, not myself."

"Of course you were. And that's why you rushed home and prepared for bed the minute the men rode out of town." The sarcasm dripped from Ruth's words like thick oozing syrup.

A deafening silence remained between them until they arrived at the boardinghouse. "I don't want to argue," Daughtie said, turning the knob of the front door.

"Good evening, ladies," Ivan Ketter greeted in an exceedingly cordial tone. He gave a slight bow from the waist with one arm carefully tucked behind his back.

"Good evening," Daughtie replied, glancing into the parlor. "You have no patients waiting to be seen?"

In a grand sweeping gesture, Ivan whisked a bouquet of flowers from behind his back. When Daughtie didn't reach out to accept the offering, he thrust the droopy gift directly in her path. "For you," he said, glancing first at her and then at the wilting arrangement. "With my sincere apologies—to make up for last night. And to ask if you would be my guest at the Merrimack House for dinner this evening."

"I'm sorry, but I've already made plans for this evening," she replied, edging toward the stairs.

"Tomorrow, then?" he asked while still holding the flowers.

"No. I'll be working at the library," Daughtie said. "Now if you'll excuse me, I really must go upstairs." Without waiting for a reply, she raced up the stairs at breakneck speed.

Daughtie was sitting on the bed darning a pair of black lisle stockings when Ruth walked in and dropped the bouquet onto the bed beside her. "You forgot your flowers. Ivan asked me to see that you got them. How could you be so cruel, Daughtie?"

"Would it be kinder to lead him on? I've attempted to convince him I have no interest in a social relationship. Unfortunately, he doesn't appear to believe me. I didn't take the flowers because I don't want to accept his gifts. Such behavior would only serve to encourage him."

Ruth grabbed a book from the shelf before turning back toward Daughtie. "You make no sense. You don't want to accept a dinner invitation from an eligible doctor, yet you'll place your reputation at risk by going to the home of that Irishman." Ruth stalked across the room and grabbed the flowers. "I'll return these for you. I wouldn't want you to keep an unwanted gift."

The door slammed, and Daughtie listened to Ruth's heavy footsteps as she descended the stairs. Prolonging an encounter with Ivan Ketter was going to make a prickly situation even more uncomfortable. Folding the darned stockings, she tucked them into a drawer, summoned her courage, and went downstairs to supper.

CHAPTER *21*

London

Barlow Kent was waiting when William arrived at Crouch's, a small pub carefully tucked between a tailor's shop and tobacconist's store on Murdock Street.

"Surely I'm not late," William said, snapping open his gold pocket watch.

"No, I arrived early," Barlow replied. "Have a seat."

William pulled a chair away from the table and sat down. "You must be anxious for my report."

Barlow leaned forward, resting his arms upon the table. "I'm *anxious* to hear something of value. For nearly four months you've been spoon-feeding us scraps of information with little substance. It's time to make our move."

"You look dour, Barlow. Did they run out of your favorite whiskey?" Chauncy Fuller asked as he approached the table.

Barlow leveled a glare at Chauncy. "If you had any sense, you'd be annoyed, too. I just told Thurston that I've grown weary of this silly charade. Either we're going to agree to do something about Farnsworth or I'll take care of this matter myself. We've been listening to these incessant reports for months, but we're no closer to making definitive plans than we were back in November. Thurston has appeared more intent on tracking down the comings and goings of Farnsworth's nephew, Taylor Manning, than on reining in Farnsworth."

William held his anger in check and gave Barlow a patronizing smile before replying. "Chauncy thought it imperative the information regarding young Manning be substantiated."

"To be honest, I think with the information you had we could have falsely accused him and no one would have been the wiser. Your continued investigation has only served to corroborate his innocence. What earthly good did that do us?"

"We don't want to be made fools when we bring in the law, Barlow," Chauncy explained as though he were speaking to a child. "And the information regarding young Manning came through *my* friendship with Wilburt Talley. Had we gone off ill-advised as you suggest, it's likely we would have caused a breach between Armstrong and Talley's design business and the Lancashire mills. Such an incident would have proved disastrous. Caution and good sense will bring a sound resolution to this situation."

"I'm weary of both of you. Talk—that's all either of you want to do. Well, I for one, am tired of your incessant chatter!"

"Settle yourself, Barlow. Whether you wish to acknowledge the value of William's information is of little consequence. This matter needs deliberate planning, and the reports we've received from William have been indispensable. I don't understand your constant wish to expedite our undertaking. As I said earlier, if we're to be successful, we must prepare well-thought-out plans using all the information available. We now know young

Manning is of no concern, and William has been able to focus his attention entirely upon Farnsworth. It makes this matter simpler knowing Manning is of little consequence to us. It appears you've become obsessed over Farnsworth leaving the country; however, all your worry serves no purpose."

Barlow set his glass down with a thud. "Don't speak to me as though I were an unruly child. You don't necessarily know what's best, and there's no guarantee Farnsworth isn't preparing to board a ship for America as we speak. William's *sources* and his unsubstantiated reports don't ease my concerns in the least. We have no idea who these shady characters are or if their information is correct."

William shifted in his chair and narrowed his eyes as he glared at Barlow. "Point out one bit of information in any report I have given you that has been inaccurate," he challenged.

"Thus far it's been correct—at least the little bit that is of consequence. Most of your reports are drivel. I don't care what's occurring in Boston or Lowell. I have no interest in how much cotton they're importing or what the output is per day in the New England mills."

"Well, you *should* be interested, Barlow. The Americans and the advancement of their industrialization have already caused a weakening of our investment in the English mills. Besides, Farnsworth and his family have been under close surveillance, haven't they, William?" Chauncy inquired.

Thurston nodded, his steely-eyed glare still directed at Barlow.

"And who is keeping watch over Farnsworth right now? He could be purchasing his passage to America, and we'd be none the wiser," Barlow countered.

"Trust me. I'll be immediately notified should he make such a purchase. I've already explained I have a man in the ticketing office—who is being well paid, I might add."

"That's just it, William. I *don't* trust you. I don't trust anyone except myself. The two of you are interested in having Farnsworth tried for treason. But I don't care if he's a spy, and I don't want to make an example of him to the English people. I want him *dead*!"

Chauncy gaped across the table in disbelief. William observed the situation unfold like a three-act play. He was now certain that Barlow's mental problems were spiraling out of control; soon the man would be a raving lunatic.

"You need to control yourself," Chauncy warned. "The last thing we need is Farnsworth showing up dead in some dark passageway. John Farnsworth is the only one who can supply the additional information we hope to gain regarding production and any new concepts they're developing for the New England mills."

William watched Chauncy continue speaking to Barlow in a soothing tone. When Barlow finally quieted and ceased his demands, William said, "Barlow may have a point. Perhaps we *should* do away with Farnsworth."

Chauncy swiveled in his chair, his features etched into an astonished stare. "What? Have you gone mad, too?"

"No, but Farnsworth will never voluntarily talk to us. Force will be required in order to gain any meaningful information. Afterward, we dare not release him, for he'd give our names to the authorities. I believe Barlow is correct: Farnsworth must die."

Barlow rubbed his hands together and leaned forward. "Let *me* do it."

William shrugged. "I don't care who kills him, but a plan is necessary. Once he's abducted, we'll need to convince him that if he doesn't talk to us, we'll use threats against his family. We may be forced to actually harm some member of his family in order to prove to him that we mean business."

"Hold up, gentlemen," Chauncy said. "I'm not

opposed to abducting Farnsworth and making a few threats to his family. However, I won't condone murder or the abduction of his family members."

"I didn't realize you were so faint of heart, Chauncy. I'm certain Barlow and I can handle this matter if you'd prefer to place us in charge. However, I could use a suggestion of someplace where we can interrogate him."

"No! I will not agree to murder. I must have your word," Chauncy said.

William glanced toward Barlow and gave a slight nod. "You're right, Chauncy. We'll turn him over to the authorities once he's talked. After all, there are three of us. We can deny any allegations he might make against us."

"Right. It's best we leave it to the authorities," Barlow agreed.

William grinned. Barlow had understood and followed his lead. The two of them would handle Farnsworth any way they pleased; Chauncy would have to live with their decision.

"Good! Since we're all in agreement that the authorities will be called in once we've questioned Farnsworth, I suggest you move ahead with his abduction, William. I have a rather unpleasant room adjacent to my wine cellar that is quite private. He couldn't possibly escape, and there's an outside entrance into the cellar. If you come by my office tomorrow, I'll have a key for you," Chauncy said.

Tapping his fingers along the edge of the table, William hoped he gave the appearance of a man deep in thought. "I'm thinking it may be wise to use Barlow's assistance with the abduction. In spite of his age, John Farnsworth is a powerful man. There's always the possibility he could wrestle free of me, and I wouldn't want that to happen. Another set of hands would provide additional backup should the need arise."

Chauncy's brow creased at the proposal. "I fear Barlow's

involvement might cause him undue stress. No offense, Barlow, but you have been troubled of late. I wouldn't want to make matters worse," Chauncy said, glancing toward his wife's cousin.

Barlow grasped Chauncy's arm. "Quite the contrary. Having this challenge will keep my mind off other more distressing situations. Give me this opportunity. You won't regret it—I promise."

Chauncy hesitated for only a moment. "If William wants your assistance and believes you're up to the task, then I'll give my approval."

Barlow's complexion turned ruddy, and he appeared close to tears. "Thank you, Chauncy."

Chauncy nodded and quickly turned back toward William. "Then we're settled. You'll stop by my office in the morning."

"Yes, in the morning," William replied, firmly shaking Chauncy's hand. "I believe we'll remain behind and formulate our plans."

Chauncy nodded his agreement, and the two men watched until he left the pub. "I was pleased to see that you picked up on my veiled message—I didn't know if you'd understand."

Barlow's lips formed a thin line. "Chauncy believes me unstable, but I am completely reliable and understand everything going on around me," he replied solemnly.

"Well, then, let's begin planning, shall we? The fact that John knows both of us presents a bit of a problem. If he should see either one of us, he may become suspicious. Because I've surreptitiously maintained a watchful eye, he's still not aware I'm in England. I'd like it to remain that way until we have him under our control. Perhaps you know a couple of less-than-reputable men who might agree to lend their assistance—for a reasonable fee, of course."

"Yes, I can make arrangements. How soon will we need them?"

"I'm not certain just yet. Tell them they'll be paid to remain available for the next two weeks. They must be accessible both night and day."

"*Two weeks?* I thought we were going to make our move right way."

William leaned forward, his features frozen into a cruel expression. "You listen to me, Barlow. I'm in charge of this maneuver, and if you want to remain involved, you'll do as you're told. If we're not prepared for every circumstance, the plan will fail and Farnsworth will slip out of our grasp. I won't attempt Farnsworth's apprehension until I'm certain we will succeed. Do you understand?"

"Yes," Barlow mumbled. "I'll put two men on alert. Anything else?"

"Outfit them with uniforms worn by the local constables. Is that possible?"

Barlow nodded. "Yes, but it might take a few days."

"Let me know when the men and uniforms are ready."

"And what are you going to be doing?" Barlow asked.

"Maintaining a close surveillance on Farnsworth and his family. If it appears they're going to sail before you've made arrangements, we'll be forced to apprehend him ourselves. I'd prefer that didn't happen, but we must be prepared in either event. Let's make this pub our meeting place. It's not far from where I'm residing, and it's fairly close to Jarrow Farnsworth's home."

"I'm not far from here, either, and I'll find suitable quarters in the vicinity for the men I hire."

"Excellent. I'll meet you here tomorrow evening. Seven o'clock?"

"Seven o'clock will be fine," Barlow replied, retrieving his felt top hat and following William to the door of the pub.

The men parted, Barlow heading off toward his empty house and William to the boardinghouse where he had taken up residence. He longed for someone he could take into his confidence, someone who could enjoy the totality of what he hoped to accomplish. But he dared not trust any of these Englishmen, who already questioned his loyalty and motivation.

He hurried past the parlor and up the stairs to his room, hung his coat, and sat down at the small writing desk. Pen in hand, he began to write:

Dear Thaddeus,
The events of this evening proved more fruitful than even I could have hoped. . . .

CHAPTER 22

Lowell
April

Daughtie waited outside Mr. Gault's office. She was exhausted and wondered if Mr. Kingman had asked her to deliver his message as retribution for today's ineptness. Two girls stood in front of her, obviously wanting to inquire about positions at the mills. Their excited chatter buzzed around her like bees swarming to the hive. She stared toward the mill yard in a half-dazed stupor before spotting Ruth coming across the yard. Daughtie waved with as much enthusiasm as her weary limbs would permit.

Ruth sprinted toward her, the spring breeze whipping at her cape. "Why are you waiting to see Mr. Gault? Planning to apply for another position?" she asked with a wry smile.

"Mr. Kingman asked me to deliver a message for him. Nothing seemed to go right today. Normally I can draw two full beams on Saturdays, and if I'm having a really good day, I can complete three. However, I struggled to get even one beam done today. Mr. Kingman came out from the weaving room several times. His scowls made it abundantly clear he was unhappy with my lack of progress. I think he decided since I was slow at the frames, he'd find a way to punish me. What better way than to consume my precious extra time off on a Saturday afternoon?"

"Don't let Mr. Kingman bother you. All of the weavers were busy today. Had you completed another beam, one of us would have been forced to work an extra loom. I'm glad you weren't successful," Ruth sullenly replied.

Daughtie gave her a weary smile. Ever since the day of the turnout, Ruth had remained irritable. Her words were generally laced with anger, and she'd become even more opinionated about the working conditions at the mill. Daughtie remained uncertain if the anger was directed at her or the Corporation. She doubted her refusal to participate in the turnout had been forgiven, although both girls pretended things were normal. Yet there remained a chasm between the two of them, especially over matters relating to their work.

"You don't need to wait with me. Go and enjoy your extra time away from the mill. I overheard you tell Margaret you'd go to the shops with her before supper. You won't have time if you wait on me. There's Margaret over there," Daughtie said, pointing across the yard.

Ruth glanced toward the gate and waved at Margaret. "Would you tell Mrs. Arnold I'll be home before supper?"

"Of course. Have fun shopping."

Ruth gave her a patronizing smile. "We're not going shopping; we're meeting with a printer. We're going to see how much it would cost to print pamphlets."

"What kind of pamphlets? What are you up to, Ruth?"

"Nothing that would be of interest to you," she replied before walking off.

"You're determined to get yourself dismissed," Daughtie

muttered as she watched Ruth march off with her head held high, resolve in her step.

By the time she'd received her pay and was leaving the mill yard, Daughtie's shoulders were slumped and there was little resolve in *her* step. She merely wanted to get home and put this terrible day behind her.

A dirt-smudged young girl with reddish-brown curls tugged at Daughtie's cloak as she rounded the corner. "Would ya be Daughtie Winfield?" the girl asked.

Daughtie nodded.

"Mr. Donohue said I should give ya this." The child thrust a paper into Daughtie's hand and disappeared before she could say a word.

Daughtie unfolded the paper and read Liam's words: *I must see you this evening. Come after supper and be certain you're not followed.*

The message was intriguing. Was Liam planning something special? Obviously he didn't want her to bring anyone else along. She smiled at the thought. Whom would she even ask to accompany her to Liam's house? Ruth wouldn't consider darkening the doorway of an Irishman's home. She read the note one last time before entering the front door. Her weariness and disillusionment were quickly replaced by an unexpected excitement and energy.

"Good afternoon, Daughtie," Dr. Ketter greeted as she walked in the front door.

"Good afternoon to you," Daughtie replied a little too excitedly.

He brightened at her reply. "You certainly appear to be in fine spirits today. Perhaps I could convince you to join me for a stroll after supper this evening."

Daughtie's enthusiasm waned. "I'm sorry, but I have plans this evening," she replied while removing her cape and hanging it on a peg by the front door. When she turned back toward the hallway, Dr. Ketter was directly in front of her, blocking her path to the stairway.

"Tomorrow afternoon, then? Or perhaps I could escort you to church in the morning, and then we could take a stroll in the afternoon—or a carriage ride. I could go to the livery right now and make arrangements for a horse and buggy. Would you find a carriage ride to your liking?" he inquired persistently.

His enthusiasm likely matched what she had felt after reading Liam's message. She didn't want to injure his feelings, yet accepting his invitation would only give him false hope. "Thank you for the offer, but I can't accept. You're a fine man, and any number of girls would be flattered by your attention. In fact, I'm certain Ruth would find a buggy ride after church much to her liking. Why don't you consider asking *her*?"

Dr. Ketter flinched as though he'd been stuck with a hatpin. "Because I don't want to keep company with Ruth. You've captured my interest, and I know it's only a matter of time before you come to trust me," he replied.

"Trust you? What makes you think I don't trust you?"

He patted her hand. "Please don't be angry with Ruth, but she's told me that you have a problem trusting men. She counseled me to move slowly and take time to build a friendship before I attempt to pursue a romantic relationship with you. However, I have let my heart rule instead of my head. Now I fear I've lost all hope of gaining your trust."

"I'm not certain how Ruth determined I have a problem with trust, but let me assure you, Dr. Ketter—"

He held up a finger. "Ivan—not Dr. Ketter."

"Let me assure you, *Ivan,* that I've never had a problem trusting either men or women—unless they do something to destroy my belief in them."

His lips turned up in a broad smile. "So you trust me?"

"I have no reason not to. But that doesn't mean I want

to take a carriage ride tomorrow afternoon. Now if you'll excuse me, I must go upstairs and complete some tasks before dinner," she said, edging her way around him and hurrying toward the stairway.

"She trusts me," he murmured expectantly.

Daughtie advanced up the stairs, pretending she hadn't heard his words. Obviously Ruth had continued to play the matchmaker, assuring Dr. Ketter it would only be a matter of time until Daughtie trusted him, only a matter of time before he could become romantically involved with her. How dare Ruth meddle in her life!

The mood at supper was stilted and uncomfortable. Ruth hadn't returned in time for the evening meal, and Dr. Ketter's attempts to draw Daughtie into conversation made her edgy. She gulped down her meal, excused herself, and rushed from the house, mumbling that she wouldn't return until just before curfew. Tucking her head against the strong wind, she hurried toward Liam's house.

A hand grasped her arm as she rounded the corner toward Worthan Street. "Where are *you* off to?"

Her gaze snapped upward and she met Ruth's questioning stare. "I have some—some errands to attend to," she stammered.

"Errands? Where? You've already passed the library and all the shops."

"Have I? I was so deep in thought, I lost track."

"Come on," Ruth said, placing an arm around her shoulder. "I'm going home. I'll walk back to town with you."

Daughtie glanced at Ruth. "Where were you?"

"After our visit to the printer, Margaret and I had a meeting to attend. Was Mrs. Arnold upset that I missed supper?"

"No. She said she'd keep a plate warm in the oven. Will you be home the rest of the evening?"

Ruth nodded her head. "Why do you ask?"

"When I get home, I'd like to talk with you."

"Why don't we stop at Clawson's Tea and Pastry Shop? We could visit over tea and cake," Ruth suggested, looping her arm through Daughtie's in the first act of amiability since before the turnout.

Panic welled up within Daughtie, threatening to cut off her breath. How was she going to get away from Ruth? Drawing a deep breath into her lungs and then slowly blowing outward, Daughtie relaxed and began to gather her wits. "That would be lovely, Ruth, but I fear Mrs. Arnold will worry if you don't return to eat that dinner she's keeping warm for you."

"Oh! I had completely forgotten. I don't want to worry Mrs. Arnold. Perhaps I shouldn't stop for tea. We can talk when you get home."

"Exactly! We wouldn't want Mrs. Arnold to fret."

A complacent smile crossed Daughtie's lips as Ruth turned and walked toward home. She waited until Ruth rounded the corner and was out of sight before changing directions and heading back toward Liam's house. A slight chill, obviously unwilling to surrender its frosty clutches to the warmth of springtime, clung to the nighttime air. Daughtie bowed her head into the cold breeze and quickened her pace, breathless by the time she reached Liam's front porch.

She lifted the heavy knocker and let it fall from her hand, permitting it to bounce against the iron striker. The silence resonated with a series of metallic thumps before the front door opened. Grasping her arm, Liam yanked her inside and quickly slammed the door.

"Does anyone know ya're here?" His Irish brogue hung thick on the air.

"No."

"And ya're certain ya weren't followed?"

"No—I mean yes, I'm certain I wasn't followed."

"What took ya so long? I was beginnin' to think ya weren't comin'."

His dark eyes sparkled with excitement—or was it fear? She wasn't certain if she should be frightened or joyful. "Why are you acting so strangely, and why do you suddenly care if someone sees me coming into your house?"

Before he could answer there was a mewling sound— weak at first, but now growing stronger. She clasped his arm. "You've baby kittens upstairs, don't you? Oh, let me see them," she begged.

He shook his head. "That's not kittens; it's a baby—two babies. Up there," he said while pointing toward the stairs. "They were born after the mother arrived here. A slave. And for sure, I don't know how she ever made it. She wasn't here more than an hour before they were born. Two boys. The mother needs tendin'—she's in bad condition. That's why I sent for ya."

Daughtie rushed up the steps at breakneck speed, the cries of the babies directing her to the proper bedroom. A young black woman lay on one side, her eyes closed and one arm protectively crooked around the two babies. The infants' cries grew increasingly louder, and Daughtie wondered at their mother's ability to sleep.

Drawing closer, Daughtie kneeled down beside the bed. The babies were so very small. "I've come to help you," she explained while leaning forward to stroke the woman's arm. However, one touch confirmed her worst fears: the woman was dead, and her infant sons would soon follow if they didn't receive nourishment.

Hurrying to the top of the staircase, she called down to Liam, who was perched on the bottom step, "She's dead, Liam, and the babies need milk or they'll die."

"The goat? Will her milk do?"

"Let's hope so. We have no other choice."

"Stay upstairs while I'm out in the barn. Should ya hear anybody knockin' at the door, keep yourself out of sight, and whatever ya do, don't open it," he instructed.

She watched as he turned a key in the lock of the burnished wooden door before striding off toward the back of the house. Daughtie returned to the crying babies and lifted them away from their mother's cold body. Pulling a soft quilt from an oak blanket chest, she wrapped the boys together in the coverlet. Perhaps they could lend each other a bit of the same comfort and warmth they had shared in their mother's womb. Lifting the bundled infants, she began pacing the floor, just as she'd done so many times at the Shaker village. Movement had seemed to work with those babies. But then, *their* bellies had been full.

The infants remained awake. Their lusty cries had turned to pitiful whimpers when she finally heard Liam's footsteps coming up the stairs. A small pail dangled from his broad fingers.

"She wasn't very cooperative," he said, extending the container toward Daughtie.

"They're newborn babies, so they won't eat much at a feeding," she said while eyeing the contents of the bucket. "We'll need a couple of clean handkerchiefs."

Liam strode out of the room and quickly returned with two folded white squares in his palm. "Will these do?"

"Yes, they'll be fine," she said, shaking the folds from each handkerchief and handing one back to him. "Fold over one corner and twist the end," she said while forming a loose knot at one end of the cloth.

"Like this?"

She smiled up at him and nodded. "That's good. Now, dip the knotted portion in the pail," she instructed, plunging her own cloth into the milk. "Once you've got it soaked, hold it to the baby's mouth and let him suck on it."

Liam watched intently as Daughtie offered the milk-soaked rag to one of the infants. "Shall I try with the other babe?" Liam inquired, gazing toward the crying infant lying on the bed.

"Please," Daughtie replied.

The sound of the babies' smacking mouths soon filled the room.

Liam glanced in Daughtie's direction as he once again saturated the cloth with milk. "I'm not sure what to do about their mother. There's a nice place with trees and wild flowers out beyond the barn. Once we've finished feedin' the babes, I could dig a grave and bury her—if ya think that would be proper."

"I don't see that we have any choice. We certainly can't go ask Mr. Livermore to build a casket and buy a plot in the local cemetery."

Liam gave a snort. "That's a fact. Ya're the only one in this room that would receive permission to push up daisies in the Lowell cemetery. They'd turn away an Irishman as quickly as they'd turn away this black girl or her babes. Maybe faster," he added.

"I'm concerned with how you're going to care for these babies by yourself. If I don't return to the boardinghouse before curfew, Ruth is certain to send someone looking for me. There's little doubt she'd have them come here first."

"Don't see as I 'ave much choice but to try and take care of them until ya return tomorrow or the others arrive."

"Others? You expect more runaways?"

He nodded and motioned toward the mother. "She thought they were less than a couple days behind her. They'd been travelin' together, but when she started feelin' poorly, they decided to remain behind as decoys. They didn't want her to be forced to give birth out in the open, with no protection. Their plan was to go spreadin' out and deflect the slave owners and hounds that had been trackin' them. I think she feared some of the other slaves had been recaptured because of her condition. I tried to reassure her as best I could."

"Our best hope is that they arrive soon and that they'll be willing to take the babies with them."

"Willin'? I don't know as I'll be givin' them a choice, lassie. I think I'd have a bit of a problem explainin' how two little black babes arrived on my doorstep," he replied with a grin.

"It's good that you haven't lost your sense of humor," she said while placing one of the babies in one end of an empty drawer. "You can put him at the other end; then if you'd get me some water and towels, I'll get their mother ready for burial."

Liam followed her bidding, fetched the items, and then left to dig the grave. Daughtie prepared the body in silence while the two tiny infants slept nearby, unaware of the fact that their mother had died so they could be born free from the slavery that had bound her.

When Liam returned, the young woman was wrapped in the sheet and blanket Liam had given her. "Are ya comin' with me?"

"No, I'll stay here with the boys and pray—for their health and God's protection over all of you."

He nodded. "Aye. Let's hope yar prayers are answered."

"Liam, I must depart as soon as you return. It's getting late."

"I'll hurry," he replied, lifting the woman's body with a care and respect that touched Daughtie's heart.

Daughtie gathered her Bible and pulled a fresh hand-kerchief from the oak chest, hoping to escape the room while Ruth was still in the midst of her preparations for church. Exiting the doorway, she hurried down the hall and reached the top of the steps before she heard Ruth's voice.

"Are you going to the Baptist church with the rest of us this morning? All the girls from the weaving room decided to go there today."

Daughtie hesitated a moment. "No. I believe I'll attend services at the Methodist church."

"Why?" Ruth quizzed in a whiny tone. "You're always separating yourself from everyone else. There are some girls who think you're aloof."

Daughtie wasn't going to continue this conversation. No doubt Ruth was attempting to delay her departure until she could have a face-to-face confrontation. "I'm sorry to hear that, but I'm certain you'll set them aright," she called over her shoulder while scurrying down the steps.

Making a turn to the right when she reached the bottom of the staircase, Daughtie walked into the kitchen, where Mrs. Arnold was busy preparing breakfast. "I'm attending the Methodist church this morning, so I'll be leaving—no time for breakfast," she explained.

Mrs. Arnold looked up and gave her a smile. "Take a biscuit or two. You can eat them on the way," she encouraged, wrapping two of the freshly baked offerings into a small cloth napkin.

"Thank you," Daughtie said, giving the older woman a grateful smile. She tucked her Bible under one arm and grasped the biscuit-filled napkin. "I have plans for the day and won't be eating my meals here at the house."

"Going on that picnic and carriage ride with Dr. Ketter after all?"

Surprised by the question, Daughtie jerked her gaze upward and was met by Mrs. Arnold's inquiring stare. In addition to formulating plans with Ruth, it appeared Dr. Ketter was forming an alliance by taking Mrs. Arnold into his confidence. "No, I haven't changed my mind. My plans don't involve Dr. Ketter," she replied before hurrying back toward the hallway.

Daughtie quickly peeked up the stairway. Ruth was nowhere to be seen. Swinging her blue worsted capuchin about her shoulders, she pulled up the hood and adjusted her Bible.

"May I walk with you?"

Daughtie turned with a jolt. Ivan Ketter was standing directly behind her. "No. Not today. I'm busy with other matters," she stammered.

He glanced toward the Bible tucked under her arm. "You're obviously going to church. Is there some reason I can't accompany you?"

"I don't think you'll find my companionship enjoyable today. Besides, I'm not going to the Baptist church," Daughtie explained. She gave a sidelong glance toward the stairway. If he didn't soon release her from this conversation, Ruth would come bounding down the steps, and she'd never get away without additional questions.

He graced her with a broad smile. "I'm willing to attend whatever church you like," he said, removing his hat from a peg and opening the front door.

"Have a nice time, you two," Ruth called from the top of the stairs.

There was no escape—Dr. Ketter was at her side, and Ruth was descending the stairs. "As you wish," she murmured, walking out the door.

Dr. Ketter's voice droned in the background as they walked the short distance to the church. Meanwhile, Daughtie's mind was focused upon Liam. How had he coped with the babies last night? Did he get any sleep? Her concerns had caused her to choose the Methodist church this morning because their services began earlier. The preacher served both the Lowell and Belvedere Methodist churches, which left no choice but to have services earlier in one of the communities. Lowell had drawn the short straw. Daughtie had taken advantage of the schedule with the hope of reaching Liam's house as early as possible. However, if she was going to free herself of Dr. Ketter's company, a plan would be necessary—of that, there was little doubt. Thus far, Dr. Ketter appeared unwilling to accept her rejection.

"Are you going to answer me?" Ivan inquired in a loud voice as they walked up the steps of the white wood-frame church.

"What?" She turned to face him, a puzzled look upon her face.

"You haven't heard a word I've said, have you?"

"I told you I wouldn't be good company," she replied distractedly.

"Obviously you're intent upon proving your point," he said, his tone accusatory.

The two of them stood in the vestibule as the members of the congregation strained to hear the couple's conversation while moving past them on their way into the sanctuary.

"Could you please keep your voice down? I really don't want to share this conversation with every person attending church services this morning," she said from between clenched teeth.

"Perhaps you'd prefer if I just left," he fired back.

"Suit yourself. You're not here at my invitation." She turned on her heel and walked into the sanctuary.

Ivan didn't follow. Although his presence was unwanted, she felt a twinge of guilt for exhibiting bad manners. She abhorred rude behavior. She bowed her head. *I'm asking your forgiveness, Lord. I was rude and behaved like a petulant child,* she silently prayed while the congregation rose and began to sing. "And I promise to apologize to Dr. Ketter," she muttered aloud before joining in to sing the chorus.

The minute services ended, Daughtie darted from her

pew and down the aisle. She willed herself to maintain a modicum of restraint as she greeted the preacher in her most cordial voice. Holding her head high, she sauntered out the front door and down the street in a most dignified manner. Rounding the corner and finding the street deserted, she abandoned modesty, hiked her skirt, and bolted off toward Liam's house. She slowed only occasionally to glance over her shoulder, assuring herself she wasn't being followed.

Bounding up the front steps, she hesitated just long enough to catch her breath and then rapped on the front door. It seemed an eternity before Liam peeked out from behind the opaque lace curtain that covered the oval-shaped glass in the walnut door.

He opened the door only wide enough for Daughtie to slip through. "Hurry," he commanded, nearly closing the door on her skirt while pulling her forward. "You weren't followed, were ya?"

"No. I was careful. Besides, folks are still at church."

"You're not," he replied, obviously unwilling to accept her simple explanation.

She pushed back the hood of her cloak and placed her Bible on a small cherrywood table near the foot of the stairs. "The streets were deserted, but I did keep a watchful eye," she said while removing her cloak. The sound of crying immediately captured her attention, and she glanced up the stairway. "Did the babies sleep last night?"

Liam gave her a weary smile. "No—and neither did I. Just as well, though, since the rest of the slaves arrived in the middle of the night. I don't know if I would have heard them had I been sleepin' soundly."

"Wonderful! I'm pleased you had help with the babies."

"Help? Those poor people were so exhausted I couldn't have possibly asked any of them to stay awake with those cryin' babes. I'm thinkin' the twins are sufferin' with what my mother called a sour stomach. Do ya think maybe the goat's milk isn't agreein' with them and that's the cause of all their discomfort?"

"Colic may very well be the problem. Let's have a look at them." Taking the lead, she hurried up the steps, the sound of the babies' cries growing louder as she neared the bedroom. Opening the door, she hurried to the babies and lifted one of them into her arms. "He's drawing his legs up as though he's having stomach pain," she said. "How long since you fed them?"

"About an hour. They shouldn't be hungry."

The muffled sound of a baby's cry in the next room caused Daughtie to turn toward Liam. "Another one?"

He nodded. "The woman that was with them has a babe—a little girl. I'd guess her to be six months old, maybe a little less."

"I think God has answered my prayers. He's sent us a wet nurse for the twins! Where is she?"

Liam nodded toward the door. "The far bedroom— across the hall," he said. "But she's likely tryin' to sleep."

"Well, her baby's awake, so I'm sure she'll be up and about. Do they know about the twins?"

"They questioned whether their friend had arrived. I told them she had and that she'd given birth, but that's all. We didn't talk much. I gave them food, put the men and boys in one bedroom and her in the other. Thought I could be hidin' them better today. I didn't figure anyone would come snoopin' around last night."

"I think those runaway slave hunters come looking any time of the day or night. You're fortunate they didn't appear during the night—or early this morning. It's probably more important the runaways are in a safe hiding place; they can always sleep once they're in a secure place. Why don't you go and instruct the men? I want to talk to the girl. I'll tell her about the twins and see if I can convince her to nurse them. Once she knows her friend has died, I'm certain she'll want to help," Daughtie replied, striding off toward the room with one of the twins in her arm. She tapped on the door and waited a moment before turning the knob and entering.

"Who's you?" the wide-eyed girl asked while shrinking back into one corner of the room. The young woman's ebony skin glistened in the sunlight that now filled the room. A baby lay cradled in her arms, contentedly nursing at her breast.

Daughtie glanced toward the infant in her own arms and pulled the piece of swaddling away from his face. "He's only a day old. He has a brother—twins—born to your friend. I'm sorry to tell you she died after giving birth. Were you close?"

"Sistas. She was my sista," the girl replied, a tear rolling down her cheek. "Can you bring 'im closer?"

Daughtie drew nearer. "We've been feeding the boys milk from Mr. Donohue's goat. It doesn't seem to agree with them. Do you think you could . . ."

The girl nodded and formed her other arm into a cradle for the newborn. "You gonna let us take 'em wid us?"

Daughtie handed over the infant and smiled at the girl. "That's our hope. We were concerned you might not be able to take them. What's your name?"

The dark-skinned girl looked up at Daughtie, her eyes still wet with tears. "Dey call me Florie."

"I'm pleased to meet you, Florie. I'm Daughtie Winfield."

"Thankee, ma'am. Where's de odder one?" she asked, peering down at the baby.

"He's across the hall in Mr. Donohue's room. I don't want to overburden you with three babies. Is there anyone who will help?"

"My husband and my brodder are with de odder men.

They'll hep tote 'em. We got a far piece to go 'fore we get to safety?"

Daughtie nodded her head. "It's still quite a ways before you reach Canada, but I'm certain there are excellent safe houses on the remainder of your journey. I know you're going to reach freedom," Daughtie said, giving the girl an encouraging smile.

Florie didn't appear completely convinced as she placed her child on the bed and began nursing her newborn nephew. "Ain't gonna be easy keeping three babies quiet. Appears we gonna need a lot of hep from de Almighty if we gonna make it."

Daughtie gave the girl a gentle smile. "If it's any consolation to you, I'll be praying for all of you, Florie."

CHAPTER 23

London

Addie fluttered into the parlor while tucking a wisp of hair behind one ear. "John, I've been sorting through our things, and we really need to finish packing our trunk. Why don't you put down that book and come help me," she urged, a rosy hue coloring her plump cheeks.

Giving his wife a fleeting smile, John enveloped her hand in his own. "I don't believe there's a need to begin this flurry of activity so early in the evening. We'll have ample time later, my dear. Besides, I'm rather enjoying my book. I'd much prefer to have you sit with me and relax for a while."

"Really, John! You men just do not understand the amount of time it takes to properly arrange for a long journey. And then there's Elinor. I need to oversee her preparations. I simply can't wait to complete everything," she explained.

When she sat down beside him, John exclaimed, "Ah, good," and patted her hand as though he were patting the head of his favorite hunting dog.

"I haven't acquiesced, John. I thought perhaps you might reciprocate my altruistic behavior if I sat with you for a while."

"I see," John replied. "It would seem your behavior is less than altruistic, then, isn't it?" he asked with a grin.

"I suppose it is," she replied with a giggle. "But do say I've been successful in gaining your assistance."

"How could I possibly refuse you after such honesty? Just let me finish this chapter, and we'll go upstairs."

Addie leaned her head against his shoulder and compliantly waited while he finished reading, her mind racing with all she must accomplish before they sailed. She jarred to attention the moment John snapped the book together.

"Ready?" he asked.

"Absolutely!" She moved off toward the stairway, glancing back to assure herself he was really following. "I can hardly wait to see Mintie. It seems ages since I've shared a cup of tea with her."

John gave a hearty laugh. "How can you miss the old girl? You receive at least one letter a week telling you every scrap of gossip that's occurring in Lowell. I dare say, I doubt you've missed out on one jot of chitchat since we departed."

"Well, that's true enough, but sitting down and talking over a cup of tea is quite different from receiving a letter. Besides, Mintie's my sister, my only living relative. She can be cantankerous, but I still love and miss her."

"I find it's been easier to accept Mintie's shortcomings since we've been in England. I fear once we set foot in Lowell, your sister's overbearing attitude will become more annoying. What does she say about Lawrence Gault? Is he still calling on her? The man must be a saint—or a fool; I haven't decided which. I can't imagine why he'd put himself through such torture. After all, there's many a woman in Lowell who would treat him like a king."

Addie turned to face John at the top of the stairs. "Mintie has mentioned Mr. Gault from time to time, but she hasn't said enough to make me think he's become a steady suitor. But who knows? She may want to surprise us. She may be wearing a ring by the time we arrive back in Lowell."

John reached up and scratched his head. "For Lawrence's sake, let's hope not."

"That's not a very nice thing to say," Addie chided gently.

"Hmm. Perhaps not, but at least it was truthful. Now, what is it you're expecting to accomplish before bedtime? And what's all that giggling down the hall?"

"I set Bella and Elinor to work before I came downstairs. They're busy sorting through Elinor's belongings. Once they've set things aside, I'll go through them one final time before packing her trunk."

"Seems it would save time to just let her pack. Why do *you* need to go through everything?"

Addie glanced toward the ceiling. How could she possibly make a man understand that a young girl could not be left to her own devices at such an early age? "She'll be packing nothing but bric-a-brac and leaving all her important belongings behind."

John shrugged his shoulders. "She has Bella helping her, and if she forgets something, we can replace it when she gets to Lowell."

She shook her head. "You don't understand—there are some things that can't be replaced, John. It will be best for me to help."

"I suppose that's up to you, but I still think you could save yourself time and effort by allowing them to complete the job they've started. In any event, it sounds as though they're enjoying themselves."

Elinor held up a moth-eaten woolen shawl and giggled. "Shall I take this, Bella?"

Bella laughed at the sight. "I think that wrap has out-lived its usefulness."

"We could put it with the pile of belongings to be packed. It would likely prove interesting to hear Aunt Addie's reaction to my choice."

"No need to cause her undue anxiety. She's already worried we won't be prepared in time to sail, and she's most anxious to return home."

"I thought she liked England."

"She does, Elinor, but she misses being in her own home—and I'm sure she's longing to be reunited with her sister. They've never been separated for such a long time."

"Well, she seems rather old to be missing her sister," Elinor whispered.

Bella carefully folded a green plaid dress and placed it on top of several others. "Age doesn't diminish feelings for those we love. In fact, our affection for others usually increases as we grow older."

"Are you anxious to get back to those you love?"

"I suppose you could say that. I long to visit with my friend Daughtie. She's my dearest friend and I miss her."

"Who is it you're missing? Your husband, perhaps?"

Bella turned to see Taylor leaning in the doorway and graced him with a glowing smile. "I'm always pleased to see you, Taylor. However, I was telling Elinor that I miss visiting with Daughtie."

"I'm sure I can't take Daughtie's place, but I'd be pleased to spend the remainder of the evening visiting with you. Surely you two have done enough sorting and folding for one night."

"I doubt Aunt Addie would agree with you, but I can

work on my own until bedtime," Elinor replied.

"Do you mind if I leave you?" Bella inquired.

"Taylor will thrash me if I keep you here," she replied, then beamed a smile in her brother's direction.

"I appreciate your willingness to go on without me. Just don't place any more moth-eaten items with the clothes to be packed," Bella warned as she and Taylor exited the bedroom.

Taylor cocked an eyebrow. "What was *that* all about?"

"A little prank Elinor was plotting."

"I trust you discouraged her childish behavior."

Bella's lips turned up in a winsome smile. "We need to remember that she is only a child; she's bound to enjoy a little mischief from time to time. If memory serves me correctly, I participated in my share of childish behavior."

"You? Why, that's difficult to believe," Taylor said with a boisterous laugh. "Now, tell me, what is it you're so anxious to discuss with Daughtie?"

Bella walked to the dressing table and seated herself. "It's her most recent letters," she said, letting down her hair.

"All that business about the walkout?"

"No. Although I must admit I'm anxious to hear all of those details, too," she said, beginning to brush her hair in slow, methodical strokes. "My primary concern is that her letters are filled with talk of Liam Donohue. I had hoped she was going to take an interest in Ivan Ketter, the new doctor. I had a letter from Ruth, who says that Dr. Ketter is quite smitten with Daughtie. However, Daughtie continues to discourage his advances."

"Exactly what is it that concerns you?"

"Daughtie is helping Mr. Donohue furnish his house, choosing the draperies and furniture—that sort of thing. From the tone of her letters, it appears as if her visits to his home are the most important part of her life."

Taylor stroked his chin. "What would you have her write about? Her day-to-day life in the mill? I doubt either of you would find that very interesting. I imagine her jaunts to Liam's house are the bright spot in her life. She merely wants to share that with you."

Bella continued brushing her hair. "She invited him to attend a meeting at the Pawtucket church—and sat beside him."

"She attended a public meeting and sat beside a man. My, that is shameful. You would never have done such a thing, would you?" he asked with a grin.

Turning on her chair, Bella stared up at her husband. "He's an Irishman, Taylor. You understand the ramifications of such a relationship. Daughtie will be ostracized if she begins keeping company with him. Her letters sound as though she's developed feelings for him. It would be better if she directed her interests toward Dr. Ketter."

"I thought she wrote that she was attending the Blowing Out Ball with him."

Bella nodded. "Yes, that's true. Perhaps I am overreacting, but Ruth—"

"Don't take too much stock in what Ruth says. You've told me over and over again what a sensible girl Daughtie is. I doubt there's any more to this than her willingness to assist Liam. She's likely finding pleasure in the diversion. Liam's an honorable man, Bella. He knows Daughtie's unavailable—at least to him."

"But Daughtie believes all people are equal. She's studied her Bible, and since we've been in Lowell, she's forsaken much of the Shakers' doctrine. However, she still holds to their belief that God is the creator of all mankind. If she believes she's living what the Scriptures proclaim, she doesn't care what others think."

"Then why are you so concerned? Daughtie's capable of looking after herself."

"That's my point—she *isn't* capable of knowing exactly what such behavior could mean to her future. She could be fired from her job in the mills; *then* what would she do? I don't want her to ruin her future."

"You're worrying needlessly, my dear. We'll soon be home and you can express your concerns. However, you need to remember that Daughtie must make her own decisions."

"I understand, but I'll still be offering my guidance and— Who can that be?" Bella asked as loud knocks sounded at the front door, interrupting her midsentence.

Taylor shrugged his broad shoulders. "I don't think we were expecting anyone. I'm not certain whether Uncle John is still downstairs," Taylor said, striding toward the hallway. "I'll be back momentarily."

The sound of angry voices drifted up the stairs. Bella moved into the hallway, listened for a moment, and then tentatively edged down the steps. She stopped before reaching the bottom of the stairway, bewildered at the sight of two lawmen threatening to arrest her husband if he didn't immediately produce his uncle John.

"If you men will give me just a moment, I'll see if I can find him. I believe he's already retired for the night," Taylor explained.

"None of your excuses. We're here to arrest him, and we're prepared to search this entire house if necessary."

Bella could listen to no more. "My husband said he would go and fetch his uncle. I think you'll find that solution much more expedient than searching the house. Once you've met with Mr. Farnsworth, I'm certain you'll see there's some mistake."

"There's no mistake. John Farnsworth is guilty of crimes against the Crown. There's ample proof of his treason," one of the men replied before turning back toward

Taylor. "Now go and get him, or we'll take matters into our own hands."

Bella watched as Taylor hastened up the stairs. "And what are these charges against Uncle John?" Bella inquired, moving closer.

"We told you—treason," the other lawman answered irritably.

"Yes, but since you've already completed your investigation, I was wondering if you could explain the exact acts of treason of which he stands accused."

The two men glanced at each other. "We're not supposed to give details," one of them replied.

"Why not? Surely a bit of clarification isn't out of line. Who instructed you to withhold details?" Bella persisted.

"Our—our—the one who gives orders," the man stammered.

"The *investigator*," the other interjected while nudging his companion in the side.

"I see. And what reason did he give for this admonition?" Bella inquired.

"He's not required to give a reason. We follow orders, and we were told to arrest John Farnsworth."

"Well, here I am," John said as he walked down the steps. "What's this all about?"

"You're under arrest for treason," one of the officers replied, thrusting several legal documents into John's hand. Without warning, the officer pulled John toward the door.

John swung around, the rapid motion releasing his arm from the hold. "I'm willing to go peacefully, but I want a moment to speak to my wife and nephew before departing. If you'll permit me this small concession, we can then leave."

One of the policemen nodded agreement as Addie came scurrying down the steps. "You're *not* going with them, John. You've done nothing to deserve this shoddy treatment. Tell these men to go away. Surely there are some dishonest scoundrels they should be arresting instead of harassing a decent law-abiding citizen."

"Now, now, my dear. We'll get this matter straightened out in due time," John reassured her as he pulled her into his arms. Reaching out, he drew Bella and Taylor near and lowered his voice to a whisper. "I want you to listen carefully. I want all of you on that ship tomorrow morning whether I'm able to join you or not. Taylor, I want you to take charge of the women should I be delayed."

"I'll not leave without you, John," Addie replied, tears beginning to trickle down her cheeks. "Please don't force me to go," she begged, taking his hand and pressing it to her lips.

"Don't cry, Addie dear. I'm hopeful this can be resolved in short order. If not, I need you to trust that I know what is best. I want you to promise me that you'll abide by my request."

"I feel totally helpless," Addie replied, her shoulders sagging as Bella pulled her into an embrace.

"We're never defenseless, Aunt Addie. We have the Lord, and we have the power of prayer."

John nodded his agreement. "Taylor, I'm not certain the paper work these men have shown me is authentic, but it's imperative you sail with the women as scheduled. Promise me you'll do as I've asked—no matter what happens."

"I promise, although if you haven't been released, I would prefer to remain in England and send the women on without me."

"No. I don't want them traveling across the ocean unaccompanied."

"If you're absolutely certain that's what you want, I'll conform to your wishes."

John patted Taylor on the shoulder. "Thank you, my

boy. It appears my escorts are growing anxious to depart. I'd best accommodate them before things become ugly. Bella, take care of Addie for me."

John leaned forward and kissed Addie. "Don't worry. I'll be back before you've time to know I'm gone."

The two lawmen followed John out the front door. He glanced over his shoulder at one of the men. "Which way?"

"To the right and down the alley."

The reply confirmed John's impression of these men. They weren't the police; the police wouldn't be escorting him down a dark alleyway; instead, they would lead him off to the nearest jail, most likely in a police wagon. He didn't know where these men were taking him, but he did know he must flee. If they managed to get him confined somewhere, he'd likely never free himself.

Slowing his gait, John turned toward the men, who were following close behind. "Why don't you take the lead? I'm having difficulty seeing in this shadowy alley."

One of the men grunted, and as he moved forward, John grasped his arm, propelling him into his companion with such force that they both plummeted to the ground. The moment the men were down, John ran off in the opposite direction as his mind scrambled with thoughts of where he might hide. He couldn't possibly return to the house; that would be the first place the men would expect him to hide. Although the homes of several acquaintances were nearby, he knew he dared not place his friends in jeopardy.

He continued running in a chaotic pattern until he finally neared the docks of the Thames. Hesitating only a moment, he surveyed the area and rushed onward. Lowering himself behind a mass of stacked cargo, he placed one hand over his pounding heart and waited until the rhythm slowed. When his breathing had finally returned to normal, John raised himself upward and peered around one of the stacks, his glance focused upon the ship docked nearest to where he stood. It was the *Liberty Queen*—the ship on which he had booked their return passage. Seeing no one in sight, John moved across the open expanse, careful to stay in the shadows. Certain he'd gone undetected, he stole on board the ship, waited momentarily, and then made his way below deck.

———

Morning came much too soon to suit Taylor. He hurried Bella and Elinor into their clothes, periodically stopping at the window to gaze into the streets below.

"Aunt Addie?" he called as he tapped on her door.

Addie appeared, her eyes red from crying. "Must we leave now? It's not even light."

"We have to go now or we'll never make it on time. The ship won't wait for us."

"But we could change the sailing to another ship—one leaving later," she challenged. But Taylor ignored the woman's pleas that he book passage on a later voyage, holding fast to the promise he'd made.

"We have to go, Addie. I've already arranged for the cab. The luggage is being loaded even now."

She nodded, tears threatening to spill again. "Very well."

It was difficult to convince his grandfather and grandmother that John had been called away unexpectedly and wouldn't be able to return to bid them good-bye. He assured them both, however, that John would be in touch soon and was profoundly sorry for such rude manners. Grandmother Cordelia eyed him suspiciously, making Taylor certain she knew something underhanded was afoot, but she said nothing.

"May God hide you all in the palm of His hand," his grandmother whispered. Taylor pulled away to meet her gaze, seeing by her resolve that she would also save Jarrow Farnsworth from any undue misery. "You will write?" she questioned.

He nodded. "Yes. As soon as I can."

Shafts of sunlight were just starting to glisten through the heavy fog as the party made their way to the awaiting carriage. Two men, who were stationed across the street, turned their backs when Taylor glanced in their direction, but he said nothing to the ladies about their surreptitious presence. He had noticed the men late last night while wandering about the house, unable to sleep. He'd seen that they were still there this morning every time he'd gone to check from the bedroom window. There was actually nothing to be done about it, but it did give Taylor cause to wonder. If the Crown was intent on arresting John, why were they having the house watched? They'd taken John to jail last night.

A thought came to mind that John might have escaped.

"They must be concerned he'll return to the house," Taylor muttered as he climbed the carriage steps.

"Did you say something?" Bella asked.

Taylor took the seat beside her. He momentarily considered explaining the situation, then decided against it. Calling attention to the fact that they were being watched would only serve to alarm Bella or Addie. And saying anything in front of Elinor would likely cause the girl to prattle on incessantly.

Keeping the surveillance issue to himself was judicious, yet he longed for someone to confide in. If John hadn't escaped, why was the family being watched? Since John was already in custody, was it possible the police had decided to arrest *him* for treason, also? Why else would these men continue observing them? He glanced over his shoulder as the carriage neared the docks. The men were nowhere in sight. Perhaps he had overreacted.

"Come along, ladies," he said, leading the three women on board and then, after receiving directions, escorting them to the first of the reserved cabins.

"This is the room Uncle John reserved for the two of you," he told Addie as he opened the door.

Addie glanced about and nodded her approval. "As soon as my trunk is available, I'll begin unpacking."

As Addie entered the room, a shuffling sound was followed by a deep groan. They watched, awestruck, as John unfolded his body from a small cloth-covered nook at one end of the bed, the disheveled piece of cloth hanging from his shoulders like an ill-fitting mantle.

"John!" Addie cried, hurrying forward to embrace her husband. "How did you get here?"

"No time to explain right now," he said while returning her embrace. "I'm guessing my captors are already on board ship searching for me."

"So *that's* why those men were outside watching the house all night," Taylor exclaimed. "I feel certain they followed us to the wharf, although I didn't catch sight of them."

"Men were watching the house and you said nothing?" Bella questioned in anger.

"We'll discuss it later," Taylor insisted. "Right now other matters are more pressing."

John nodded. "There's no time to waste, my boy. Why don't you see if you can search out a hiding place and perhaps find something to help me disguise myself? Then get back here as soon as possible."

"I'll see what I can locate. If you're forced to answer the door, be certain Uncle John is well hidden," Taylor told Addie before motioning toward his sister. "Elinor, you stand in front of that nook with your skirt spread wide to help camouflage the area, should the need arise, and remain calm," he instructed before striding out of the cabin.

Avoiding several deckhands, Taylor made his way through the narrow passages below decks, noting several places where John might safely hide. He paused and glanced about before stealing into a large area that was obviously used by the sailors for sleeping. Stacked beneath the hammocks, he discovered items of worn clothing that likely belonged to the sailors who were now hoisting sails above deck. Choosing a frayed shirt, knitted Monmouth cap, checkered neck square, and a pair of canvas trousers, Taylor slipped the items beneath his arm and hurried back toward the cabin.

He knocked on the door several times. "It's me," he finally announced through the closed door.

Bella opened the door only a crack before peering into the hallway, a questioning look etched upon her face.

"I'm alone," Taylor said.

Opening the door only wide enough to permit her husband entry, Bella took the clothing and handed it to John.

"Why don't you ladies take a stroll down the passageway while I change into these clothes?" John suggested. "Taylor can remain with me in the event someone should appear at the door."

John quickly changed into the garments. "I'll wait until the women return before I depart. Addie will be unhappy if I hurry off without a word. These breeches obviously belong to someone shorter than I," he said while tugging at the waist.

"I'm sorry. It's the best I could do with so little time to choose."

"No need to apologize, my boy. This is excellent," John replied. He was pulling the knitted woolen cap down over his thatch of graying hair when the women returned.

Addie gave her husband an appraising look. "You make a convincing sailor, my dear."

A loud knock sounded, and John nodded for Taylor to open the door. The captain stood centered between two broad-shouldered men dressed as police officers. Taylor immediately recognized them as the men who had been watching the house. "Gentlemen, what can I do for you?" he inquired with a false sense of bravado. Taylor noticed that his uncle had turned his back to the door and busied himself with something.

"We'd like to search this cabin. The police tell me they're looking for John Farnsworth. My manifest shows he and his wife are assigned to this cabin. They'd like to satisfy themselves that he's not here."

Addie stepped forward. "I'm Mrs. Farnsworth. Surely you know that two of your fellow policemen were at the home of my father-in-law last night and took my husband into custody."

One of the officers pushed the captain aside, his gaze darting from person to person as he pressed through the doorway. "Who might you be?" the officer inquired, his gaze resting upon Taylor.

"Taylor Manning, the nephew of John Farnsworth," he replied with a note of pride.

The captain moved forward, the room now filled to capacity. "And what are you doing in here?" the captain inquired of John while the two men in police uniform searched under the bed and in the tiny closet. "I haven't seen you before. Are you Cookie's new helper?"

"We have some special problems with my aunt's diet and asked to speak to the cook," Taylor replied before John could answer. "This man was sent to pass along the information to your cook."

"I'm surprised Cookie is willing to consider a special request. Gauging from past experience, don't be surprised if he immediately dismisses your demands," the captain said, his gaze directed toward Addie. "Of course, a few coins might change his mind."

"I'll find a way to manage if he's unable to accommodate my needs," Addie responded sweetly.

"Well, then, have you finished with him?"

Taylor nodded. "I believe so."

"Then you best get back to the galley. Cookie will be needing your help," the captain ordered John.

"Aye," John replied, edging through the group and making a hasty exit.

Taylor turned his attention to the captain. "If there's nothing further, I'd like to leave my aunt to rest, and I imagine these police officers would like to disembark before we set sail."

The captain glanced toward the two men.

"We'll be going ashore; however, I would ask that you keep a watch out for Farnsworth, Captain. Should he appear, I'd request that you place him in chains and keep him on board until you return to England," one of the men replied.

The captain's forehead creased with his eyebrows knitting into a tight woolly row. "I'll do my best, but I'm not making any promises. I've a ship and passengers that need my attention while we're at sea. If you still believe Mr. Farnsworth is aboard, I'd suggest you purchase passage and seek him out. Then you'll have ample time to search every nook and cranny of the ship," he said with a loud guffaw.

"Since we can't leave our posts, I fear we must rely on you and your men for assistance. Perhaps you'd be willing to inform your men that there will be a tidy bounty offered to the man who brings Farnsworth back to us?"

"And what about the ship's captain? Will there be a reward for him, also?"

"Of course, my good man. We wouldn't expect you to

haul a criminal across the ocean without recompense."

"In that case, I'll be certain my men are aware of the possibility that Farnsworth is a stowaway," the captain replied as they turned and walked down the passageway.

All color drained from Taylor's face. He closed the door and waited a moment before turning toward the women. "I'll be back shortly. With the promise of a reward, every man on this ship will be on the lookout for Uncle John. I must get word to him."

CHAPTER 24

William Thurston stood beside a stack of crates along the wharf, watching as two of his hirelings, known to him only as Hobbs and Jones, disembarked the *Liberty Queen*. They were alone. He felt the blood rise in his cheeks. Incompetent fools!

The men skulked toward him like two disobedient schoolchildren. "Where's Farnsworth?" he seethed.

"He's nowhere to be found on that ship. We searched it high and low—even had the captain helping us in our attempt to locate him."

"I *know* he's on that ship," Thurston fumed.

"You can go and look for yourself, Mr. Thurston, but you'll not find him, either. The man's vanished into thin air. My guess is that some friend of the family has hidden him, or he may be hiding in his father's house," Hobbs said.

"I'm not interested in what you think. His father's home has been thoroughly searched. Besides, Farnsworth wants to get out of England, and I *know* he's on that ship!" Thurston insisted.

Jones shrugged his shoulders and began to turn away. "Maybe you should go on board and see if you have any better luck finding him. We told the captain you'd pay a reward if anyone was able to find and capture Farnsworth."

William's irritation increased as he watched the two men walk off without another word. "Slackers! I should have saved my money and done the job myself," he muttered as he neared the ship.

"Where d'ya think you're going?" a raggedy-appearing sailor shouted at William when he reached the top of the gangplank and attempted to board the ship.

"Step aside," William commanded.

"Can't let anyone except passengers on board. We'll soon be casting off. Captain's orders."

"I *must* come on board," William insisted.

"Not unless you're a passenger," the sailor repeated.

Making a hasty retreat down the gangplank, William rushed into one of the many shipping offices that lined the wharf. "I need to purchase passage on the *Liberty Queen,*" he called out to a clerk sitting at his ledgers.

"Hasn't she sailed yet?" the young man inquired, slipping off his stool and moving toward a window.

William pushed the clerk back to the desk. "No, and I need to purchase passage immediately—before she sails. Hurry!"

The clerk peered across the desk with a look of irritation as he took Thurston's payment. "There'll be no refunds if she sails without you," he called as Thurston hurried out of the office.

William didn't answer. He was certain there would be sufficient time to search the ship, find John Farnsworth, and return to dry land before the ship sailed. He'd worry about recouping his fare when Farnsworth was in his grasp. The same raggedy sailor met him as he attempted once again to board the ship. With a smug grin, he waved his passage papers in the air and pushed past the man.

"We're setting sail any minute now," the sailor called after him.

William turned, his lips curved into a wry grin. "You gave me that same information fifteen minutes ago, and you still haven't set sail," he replied before stalking off to begin his search.

"Don't say you wasn't warned," the sailor bellowed.

William didn't reply, his gaze darting about the ship for some sign of the elusive Farnsworth. He made a wide turn to go down the steps and check the cabins when he spotted a tall man leaning on the ship's railing facing the dock. Farnsworth! He moved forward, his focus steadied upon the tall lean figure with graying hair. As he grew nearer, a young woman with her skirts billowing in the breeze and a small child at her side blocked his path. He could no longer see Farnsworth, and by the time he'd gotten the woman and child out of his way, his quarry had slipped away.

William hurried to the rail, his gaze flitting about as he surveyed the amassed passengers. He caught a glimpse of Farnsworth going below decks and followed at breakneck speed. However, a sailor was coming up the steps as William approached. "Best slow down, sir. The steps are wet and we don't want you falling."

William gritted his teeth. Who did this insolent tar blocking the stairway think he was? He wanted to shove the sailor aside but knew he dared not lose his temper. "I'll do my best," he said, forcing a smile.

The moment the sailor stepped aside, William fled down the stairs. Farnsworth had once again eluded him! He walked through the ship's passageway and then slowly retraced his steps. He heard the orders to cast off, and the ship lurched slightly as it began to move away from the dock. Mounting the steps two at a time, he reached the deck and once again his gaze locked upon Farnsworth at the railing. This time he headed straight for his prey and in a swift, calculated motion, William grasped the man's arm and pulled it back in a painful twisting motion.

Yelling in pain, the man attempted to turn toward his assailant as the ship lurched unexpectedly. Breaking Thurston's hold, the man gave a shove and pinned Thurston against the ship's railing.

The man appeared incredulous. "What are you doing?" he screamed while staring into Thurston's bulging eyes.

"I thought you were someone else," Thurston hoarsely whispered.

The man shoved William away from him. "Next time you decide to accost someone, make sure you've found the proper person."

"My sincere apologies," William said. "If there's anything I can do to—"

"Just stay away from me for the remainder of the voyage," the man said in a warning tone.

"I'm not making the voyage to America. I merely came on board to find a man who's hiding on board—he's done me a grave injustice. In fact, you resemble him, and that's why I acted in such haste. Once again, I do apologize."

The man shook his head. "It appears to me you *will* be making the journey," he said while pointing his thumb toward the dock, which was growing more and more distant as they talked.

Forgetting his apology, Thurston rushed toward the ship's railing. The sailor who'd forced him to purchase passage nodded toward land with a smug look etched upon his face. "Guess you'll be sailing with us, Mate," he said with a snigger.

"I want off this ship," Thurston angrily commanded.

"Unless you plan on swimming for land, I'd say the next time you get off this ship you'll be setting foot in Massachusetts."

"You go and tell the captain I *must* return," William insisted.

The sailor bellowed a loud guffaw. "Tell him yourself, mister."

William watched the sailor walk away, an insolent swagger in his step. "I'll report you to the captain," he hollered.

The sailor pulled his knitted cap from his head and waved it in the air. "You do that. Tell the captain I wasn't willing to bother him with nonsense about dropping anchor for someone who knew we were setting sail. If I know the captain, he'll toss you overboard," he replied in a loud voice.

Many of the passengers had stopped, listening to the barbed exchange, their gazes flitting back and forth between the two men as they argued. William felt the heat rise in his cheeks. He disliked being made the fool in front of one person, much less a crowd.

He glanced about the group and then gave them a dismissive wave. "You'd just as well go on about your business. There's nothing more to see or hear." A few passengers walked away, but most remained, staring at him and waiting for the next lick of excitement he might send their way.

Wending his way through the curious assembly, William's anger continued to mount. *Why won't they just go away!* A seaman was in front of Thurston, but when he didn't move rapidly enough, William gave him a hefty shove and continued off toward the stairway. He held his shoulders straight and head high until he was securely inside his cabin. Then, behind the closed door, he vented his rage, yelling in anguish as he hurled the few unbolted furnishings into the walls.

When his anger had finally subsided, he picked up the husk-filled mattress and threw it back across the ropes attached to the wood frame bolted to the wall. He'd broken the only chair in the room. Disgusted he now had no place to sit, he flung himself onto the bed, weary from a day that had gone amiss at every turn. He was on a ship with little money and no personal belongings, not even a change of clothes. Soon he would be in Boston—a place he dare not be seen. If even one of the Boston Associates should gain knowledge he was back in the country, there would be a manhunt to see that he was placed behind bars. Of that fact, there was no doubt! He would have to carefully lay his plans before the ship docked.

A soft knocking at the cabin door caused Taylor to look up from his reading. "I'll answer," he said, placing his book aside. "Uncle John," he uttered as the older man slipped through the open door and then leaned against it, his breathing rapid and his complexion a pasty white. "You look as though you've seen the devil."

John loosed the checkered kerchief from around his neck and wiped the sweat from his brow. "If not the devil, then one of his faithful followers," John replied.

Bella set her stitching aside and stared at John. "You're not making any sense. Whom are you referring to?"

"William Thurston."

"On this ship? Surely not," Taylor replied.

John narrowed his eyes. "I know William Thurston, and he *is* on this ship. He pushed me out of his way only minutes ago."

"He's seen you?" Taylor asked, his voice tinged with concern.

"No. He was too busy attempting to get below decks to his cabin. There's no doubt in my mind he's behind this whole charade of having me arrested by those hooligans who pretended to be police. I'd venture to say that those men with the captain this morning weren't truly policemen, either. They're probably a couple more of Thurston's hired thugs."

Bella frowned. "Exactly what is Mr. Thurston hoping to gain through all of this?"

"I suppose he's seeking to earn himself a place of prestige among propertied Englishmen since he's no longer welcome in America. If Thurston has successfully convinced them I'm a traitor and can hand me over to these men, he'll gain gratitude and respectability."

Taylor nodded. "I agree, Uncle John. He's likely told them a pack of lies in order to persuade them you're a traitor and has probably promised to deliver you as a token of his goodwill. I can just hear him telling all those stiff-necked aristocrats how much he loves the homeland."

"Not to mention the fact that he's probably counting on a tidy sum for capturing a treacherous villain such as I."

"But it appears his plan has gone awry. Surely he didn't plan on sailing to America."

John moved away from the door and seated himself. He had finally regained some color in his cheeks. "You're right, but he waited too long and was unable to disembark. Now he finds himself in a quandary. Taylor, you're going to have to talk with the captain. Explain what occurred back in Massachusetts, including the fact that William Thurston escaped a couple years ago, evading just punishment for his heinous crimes. And since the captain believes those men were truly the police, you'll need to be at your most eloquent."

Taylor smiled broadly. "I'll do my best. Perhaps it would be wise to schedule an appointment with the captain. Arranging a definite time to meet would ensure an adequate period in which to explain our dilemma."

"Excellent! You're already planning a strategy. I believe you'll be able to handle this matter in fine fashion. As for me, I believe I'll go and visit with Addie in our cabin. I'll await word from you."

"No need postponing matters. I believe I'll go and see the captain now. Perhaps he'll have time to visit with me today," Taylor said while straightening his cravat.

Bella picked up her stitching, her lips turned upward in an endearing smile as she gazed at her husband. "I think that's a prudent decision," she agreed.

While mounting the steps and striding toward the captain's quarters, Taylor began formulating his plea. His argument must be incisive, for without the captain's assistance, they would be helpless in gaining control over Thurston and having him placed under arrest once they arrived in Boston. Surely the captain would be willing to assist in bringing his reluctant passenger to justice once he realized the fact that Thurston had been the primary architect of kidnappings and thievery in Lowell.

Taylor knocked on the cabin door and then waited a few nervous moments until the captain shouted for him to enter. "Good day to you, Captain. I'm Taylor Manning, one of your passengers."

"What can I do for you, Mr. Manning?"

Taylor met the commander's gaze. "I'll need an hour or so of your time to totally explain my dilemma," Taylor explained. "I wanted to see if you might have that much free time available today or tomorrow."

The captain cleared his throat and leaned back in his leather-covered chair. "Must be a mighty thorny issue if it's going to take you an hour to state your case."

Nodding in agreement, Taylor said, "It's complex, and I don't want to leave you with unanswered questions."

The captain gave him a lopsided grin. "You've managed to rouse my interest. I've got time right now. Why don't you take a seat over there and begin telling me your story."

Taylor's lips twitched nervously. "Now?"

The captain pointed to the empty chair. "No time like the present. Sit down."

————————

"You've already talked to the captain?" John asked in an incredulous tone.

Taylor smiled at his uncle, unable to hide his pleasure. "Yes. And he's agreed to help us."

John pulled Taylor into a husky embrace. "I'm proud of you, my boy. Has the captain secured Thurston in chains?"

"No. He explained that Thurston had taken to his room, and since there was no place for him to go, he'd wait until we docked to take him into custody and place him in irons. If William remains unsuspecting, there should be no problem; at least that's what the captain believes."

"I'd prefer he be placed in shackles right now," John replied.

Taylor nodded. "I attempted to convince the captain. However, he feared the passengers would be unduly upset by the tumult. He thought it best to wait."

"Well, we'll abide by his decision. I'm just thankful you were successful in winning over the captain. You performed admirably."

Taylor beamed. "Thank you, Uncle John."

CHAPTER 25

Boston Harbor
May

Taylor moved away from the crowd of passengers beginning to gather on deck. The sun was shining brightly as the *Liberty Queen* neared Boston's harbor. He wanted to ensure William Thurston was detained before the ship docked. The captain clenched an unlit pipe in his fist as he moved about the deck of the ship shouting orders to his crew.

"Good morning," Taylor greeted as he approached the captain. "I was wondering if it might be wise to take Mr. Thurston into custody before we docked."

The captain turned his attention to Taylor. "Glad you reminded me. I had nearly forgotten our unwelcome passenger."

With no more than a nod of his head and a wave of one hand, several sailors scurried to the captain's side. He issued their instructions and soon they were all outside the door of William Thurston's cabin. The captain knocked, waited, and then knocked once again. When there was no sound from within, he unlatched the door.

"He's gone," one of the swabbies announced. He spoke the words as though the others would not realize the cabin was empty without his verbal declaration.

"Search the ship. I want him found," the captain commanded.

Taylor stared after the sailors as they scurried from the cabin. He dreaded taking the news to his uncle, but the older man was awaiting word of Thurston's detainment. No doubt he would grow concerned if Taylor didn't soon return.

He entered John and Addie's cabin and gave his uncle a feeble smile. "It appears Thurston has eluded us. He's obviously hiding on board somewhere, but he's not in his cabin."

John rubbed his forehead while listening to the news. "Just as I feared. That scoundrel should have been placed in shackles when he was first discovered on board."

"We'll hope they locate him before we disembark," Taylor replied.

"I don't hold out much hope they'll be successful," John put in.

"If not, we'll notify the authorities here in Boston when we go ashore. Perhaps if we offered a reward, the sailors would continue searching for him after we dock," Taylor suggested.

"If the crew doesn't find him before we dock, ask the captain if he'll notify his men we've posted a reward, and if found, Thurston should be delivered to the police," John replied. "I'd much prefer to remain in Boston until he's arrested, but I know the women are going to want to be on the first canal boat to Lowell. Once we've talked to the authorities, we'll depart."

Lowell

Daughtie edged her way down the spiral staircase of the Appleton and into the mill yard, anxious to return home to supper and a quiet evening. Perhaps there would be a letter from Bella waiting for her. During the noonday meal, Mrs. Arnold had mentioned that she would stop and check the afternoon mail. The thought of a letter caused Daughtie's step to quicken as she passed through the gate and turned toward the boardinghouse.

"A message for ya, ma'am." The young Irish girl who had once before come to fetch her now impatiently tugged at Daughtie's arm. The girl's wary gaze darted about in every direction before finally settling upon Daughtie. With deliberate determination, she shoved the piece of paper into Daughtie's hand and hurried off in the direction of Liam's house.

"Was that an *Irish* girl?"

Daughtie startled at the sound of Ruth's voice. "You frightened me. It's impolite to sneak up on people," she chastised while continuing her rapid pace toward home.

"Sneak up? I walk home with you three times a day, six days a week. I would think you'd be expecting to see me," Ruth rebutted. "What did the girl want? I saw her say something to you. She was over here begging, wasn't she? We ought to turn her in to the overseer or tell Mr. Gault down in the office. Those Irish vagrants aren't permitted to come over to this side of town and beg. You didn't give her any coins, did you? If so, she'll be waiting outside the gate for you every day."

"No, I didn't give her anything," Daughtie tersely responded.

"There's no need to become haughty. I was merely looking out for your best interests. I know how you tend to take pity on every pathetic creature you encounter, and

I don't want the girl taking advantage of your kind nature."

Daughtie ascended the steps leading to the front door of the boardinghouse. "Thank you, Ruth, but I do believe I can take care of myself. And it's not my nature that causes me to take pity on the less fortunate; it's the love of God. The Bible says we should be kind to one another."

"But she's not one of us," Ruth said sternly as she pushed open the front door. "She's Irish."

"I am quite certain that I've never yet seen a verse in Scripture telling me to be kind to everyone but the Irish."

Both girls were met with the inquisitive stares of half a dozen people. The parlor was filled with Dr. Ketter's patients, all of whom appeared immensely interested in the girls' conversation. Daughtie ignored the obvious interest, her gaze focused instead upon the candle table near the foot of the stairway, where she spotted a letter. Moving quickly, she picked up the missive and read the inscription. It was a letter from Bella.

"Oh, Daughtie, I'm pleased to see you. I'm running behind with my patients. Could you possibly assist me?" Dr. Ketter inquired expectantly.

"I'm sorry, but that's impossible, Dr. Ketter. I'm going to have a quick bite of supper and be on my way—errands. I'm sure Ruth would be most pleased to help, wouldn't you, Ruth?"

Ruth appeared surprised by Daughtie's suggestion. "I thought you planned to stay in and do your mending and read this evening."

"My plans have changed," she replied. "If you'll excuse me, I want to read Bella's letter and be on my way within the hour." Without waiting for a response, she raced up the stairs and unfolded the note delivered by the Irish girl.

As she'd expected, the missive requested she come to Liam's house at the earliest possible moment. Tucking Bella's letter into her reticule, she hurried back down the stairs and into the kitchen, and with Mrs. Arnold's permission, helped herself to a piece of ham and a slice of thick, warm bread.

"Cut yourself a slice of apple pie," Mrs. Arnold instructed considerately.

Daughtie nodded and helped herself to a thick piece of the fruit-filled pastry. "I'll eat it on the way. I promise to return your napkin," she said, folding the checkered square cloth around the pie.

Mrs. Arnold gave her a cheerful smile. "That'll be fine," the older woman replied as Daughtie rushed back down the hallway and out the front door.

Fortunately, Ruth was nowhere to be seen. Either she was in Dr. Ketter's office assisting him, or she'd gone upstairs. Regardless, Daughtie had been able to make her exit without an explanation or argument, and for that she was most thankful. The evening air was warm and thick with the scents of budding lilac and honeysuckle. She breathed deeply to enjoy the spring aroma as she hurried onward. Finally reaching Liam's house, she raced up the front steps and knocked on the door, her heart pounding with excitement and fear.

The door opened and Liam smiled down at her. "Come in."

"More runaway slaves?" she whispered.

He nodded. "Aye, but no babes," he replied with a wan smile. "Only two lasses. The rest were restrained by their owners sometime yesterday."

"How many did they manage to recapture?"

"Six—all men and lads. The girls are thinkin' their owner quit searchin' for them once he had the men back in his possession. They didn't see any sign they were bein' followed last night or today. I've got them hidden in the upstairs room. I was expectin' them to arrive last night and feared something had gone wrong. And for sure, when the girls arrived, they were confirmin' my fears. Doesn't seem many of them are bein' liberated," Liam lamented.

Daughtie could see the anguish in his expression and took his hand in her own. "I understand your feeling of helplessness, but we must remain positive and celebrate the fact that at least some of them are reaching freedom."

"I know ya're right, but those poor girls are worried sick about their friends and family. They know what 'appens to runaways when they're recaptured. And now I must pass along more bad news."

"What do you mean? What's happened?"

"These girls and the rest of their group were expected last night. I was to be deliverin' them to me contact a short distance north of Lowell. When they didn't appear, I met up with me contact to tell him of the situation. He said the group had likely been recaptured."

"And? Didn't he realize they might only have been detained? Did he tell you what to do if they arrived?"

Liam shook his head. "No. I should've been askin', but I wasn't thinkin' straight. He seemed nervous and was anxious to be goin' on his way. Now I don't know what I'm to do with these girls. I don't know the proper route they're to take, and there's no man to travel along with them. The only instructions I've ever had were to either deliver them to their next contact or give instructions to the next safe house."

"Can't you do that? Direct them to the next safe house?"

"The safe houses change frequently. We're given new instructions each time a group is expected. My house isn't used every time runaways come this direction. It would be too risky for them to always move in the same direction and to use the same houses. So I'd be needin' to have some assurance they'll reach safety before I send them on."

"You're right, of course," she said as she began to wring

her hands, attempting to contemplate their options. "I think we need to pray."

Liam's eyes widened, apparently startled by her pronouncement. "Pray? Here? Now?"

Her lips curved into a gentle smile. "Yes, here and now."

"Ya're beginnin' to think ya shouldn't be involved in such a thing as this, aren't ya?"

"No, not at all, but I *am* feeling as though we need divine intervention to find a solution. It's clear neither of us knows what to do."

"'Tis true that a little help from above couldn't hurt. I'm thinkin' ya know more about what God might be wantin' to hear, so you go ahead and pray. I'll listen and agree," he said with a grin.

"There aren't any set rules about prayer, Liam. God wants to hear whatever is in your heart; how we say it doesn't really matter."

"Maybe so, but I'd still prefer you do the talkin'."

She nodded her agreement, bowed her head, and asked God to send them a plan, some resolution that would protect all of them.

"That's it?" he asked when she'd whispered a soft amen.

"Did I forget something?"

Liam wagged his head back and forth. "No. It's just that your prayin' was kind of simple."

"The Shakers taught me to be simple and direct; I carry that same concept into my prayers. I like to believe God appreciates the fact that He doesn't have to sift through all the inconsequential words before getting to the heart of my supplications—not that He doesn't already know my needs," she added.

"So if He already knows what ya're needin', why do ya pray?" Liam inquired.

"Because God's Word instructs us to pray. Even Jesus prayed to the Father."

Liam rubbed his forehead, a confused look in his eyes. "So ya pray in order to let God know ya're doin' what the Bible instructs, which is countin' on Him to solve your problems, even though He already knows what's goin' on before ya pray?"

Daughtie reflected on Liam's statement for a moment. "God is certainly all-knowing. He *could* solve our problems without hearing our prayers, but He created man for communion. Prayer is our way to fellowship with God."

"I can understand the Almighty wantin' to hear from a sweet lady like yarself, but why would He want to hear the blatherin' of an ungodly Irishman?"

"Because He loves you, Liam. It's God's fondest desire that every man love Him in return. God *wants* to bless all of our lives, but many refuse Him. They miss out on the wondrous gift of His love and protection. Isn't that sad?"

"Are ya tryin' to make a point with me, lassie?"

Giving him a gentle smile, Daughtie nodded. "I don't want you to miss *any* of the blessings God has stored up for you, Liam. I know you're a decent man, but doing good deeds and caring about others won't gain you access into God's kingdom."

He appeared puzzled by her words. "I thought that's what godly people were supposed to be doin'—helpin' the poor and downtrodden."

"Yes, of course they are. Good deeds are exactly that— a way of ministering to our fellow man. But that's all they are—charitable acts, not a key to eternity with our Heavenly Father," she explained.

"What more *am* I to do?"

"You must acknowledge that Jesus is the Son of God, confess your sins and ask His forgiveness, and invite Him into your life, Liam," she explained.

He remained silent for a moment and then slowly rubbed his jaw, appearing to contemplate her words. "I'll be thinkin' about what ya've said. Yar beliefs are a far cry from the peculiar ideas my mother adopted. Sometimes it's hard to be knowin' what to believe."

Daughtie nodded in agreement. "Exactly! Rather than accept what I've said here tonight, you need to search out the truth for yourself. Read your Bible. Pray. Seek God. He'll reveal Himself and the truth of His Word to you, and then you can make a sound decision."

"How is it that such a young lass can be so wise?" he asked, his dark eyes reflecting the golden glow of the flames dancing in the fireplace.

For a moment she felt mesmerized, captive to his unyielding gaze. A thump, immediately followed by the sound of breaking china, pulled her attention to the stairway. "The girls?" she inquired, looking back at Liam.

"Sounds as though they're having a bit o' trouble. I'd best be checkin' on them."

"May I go with you?" she asked. "I'd like to meet them."

"Of course," he said, leading the way.

Two dark-skinned girls, both attired in ragged dresses made from the white cotton known as Negro cloth, which was produced in the Lowell mills, were on their knees gathering broken pieces of a hand-painted china bowl and water pitcher. Both gazed upward with a look of terror filling their large chocolate brown eyes.

"It was an accident," the older of the two explained in a shaky voice while inching herself in front of the younger girl. "It were *my* fault, Massa; you can whip me," she continued.

"There won't be any whippin' around this house," Liam replied in a firm tone.

"But I broke—"

The younger girl peeked around from behind her companion. "She din do it—I did. You can whip me, but please don' hurt her," she pleaded.

"I've never seen folks so anxious to take a whippin'. There's nothin' in this house that can't be replaced or repaired, so don't concern yourselves over a broken piece of china. Just be careful you don't cut yourself," he said while pointing toward a shard of the porcelain.

"Thank you, suh," they replied in unison.

Daughtie stepped forward. "I'm Daughtie Winfield, a friend of Mr. Donohue. We're hoping to find a safe place for you girls to call home."

"I'm Minerva, and this here be my sister, Nelly. Ain't we goin' on up north ter Canada?" the older girl asked.

Liam squatted down in front of the girls. "Here's the problem. The two of you can't make it on your own all the way to Canada, and I don't know when another group of runaways may be passin' through that I could be sendin' you with. I can't risk keepin' you here too long, and yet I can't just send you off without havin' a place arranged for you to go."

"Can't we move on ter de next station? We'll keep a lookout fo the signal."

"What signal?" Daughtie asked.

"A single candle in the window," Liam replied before turning his attention back to the girls. "You'd be travelin' at least twenty miles, and even if ya found the signal, I don't know the password. That's what I've been tryin' to explain. We missed our connection last night. We're goin' to try and devise another plan."

Daughtie gave them a confident smile. "We've been praying for God to send us the perfect answer."

"Den we'll pray, too," Minerva said.

"Oh, that would be most helpful. With all of us praying, I'm certain God's going to send us a magnificent solution. You should be careful to remain hidden when Mr. Donohue's gone from the house. Don't answer the door, and don't burn a candle upstairs. Folks around here know Mr. Donohue lives alone," she instructed and then turned back toward Liam, who was grinning at her. "I should take my leave. I'm sure Ruth will be questioning me concerning my whereabouts since I told her I had errands to complete. Why are you grinning at me? Have I said something to amuse you?"

"Your orders to the girls—I gave them all that information when they arrived," he replied, escorting her down the hallway.

"Oh! Would you extend my apologies to them?" she asked, her cheeks flushed red with embarrassment.

"I doubt they were upset over your reminder." A smile tugged at the corner of his lips. "Any special orders for *me*?"

She gave him a sidelong glance, uncertain if he was toying with her. "Be certain you keep to your normal routine so you don't arouse suspicion," she warned. "And pray," she hastily added as he opened the front door for her.

"I think I can remember all of that," he said, a twinkle in his eyes.

"Even if you should forget everything else, don't forget to pray—that's the most important of my instructions." She stared up into his eyes, remembering the night he'd kissed her on the cheek outside the boardinghouse. She wondered now if that had just been a passing kindness—a tenderness because she'd talked of her loneliness. Her own feelings for him seemed to spill out from her heart and into her every thought. If only she could be sure of what he was feeling—thinking.

Liam leaned down, and before she realized his intent, she felt the softness of his lips upon her cheek. "Good night, Daughtie. And thank you for your help."

"You . . . you're welcome," she stammered.

She headed toward home, her fingers touching the spot Liam had kissed, her heart thumping in wild delight.

———————

It was nearly eight-thirty when Daughtie returned home—early enough Ruth ought not quiz her at length, but late enough that Dr. Ketter's patients would be gone. Hopefully he wouldn't see her come in.

"There you are!" Ruth exclaimed.

Daughtie turned toward the parlor, where Ruth sat with her hands neatly folded atop her lap.

"You went sneaking off without so much as a word, and now you've missed all the excitement." There was no mistaking the smugness in Ruth's voice.

"What have I missed?" Daughtie inquired.

"Bella has returned from England and sent word for you to come and visit her tonight. Their ship docked yesterday, and they returned to Lowell by canal boat early this evening."

"Oh, that's marvelous!" Daughtie exclaimed, turning again for the door. "I'll be back after a while."

Daughtie hurriedly made her way to Bella's and knocked at the front door. She waited several anxious moments before it swung open. "Bella!" Daughtie greeted, pulling her friend into a warm hug. "It's so good to see you."

Bella returned the embrace and then led Daughtie into the parlor. "I was beginning to think you weren't coming—or that you hadn't received my message."

Daughtie sat down on the overstuffed settee. "I left the house before your message arrived. I came as soon as I heard you'd returned. I want to hear all about the wonderful places you visited."

Bella giggled. "I haven't enough time to even begin

telling you of the wondrous sights we visited in the short time before you must return to the boardinghouse. We'll have to save that for a lengthy visit after church on Sunday. But I couldn't wait to tell you of the excitement that occurred on board ship. However, the story really begins before we left England," she said, taking time to explain about John's kidnapping and William Thurston's connection to the incident.

Daughtie clasped a hand over her mouth. "So William Thurston is alive and well, living in England?"

"He *was*. As I told you, by the time we boarded the ship, Uncle John had already escaped and was hiding on the ship. Then, lo and behold, he spotted William Thurston on board. In fact, Mr. Thurston, whom we believe was searching for Uncle John, pushed John out of the way thinking him to be no one of importance—since he was dressed like a sailor. We set sail before Thurston disembarked."

"Oh, my! What a turn of events!" Daughtie exclaimed.

"And that's not the worst of it. Taylor went to the captain with the arduous task of explaining the situation. Fortunately, the captain believed him and agreed to take Thurston into custody before we docked in Boston."

"I am so *very* thankful to hear that evil man is going to be held accountable for his crimes. And Ruth will be elated to hear the good news. She's always harbored anger that William Thurston was the one who planned all of the kidnappings and yet slipped away before receiving punishment," Daughtie said.

"That's just it—he's escaped once again."

"*What?* How did that happen?"

"When Taylor and the captain went to Thurston's cabin to place him in shackles, he was missing. The sailors searched the ship, but to no avail. John has offered a reward and is hopeful some of the crew will continue the search— at least until they set sail back to England."

"How disappointing. Do you think he's still on board the ship? Surely he would want to return to England rather than remain a hunted man in the United States."

"I'm not certain. Uncle John is hopeful he'll be captured and brought to trial, but I fear he's managed to slip away again. But enough of this gloomy talk. I've more news to share."

"What else happened?"

"We brought Taylor's sister Elinor home to live with us!"

"Truly?"

"Yes. It was getting a bit much for her grandparents to continue to care for her, so they decided we would be the best candidates to raise her."

"Well, that's very exciting and scary all at once, isn't it?"

"It certainly is. I want to introduce you to her and tell you all about our journey. Do say you'll come to church with us on Sunday and join us afterward for the noonday meal."

Daughtie hesitated a moment, her mind racing. "I'll try," she said.

The smile faded from Bella's lips. "*Try?* Have you more important plans?" she asked, obvious disappointment in her voice.

"I may be needed to assist some friends," she hedged.

Bella arched her eyebrows. "You're keeping something from me, Daughtie Winfield. What is it?"

"What makes you think I'm keeping secrets?"

"Because you've been my dearest friend since the day I arrived at the Shaker village in Canterbury. I know you almost as well as I know myself. You may as well take me into your confidence, for you surely realize I'll give you no peace until I know what's going on," Bella replied. And then, as if struck by a bolt of lightning, Bella grasped Daughtie's hands in her own. "Does this have something to do with Liam Donohue?" When Daughtie didn't immediately answer, Bella squeezed her hands. "I've guessed correctly, haven't I? I can see it in your eyes."

Daughtie's voice caught in her throat. "It's not what you think," she argued, her voice raspy.

"Then tell me," Bella insisted. "You know I've always kept your confidences."

"Runaway slaves," Daughtie whispered. "We're helping runaway slaves."

Bella clasped a hand across her mouth. "You're placing yourself in extreme danger."

"Given the opportunity, you'd do the same thing."

"Perhaps," Bella conceded. "Give me the particulars—who else is involved? How did this all begin? All you said in your letters was that you had attended an antislavery meeting."

Daughtie nodded. "Yes, Prudence Crandall came and spoke."

"And your letter said you had invited Liam Donahue," Bella continued. "That was an even greater mistake than helping runaways."

Shifting on the settee, Daughtie met Bella's gaze. "Really? Is that how you truly feel, Bella? That if a person was born in Ireland, that makes him less acceptable than someone born in—shall we say—England?"

"Whether it's what *I* believe or not isn't what matters. People consider the Irish to be less . . ." Bella hesitated, obviously unable to find the right words.

"Less *acceptable*?"

Bella fervently bobbed her head up and down.

"But they're not. They're made of the same flesh and blood as you and me. We all are—the Negroes, the Irish, the English—all of us. Neither the country of our birth nor the color of our skin makes a difference."

"Those things don't matter to you or me, and they

shouldn't matter to others, but they do," Bella replied.

"Well, I won't accept that way of life. I believe we're equal—all of us—and that's how I intend to live. I'll not let others dictate the acceptability of a person based upon dark skin or an Irish brogue. I'm thankful I grew up among people who taught me we're all created in the image of God. Sister Mary is Irish—and what about Brother Lemuel? He's black, and he's also one of the finest men God ever placed upon this earth. You loved both of them, didn't you?"

"Your argument isn't with me, Daughtie. I don't disagree with you. But this isn't Canterbury—you're not living in the secluded Shaker village anymore, and the rest of the world doesn't hold to Shaker theology. Besides, you left the Shakers because you didn't agree with their beliefs."

"*Some* of their beliefs—the ones that I couldn't justify with the Scriptures. However, I continue to embrace those tenets of the Society that are irrefutable, and I believe equality is one of those basic truths that is undeniable."

"You know I believe in equality, too, Daughtie, but there are barriers that can't be crossed when you're living among the rest of the world."

"Nothing will ever change unless we promote an attitude of accepting everyone. We can't sit back and remain complacent. Someone must lead the way and cross the barriers. How else will slaves be set free? How will Irishmen ever be permitted to live alongside Englishmen? Or how will equality ever truly exist in this country?"

"Or the Shaker girl be permitted to fall in love and marry an Irishman?" Bella whispered.

Daughtie silently stared back into her friend's questioning gaze.

"You're in love with Liam Donohue, aren't you? That's what all of this is about, isn't it?"

"No. That's not what this is all about. I won't deny my feelings for Liam. However, the slavery issue and mistreatment of the Irish did not evolve out of my feelings for him. Rather, I grew to care for him because he so passionately desires to help those less fortunate, no matter their color, creed, or native land. He's a fine man, deserving of a good wife," she adamantly proclaimed.

Bella stared at her, mouth agape. "You—you're going to marry him?" she finally sputtered.

"No," Daughtie replied calmly.

"Oh, Daughtie, for a moment I was so frightened."

"He hasn't asked me," Daughtie quickly added.

Bella clutched Daughtie's hand. "But you wouldn't accept if he did?"

"Yes, I believe I would. I'd be proud to call Liam Donohue my husband."

Bella leaned against the back of the settee. "I believe I'm going to faint," she announced, blotting her face with a lace-edged handkerchief.

Daughtie grabbed the cloth from Bella's hand and began fanning it back and forth in front of Bella's face. "Dear Bella, *please* don't faint. You should be pleased that I've grown so independent in your absence. Remember how you used to worry about my inability to make decisions?"

"I fear you've learned too well," she said with a weak smile.

"I'm sorry I've upset you first thing upon your return. I've so looked forward to having you back, and now look what I've done!"

"It's not your fault. I insisted you take me into your confidence. Although I fear for your safety and happiness, I'll never betray you. You will always be my dearest friend," Bella replied. "If your other plans don't interfere, will you promise to spend the day with me on Sunday?"

Daughtie smiled. "Of course."

CHAPTER 26

Boston

William Thurston hurried through the back streets of Boston, his haste causing him to occasionally stumble on an uneven cobblestone or piece of scattered garbage. Undeterred, he continued onward until he chanced upon a seedy tavern along the alleyway he was traversing. Pushing through the door, he welcomed the darkness that shrouded the interior. He knew immediately this would be his hiding place until the sun set.

He sat down at a rough-hewn table in a rear corner where he had a view of the door. Pushing aside the remnants of an unfinished meal, he ordered a mug of ale and remained silent while the barkeep placed it on the table. He placed a coin on the sticky tabletop before taking a swallow of the brew.

Drinking slowly, he began to take stock of the circumstances that had sent his clever plans plummeting into disaster. Had it not been for the ineptitude of the thugs he'd hired to detain Farnsworth in England, he would now be considered a champion to Chauncy Fuller and his friends.

Instead, he was hiding out in a vermin-infested pub in Boston. However, he reasoned, he couldn't take the chance of being spotted by one of the Boston Associates. Worse yet, the wife he'd left behind or one of her voluble matron acquaintances might see him should he wander about town.

The day wore on, and by nightfall, William walked out the door of the tavern, his latest plan firmly in place. He'd spent the day watching and waiting. Now he stood outside the door, pausing until he was certain no one was lurking about. He untied the reins of an agile-looking mare, slipped his foot into the stirrup, and hoisted himself up into the saddle. Waiting until he was only a short distance from the tavern, he then dug his heels deep into the horse's flanks, pleased when the animal responded and raced off at full gallop.

The next morning William was knocking at the front door of the Litchfield, New Hampshire, boardinghouse Thaddeus Arnold now called home.

A thin small-framed woman opened the door. "My rooms are full," she said before William could speak.

"I'm not looking for a room. I'm looking for Thaddeus Arnold. I understand he's one of your boarders."

"He is. Come in and sit down," she ordered, pointing a flour-covered finger toward the parlor. "I'll go and get him. He hasn't yet come down for breakfast."

"Thank you."

"You friend or family?" the woman asked, peering down at him while mounting the steps.

"Friend."

The woman stopped her ascent. "Haven't seen you around here before. Where do you hail from?"

"England."

The woman appeared impressed only momentarily. "You don't sound like an Englishman," she snorted and then continued upward.

The sound of muffled voices could be heard from above, and then the woman reappeared, stopping outside the parlor door. "Mr. Arnold will be down in a minute. He didn't seem to be expecting any visitors from England."

William ignored the remark, keeping his gaze fixed upon the stairway until he spotted Thaddeus peeking through the banister. "It's me, Thurston. Get down here and quit acting like a frightened schoolboy," he ordered.

Thaddeus hurried into the parlor, patting his hair into place as he rounded the corner. "William! What an unexpected surprise. I couldn't imagine who might be here. I've not given my address to anyone—except you, of course. And I certainly wasn't expecting *you* to make an appearance. What brings you back from England?"

"Sit down and I'll explain," William said, attempting to keep his irritation under control.

Thaddeus did as he was told, appearing spellbound while William related how his plot to be accepted among England's elite had gone afoul, causing him to now be sitting in New Hampshire instead of the well-appointed drawing room of Chauncy Fuller's mansion.

"How did you manage to get off the ship undetected?" Thaddeus asked, his eyes glinting with excitement.

"I went into steerage and rummaged through the trunk of a buxom woman when she and her husband were on deck, and I found a dress and a bonnet that had a wide brim to help cover my face."

Thaddeus appeared shocked. "You disguised yourself as a woman?"

"Don't act so appalled. My idea worked, didn't it? The captain had his whole crew looking for a man. I strolled by them in that woman's ill-fitting gown, my own clothes tucked underneath, and not one question was asked. Personally, I felt my performance was a stroke of genius."

Thaddeus bobbed his head in agreement. "So it was. You truly are brilliant."

"I'm certain you realize my unexpected departure from England has left me financially embarrassed. My funds are in England, and I'm going to need money to book a return passage. That's where you come in, my friend. I need to borrow enough money for passage and a little extra to take care of my needs until I sail. Of course, I knew you would be the one person I could count on for such a loan."

"Your request comes at a bad time, William. I was at the gaming tables yesterday and find myself without funds to assist you," Thaddeus replied, his voice a hoarse whisper.

William stiffened, and his gaze narrowed into what he hoped was an icy stare. "Then you need to determine how you're going to get your hands on enough money to help me."

Thaddeus squirmed in his chair for several moments and then slapped his leg, obviously pleased with himself. "I know where I can get the money. Naomi! She was always tight with her money. I'm certain she's tucked away every cent the Corporation has paid her. After all, Naomi expects me to leave her a few coins every time I stop to see Theona. I've always complied because I didn't want her to stop me from visiting," he said. "The visits give me a reason to be in Lowell without questions being asked," he explained.

"Your former wife will loan you the money?"

"No, of course not. I'll steal it from her. If you can pass yourself off as a woman, surely I should be able to pilfer the money from the home of my former wife," he said with a coarse laugh.

"She doesn't keep her money in the bank?"

"Naomi was never one to use the bank. Unless one of those mill girls has recently convinced her to begin using the Thrift Savings where they keep all of their earnings, I'm certain I'll find her money hidden away in the bedroom. The blanket chest was always her favorite hiding place. I'll call on her tomorrow," Thaddeus said.

"Thank you, my friend. Of course, you'll be handsomely rewarded once I return to England."

———

A sign on the front door advised patients to walk in and be seated. Although Thaddeus wasn't a patient, he walked in the front door and down the hallway of what now served as both Naomi's boardinghouse and Dr. Ketter's office.

"Hello, Naomi," he said, enjoying the opportunity to make a surprise visit upon his wife. He knew she despised having him appear, but that fact made his visit even more appealing.

She whirled around, the apple she was peeling suddenly falling to the floor. "Thaddeus! What are *you* doing here?" Picking up the apple, Naomi rinsed it in a pan of water and sliced it into thin pieces before handing it to Theona.

"Paying a visit to my daughter," he said in an even tone.

The wide-eyed child remained partially hidden behind Naomi's skirt, her round rosy cheeks moving up and down as she chewed the apple. "You were here only days ago. Usually it's at least several weeks between your visits," she replied while giving him a hasty once-over. "I'm merely surprised your visits with Theona are so stimulating that you'd make the journey twice in one week. Are you certain you're not in some kind of trouble?"

Thaddeus beckoned to the child. "Quite the contrary, my dear," he amicably replied before lifting Theona to his lap. "I see you've water boiling over the fire. Would it trouble you too much to prepare a cup of tea?" he asked in his most pleasant tone.

She eyed him suspiciously. "I suppose a cup of tea wouldn't be out of order."

Naomi's wary attitude didn't surprise him. After all, his amiable behavior toward her was utterly out of character, but he needed time if he was going to find a way to get into the blanket chest in her bedroom. Watching as she brewed the tea, he bounced Theona on his knee, hoping to appear the doting father.

Naomi placed his tea on the table beside him. "Won't you join me?" he asked.

She pushed a stray wisp of hair behind one ear. "No, I have laundry to hang," she responded.

"Surely you can take a few minutes," he urged.

She hesitated and then sat down. "You talked as though things are going well for you. Have you found new employment?" she inquired.

"A new business venture," he replied, finding pleasure in divulging the information. He continually hoped to make her regret the fact that they were no longer married.

"Business venture? That sounds risky. I hope it's a sensible investment," she impulsively responded.

He inwardly bristled at her comment, wanting to launch into a verbal assault upon her. How would *she* possibly know anything about business? Her only concern was his ability to pass along a few coins for Theona's care. Forcing himself to remain calm, he gave her an affable smile. "I believe this particular activity will prove extremely beneficial. In fact, one of the primary partners in the venture has been visiting from England only this week. He came specifically to see me and encourage my participation in the undertaking," he boasted.

She leveled a look of skepticism toward him. "An unknown man came all the way from England to talk to *you* about entering into a business enterprise?"

"I didn't say he was unknown," Thaddeus countered.

"Whom do you know in England?" she quizzed.

Without thinking, he blurted out William Thurston's

name. Too late, he caught himself, realizing he ought not be speaking of William's whereabouts.

"I don't believe I've ever heard you speak of him," she replied.

Thaddeus breathed a sigh of relief, pleased that while they were married he'd managed to keep his wife at home, well away from the gossip that circulated about Lowell. She'd likely never heard of William Thurston or his involvement in the kidnappings that occurred three years ago. Perhaps she would forget the name as quickly as she'd heard it.

"I must get to my laundry. Theona, stay here with your father while I go outside," she instructed. "I won't be too long," she called over her shoulder while exiting the rear door.

"Take your time. I'll just have another cup of tea," he replied, listening until the door closed and then lifting Theona off his lap. "I'll be right back, Theona. You stay here and finish your apple."

Assuring himself the doctor and his patients would not see him, Thaddeus hurried down the hallway and up the stairs to Naomi's bedroom. Spotting the blanket chest, he moved quietly across the floor, uncertain if sounds from above would alert the doctor. The hinges on the chest squealed in protest as he lifted the lid. He waited a moment—his heart hammering wildly as he listened for the sound of footsteps. Only the sound of murmuring in the office below could be heard. He exhaled deeply as he began rifling through the stored coverlets, pleased when his fingers finally touched upon what he knew was Naomi's leather pouch. Circling his hand around the supple doeskin, he pulled it from between the folded blankets and momentarily savored his victory.

"Theona!"

The child stood in the doorway watching him, her blue eyes wide and unyielding.

"What you doing?" she innocently inquired.

He didn't respond to her question. Instead, he took her by the hand and led her out of the room. "Come along, let's go back downstairs."

"Mr. Arnold! What are you doing upstairs?"

Thaddeus startled at the voice and immediately turned his gaze to the downstairs hallway, where Dr. Ketter stood staring up at him.

Pointing toward his daughter, Thaddeus gave the doctor a cautious smile and nodded. "Just retrieving Theona. I didn't want her falling down the steps," he replied. Taking the child's hand, he descended the stairs and hurried back to the kitchen.

"Come along, Theona," he said to the child, pulling her along toward the rear door.

Pulling open the door, he glanced about, finally spotting Naomi's feet beneath a sheet she was hanging on the line. "I've some business to attend to, Naomi. I really must be going. Shall I send Theona out with you?"

She pulled the sheet aside and gave him a questioning look. "You're leaving already?"

"Yes, I had forgotten a matter that needs my immediate attention," he said.

"Come along, Theona," she said.

With his back toward Naomi, Thaddeus leaned down and placed a kiss upon the child's cheek. "It isn't safe for you to be going upstairs by yourself. You might fall," he said, making certain his words were loud enough to be heard by Naomi.

The child gave him a confused look. Narrowing his eyes, he leveled a menacing glare at Theona. "Yeth, thir," she obediently replied.

He tousled her dark hair. "That's a good girl."

Daughtie placed her cape on the peg inside the front door and then greeted Theona, who stood in the doorway of the kitchen. "Did you have a fine day, Theona?" she asked, walking down the hall.

Theona bobbed her head up and down, her bow-shaped lips turning up in a sweet smile. "Papa come," she said as Daughtie drew nearer.

Daughtie turned and gazed toward Naomi. "Was Mr. Arnold here again today?"

"Yes. It was a strange visit. He came in talking as though he was anxious to spend time with Theona, but he didn't stay long."

"It hasn't even been a week since he last called upon you, has it?"

"No," she replied while pulling a stack of plates from the shelf and then gathering silverware in her other hand.

"Papa upthtairs," Theona said as her mother walked into the dining room to set the table.

Naomi turned on her heel. "No. Papa's gone home. He's not upstairs."

"Papa upthtairs," the child repeated.

"No, Theona! Your papa has gone home."

"She likely means that he was upstairs earlier—before he left the house," Dr. Ketter explained as he helped himself to a sweet pickle.

Naomi turned her attention to the doctor, a startled look etched upon her face. "What? Thaddeus was upstairs?"

Theona's head bobbed again. "Papa upthtairs."

Naomi stooped down in front of the little girl. "Why was Papa upstairs?"

The child gave her mother a winsome smile. "Blankie," she said.

"The blanket chest—my money," Naomi cried, racing toward the stairs. "He's stolen my money. I know it!" she shouted.

Theona whimpered, tears threatening to spill down her cheeks at any moment. Daughtie sat down and opened her arms to the child, lifting her into a warm embrace. Theona snuggled close and rested her plump cheek against Daughtie's chest.

Naomi returned to the dining room, a faraway look in her eyes. "He took all of my money—even the leather pouch."

"You must go to the police," Daughtie encouraged.

"Absolutely. I'll go with you and confirm that I saw him upstairs while you were outdoors," Dr. Ketter said. "I'll get my coat."

"No. Wait. I don't want to go to the police. Let's have dinner."

Daughtie stared at the older woman in disbelief. "But, Mrs. Arnold—"

"No, I'll not go," she interrupted. "I don't want to discuss this any further," she said, casting a glance at Theona.

Daughtie nodded. "As you wish."

"Ruth said she wouldn't be here for supper, so we may as well eat," Mrs. Arnold said. "I'll get the bread."

Except for the sound of clattering dishes and an occasional word from Theona, the four of them ate their meal in silence. Ivan excused himself as soon as he'd finished eating a piece of pie and headed back down the hall to his office.

Daughtie took a sip of tea and glanced over the top of her cup at Mrs. Arnold. "You really should go to the police," she softly urged.

Theona scooted down from her chair, marching off to entertain herself in the other room.

"I haven't forgotten the years of abuse I suffered at his

hand. He's a cruel man—no one knows that better than I do. I still bear the scars from his beatings. If I go to the police and he convinces them it's all a lie, he'll retaliate. I'm not willing to take the chance that he'll return and harm Theona."

Daughtie longed for words to comfort Mrs. Arnold, but none came to her. "I understand. You must do what's best for both you and Theona. I hadn't considered that he might strike out against Theona—or you," she said, taking Naomi's hand in her own. "I don't want you or Theona placed in harm's way."

Mrs. Arnold gave her a faint smile. "I don't understand Thaddeus. I never have. It's abundantly clear that he came here to steal from me, yet he spent a great deal of time telling me about a new business venture. He seemed genuinely excited, going into detail about a Mr. Thurston who'd come from England to encourage his participation in this innovative enterprise. None of this makes any sense."

"Thurston? William Thurston?" Daughtie's mind reeled with Bella's tale of William Thurston escaping before the authorities could apprehend him. Apparently he was nearby, possibly in Lowell. She must get word to Bella and Taylor.

CHAPTER 27

Daughtie remained in the kitchen with Mrs. Arnold and Theona until the older woman composed herself.

"There's really nothing anyone can do, and there's no need for you to remain here in the kitchen with me," Naomi said. "You go on. I've got dishes and mending I need to complete before bedtime, and Theona's here to keep me company, aren't you, dearest?"

The little girl smiled at her mother while clapping her hands. "I will help," she said.

Theona's sincere offer caused Daughtie to smile. "If you're certain you don't need me, I believe I'll call on Bella and Taylor Manning. We had time for only a short visit last evening," she explained.

"What a pleasant coincidence," Dr. Ketter commented.

Daughtie turned toward Dr. Ketter, who was now standing in the doorway of his office.

"I'm preparing to leave for the Farnsworth residence, also. Taylor and his bride *do* reside with Mr. and Mrs. Farnsworth, don't they?"

"Yes. Their new home isn't completed yet," she replied. "Is someone ill?"

"No, at least not that I'm aware of. They extended an invitation to call, saying they would like to meet me."

"I see. I'm surprised they're entertaining so soon after their arrival home. Perhaps I should call upon Bella some other time."

"Nonsense! Mr. and Mrs. Farnsworth merely wish to become acquainted since they find themselves without a doctor now that Dr. Barnard has retired. I'm sure your friend will be delighted to have you visit, and *I'll* be pleased to have you accompany me," he said with a bright smile. "I was planning on walking because it's such a fine evening, but I could fetch a carriage if you'd prefer."

"I'm accustomed to walking. Besides, this is the first day we've been without rain this week. The spring weather will make for an enjoyable stroll," Daughtie said, unable to think of any excuse to avoid Dr. Ketter's company. After all, it was imperative she inform Bella and Taylor of William Thurston's activity.

Dr. Ketter was smiling profusely as they crossed the street, careful to lead her around several large mud-filled puddles. "I'm pleased to have some time alone with you. Sometimes I wonder if you're intentionally attempting to avoid me," he said, hesitating and obviously hoping she'd reject his idea.

His comment mirrored her feelings, yet she knew to simply agree with his remark would be insensitive. Finally she settled upon a vague reply. "I keep very busy with a number of activities."

"I may consider joining into some of those activities in order to spend time with you," he said with a bright smile.

Clearly Dr. Ketter wasn't easily deterred, and Daughtie wished she had given a more direct reply after all. "The groups to which I belong are for women," she curtly stated.

"I was purely jesting with you. I'm hopeful you won't make it *quite* that difficult for me to call upon you."

"I have no time for gentlemen callers," she answered, attempting to hide her irritation. She wanted the discussion of her free time to end. "You might consider directing your attention toward Ruth. As I've said before, I believe the two of you would have much in common, and she has expressed a keen interest in attending several lectures that will soon be presented in Lowell."

They stopped while permitting an approaching carriage to pass, then began crossing the street to the Farnsworth home. Ivan gazed down at her. "Is it truly your desire that I pursue Ruth, or are you being coy? It's sometimes difficult to discern if women are saying exactly what they mean."

"I cannot speak for other women, but you may take *me* at my word. While you appear to be a fine, upstanding man, I am confident that you and I have very little in common. I have not pursued your interest but rather have tried to make my disinterest more than apparent. I believe if anyone is to blame for this, it is Ruth for her encouragement of your attention toward me. I am certain she had the best intentions, for she worries after me like a mother hen; however, she was misguided in this pursuit and I am afraid we have both suffered for it." She paused, eyeing him quite sternly. "So please be assured, I am not attempting to lure you with game playing. There is no reason for you to continue pursuing me. I will not change my mind."

"Well, that was certainly clear and concise," he replied dejectedly. "I'll keep my distance."

His disappointment was evident in his voice, but Daughtie knew that this time she could show no mercy. One kind word and he would resume his pursuit of her. "Here we are," she said, turning up the steps to the Farnsworth house as he followed close on her heels. Her knock was answered by a young girl with a mischievous grin on her face.

"I'm Elinor. Who are you?" the bundle of energy asked.

"Why, it's so nice to meet you, Elinor," Daughtie answered. "I'm Miss Daughtie Winfield, and this is Dr. Ivan Ketter. What do you think of America so far?"

"I think it rains all the time!" Elinor laughed as she let the guests into the house and turned to find Addie and John waiting patiently behind her. Bella joined the group, and soon Addie and John whisked Dr. Ketter into the formal parlor for a visit while leaving her to chat with Bella.

A clap of thunder sounded overhead. "What's wrong, Daughtie? Is the storm disturbing to you? You've appeared anxious ever since you arrived this evening," Bella said while pouring a cup of tea.

"It's not the storm that's upset me. I've news to share with you—about William Thurston."

"William Thurston?"

Daughtie startled at the deep male voice that echoed her words. "Oh, Taylor! You surprised me," she sighed.

"I'm sorry, but hearing William Thurston's name certainly captured my attention. You have news of him?"

"Yes," Daughtie said, while giving a quick nod of her head. "Thaddeus Arnold was in Lowell earlier today. He said he came to call upon his daughter, Theona. In the midst of Mr. Arnold's visit, he mentioned he had entered into a business venture with someone who had recently sailed from England. As he continued with the story, he mentioned that William Thurston is his newly arrived business partner."

Taylor appeared stunned. "He told you this?"

"No, he told Mrs. Arnold and she passed along the information to me."

"Do you know where Thaddeus makes his home?"

"A village in New Hampshire, but I don't recall the name. I can ask Mrs. Arnold. I think she'll cooperate. However, she's fearful of retribution from Mr. Arnold should she go to the police."

"She should be more fearful of the company her former husband is associating with. Did he tell her anything more?" Taylor inquired.

"I didn't finish my story," Daughtie said. "While Mr. Arnold was at the boardinghouse, he went upstairs to Mrs. Arnold's bedroom and helped himself to her savings. I encouraged her to report the matter, but she wouldn't."

"She's *certain* he absconded with the money?"

"She didn't actually see him with it, but when Dr. Ketter was coming out of his office, he noticed Mr. Arnold upstairs. The rains had abated, and Mrs. Arnold was outdoors hanging laundry. There was no reason for Mr. Arnold to be in her room except to steal," Daughtie declared.

"Did I hear my name mentioned?" Ivan inquired as he entered the room, flanked by Addie and John.

"I mentioned your observation of Mr. Arnold in the upstairs rooms today," Daughtie replied.

"Seems William Thurston may be in New Hampshire or possibly even here in Lowell," Taylor told his uncle as the group joined them.

"Do tell," John said, his face flushed with excitement. "How did you come by this piece of information?"

"Daughtie," Taylor replied. "Tell him what you related to me," he instructed.

Daughtie repeated the story, with Dr. Ketter interrupting to add a piece of information from time to time. John's interest was obviously piqued as she related details of William Thurston's dealings with Thaddeus Arnold.

"I'm not at all certain I understand why you're all so interested in this William Thurston," Dr. Ketter remarked when Daughtie had finished speaking.

"He was a primary participant in thefts and kidnappings that took place here in Lowell three years ago. In fact, he was the instigator who stayed behind the scenes, ordering his henchmen to conduct the reprehensible deeds," John explained.

Daughtie leaned forward, peeking around Bella. "Ruth and Bella were both among those who were kidnapped. Fortunately, they were rescued, thanks in large part to Taylor and Mr. Farnsworth," she said, giving both men a charming smile.

Dr. Ketter appeared aghast at the mention of the kidnappings. "And this Thurston fellow managed to escape before being brought to justice?"

"Quite so. But with a modicum of good fortune and careful planning, we may be able to detain him before he's able to slip out of our grasp. To be frank, I'm astounded he's remained in the country this long. Of course, we alerted the police in Boston. They agreed to assist by checking the manifests of passengers sailing to England. If he became aware of police involvement, he may have decided to wait until activity quiets around the docks," John surmised. "I think we should talk to Mrs. Arnold, learn exactly where Thaddeus resides, and pay him an unexpected visit."

"Exactly!" Taylor agreed. "I'll get my hat."

Daughtie rose from her chair. "Please wait. After today's events, I think your appearance at the door may upset Mrs. Arnold."

"Possibly," John agreed. "And the hour *is* growing late for calling."

Taylor stopped midstep. "Perhaps you could talk to her in the morning, Daughtie. Bella tells me you're attending church with us. You could bring us word when we meet."

"I'll do my best," she cautiously replied.

John nodded. "She may still be up and about when you arrive home. I understand the mills will be closed Monday and Tuesday, possibly longer, if these rains don't subside. With these spring freshets flooding the mill pond, it may be impossible to regulate the waterpower for even longer if we don't soon get some relief from the downpours."

"I didn't know a decision had been made. Mr. Gault sent word to each foreman late today simply advising the possibility of a shutdown existed," she said.

"I should think all of you girls would be pleased to have a little time away from the mill," John commented.

"For some of us the break from work is a blessing; for others, the loss of pay caused by the spring freshets can be most distressing."

Addie nodded in agreement. "Ah, yes. I remember only too well those poor girls who were placed in dire financial straits by the loss of wages. Let's hope they've been able to monetarily prepare themselves for the spring rains."

Daughtie and Dr. Ketter moved toward the door and bid farewell. She then stepped outside, knowing that Ivan Ketter would follow her, yet hoping he wouldn't begin his pursuit anew.

"I've been thinking," he said softly as they headed for Mrs. Arnold's house. "I want you to know it was never my intention to make you uncomfortable. I'm generally not so bold, but I was encouraged."

"Yes, I know," Daughtie replied, uncertain where this conversation was leading.

"I'm not a difficult man," he said in a reflective manner. "I'm sorry that I made you uncomfortable. I would never have pursued your affections had I not believed it all to be part of the ritual."

Daughtie couldn't help but chuckle. "I grew up with the Shakers, Dr. Ketter. Men and women were not allowed to share their affections or play a part of any ritual, as you call it. I'm sorry you felt misled."

"Well, truth be told, I wouldn't mind getting to know Miss Ruth better."

Daughtie looked up at him with a huge smile. "I think I can help arrange that."

He perked up at this. "Truly? You don't think she'll feel the same as you?"

Daughtie shook her head. "No, in fact, Ruth was quite jealous of the attention you showed me those first few days. I do not believe it will be a difficult task at all to win her interest."

"And you would consent to helping me?"

Daughtie laughed. "I hardly believe you'll need my help, Dr. Ketter. I believe Ruth's heart will speak for itself once she realizes you are interested."

They reached the house just then. Daughtie turned at the door. "I'm glad this has been worked out between us. I never wished to make an enemy of you."

"You most assuredly will never be my enemy," Ivan replied.

"Nor you mine," Daughtie answered, glad to have things work out much better than she could have hoped for.

Dr. Ketter opened the door to find Ruth conveniently nearby. "Ah, Ruth. Just the woman I hoped to see."

Ruth appeared rather shocked as she looked past Dr. Ketter to Daughtie. "Me?"

"Indeed. Have you a few moments to join me by the fire?"

Daughtie wanted to giggle at the look on Ruth's face. *Good,* she thought, *let her have some of her own medicine. Let her be the recipient of Dr. Ketter's persistent attention.* Somehow, Daughtie believed Ruth would receive it in a much more welcoming manner.

Daughtie readied herself for church the next morning, now armed with the information Taylor had requested the evening before. She would need to depart early if she was to arrive at the Farnsworth home as scheduled. Hurrying downstairs, she sighed, weary from the night of thunder and lightning that had interrupted her sleep. The rain had subsided a bit, but the clouds overhead appeared ominous as she hastened her steps.

"Psst. Ma'am!"

Daughtie turned toward the sound, surprised to see the Irish girl who had always delivered Liam's messages hiding in the brush along the fence line. The girl glanced about and then hurried toward Daughtie, waving a piece of paper in front of her. She shoved the scrap in Daughtie's direction, obviously anxious to be rid of it and on her way. Unfolding and smoothing the rumpled paper, Daughtie scanned the carefully penned words. Her heart plummeted. How could she possibly handle another complex situation at this time?

In a few moments Daughtie was staring at the front door of the Farnsworth house. In order to help Liam, she'd *have* to place her trust in Bella. She knocked, fervently praying Bella would be the one to answer.

"Daughtie! I told Taylor it would be you," Bella replied. Her blond curls were held in place with a tortoise-shell comb inlaid with green stones that matched her dress.

Grasping Bella's hand, Daughtie pulled her into the parlor, where they couldn't be heard. "Mr. Arnold is in Litchfield, a small hamlet north of Nashua."

"Why are you whispering, and why have you forced me into the parlor?" Bella asked, her pink lips forming a diminutive pout.

"You must make some excuse for my absence today,

both at church and afterward."

Bella's pout intensified. "You're not going to be here for dinner and visiting this afternoon?"

"Please don't be angry. I've had a note from Liam requesting I come to the house. He truly must get the girls moved, and I've had a brilliant idea. We may even be able to execute the plan today if we begin immediately."

"Oh, do tell me all about it," Bella replied, smiling as she clasped her hands together in excitement.

"I haven't time right now. Besides, it's better if you don't know. That way you'll not be forced to tell a lie."

Bella's smile faded, and she began tapping her right foot at a rapid tempo. "You know I can maintain a confidence."

"I never questioned your loyalty, but I don't want to put you at risk or cause you any difficulty. Besides, there's no time for discussion—I should already be on my way to Liam's. I must hurry," she said, giving Bella a quick hug.

"You know I wish you well. I'll be praying for you."

"Oh, thank you, dear Bella. You are the very best friend I could ever hope for. We'll need your prayers if the girls are to find safety," Daughtie replied.

Bella nodded. "Is there *nothing* I can do to help?"

Daughtie hesitated. "Perhaps there is. Would you send word to Mrs. Arnold that I've gone to Canterbury? I think I can make good use of this time away from the mill."

"Please send me word when you've returned. Otherwise, I'll continue to worry about your safety. And give my love to Sister Mercy."

"Sister Mercy? Oh, yes. If I see her I'll send your regards," Daughtie replied before making a hasty retreat.

———

The drizzle continued, and thunder rumbled above as if drumming out a warning that the threatening dark clouds would soon deluge the town with further pelting rainfall.

Daughtie bent her head against the wind, thankful her hooded cloak offered a modicum of protection against the onslaught. The glow from a whale oil lamp shone through the curtained window of Liam's house, and she quickened her step, anxious to be out of the miserable weather.

Liam approached in answer to her knock, a look of surprise crossing his face as he pulled open the door. "I didn't expect ya quite so early. How did ya manage to depart the boardinghouse undetected? Won't Ruth be expectin' ya to attend church services?"

Daughtie rubbed her hands together, the rain leaving her chilled. "She knew I was leaving early in order to deliver a message to Bella. She's expecting me to attend services with Taylor and Bella. However, I asked Bella to inform Mrs. Arnold that I would be going to Canterbury."

He frowned as he led her into the parlor. "Canterbury? What would be takin' you back to visit the Shakers?" he asked. "I don't mean to appear single-minded, but I truly need your help with the two slave girls hidin' upstairs."

Daughtie moved in front of the fire, extending her hands toward the warmth. "Not Canterbury, New Hampshire, although that's where Bella surmised I was going, also," she explained. "Canterbury, Connecticut."

He stared at her, his eyebrows furrowed. "Sit down and tell me what you're thinkin', lassie."

"The safety of the girls has been in my prayers since I left here the other evening," she began. "I've prayed that another group of runaways would arrive and the problem would be solved, but that obviously hasn't occurred. However, when I opened my Bible last night, my most recent letter from Prudence Crandall fell to the floor."

Liam nodded and leaned forward. "Aye?"

"As I picked up the letter, I was struck by an idea. The very best place for these girls would be at Prudence Crandall's school in Connecticut," she said, somewhat surprised he needed clarification.

"I see," he said, rubbing his forehead. "With all the problems Miss Crandall's had with the townsfolk, do ya think her school is safe? Would it not be less dangerous to take them to the Shaker village, perhaps? You once spoke of the Shakers takin' in some runaways."

"No," Daughtie replied. "Both Minerva and Nelly have religious convictions that are in opposition to those of the Shakers. To force them into that world would be particularly unfair. Besides, in her latest letter, Miss Crandall was pleased to relate that her difficulties had subsided and there had been no further incidents at the school. In fact, she even mentioned she was going to once again begin seeking new students. Then she went on to say that she believed our prayers were being answered," Daughtie replied.

Leaning forward, Liam rested his arms on his thighs and met Daughtie's intense gaze. "So ya believe this is *God's* plan?" he quietly inquired.

Daughtie nodded her agreement. "Yes, I do. I believe it's His answer—and now that the mills are closed due to the rains, I can go with you and speak to Miss Crandall on their behalf."

"If ya believe God wants us to take them to Miss Crandall's school in Connecticut, then I think we should comply. It won't take long to make preparations."

She peered into his eyes, hoping to assure herself he wasn't scoffing. He appeared sincere. "I'm pleasantly surprised at your desire to follow God's direction. You've apparently given additional thought to our recent conversation," she replied cautiously.

"Aye. I've been spendin' some time readin' the Bible and prayin', but those two girls make quite a proclamation for God, also. Their faith would be an inspiration to any heathen," he said with a grin. "They don't waver from what they believe. In fact, they told me their faith in God is what sustains them durin' difficult times. When she's havin' trouble or feeling sorry for herself, Nelly said she thinks how Jesus suffered in order to grant her the gift of eternal life. We've talked a great deal since they arrived—mostly about their faith," he continued. "It appears I've been surrounded by devout young women who aren't afraid to express their belief in God."

A smile tugged at Daughtie's lips. "Seems as though God's found a way to present His message."

Liam smiled in return. "He's found *three* ways. I guess He figures a hard-headed Irishman needs to hear things more than once."

"I've discovered God is more than willing to use any method necessary in order to gain *my* attention, and it seems He's doing the same with you."

Liam arched his eyebrows, obviously taken aback by her remark. "One thing is certain. I've had plenty to mull over the past few days. Now with your idea that the girls should go to Prudence Crandall's school, it's become obvious to me that God's concerned with the future of these girls. We'd best be prayin' that He remain involved if we're going to get them safely delivered to Connecticut."

"Do you think there's any possibility we might be stopped along the way?" Daughtie asked.

"Perhaps. But since we'll be taking the wagon, I can say I'm going to Connecticut for my stonemasonry business."

Daughtie nodded. "I'll go upstairs and tell the girls we're leaving. We'll gather some food while you hitch the wagon."

"Good, but don't be too long. With these rains, I fear we'll be forced to move slowly. We can hope the weather clears as we move south," he said while moving toward the door. "I don't think there's anyone lurkin' around, but I'll bring the wagon up close to the back o' the house. The three of you can come out the kitchen door."

"We'll be ready," Daughtie said, the sound of her shoes echoing as she clattered down the hallway at full tilt.

CHAPTER 28

John greeted Matthew Cheever with a warm handshake while entering the foyer of St. Anne's Episcopal Church. "Good to see you, Matthew. I understand that even after being gone all these months, I still won't be returning to work tomorrow."

Matthew nodded. "These spring rains seem to wreak havoc upon us every year. I received word your ship docked earlier this week. Forgive me for not calling upon you and Miss Addie, but the rain has managed to keep all of us indoors more often than not. And now with the water continuing to rise, it's simply impossible to continue operations until the rain lets up. Needless to say, the Associates are unhappy."

"And when the Associates are unhappy, Kirk Boott is *very* unhappy," John added. "There's no doubt this troublesome weather places an additional burden upon you. Production stoppage isn't good for any of us."

Addie tugged at John's arm. "That's enough talk of the mills for now. Services are about to begin. Did John extend an invitation to join us for dinner?" she asked with a cheery smile.

John's eyes widened. "It appears you've taken care of the assignment for me," he teased.

"John!" A playful look of recrimination was etched upon Addie's face. She took hold of John's arm before turning her attention toward Matthew. "Would you and Lilly consider joining us for dinner after church services—if you don't have other plans? We'd enjoy the opportunity to visit, and I'm certain John wants to hear what's been happening at the mills since our departure."

John moved closer to Matthew. "There's a matter of importance I must discuss with you as soon as possible," he confided.

Matthew beckoned to Lilly, who stood visiting with Bella and Taylor. "Mr. and Mrs. Farnsworth have invited us to join them for dinner this afternoon," he said with mock formality. "I didn't know if you'd be feeling up to it. Have you made prior arrangements?" he questioned.

Lilly Cheever, clearly expecting, patted her rounding stomach. "I made no plans for this afternoon. Your mother has offered to take Violet home for the day. I think dinner and visiting with our dear friends will ease the gloom of this frightful weather and be a delightful way to spend our free time. We would *love* to come," Lilly replied happily.

Addie's lips turned upward in a broad smile. "Good! Now I think we had best get to our pews, or Reverend Edson may be forced to conduct the services out here in the foyer."

John smiled at his wife while leading her down the aisle of the church. "I believe your sister is glowering at us," he murmured, catching Mintie's poignant frown.

"She doesn't approve of making a late entrance," Addie whispered in reply.

"Obviously she believes it's perfectly acceptable to

crane her neck and stare down her nose at those of us breaching her rules of etiquette," he mused.

"I've likely hurt her feelings by not rushing to her side as soon as we arrived this morning. She becomes easily wounded by my thoughtless behavior."

"Goodness, Addie. How did Mintie succeed in convincing you you're thoughtless? There isn't an inconsiderate bone in your body."

Mintie pushed open the pew door and gazed up at her sister and brother-in-law. "You're late," she charged, thumping the tip of her umbrella on the hardwood floor for emphasis.

"We're *not* late, Mintie. Services haven't even begun," John curtly replied. "We were in the vestibule."

Mintie arched her thin eyebrows high above the wire-rimmed glasses perched on her beaklike nose. "Visiting, no doubt!" she accused.

"Extending dinner invitations," John brusquely replied while seating himself at the end of the pew.

Leaning across Addie's portly figure, Mintie extended her long neck and leveled a thin-lipped look of disapproval at John. "I don't believe *I* received a dinner invitation."

John gazed into his sister-in-law's stern brown eyes. "Where's Lawrence this morning?" he asked, hoping to soften her a bit.

Mintie glanced to the left as though she momentarily thought Lawrence was beside her. "He's gone to Rhode Island. He decided a short visit with his sister might be in order since the mills will be closed for several days. He left by coach early this morning. I told him the coach would likely be hindered by mud before reaching the outskirts of town, but he thought otherwise."

"He was probably anxious for quietude and pleasant company," John murmured, flinching as Addie's elbow jabbed into his side.

"What?" Mintie asked, cupping one ear. "I couldn't hear you over those chattering girls."

Addie bent toward her sister. "He said Lawrence's sister is probably anxious for some pleasant company."

Mintie gave a curt nod. "I'm certain she is. Lawrence tells me the poor woman is married to a disagreeable sort— rigid and difficult to please."

"Sounds as though she's describing herself," John whispered mischievously.

Addie turned and grinned. "Stop, John," she muttered genially.

"So you're having a dinner party?" Mintie asked.

"No, not a dinner party. I must discuss some business matters with Matthew, and since the mills are closed, I thought it expedient to invite the Cheevers to dinner after church services. We knew you'd be busy preparing dinner for your boarders or we would have included you," John replied. "However, if you'd like to come over later in the afternoon for tea, I'll send a carriage," he offered.

"Well, let me think." She hesitated, her forehead crinkled into deep ridges. "I believe I *could* fit tea into my schedule," she finally replied. "You may send your carriage at three o'clock."

John nodded, leaned back against the pew, and grinned at Addie.

"Thank you, John. That was very kind," she whispered.

"You're welcome, my dear. So long as you realize that I invited her only so she wouldn't press you."

"Ssshhhh!" Mintie hissed, extending her umbrella menacingly in John's direction.

"You keep that umbrella under control, Mintie, or you'll not be joining your sister for tea this afternoon," he warned.

Mintie jerked the umbrella away from his leg and

pointed a thin finger toward the pulpit. "Quiet! Church has begun."

John leaned close to Addie's ear. "That woman insists upon having the final word. No wonder Lawrence went to Rhode Island," he muttered.

With dinner completed and the women off to the parlor, John led the way into the small library adjacent to the dining room, where he offered Matthew a cigar.

"No, thank you, John," Matthew said, seating himself on one of the tapestry-covered overstuffed chairs opposite Taylor. "I'm glad both of you have returned, and of course, I'm anxious to hear about your journey. Any new designs or innovative ideas to report?" he inquired.

"There are a few new concepts I'd like to see incorporated, and I believe Taylor has a few ideas to report, also. However, those matters can wait."

Matthew appeared surprised. "Really? I thought that's why you'd invited us to dinner."

"No. What we must discuss is of grave concern and will require your immediate involvement."

Matthew sat up in his chair and tugged at his waistcoat. "You're acting terribly mysterious, John. Is there anything illegal or immoral involved in this situation you wish to discuss?" he asked with a chuckle.

"Thurston—William Thurston. He's returned to the United States."

Matthew jumped to his feet. "You're certain? Where is he? How long have you known?"

"Sit down. It's a lengthy story," he said, waiting until Matthew had settled himself before relating the tale of his own kidnapping and escape in London, William's appearance on the ship, and the information recently divulged by Thaddeus Arnold. "So you see," he concluded, "there's every reason to believe William Thurston may be hiding out somewhere in close proximity to Thaddeus Arnold."

Matthew nodded. "And if not, I'd wager Thaddeus must know how to make contact with Thurston."

"If he's still in the country," Taylor remarked.

Matthew appeared confused. "I'm surprised he didn't immediately board the first ship sailing back to England. Why would he remain in Massachusetts when he knows his only future is in jail?"

"Or worse yet, having the fury of his outraged wife vented upon him," Taylor replied in a jesting tone.

"I imagine Mrs. Thurston would be one of the first to contact the police. In addition to all his other crimes, word has it that William made off with some of her family's gold and jewelry before departing the country."

"I don't doubt it," John replied firmly. "I don't believe that man has a shred of moral fiber in his whole body. So what do you say, Matthew? Shall we head out for New Hampshire in the morning and pay Thaddeus Arnold a visit?"

"I can't think of anything else I'd rather do. If you have no objection, I'd like to pass this information along to Mr. Boott. He may want to accompany us."

"Whatever you decide is fine with me," John replied.

A spindly woman answered the door, strands of wiry hair poking out from beneath a white mobcap. She wiped her hands on a stained cotton apron that partially covered her worn print dress. Pointing a thumb toward a wooden sign with faded letters announcing rooms for rent, she wagged her head back and forth. "I'm full up. Never take the sign down—just in case one of my boarders leaves unexpectedly."

"We're not looking for a room. The tavern owner told

us Thaddeus Arnold is one of your boarders," John said. "We've come to call on him."

"You friends of his from down in Lowell?" she asked.

John nodded. "We worked at the same mill."

"Hear tell it's been raining hard down that way," she said. "Coach driver said he had trouble making it through. Not that far from Lowell to Litchfield, but we ain't had a drop. You reckon it's heading this way?"

"I think the rain's headed away from the area, so it's not likely you'll be getting much, if any," he replied. "Is Mr. Arnold here?" he asked, hoping to curtail her conversation.

"He's become mighty popular all of a sudden," she remarked. Turning away from the doorway, she beckoned toward the men. "Come on in. I'll fetch him for you."

"We truly would enjoy the pleasure of surprising him, if you don't mind," John whispered, as though taking the woman into his deepest confidence. He put a coin in her palm and smiled broadly.

She grinned in return. "I always did like surprises myself," she said. "You go on up and knock—second door on the left."

"Thank you," John replied while motioning Matthew and Taylor to follow him.

Matthew rapped soundly, and the three men waited silently. The sound of shuffling feet approached on the other side of the door, followed by the squeak of the door as it opened to reveal an obviously stunned Thaddeus Arnold.

"What are *you* doing here?" he gasped, his gaze darting about like a trapped animal seeking escape.

"Let's go in your room and talk," Matthew suggested. "I'm sure you don't want the other tenants or the boarding-house owner hearing our conversation."

Thaddeus tentatively backed into the room, watching as

Taylor closed the door and then firmly leaned his body against it.

"You can sit here," Thaddeus offered while looking at Taylor.

"I prefer to stand," Taylor replied.

"You know why we're here," John said in a menacing tone. "Why don't you just tell us where Thurston is and we'll be on our way."

"Thurston? I don't know what you're talking about. Why do you think *I* know the whereabouts of William Thurston?"

"Because you've been seen together," John bluffed.

"If someone's made such an allegation, he's mistaken. William Thurston's a wealthy man of social standing; he wouldn't keep company with someone like me. Anyway, I heard he left the country and lives in England."

"He does live in England. However, he's currently in Massachusetts, and we're certain you know where to find him. If you don't cooperate with us, we'll see to it that you're arrested for aiding a criminal. And then there's the matter of the funds you stole from your former wife."

"How do you know about Naomi?" he screeched.

"At least you're willing to admit you've wronged Mrs. Arnold. Now, why don't you make a clean slate of matters, admit to your involvement with Thurston, and help us apprehend him. Otherwise, I plan to have Taylor go and fetch the authorities. I'm certain they'll be willing to hold you in the local jail until we can return you to Lowell," John threatened.

Thaddeus slipped a finger between his thin neck and the starched collar. Beads of perspiration formed along his brow and then trickled downward, casting a sheen upon his pallid complexion. "I may be able to help you," he ventured in a warbling voice.

"Now, there's a good fellow," John amicably responded

while giving Thaddeus an encouraging smile.

His lips quivered, his uncertainty obvious. "I'm expect-ing William within the hour," he admitted grudgingly.

"Really? Well, perhaps we should wait for him. Taylor, why don't you see if there's an out-of-the way spot to secure the horses, someplace where William won't catch sight of them when he arrives," Matthew suggested. "While you're taking care of the horses, I believe I'll see about getting some assistance from the police. Do you think you can manage Mr. Arnold by yourself for a short time, John?"

"I don't think we'll have any problems," John replied evenly.

Taylor opened the door and then glanced over his shoulder. "Any place you'd care to suggest for our horses, Mr. Arnold?"

"There's a lean-to out back," he grumbled, watching Taylor and Matthew leave the room.

Speculating Thaddeus would likely attempt an escape, John assumed a position in front of the door, folding his long arms across his chest.

"If only I hadn't changed the meeting time, William would be safe. I'm sure I'll be blamed for this entire fiasco. Bad luck seems to follow me like a thundercloud," he lamented.

"Has it occurred to you that your difficulties are self-imposed, Mr. Arnold? If you behaved in a proper fashion, I doubt you'd find yourself surrounded by these intimidating difficulties."

"Save your sermon—it's too late now."

"It's never too late to turn your life around and receive forgiveness," John replied with certainty.

"Forgiveness? You think that's possible?" Thaddeus asked, his eyes glimmering.

"Of course. If you genuinely seek absolution, God will

be faithful to His word and forgive you. However, Thaddeus, you mustn't confuse the forgiveness of God with the forgiveness of man."

A scowl replaced his look of expectation. "In other words, I'm going to jail."

John nodded. "Most likely."

Thaddeus slumped down in the chair, his eyes filled with fiery anger. "Well, if that's the case, I'm not asking God or anyone else to forgive me," he snapped.

"As I thought! You're not seeking forgiveness; you're looking to escape punishment," John replied as the sound of footsteps echoed in the hallway.

A knock sounded at the door. "Uncle John, I've a policeman here with me," Taylor announced.

John opened the door to permit them entry and remained silent as the policeman pulled Thaddeus to his feet. "Turn around," he said.

John and Taylor watched as the officer bound Thaddeus's hands behind his back and then led him out of the room and down the stairway.

"Matthew has gone to fetch more lawmen. He should be back directly. They'll wait across the way until Thurston shows himself," Taylor explained.

Time weighed heavy as the men crouched alongside the boardinghouse, their anticipation rising each time they heard the sound of horses' hooves drawing near. Nearly two hours had passed, and they had almost given up all hope of apprehending Thurston when Taylor announced that another rider was approaching in the distance.

"It's him!"

They watched from their hiding place until Thurston began to dismount his horse, and at the policeman's approach, they descended upon him. With an ease that surprised all of them, the elusive William Thurston was quickly under their control.

"You!" Thurston spat in John's direction. "I should have put a knife through your heart when I had the opportunity. Instead, I waited, giving the English gentry the right to make my decisions regarding your future."

John stared at Thurston in disbelief. "Your hatred of me is obvious, yet I'm at a loss to understand the root of your contempt. You successfully escaped punishment for the unspeakable crimes you committed in this country, and still you're willing to place yourself in harm's way in order to damage me. What unfathomable reasoning causes your reckless behavior?"

Thurston emitted a chilling laugh. "This isn't about *you*! This is about much more: This is about the Boston Associates. Without you, they will suffer irreparable damage. Without the knowledge you stole from England, their expansion will be thwarted. I'm certain you're aware the English want you punished for treason. I promised to deliver you to them," he snarled, his face twisted into a picture of demented torment. "You foiled my plans!" He lunged toward John as a gunshot reverberated from the woods nearby. John stared in alarm as he watched Thurston's body crumple forward and then drop to the ground.

With eyes glazed and lips curled in a menacing contortion, a figure emerged, throwing aside his rifle and reaching for the ivory-handled pistol jutting from his waistband. He waved off Matthew and the police officers. "Put down your weapons and back away. I've no grievance with you." He turned with a sarcastic smirk. "Do you remember me, Farnsworth?" he hollered, brandishing the weapon. "Barlow Kent?"

John nodded. "Of course I remember you, Mr. Kent. You worked at the mill in Lancashire. I'm surprised you've left England," he said, attempting to maintain a calm demeanor.

Barlow glared into John's eyes. "To see you receive the

punishment you so richly deserve, I would have sailed to the ends of the earth. You ruined my life, and now I'm going to end your time on this earth."

"*I* ruined your life? How can that be, Mr. Kent? We barely knew each other."

"You had me fired from my position. Do you recall telling my supervisor I should be terminated from my job at the mill in Lancashire?"

"Yes. You were a poor employee who wouldn't take instruction or give an honest day's work for your pay. As I remember, you were given several opportunities to mend your ways, but your behavior never really improved," John detailed precisely.

Barlow appeared dazed, as if he'd not heard a word. "You caused the death of my wife—and unborn child," he accused determinedly.

"What? That's a preposterous allegation. I didn't even know your wife. How could I possibly be responsible for her death?"

A spark of anger once again ignited in Barlow's eyes as he gestured wildly with the gun. "My Nancy died in childbirth. We had no money to pay for a doctor because *you* had me discharged from my employment at the mill. Are you finally beginning to understand, Mr. Farnsworth?"

John's gaze remained fixed upon Barlow while Taylor moved with a quiet, determined step and positioned himself behind the crazed man. The officers and Matthew also inched closer.

"You don't claim any of the responsibility for losing your job?" John quietly inquired, hoping he could maintain Barlow's attention. "Surely you don't blame me for this tragic occurrence in your life. Such an idea is outrageous."

John's words appeared to fan the embers of hatred burning deep inside his assailant, who now leveled the weapon directly at his heart.

"You're going to die," Barlow seethed, his anger at fever pitch.

The words had barely been spoken when Taylor and the others jumped forward. Taylor grasped the attacker's arm, wrenching the gun from his hand. Following his lead, Matthew wrestled Barlow to the ground while the lawmen neatly took matters in hand and arrested the man.

John bent down, placing one knee on the ground beside the collapsed body of William Thurston, and felt for a pulse. He looked first at Taylor and then turned his gaze toward Matthew. "William is dead. I guess Thaddeus finally got the better deal," John said, shaking his head. "He may be in jail for a long time—but at least he'll live to tell about it."

CHAPTER 29

Canterbury, Connecticut

Daughtie rapped on the front door of Miss Crandall's School for Young Ladies of Color upon their arrival in Canterbury, Connecticut.

"Good afternoon, my dear," Miss Crandall greeted as she opened the door, her thin lips brightening into a welcoming smile.

"Good afternoon, Miss Crandall. I was wondering if I might have a few words with you concerning a matter of grave importance. You may not remember me, but we've corresponded. I'm Daughtie Winfield of Lowell, Massachusetts."

"Ah, Miss Winfield. I didn't recognize you, but it's an unexpected pleasure to have you call. I was in the midst of a class, but if your visit requires my immediate attention, I can make arrangements," she said, her gaze drifting toward Liam, who was still perched in the wagon. "You can have your driver take the wagon to the barn behind the house," she offered.

"There are four of us," Daughtie whispered. "We have

361

two runaways hidden in the back of the wagon."

Miss Crandall's eyes widened slightly. "After you place the horses and wagon in the barn, the four of you can come in through the back door. I'll be waiting there for you."

"Thank you, Miss Crandall," Daughtie said, warmly clasping the older woman's hands.

"Don't thank me yet. We need to talk."

Daughtie didn't wait for further explanation. The fact that Miss Crandall had said the runaways could come into the school was affirmation enough. She ran to the wagon and hoisted herself up beside Liam. "We're to park around back in the barn," she instructed.

"She said the girls could stay?" he asked.

"She said we could all come in and talk. I didn't go into detail."

Liam's shoulders visibly slumped. "Do ya think she'll be willin' to keep them?"

"I don't know. I haven't asked," she replied more abruptly than she had intended.

"I'm not meanin' to make you angry with my questions," he said, his voice low and calm while he directed the horses into a space near the door of the barn.

"I know, Liam," she said hastily while turning on the seat and pulling back the covers that served to obscure the two girls from view. "Come on, girls."

The four of them moved quickly across the small open area between the house and barn, each walking with a hurried determination.

"Is dis da place you was tellin' us 'bout?" Nelly asked as they neared the back of the house.

"Yes," Daughtie replied simply as she ushered the girls through the door. "Miss Crandall, these are the girls I mentioned. This is Nelly. And this," she said, pulling the other girl forward, "is Minerva, her sister." Turning toward Liam, she gave him a bright smile. "This is my friend Liam

Donohue. He's been hiding the girls in Lowell."

"I'm pleased to meet all of you," she said warmly, glancing among them. "Girls, I'd like to have you visit one of my classrooms while I visit with Miss Winfield and Mr. Donohue. Would that meet with your approval?"

Nelly and Minerva glanced at each other, obviously surprised their approval was deemed of any importance. "Yessum," they replied in unison.

Once the girls were ensconced in another room, Miss Crandall returned and led Daughtie and Liam into the parlor. "Please make yourselves comfortable," she said before taking a seat in one of the blue-and-beige upholstered chairs. "Now tell me, what brings you to my school?"

Daughtie's lips twitched in a nervous smile. "The girls. We need a safe place for them. They have no family to rely upon, and they can't possibly make it to Canada on their own. We discussed waiting until another group of runaways arrived at Mr. Donohue's house, but we had no idea when the next slaves might arrive, and we were afraid the girls might be discovered if we waited any longer," she hastened to explain, the words tumbling over each other as she spoke.

Miss Crandall's thin lips tightened until they nearly disappeared. "You never said one word in your letters about aiding runaways. Did someone tell you I was harboring runaway slaves?"

"No, not a soul. But your speech at the Pawtucket church addressed the evils of slavery, as did your letters to me—and, of course, you're operating this school for Negro girls," Daughtie replied. She stared at Miss Crandall, her hands folded and resting in her lap, a look of expectation etched upon her face.

Miss Crandall stared back, her eyes narrowed. "So why would you bring these girls to me?" she asked warily.

"Oh yes. Let me complete my explanation. I had been

spending a great deal of time thinking and praying about this situation with the girls and how we might help them, knowing we soon must come to a decision. As I picked up my Bible to see if God's Word might reveal an answer, your last letter to me dropped upon the floor. You'll recall you had written that things here in Canterbury had grown more peaceful and that you were giving thought to the possibility of enrolling a few new students. Needless to say, your letter appeared to be an answer to prayer. The more I prayed, the more I believed the Lord was directing me to bring the girls here—to your school—a place where they would be safe and could receive an education among people they can trust."

Miss Crandall leaned back in her chair and gave Daughtie a kindly smile. "I believe you're telling me the truth, Miss Winfield. And if I weren't in such financial straits, I would consider admitting the girls. But I simply cannot manage to feed and clothe them. When all of this difficulty began, there were some parents who withdrew their daughters. Consequently, I had to begin charging higher fees. If the parents of my students discovered I was permitting these girls to stay here free of charge, I'd likely have further withdrawals from my enrollment, and I can ill afford to have that occur."

Liam shifted to the edge of the settee. "What if ya received full payment for the girls, Miss Crandall? Would ya have any objection to boardin' them?"

Prudence hesitated a moment. "If they paid for tuition and boarding fees, I would be delighted to have them remain, but since that's impossible, I think we must devise some other plan."

"I'll pay for them," Liam modestly replied.

"I mean no disrespect, Mr. Donohue, but I'm not sure you understand the financial commitment involved."

"I believe I can afford your charges, Miss Crandall. I'll

sign a note if ya like, but you'll find my payments will be made as promised. I'll be leavin' funds with ya to purchase some clothes and any other necessaries they might be needin'."

Miss Crandall glanced toward Daughtie with a questioning look in her eyes. "If you're absolutely certain you want to do this, then my answer is yes. But you must remember that if matters should begin to worsen with the townspeople, the school may be closed, and the girls will once again be placed in jeopardy."

"We understand, but they'll be safe with you for now. If problems arise in the future, we'll make other arrangements."

Prudence nodded. "Have you told the girls they'll be staying here?"

"We told them a little about the school. They seemed excited with the thought of receiving an education. I did explain that all the girls in your school are daughters of freemen, and they appeared astonished at the concept. However, I believe they're a bit concerned by our decision to bring them to Connecticut. Liam explained this was the safest possible place for two young runaway girls right now. The men they were traveling with were recaptured, and we truly don't believe we should send them off toward Canada by themselves," Daughtie said.

"I agree with you. I'm doubtful they could make it to the border on their own. There are too many tragedies that could befall two young girls traveling alone. However, they won't be content if they're forced to remain in Canterbury against their will," Miss Crandall replied.

Daughtie glanced at Liam. "I think the girls realize this is the wisest possible choice. Perhaps if you talk to them before making a final decision, you'll feel more assured," Daughtie suggested.

"I think that's an excellent suggestion. I'll emphasize

the complications and dangers of sending them off on their own and Mr. Donohue's willingness to pay their fees to remain here and attend school. If they choose to stay, we'll need to begin their instruction separate from the other students. I doubt if they read or write, and I wouldn't want them to feel overwhelmed. I'll have to rely upon the discretion of my girls to keep this matter a secret. However, with the inequity and hurtful behavior heaped upon us by the residents of Canterbury, I'm certain my students will be quick to protect Nelly and Minerva."

Daughtie sighed and gave the older woman a broad smile. "Thank you, Miss Crandall."

"Why don't you two relax for a short time? I'll have the girls come to my office, where we can visit privately, and then I'll be back."

Daughtie watched Miss Crandall exit the room and then turned toward Liam, her eyes revealing a modicum of apprehension.

He placed his hand atop hers for an instant. "No need for worryin', lassie. Let's sit back and let God work out His plan."

As they reached the outskirts of Canterbury, Liam snapped the reins, and the team of horses broke into a trot. "It's been a pleasure havin' the sun shinin' down on us while we've been in Connecticut. Can't say I've missed the rain," he commented.

Daughtie nodded her agreement and settled back on the wooden seat. "I'm relieved the girls decided to remain in Canterbury. They actually appeared happy by the time we left, don't you think?"

Liam remained silent, his lips turned upward in a self-satisfied smile.

Daughtie stared at him, waiting. "Why are you smiling?

Did I say something humorous?"

"Ah, lassie, you do make it difficult for me to be trustin' in your Lord," he finally replied with a lilt to his voice.

Daughtie's cheeks flushed. The truth of his words pricked her heart. "You're right, Liam. God provided an answer, but I didn't have faith He would see the plan through to completion. How can I expect others to believe when my own faith is so weak?" she lamented.

"Now, don't go bein' so hard on yourself. God managed things just fine without ya this time. Surely He's willin' to accept a misstep now and again, don't ya think?"

Daughtie smiled and nodded. "Seems as if you've gotten to know quite a bit about God since the arrival of Nelly and Minerva."

"That's true. Those girls have an unwaverin' love for God that's hard for me to understand. Even through the difficulties they've endured, they don't doubt God's love for them and they want everybody to know Jesus. 'Course, both Matthew Cheever and John Farnsworth have talked about their faith with me from time to time. However, while those girls made me long to learn more, it was you who made me aware of what I was really missin' by tellin' me to search the Scriptures for myself and pray." He shifted on the wooden seat and took a deep breath. "Tell me, what do you think of the new doctor?" he asked.

Daughtie gave him a sidelong glance. "Aren't you the man who accused me of abrupt changes in conversation not so very long ago?"

Liam gave a hearty laugh. "Now, don't be avoidin' my question, lassie," he teasingly replied.

Daughtie gave him a faint smile. "Dr. Ketter appears to be quite capable. Why do you ask?"

"I saw him escortin' you to the Farnsworths' the other night. He looked to be enjoyin' your company."

Daughtie's brow furrowed as she thought for a moment.

"I didn't see you at the Farnsworths'."

"I know. John asked me to stop by and visit with 'im about some stonework. I thought I'd stop on me way home, but when I saw you and the doctor goin' up the steps, I figured there was a party or some such thing goin' on, so I went home. That doctor would make a good match for ya."

"Match? As in marriage?"

Liam nodded.

"Why would you even think such a thing? Dr. Ketter will likely make a good husband for some woman, but *I'm* certainly not interested in becoming his wife."

"And why would he be such a poor choice for you?"

Daughtie swallowed down the lump that was rising in her throat. Obviously she had misconstrued Liam's words and actions these past months. What a fool she was! He had merely wanted someone to decorate his home and help him with the runaways, when all the time she had secretly thought he was interested in her affections. Their long discussions, the playful banter, his kisses upon her cheek— they had all been nothing more than brotherly companionship.

Liam gave her a lopsided grin. "Have ya lost your tongue, Daughtie? Never known ya to be so slow to answer," he teased.

Daughtie choked back her tears and inhaled a deep breath of the cool morning air. "Dr. Ketter and I don't share the same values."

"Ya don't? Why, the two of ya go to the same church most of the time, and ya said he's a good man." His brogue thickened.

Why wouldn't Liam let the matter rest? "He is a good man, but he's not the man I want to marry," she replied with finality.

"Ya already told me that much. I'm askin' why he isn't the man for ya."

"And I answered you. Perhaps not to your satisfaction, but I *did* answer you."

"You're soundin' a wee bit ill-tempered, lassie. I'm only tryin' to find out why you don't want to marry this fella."

"Because I don't love him," she snapped.

Liam gave her a broad smile. "Now, *that* was an answer!"

Her eyes flashed with anger. "Can we talk about something else now?"

"I'm guessin' he's in love with you. Has he asked ya to marry 'im?"

She clenched her jaw. "No."

"And ya don't want him to ask ya?"

"No!"

"Strange," he mused. "Most girls want to get married. Do ya not want a husband?"

Why wouldn't he quit badgering her with these questions about love and marriage? "Yes, I want a husband."

"So it's just Dr. Ketter ya're not wantin'?" he continued.

"Yes," she sighed in exasperation. "I want to marry a man who has a heart for the downtrodden. Dr. Ketter's a physician, but his interest is directed toward those who can pay for their medical treatment. Even though he possesses the skill, Dr. Ketter's not the type who would go into the Acre and help the sick merely because they are in need. I want to marry a man I love, a man who is willing to sacrifice for others—a man who would be willing to take the type of risks you've taken helping runaways. A man like you."

"Ah, but that could never happen, lassie, for ya know folks would never be acceptin' a fine girl such as yourself takin' up with someone of the lower class. They'd condemn and forsake ya for sure. Now think about it, what kind of life would that be?"

"Two people of differing classes could still have a good

marriage and a good life if they didn't put stock in what others thought and believed. Besides, look at what Prudence Crandall has endured for the sake of girls she doesn't even know. Do you think I'd be willing to do less for someone I love? The opinion of others is not what's of importance to me. Besides, if a person truly cares for another, their country of birth should make no difference."

"What if your friend Bella and her fine husband would be havin' nothin' more to do with ya should you marry a man such as meself?" he ventured.

"Are you asking me to marry you, Liam?"

"And if I were askin', what would you be answerin', lassie?"

She looked toward a distant spot in the road. "I'd be required to tell you no—but not because you're Irish," she hastened to explain.

He slowly nodded and hesitated, as if weighing her reply. "I'm almost afraid to ask this next question, but if it's not because I'm Irish, and you're unafraid of retribution from your friends, then why?"

Daughtie nervously straightened the pleats in her yellow muslin dress. "You still haven't told me exactly where you stand in your relationship with God. You've hinted that you've read the Scriptures and mentioned you've been praying, and although I would marry an Irishman, I could never marry a man who hasn't avowed his belief in Jesus and accepted Him as his Savior. I fear such a match would lead to nothing but disaster and heartache," she replied, her voice barely above a whisper.

Liam had leaned in close, obviously eager to hear every word. As soon as Daughtie finished speaking, he straightened and shifted back against the wagon seat. A deep sigh escaped his lips.

She turned to face him. "What does that mean?"

"I think ya're looking for an excuse! If ya can't see how

much I've changed and grown in my beliefs, well, I doubt I could convince ya by any words I would say. Why, my poor mother would be horror-struck if she knew the changes I've gone through since movin' to America."

"What kind of changes?" she asked, squelching her instinct to argue against his comment about excuses.

"Changes such as discoverin' that what I've needed all my life is to know Jesus—and that I've been able to go through the steps of transformin' my life by acceptin' Him as my Lord and Savior. Not only would she be dumb-founded by the statement, she'd likely believe I've lost my mind."

"And have you lost your mind, Liam?"

He reined back on the horses. "No," he replied softly. "But I have lost my heart."

Daughtie trembled. "Oh?"

"I, too, want to be marryin' for love, but I fear my desire might never be fulfilled."

Daughtie stiffened and lifted her chin ever so slightly. "Well, of course it won't be fulfilled if you don't ask her the question."

Liam raised a brow. "And what question would that be, lass?"

She maintained her serious demeanor and leaned closer. "Will you marry me?"

Liam looked at her for a moment and then began to smile. "Of course I will," he replied. Then with a flick of the reins he put the horses into motion. "Besides," he added, "I'll have to be doin' somethin' to keep yar reputa-tion from bein' ruined after us bein' alone like this."

Daughter giggled and then began to laugh even harder. "Oh, Liam."

He stopped the horses again, looking at her with grave concern. "What madness has taken ya now?"

She shook her head and wiped tears from her eyes.

"You're worried about marrying me to keep my reputation intact."

He looked at her as if she were daft. "And what's wrong with that?" he asked, his voice taking on an indignant tone.

"There's nothing wrong with it, except marrying you isn't going to exactly save my reputation."

From the grin on his face, Daughtie realized he finally understood. "Well, if the town's goin' to be up in arms over ya, then we may as well give them plenty to be up in arms about. This way will make me a whole lot happier than the other." He reached out and pulled Daughtie close.

Daughtie looked up, knowing he would kiss her. She longed for his kiss—his touch—like nothing she had ever longed for before. Reaching up, she toyed with the black curls at the nape of Liam's neck.

"I think I've loved you for a very long time, my handsome Irishman," she whispered.

He pressed his mouth to hers in a very gentle, tender kiss. Daughtie tightened her arms around his neck and sighed as the kiss deepened and she seemed to melt against him.

He pulled away, pushing back a loose wisp of her hair. "I love you, my darlin'. But lovin' ya won't make others accept us together as man and wife. I want ya to think long and hard about this. I want ya to be sure before we make our vows."

Daughtie straightened and relunctantly left Liam's hold. "I am certain, but I'm quite willing to pray on it." She smiled and folded her hands in her lap. "But don't ya go thinkin' to get out of yar agreement to marry me," she said, trying hard to imitate Liam's Irish brogue. "I'll not be havin' it."

CHAPTER *30*

"Isn't that ten feet?" Daughtie questioned as Liam shoveled yet another load of dirt onto the tarp. They'd connected a pulley to the tarp in order to bring the dirt out of the hole and still it was an exhausting process.

"Not quite. It's close, but not quite ten," he said, looking at the small area.

Liam had gotten the brilliant idea to dig a hiding place for the slaves. Here in the barn, they could easily conceal it, and if anyone should find it, they would simply say they'd dug a root cellar. The plan was quite simple. The dimensions were to be eight by ten and seven feet deep, with shelves on the wall for supplies and a hidden airway near the wall of the barn. They'd been working on the hiding place since late summer, as time permitted. Daughtie thought the process was taking too long, but Liam assured her they were doing just fine.

"It's not going to be very light down here and they won't be able to burn a lantern," Daughtie said as she surveyed the room. "The air will quickly grow bad."

"Aye, but 'tis only goin' to be used for emergencies," Liam reminded her. "A place to hide them away in case the house is searched or they arrive when no one is to home."

"I know. It just seems . . . well . . . almost like a grave."

He stopped what he was doing and pulled her close. "Daughtie, my darlin', you worry too much." He turned her toward the ladder. "Let's get this dirt out of here and go have some tea."

Daughtie nodded. She hiked her skirts and climbed to the top, knowing Liam would finish tying the tarp to the pulley rope. It was only a moment or two before he bounded up the ladder to join her. He took hold of the rope and heaved the heavy weight ever upward. Daughtie's job was to guide the mass once it cleared the hole and pull it to the side, where Liam would deposit it.

Reaching out, she pulled the tarped bundle toward her, but just as she had the bundle in place the load shifted. Daughtie lost her footing and fell backward onto the straw-covered floor—landing with surprising impact despite the cushioning. Liam quickly lowered the load and hurried to her side.

"Are ya hurt?"

She laughed and rubbed her backside as he helped her to her feet. "Only me pride, luv." They laughed at her mimicking Irish.

"Well, for sure ya have straw in yar hair," Liam said, allowing his brogue to become heavy.

"And for sure, ya have straw in yar hair, too," Daughtie said, reaching down to grab a handful to sprinkle over Liam's head.

He laughed and lifted her in his arms. "Ah, my darlin'—my wife," he murmured between kisses.

Daughtie reached up to take hold of his face as he stared down at her. "I am so very happy to hear you call me that." She thought back to the difficulty they'd had in finding someone to marry them. No one wanted to allow a Yankee girl to marry an Irishman. The prejudices were strong— even among men of God who should have been able to see each man as God's child. They'd finally been forced to drive several miles to another town, where Liam managed to convince the Methodist preacher that they were both of age and in love. Daughtie had remained quiet except for an occasional reply in her attempted brogue. The preacher had seemed hesitant until Liam had added that they weren't Catholic and because of this, the Catholic Church would not marry them. The man then took pity on them and performed a hasty ceremony.

"I love—"

"Shhh!" Liam declared, putting his finger to Daughtie's lips. "Someone's coming."

They got to their feet quickly, dusting off the straw as best they could. "Sounds like the entire town is coming," Daughtie said, hurrying to the barn door with Liam following behind.

"Looks like at least three wagons—maybe four," she said, peeking from the narrow opening in the door. She glanced back with apprehension toward the hole in the floor.

"Relax. If someone questions it, we'll just tell 'em we're puttin' in a root cellar. There's no need to be afraid."

Daughtie nodded. "I know, but we didn't want anyone knowing about it. The whole idea was to hide it away after we completed it."

"Aye, and for sure ya're right. Let's just go on outside and greet whoever it is and hope they'll not be wantin' to come to the barn."

Daughtie knew it was the sensible thing to do, but a part of her was still afraid. What if the visitors had come to do them harm? People had not been happy to learn of their union. Daughtie was still snubbed whenever she went into town, and more than once she'd been turned away when a storeowner pointed to a sign that strictly forbade Irish to enter.

Taking a deep breath, she opened the door and stepped outside. The sunlight was warm on her face and hard on her eyes. She squinted and shielded her eyes with her hand. "Oh, it's Bella and Taylor!" she squealed in excitement. "And I do believe that's Miss Addie and John Farnsworth behind them."

Liam took hold of her hand, and together they walked to the front of the house. Taylor brought his wagon to a stop just beyond the front walkway. Bella was already waving in anticipation.

"Hello, Daughtie—Liam! We've brought you some gifts."

John and Addie pulled their carriage up alongside the wagon, while Matthew and Lilly Cheever came up behind them.

Daughtie turned to Liam as the party dismounted. "Oh, my. I had no idea they were coming. Did you?" She frantically tried to check her dress for dirt.

"No, to be sure I didn't."

After Taylor helped Bella to the ground, she came rushing to see Daughtie. "I feel like you've been gone forever. We decided it was time to come for a visit."

"Absolutely," Addie said, coming to join them. "The Ladies Aid Society has missed you at the sewing circles, but they sent along some little gifts to remind you to join us again soon."

Daughtie looked to her husband and then to the ladies. Lilly Cheever had now joined them. "I didn't think . . . well . . ." Daughtie paused and looked again to Liam. She didn't want to hurt him. "I didn't know if I'd be welcome to come sew with the ladies . . . now that I've married."

"Pshaw!" Addie said with a wave of her hand.

Lilly reached out to take hold of Daughtie's hand. "I second that. You are always welcome in my home. If the other ladies have a problem with that, then it is something they will have to deal with. Not you."

"We feel the same way, Liam," John Farnsworth declared as he joined the party. Matthew and Taylor were at his side. They nodded in complete agreement.

"I must be sayin' this comes as some surprise. I didn't think any of ya approved," Liam said, speaking his mind.

"Well, we must admit," Taylor began, "there was concern because of the situation being what it is. We know you've not been treated well at times, Liam. And you aren't even poor Irish. You have money and a good job skill. Still people ostracize you."

"We didn't want that for either you or Daughtie," Lilly Cheever threw in. "However, now that the deed is done and we were cheated out of a wedding, we've decided to come and celebrate with you. We've brought supper, gifts, and a few surprises."

"Surprises?" Liam questioned.

"Definitely," Matthew said, grinning.

Daughtie looked beyond them to the wagon and carriages. "Where are your children, Mrs. Cheever? I must admit I've been quite longing to see that new baby. Has he grown very big?"

Matthew laughed, but it was John who spoke. "Michael Cheever is a fine specimen of a young man. He will no doubt rival his father in height and intelligence."

"He's definitely worth the trip to see," Addie teased.

"Yes, you must come," Lilly agreed. "Maybe you and Liam would take dinner with us after church tomorrow."

Daughtie looked to her husband. Liam nodded. "That sounds quite nice."

"What does Violet think of her new little brother?"

Daughtie asked. She began to relax a bit in the circle of friends.

"She is completely delighted—spends her afternoons mooning over him," Matthew declared.

"Say there, is that straw in your hair?" Bella questioned, reaching up to pluck a piece from Daughtie's hair.

Daughtie looked at Liam, who instantly looked away, as if embarrassed. He attempted to casually run his hand through his own hair while Daughtie stammered to answer. "I . . . well, we were . . ." She didn't know how to finish the sentence. The group began to laugh uproariously until John Farnsworth finally put an end to it.

"Well, in spite of what we may have interrupted, I think we need to unload the wagon, gentlemen."

"I'll take care of this," Liam whispered in Daughtie's ear. "You visit with your friends." He turned to the men. "Let's go. Oh, by the way, how did that uprising with the farmers at the Pawtucket dam turn out?"

"Well," Matthew began while striding toward the wagon, "it's under control for now. We don't anticipate any more problems for the time."

Daughtie watched as they walked away talking and enjoying the news to be had. She felt silly for the way Liam's absence from her side was almost a loss. They spent so much time together of late, it was as if they were two sides of the same coin.

"I hope we didn't come at a bad time," Bella said, interrupting Daughtie's thoughts.

"No, not at all. Since it's Saturday evening we were working to get some of our chores done. These September evenings have been quite pleasant." She paused and offered them all a smile. "I'm so touched that you would come here today," she told her friends. "I know this is difficult. I know the world doesn't think highly of what I've done, but . . ." She paused as the men moved past them with various parcels and crates. "But I love him and I know he is the man God gave me to marry."

Bella nodded and wiped at a tear in her eye. "I'm sorry we weren't more supportive. I spoke with Ruth the other day and she was so very ugly about the entire matter. The things she said were echoes of some of the very things I had spoken to you of, but coming from her mouth they seemed so much harsher—less Christian. I suppose I let my fears for you cloud my judgment. Please forgive me."

Daughtie hugged Bella close. "Of course."

They pulled away, this time laughing at each other's tears. "Here this is a happy occasion," Daughtie sniffed.

"It is a happy occasion," Lilly declared. "We want to celebrate and set things off on the right foot." Addie nodded in agreement.

Daughtie reached out to hug all three women. "Oh, I'm so grateful to have good friends like you."

The men made one more trip to empty the wagon and disappeared into the house. Daughtie pulled away and smiled. "So shall we join the men in the house?"

"I think that would be splendid," Addie declared. "We can . . ." Her words faded as the sound of yet another carriage came from far down the lane.

"Who could that be?" Daughtie asked, straining to see.

"Well, I'll be," Addie said with a gasp of surprise. "It's Lawrence and Mintie."

"Oh my," Lilly Cheever said softly.

"Whatever is she doing here?" Bella asked.

The carriage pulled up and a very prim and proper Miss Mintie allowed her escort to help her from the carriage. Her walking-out suit of dark burgundy seemed almost flamboyant on the woman who rarely wore anything more lively than blue.

"Mintie, I didn't think you were going to come here today," Addie said as her sister and friend joined them.

"Hello, Mr. Gault." He gave a slight bow. Addie turned back to Mintie for an explanation.

Daughtie wondered if the old woman had come to criticize her choice of husbands. Mintie Beecher had been known for her hatred of the British. Did she feel the same way about the Irish?

"I told you that I couldn't be ready by four. I did not say that I wouldn't come," Mintie announced. She turned to Daughtie, her pinched features as stern as ever. "So they tell me you have married."

Daughtie stiffened. "Yes. Yes, I have. His name is Liam Donohue."

"I see," Mintie said, eyeing the girl as though weighing each word. "So you *did* marry the Irishman."

"Sister!"

Lilly started to protest. "Miss Beecher, that's hardly—"

"Silence!" Miss Mintie declared. "I'm speaking with Mrs. Donohue."

Daughtie swallowed hard. Miss Mintie could be most difficult to deal with, and this occasion was certainly no exception. "Yes," she finally answered. "I married an Irishman."

Mintie hurrumphed and nodded. "Well, it's better than marrying an Englishman."

"But John's English!" Addie protested.

"No," Mintie said quite stoically, "he's an American."

For a moment there was no sound, but only for a moment. After that, Bella began to snicker and Addie to laugh with a great wheezing gusto. Lilly bent double in laughter, while Daughtie and Mintie faced off like two lionesses over a kill.

Slowly Mintie and Daughtie looked to the others. "A great bunch of ninnies," Mintie declared.

Daughtie looped her arm through Mintie's. "I quite agree, Miss Beecher. I think we should leave them here and let them laugh themselves silly."

The old woman looked up to meet Daughtie's gaze. She gave the slightest hint of a grin and declared, "On that matter, my dear, we are already too late."

As they approached the house, Daughtie and Mintie were nearly knocked aside by the men. They bounded out the front door holding Liam high in the air. Liam, kicking and hollering, seemed not at all impressed with their revelry.

"What are you doing?" Lilly questioned from behind Daughtie.

Matthew called over his shoulder, "We're celebrating with the groom. We'll be back shortly—after we've dunked his highness in the pond."

The men laughed and Lawrence Gault hurried to join the fun.

Liam called out as they passed, "Don't ya dare be givin' 'em even a spot of tea. They've come to make mischief on this house—I'm thinkin' they're all leprechauns in the guise of our good friends." And then they were gone, disappearing behind the barn on their journey to the cattle pond.

Daughtie got over her surprise and gave a contented sigh. She knew exactly what this kind of camaraderie meant to her husband. Turning to Mintie, she smiled. "Would you care to take tea with an Irishman's lady?"

Mintie straightened and gave a very curt nod. "I have come with no other idea in mind."

Daughtie felt the warmth of the old woman's approving words. To imagine Miss Mintie offering her support was more than she could have ever hoped for. If Miss Mintie and her sister and Lilly Cheever and Bella could all accept her marriage to Liam, then maybe others would come around in time. And if not, then these ladies were sufficient to bless Daughtie with enough friendship and love to last the rest of time.